VENGEANCE WEARS
A STAR

PRAISE FOR THE CORRIGAN BROTHERS SERIES

VENGEANCE WEARS
A STAR

CORRIGAN BROTHERS
BOOK THREE

SCOTT F. SMITH

WOLFPACK
PUBLISHING
— EST 2013 —

To my mother, Sonya, and my father, Cotton.
You showed me a world of happiness and possibilities.
Your forever love story is an inspiration.

AUTHOR'S NOTE

"In the Spirit of a Classic Cotton Smith Western Adventure!" Pressure-packed words to be sure. Following in the footsteps of a beloved, award-winning author is no easy feat.

Although my father, Cotton, was short in stature, he was a larger than life leader. Ask the thousands of little league ballplayers, Scouts, clients, fellow Western Writers of America authors, friends, and anyone who knew him or crossed his path. I tell you this not to rewrite Cotton's obituary, but to let you know what he was like and the influence he had on me.

Dad loved American history, reading and Western movies. One of the first movies I watched all the way through—with him, I was eight—was *The Magnificent Seven*. That grew into my fondness for movies that had three things: horses, cowboys, and horses. I can't count how many times I've rewatched classics like *Winchester '73*, *Silverado*, *Rio Bravo*, and *Tombstone*, but it's more times than soldiers who went after Butch and Sundance.

Family vacations—those old-fashioned long epics we

all used to take in the car—were amazing because we often went to places that breathed with Old West history: Deadwood, Santa Fe, Cheyenne, all of 'em. It was on one of those epic journeys that Dad introduced me to the joys of reading Louis L'Amour. I was about ten or eleven and that first one was *Flint*. Somewhere on the highway between Casper and Cody, I got hooked. *The Daybreakers* and *Hondo* followed. Later when those movies with Tom Selleck and Sam Elliott came out, I wanted to be a Sackett.

It was with great pride that the Smith family celebrated Dad's first book, *Dark Trail to Dodge*. We even had special "Dark Trail" beer brewed for the occasion, with his cover as the label. You see, the Smith family is a rowdy bunch. Our backyard croquet games are noisy and highly competitive. Our wiffle ball games have been known to include beanballs and charging the mound. And that's just the six-year-old nephews. We don't *sing* the happy birthday song, we literally holler it at the top of our lungs. We're a full contact family. Always have been.

Holidays, birthdays, and ballgames were always accompanied by family meals. Often, we'd go around the table, everyone getting the opportunity to share what they were thankful for or impart wisdom or report some news. Sometimes there were tears. Sometimes debate. Always good stuff and always laughter. Lots of it. Cotton sat the head of the table with Sonya at the other end, holding court.

After Cotton unexpectedly died in 2015, I vowed that I would keep the stories he created alive by finishing his Corrigan Brothers series. But life kept getting in the way and my promise went unfulfilled. That is, until my retirement and Covid isolation joined forces and gave me time to focus on writing. Flash forward to 2024 when my friends at Wolfpack Publishing believed in the concept of my continuing on, *in the spirit of a Classic Cotton Smith Western Adventure*. The Corrigan saga now stands at five books instead of two. I'm eager to see what Holt, Deed, and Blue do next.

So Dad's gone now, Mom too. But their spirits live on. The Smith clan is still full contact. We still belt out *Happy Birthday*. The family meals are still lively. But now it's my turn to tell a story. As Dad would say, it's "good stuff."

My reader friends, I hope you think so too.

VENGEANCE WEARS
A STAR

CHAPTER ONE

"I did'ent know you was in town." Judge Oscar Pence looked up, grinning.

"A very good morning to you, sir." The calm reply came from the dark, barrel-chested man wearing a *serape*.

"Lemme get rid of this." The gray-haired magistrate spit out a wad of chewing tobacco into the surrounding snarly brush. The small tin can of spit juice remained in his hand. "Nasty habit; one o' my vices I guess."

The two stood silently watching their horses drink from a small cistern outside of Wilkon, Texas. The early morning sun promised a beautiful warm day.

"Are you coming or going, Judge?" the man with a messy mop of shaggy brown hair asked.

"I s'pose I'm comin', my good man. Jus' spent the night at the Lazy S. Felix n' I got inta our chess games an' talkin' 'bout his land. We enjoyed more'n a little of his glorious Spanish wine!"

"His land?"

"Not ta reveal too much, it ain't my place, but he's made some interestin' discoveries across his property."

"You don't say."

"And there're more places like it. If'n you know how an' where ta look."

"I see…" the reddish, brown-skinned man began to intone softly. "Food grows from the earth, but underneath all is torn up and crushed. The stones of the earth contain sapphires and its dust contains gold."

The judge raised his eyebrows at the response. "He ain't talkin' sapphires or gold, but he's got somethin' thar that's fer sure."

"We search the depths of the earth and dig for rocks in the darkness. But where can wisdom be found?"

"Huh? That sounds biblical. Don' know too much 'bout that. I s'pose wisdom cain be foun' most anywheres. Like a good game a' chess."

"Or the Good Book," the shaggy-haired man interjected. "To be wise, you must have reverence for the Lord."

"Sure, but I'm talkin' down here on earth. There be truth n' honesty in chess. The game is always constant, always within the boundaries. Rules that cain't be broken. The pieces never lie. It ain't corrupt like the world we live in."

"Life and chess. A battle on a board," the large man mused. "The Kingdom of God is intense warfare too. Protection. Sacrifice. All that matters is delivering the final checkmate."

"I dunno 'bout all that. So you play?"

"I play," the man declared. "Like life, humans are pawns; the knights, rooks, bishops, and queen are angels and divine forces. The whole point is to protect the king.

God. Pawns can only move forward, they can't go back. Like people. They must give their lives to protect the king. Pawns that reach the end of the board can become a divine force. An angel."

Judge Pence was not sure what to make of this conversation. Besides, his horse had its fill. It was time to mount up.

"If you were to play the perfect game of chess, would you ever play again?" the man abruptly asked.

"I 'magine I'd keep playin'. The game teaches you 'bout yerself. It's good fellowship. Felix n' I have figgered out a great many things o'er a game an' a coupla bottles of wine." He smiled and turned from the barrel-chested man to check his saddle cinch.

"The end is the measure for everything that happens within the game," the serape-wrapped man countered. "And how God deals with us."

Suddenly, the judge felt a powerful grip on his shoulder and a sharp blow to his back. And another. And another. He gasped as the air left his body.

And another. And another…

The tin can fell from his hand.

CHAPTER TWO

"Aww, Judge, who the hell did you cross paths with?"

Cassidy County Sheriff Holt Corrigan kneeled over the corpse, taking in the grisly scene as he smoothed his thick mustache in grim thought. He tugged on the brim of his hat and ran his fingers across the cardinal feather in the hatband in silent ceremony.

Judge Oscar Pence had not been dead very long.

Two men from the Sanchez Lazy S had found the body of the murdered federal court magistrate on their way into town. One of the riders dashed ahead to report their discovery while the other stayed behind.

Pence had been stabbed in the back. Multiple times. A large patch of reddish-brown mud marked where his life bled away. The judge's dress coat and white shirt were covered in muck and sticky blood. A few of the deadly thrusts had pushed completely through his body.

Holt had seen damage like this before—these gruesome punctures could only have been delivered by a bayonet.

The sun was pushing its way through the fall Texas morning, gathering in intensity. Holt squinted his light-blue eyes through the glare. He was an imposing figure even though he was only of average height, hard-faced with high cheekbones of bronze. The long scar on his right cheek, a reminder of a cavalry battle, was faded now into a mark that some said made him more hand-some, more mysterious. A breeze fluttered his shoulder-length brown hair like a cavalry guidon.

Holt turned away from the body and focused on the man standing next to him. Cliente, the foreman of the Lazy S ranch, was a friend. The location of the Sanchez property made them neighbors to the Corrigans Rafter C and Bar 3 compound. The two families looked out for one another, combining roundup duties, driving cattle together, and sharing ranch hands.

And both had been through hell together these past months.

The families and their ranches had been menaced by the evil scheme of Agon Bordner. Earlier that spring, the villainous El Paso businessman launched his treacherous bid for the most notorious land grab in Texas history. His strategy was simple and brutal—target local ranches, kill the families, and steal the land. After just a few months of terror, the Corrigan and Sanchez ranches were the final ones remaining on Bordner's blacklist.

They paid a price.

The Sanchezes lost their middle son, Thomas, in an ambush led by a crooked Bordner lawman. Their youngest son, Paul, was shot in a direct attack on the Lazy S ranch house. Deed Corrigan, the youngest Corrigan brother, had been wounded in the same ambush that killed Thomas.

Holt, a Confederate soldier who had not surrendered, continued to wage war by riding the outlaw trail, robbing Union-owned banks and stages carrying federal military payrolls. He had just returned to Wilkon after hearing first-hand of Agon Bordner's plans to control the region. Had it not been for Holt's resolution to finally come home when he did, he would not have arrived just in time to save his wounded brother and help defend the Corrigan and Sanchez families.

"Was he lying like this when you found him?" Holt asked.

"No. He face down. In his own blood," Cliente responded. "We roll him over. Find out who this be. If still alive. *Ya estaba muerto*. We no help. He already dead."

"And his horse? Where was it?" Holt continued.

"Judge's *caballo* out in road. Saw it first, near trail to *la cisterna*. It *estaba pastando*. Grazing," Cliente answered. "*No había sido robado*. It not stolen or run far."

Cliente and one of his vaqueros had been on their way to Wilkon's tack and general store when they came upon Pence's Appaloosa, riderless, on the road about a mile outside of town. A quick search nearby revealed the body of the judge lying by an old brick cistern. The tiny reservoir just off the road held rainwater and was used to water horses. Lazy S men often stopped here since the riders' brown skin was sometimes a barrier for using the public troughs in town.

Trying to put the pieces of this riddle together, Holt kept up the questions. "Did you see anyone—anyone at all? Before or after you found him?"

"No. *Nadie más*. No one else. U*un paseo tranquilo*. A quiet ride."

The road was usually heavily traveled, one of the common routes into Wilkon. Holt glanced around, studying the landscape near the cistern.

"What do you think, Cliente? Was this a robbery gone bad?"

"No think so. *El bandido mas interesado in matar*," he uttered, shaking his head. "Only interested in killing."

Holt looked him in the eyes and nodded in agreement. He had not wanted to believe the words from Cliente's rider this morning. Now, the stark reality of the judge's death hammered one name through his mind—Bordner! What if this was a revenge killing? What if there were *more* of the wicked man's gang still around? The thought punched him hard.

Just two days ago, gun smoke from what he believed was a last-ditch assault from the remaining Bordner men had blanketed the streets of Wilkon in a shroud of violence. Three surviving outlaws now sat in the Wilkon jail.

The possibility of more Bordner devilry put Holt's senses on battle alert.

"Stand where you can see the horses," he instructed Cliente, who was still holding a rifle he had drawn when he discovered the riderless horse. "Stay ready. This may not be over. Keep an eye on them. And watch the dog. Tag's a good sentry. He'll let us know if something's around that shouldn't be."

Tag Along, Holt's gray and brown dog with large floppy ears had been left with the horses at the road. Known as Tag, the dog had adopted Holt during a shoot-

out with members of the Bordner gang. Holt figured they
got along because they both were a couple of strays.

Only a month before, it was Judge Pence who
presided over a hearing on Bordner's concocted accusa-
tions that the Corrigans robbed the Wilkon bank. The
brothers' defense was so strong that they were all ruled
innocent. Instead, the judge drew his long-barreled
revolver and aimed it at Bordner, ordering the arrest of
the businessman and his gang for murder, robbery, bank
fraud and cattle rustling. To assist with their capture, he
requested the armed help of Texas Rangers and the
Sanchezes. Suddenly, Bordner and his men pulled hidden
guns with no intention of going quietly.

"Drop your guns...you too, Judge," Bordner had
declared. "You bastard Corrigans are going to die now.
You've caused me too much trouble."

Instead of complying, Judge Pence fired and clipped
a Bordner man in the shoulder. A fierce gun battle ensued
in the courtroom with Bordner and his gang facing off
against the Corrigan brothers and their friends, including
the judge. Bordner and most of his men were killed in the
shoot-out. The rest of the outlaw crew was thrown in jail.

In the calm aftermath of the firefight, Judge Pence
acknowledged Holt's role in helping bring down the
notorious businessman and gave him amnesty for his
post-war actions. In addition to the pardon, the judge
promptly appointed Holt to be Cassidy County's top
lawman. He had realized that most of the allegations
against Holt were linked to Bordner's attempts to frame
him and to yellow newspapers emphasizing sensation-
alism over facts.

"I reckon one o' the heroes of Sabine Pass deserves a
badge," Judge Pence had said to Holt that day. "So let's

resolve this outlaw issue ri't now." Smiling at Holt, he said, "Texas needs good men like ya, helpin' it grow, not runnin' from past mistakes." As he pinned the sheriff's badge on Holt's shirt, Pence had patted him on the shoulder and said, "Do good, boy."

Now, Holt was standing over the lifeless body of the man whom he considered to have resurrected his life. The bile that wanted to rise in his throat was not because of the brutality of the murder, but the tremendous sense of loss that was growing inside him.

Holt searched the ground near the body. The short path leading from the road to the cistern was wide enough for three, maybe four horses and free of vegetation, as was the open ring around the little water tank. This circle, like the road, was worn down by repeated use. Outside that loop, snarly brush and thin trees surrounded the area, attracted to the water.

He was no stranger to surprise attacks. War had taught him well. Holt noted that this nearby area offered some cover, but not enough for an ambusher to be completely hidden. "If I'm going to stab someone here," he muttered under his breath, "my victim would see me coming." There was nothing revealing the reason for the violence that had occurred here, just lots of horse and mule tracks, and an occasional boot or sandal print. No obvious sign of a struggle.

Except for the body of the judge.

Holt moved toward Cliente and peered out to the wide main road. It was sandy with dusty stones lying in wait just under the surface. The dry weather meant that most of the trail was pounded nearly into powder by all the wagons and four-legged traffic. Tracks blended into tracks which blended into more tracks. As he stepped out onto the road, his gaze took in the sea of mesquite, prickly pear, tall bluestem, and cat's claw that guarded either side. Live oak, pecan, and cottonwood trees stood here and there. He never really noticed before, but he spotted more than a few places where a sharpshooter with a gun could possibly hide.

"Good cover for bad intentions," he commented to Cliente. "If you're a sniper."

"*Si*, someone could hide, do harm here."

"But the judge's murderer needed to get close. You can't sneak up with a bayonet like that and not be seen."

Holt's mind raced as he returned to the body. He did not think the judge fell from his horse. The Appaloosa would likely have been spooked and run further away. The judge's clothes weren't dirty from fighting. They only got that way because he ended up on the ground.

Holt called out to his friend, "Cliente, if you were attacked and couldn't react with a weapon, what would you do?"

"No weapon?" Cliente rubbed his chin. "*Reaccionar.* Cliente fight back. With fists. Feet. *La protección. Defender hasta la muerte.*"

"Exactly. You'd protect yourself. You'd fight, to the death if need be. But the judge has no injuries other than the stab wounds in his back. His sleeves aren't torn. There aren't any slashes on his arms or hands as if he tried to defend himself. In fact, he's got a newspaper in one hand and a...a..."—he bent over to get closer—"a prickly pear bloom in the other." It was becoming obvious to Holt that Pence was attacked right here and fell where his body was found.

The gray-bearded judge had a distinct Missouri twang and always looked like a man in charge of the world. He had a manner that was more woodsman than magistrate. The long-barreled revolver he carried in a shoulder holster was not for show. He knew how to use it.

Did the judge know the person who did this? Was that why his guard appeared to be down? That possibility was seeming more likely to Holt. Judge Pence was a gregarious man, but he was cautious too.

Holt finished his thought, "Oscar was no coward. He would have fought."

He kneeled and gently closed the judge's eyes. With a bandanna from his own pocket, he wiped Pence's face to try to clean away the brutality the blood and dirt painted there.

Holt carefully went through the judge's jacket and vest, removing everything from the pockets and placing the smaller items inside the dirtied neckerchief. The judge was wearing the shoulder holster inside his jacket, the long-barreled Smith & Wesson still tucked there safely. One inner pocket held his wallet with a fair amount of cash. The other breast pocket held a compact leather portfolio containing papers. Side pockets on the jacket held a variety of personal items—a small sack containing a plug of chewing tobacco, a clasp knife with the blade worn down from years of cutting chews, a handful of cartridges for the pistol, some hard candy, and a stub of an old pencil. A silver dollar and brass key were nestled in the chest pocket of his vest. A nice gold watch on a chain was attached to a buttonhole on the vest and tucked into a side pocket. His pants pockets held a few coins and a couple of handkerchiefs. Last, he removed the rolled-up newspaper from the judge's right hand and prickly pear flower from his left.

Holt stood and adjusted his own twin shoulder

holsters which carried Russian Smith & Wesson .44s. An ivory silhouette of a panther was inlaid in each black pistol grip. He walked back to the road where Cliente had tied up the judge's horse. He added the personal belongings to the judge's saddlebags, planning to go through everything back at the office.

From his shirt pocket he pulled out a small red rock with a star-like white spot in its center. His medicine stone. The rock was a spiritual support, a ritual he embraced from Indian beliefs. He credited its special medicine with getting him through some tough times. His thoughts drifted as he rolled the stone in his fingers. He also carried a mountain lion claw in another pocket and had done so since he was twelve. It was a gift from his mother. Now it was sacred to him, like his stone.

Holt retrieved a small pouch of shredded tobacco from his trail coat tied to his horse's saddle. Returning back to where the judge lay, he took some of the tobacco and sprinkled it in all directions, a ceremony he had also adopted from Indians. "Spirits of the land..." he began, speaking to the sky. "Walk with this man...lead him on his journey...and continue watching over those who cared for him."

Kneeling again over the body, Holt whispered, "Thank you, my friend." After a moment of thought, he added, "I bet you'll be back as an owl. Or a bear." He stopped as his emotions rose. He stood with the medicine stone gripped tightly and shook his fist, angrily vowing, "I will find who did this to you. You will have justice."

CHAPTER THREE

Back in the Wilkon jail, town marshal, James Hannah, was operating with limited information and an abundance of concern. He had reported for duty that morning only to hear Deputy Logan Wheeler tell him a rider had brought word that Judge Pence was found dead. Likely murdered. Holt had rushed out to investigate. The deputy was to join Holt with a wagon for the body as soon as Hannah got situated.

To Hannah, it seemed obvious that the magistrate who helped bring down Agon Bordner could be a target for revenge. He also considered that the report of the judge's murder could be a ruse. Drawing Holt and Wheeler away like that could leave the jail a bullseye for any remaining Bordner men looking to free their friends. Either way, he was concerned that all hell could break loose.

Again.

In the thunderous courtroom battle that ended Bordner's life, Hannah had cut down notorious gunman Macy Shields and another henchman. Other gang members hammered Hannah with gunshots and he had collapsed, seriously wounded. It had only been in the last week or so that he truly felt himself again.

As far as anyone knew, there were only three Agon Bordner gang members still alive and they were sitting here in Wilkon's jail. The first was Bordner's right-hand man, Rhey Selmon, a veteran of New Mexico cattle wars and excellent with a gun. He wore a long bearskin coat regardless of the season. Also locked up was Sear Georgian, a huge cruel beast who liked to kill with his bare hands. A third Bordner outlaw—not as much of a threat as the first two, but still dangerous—was a diminutive mongrel of man named Pickles, an unbalanced bandit nicknamed for his love of the briny treats. These were supposedly the only remnants from the gang.

While the Texas Rangers were transporting the Bordner criminals jailed after the courtroom shoot-out to prison, Rhey Selmon's half brother ambushed the lawmen and broke them out of custody. In the violent frenzy that ensued, the fugitives attempted to rob the Wilkon bank and made an ill-fated getaway attempt by trying to kidnap Corrigan women.

Thanks to the Corrigans and Marshal Hannah, the desperate scheme ended badly for the outlaws. Rhey's half brother and three other gang members died on the main street of Wilkon. The three survivors—Rhey, Sear, and Pickles—were once again behind bars. The judge had already sentenced them to life in prison. With their involvement in the murders of the Rangers, prison life was likely to be cut short by a rope.

Hearing the rider's report about the judge, Mayor Patterson Cooke had run to the jail. Being the town gossip, the German lumberyard owner sought out

Marshal Hannah to acquire information he could spread around town.

"'Tis *ein* desperate situation, for zure," Mayor Cooke said. "Iss *zer* anyting I can do to help, *Herr* Hannah?"

"Thank you, mayor, but with Holt already gone and Logan leaving to investigate what's happened to the judge, I'm too shorthanded for comfort. The only thing I need is someone who's handy with a gun. And I need him right now."

"Ahh, *das* judge. Vat do you tink happened?"

"I can't give you information I don't have." Hannah sent the mayor away and shut the heavy jail door with a bang.

The mayor left disappointed, but within minutes there was an insistent knock at the jail door.

"Marshal Hannah! Marshal, open up! It's Bradley."

Standing on the planked boardwalk outside the jail was Bradley Cooke, the twenty-year-old son of the mayor, volunteering his services.

Wheeler opened the door carefully while Hannah had his shotgun leveled at the opening. The young man was quickly let in.

"Dad said you needed an extra hand," the long blond-haired Bradley announced. An old carbine was in his hands and a beat-up Army Colt strapped to his hip. "I'm here to help."

"Good to see you, Bradley," Wheeler nodded. "Thanks."

"What's that you got there?" Hannah indicated the rifle in Bradley's hands.

"M-My rifle, Marshal," Bradley answered, trying to stay confident.

"You any good with it?" Hannah asked with a wry smile.

"I've been putting food on our table since I was eleven," the young man declared.

"That's not what I meant."

"I hit what I aim at and make every shot count," Bradley said defiantly.

"All right. Put that down on the desk. You're going to use this." Hannah tossed the double-barreled Greener he was holding to Bradley. The young man caught the weapon with one hand and immediately flipped the top lever, popping open the breech ends. Like a seasoned gunman, he checked the loads and closed the break-action with an upward flick of his wrist.

Hannah nodded.

Just then, they could hear José Vaca, the Lazy S rider who brought the news of the judge to town, pulling up outside the jail with a wagon.

"Logan, before you go, let's move these idiots into one cell," Hannah said, drawing out another double-barreled shotgun from the rack behind the desk.

With scatterguns aimed directly at the three prisoners, they wrangled the outlaws all together into one cell.

"There now, all cozy, aren't you boys?" Hannah scoffed. There were no responses from the cell.

Grabbing his Henry rifle from the rack as he left, Logan called out, "We'll be back as soon as we can, Marshal!"

Hannah locked and barricaded the door as soon as Logan slammed it shut.

Two of the prisoners, Sear Georgian and Pickles, relaxed quietly into their new arrangement. Georgian dozed on the bunk, and Pickles sat against the wall amusing himself with lint from a pocket. The third, Rhey Selmon, paced like a caged animal. His eyes were ice blue and slightly crossed. Black hair strung from under a narrow-brimmed hat. He had been Agon Bordner's right-hand man, the only member of the gang that dared to call him by his first name and the only one Bordner trusted. His ever-present bearskin coat had been searched and he was allowed to wear it.

"I knew you'd be trouble for us from the very moment I laid eyes on you in El Paso." Selmon sneered at Hannah. "I shoulda killed you then."

"I wish you would've tried." Hannah chuckled. "You ain't that good."

Hannah, a notorious hired gun, was initially enlisted by Bordner to kill Deed Corrigan. Unbeknownst to the crooked businessman, Hannah had already befriended Deed and his brothers. Bordner's intended recruit instead became a deadly adversary to his plans. Hannah had played an important role in staving off the far-reaching evil. Now he had found a new life wearing a star, protecting his new town.

Quickly deputized, Bradley Cooke now sat directly in front of the packed cell. The double-barreled shotgun sat comfortably in his hands and a box of shells lay next to him.

Hannah made his orders clear. "Bradley, if anyone we don't know tries to get in, start firing into that cell until I say 'stop' or you run out of shells." Hannah looked the young man directly in the eyes. "Understand? There can be no thought, no hesitation."

The new deputy nodded solemnly. He vowed that he would not let the marshal down.

Selmon spit his defiance from the cell. The glob of spittle landed near the box of shells.

In an eye blink, Bradley stood and forcefully jabbed the barrels of the shotgun into Selmon's belly, making the outlaw lurch backward.

"Didn't your mama teach you better than that, bear boy?" Bradley growled.

At the unexpected response from Bradley, Hannah rubbed at his face to hide a grin.

"Selmon, unless you want some of that in your food, you best sit down and shut the hell up," the marshal barked.

Selmon did not respond and pushed Georgian's legs out of the way to make room at the end of the cot. Bradley sat back down and made sure the outlaw saw that his shotgun was now trained directly on him.

CHAPTER FOUR

As Holt was vowing justice over his murdered friend, a wagon bustled up to where Cliente stood guard.

"We came as quickly as we could," Deputy Wheeler declared. José Vaca nodded in agreement.

Cliente greeted the deputy and gestured toward the cistern. "Holt and judge this way."

Holt, Cliente, and Vaca gently laid the judge on a blanket while Wheeler stood guard. They carefully folded it around his body and placed him in the back of the wagon.

"When we get back, I need you to go check the judge's cottage," Holt instructed the deputy. "See if anything looks out of place. Marshal Hannah and I will go through the things from his pockets and his saddle-bags. Maybe something in there can answer why." Wheeler nodded his understanding.

"And Logan." Holt looked him square in the eye. "This may be more Bordner crap."

"Yeah, Hannah wondered that too." Wheeler shook his head, staring at the covered body. "He and Mayor Cooke's son have got the jail locked and barricaded. I know there's plenty of shotguns in there."

"Good move." Holt acknowledged the deputy's report. A former hired gunman, Wilkon town Marshal James Hannah was someone who knew how to handle himself when things got hot.

"Even though he's dead," Holt stated to the men assembled around him, "this could be one more card in Bordner's evil game. That fat bastard could still be playing with us."

With that, Holt's thoughts rushed to his brothers. What if this meant danger back home?

"Wheeler, did Hannah send out any word or alarm?"

"Yeah, the marshal sent a rider out to your Rafter C."

It was time to go. It was not good to be out here, isolated. Holt called to Tag and put him up on the wagon seat. "You stay here, Tag."

Vaca climbed onto the wagon and steadied the reins. Deputy Wheeler joined him. Cliente put a lead rope on Judge Pence's horse to pony it back to Wilkon. Holt took one last look around.

"Keep watch. It's possible whoever did this may still be lurking,"

Vaca clicked the wagon team into motion. Holt and Cliente fanned their horses out around the wagon. Their rifles, eyes, and other senses were on high alert.

Seated between the deputy and Vaca, Tag sat tall to guard the judge's final ride into town.

———

Their watchful trip on the dusty trail into Wilkon was uneventful. Only a few travelers passed them on the road, not knowing anything about the wagon, only intent on getting to their own destinations.

At the outskirts of town, three riders approached the small caravan.

A brief smile crossed Holt's face. He would recognize those silhouettes anywhere. The first rider was his older brother, Blue Corrigan. His left sleeve was pinned to his side, most of the arm taken by Union artillery. In the middle was his younger brother, Deed. A near copy of Holt, except for shorter hair, the stock of his rifle rested on his thigh. The third rider was their friend, Nakashima Silka, an older, brawny, former *samurai*. He was unmistakable, carrying a long, curved sword sheathed across his back and a shorter sword belted at his waist. They had received word from the messenger sent by Marshal Hannah and hurriedly took a shortcut to town from their ranches.

Cliente spoke first in his clipped English. "Is Corrigans. More help."

Holt's gaze met his brothers. No words. Eyes full of concern.

Since springtime, the Corrigans were the major force that stood between Agon Bordner becoming the baron of northwest Texas. Bordner-related mayhem had also continued after his death. They had reason for unease with the news of Judge Pence's murder.

Blue and Deed had left their Rafter C and Bar 3 ranches with all hands and riders on alert. The Lazy S was warned too. The morning's simple chores were now being completed with everyone at all the ranches fully armed, watchful eyes wary for an attack. The defenders felt the strain of always needing to have their guard up, but they would be ready.

Holt filled them in on where the judge was found and who discovered him.

Blue responded, "Bordner's men responsible?"

"Not sure." Holt shrugged his shoulders. "It wouldn't surprise me though."

"I thought everyone was spoken for, either buried or locked up," Deed asked.

"It wasn't a random robbery gone bad?" Blue wondered.

Holt shook his head grimly. "He was bayoneted from behind. Too many times to count. Someone wanted to be absolutely certain he was dead."

"Damn," muttered Deed.

"Aiiee, that is not good," Silka added.

Resuming their trek into Wilkon, sounds of the town reached them when they hit city limits. The rumble and creak of large freight wagons. Bangs and clatter of construction. An unseen dog barked at something it didn't like. A door slammed. Somewhere a tinny piano accompanied the merriment of laughter.

The wagon stopped in front of the undertaker's office. The men all tied up their horses and climbed down. A portly man with a rumpled shirt and wrinkled vest stepped out from the office. Claude Gausage, the town's undertaker and woodworker, met them on the planked sidewalk.

"We got Judge Pence here," Deputy Wheeler said, motioning to the back of the wagon.

Together, the Corrigan brothers carefully carried the

blanketed body inside. Silka followed them in. Tag stayed on the walkway out front.

"Set him up with the best, Claude. Send me the bill," Holt said quietly as Gausage unwrapped the blanket. Blue said a silent prayer. Deed solemnly touched a medallion at his throat. "He has no relatives that I know of. We're his family now," Holt added.

Stepping back out into the bright sun, the brothers planned to join Marshal Hannah at the jail.

Blue stepped up, putting his arm on his brother's shoulder. "I'm sorry, Holt. He was a good man."

"Thank you, big brother," Holt nodded. "He gave me my life back. I owe him."

Silka, who had been quiet in the *samurai* way and in respect to their dead friend, suddenly declared, "Something tell Silka this not work of Bordner. Judge's body hold…something *akugō*…more evil." He uttered something else in Japanese and spat into the dirt.

Holt acknowledged, "You may be right, my friend. And I'm damn sure going to find out."

Silka agreed, "It is so," and murmured some more undistinguishable words. He touched a small brass circle on a rawhide thong worn around his neck. The Japanese symbol for the word *Bushido* was engraved on the disk. Deed wore a similar medallion, a gift from Silka years before, except his rawhide had a throwing knife fastened to it which was concealed behind his neck.

"I dunno," Deed joined in. "I wouldn't put anything past that Bordner sonuvabitch, even from the grave."

With everything handled at the undertaker, Holt reminded Logan that the judge's cottage, just outside of town, needed to be checked.

"Not sure what you'll find. Take someone with you if

you want," he advised the deputy. "In fact, that might be a really good idea."

A small group of townspeople now gathered on the sidewalk around them, peppering the sheriff with questions. The rider, earlier, roaring into town shouting that the judge had been murdered had triggered the spreading of stories through town. The arrival of the wagon guarded by Holt and all the men with guns was ominous. The town was already drained from the violence of the past few months.

"Yes, I'm sorry to say," Holt spoke loudly and clearly to the assembled citizens. "Judge Pence is dead."

Gasps of horror and shock resounded through the gathering. A jumble of conversations launched at once. A couple of women burst into tears.

Through the clamor, a high reedy voice broke through, "Judge Pence? Dead?" Butting his way through the group that had gathered, Leroy Gillespie, the owner, editor and chief reporter for the *Wilkon Epitaph* newspaper, interrupted everyone and placed himself in front of Holt.

"Was the judge murdered?" asked the thin-faced man with sad-dog eyes, notepad at the ready. "Someone said a rider brought the news to town, yelling he'd been killed."

"We don't know much of anything yet," Holt answered.

"Who do you think did it?" The small crowd let the reporter do their talking.

"I'm not saying anyone did it, did I? I don't know many details." Holt was not going to engage with this bothersome reporter who was always trying to build interest in his paper by running all manner of stories, the more lurid or sensational the better.

Right after the Bordner shoot-out in Judge Pence's court, the *Epitaph* had run a big story about the Corrigans standing up to the crooked man from El Paso. Much to his chagrin, Holt had been a major part of the article. The report exaggerated his post-war exploits and embellished the brothers' efforts in saving the town. There was no mention of the Sanchez family's role. Or of Hannah's. At least the detail about Holt receiving amnesty from Judge Pence was accurate and not overstated. In the account, Gillespie included a reference to Wilkon as "Kill Town." Holt did not like being the center of attention, but the thing that galled him the most about the article was this yahoo calling his town that name. A name he felt was insulting and downright wrong.

Gillespie adjusted his thick eyeglasses and continued, "Where exactly was he found?

"Outside of town. Like I said, I don't have much to tell." As a lawman and especially as a friend, he did not want to speak about Oscar Pence right now.

Jotting a quick note, Gillespie persisted, "How long had he been dead?"

Holt was growing more irritated by the second. Gillespie's snooping was painful—and annoying.

"We don't know anything for sure right now other than a damn good man is dead," Holt shot back testily. Hoping to bring an end to the gathering, he called out, "Okay, everyone...go back to what you were doing. There's nothing more here."

The townspeople obeyed the sheriff and began to disband. Conversations became a fading jumble of disbelief and shock. But Gillespie had not given up.

Bobbing and weaving through the dispersing crowd

around him, the reporter chirped at Holt, "How did he die?"

Enough was enough.

Glaring at Gillespie, Holt snapped, "He stopped breathing. Got it?" He placed his forearm against the reporter's chest in order to move quickly past. "If you want to help, go find out if Judge Pence had any kin," Holt growled. Moving to the wagon and horses, his words spat angrily, "Otherwise, stay out of my way."

Holt checked his horse's cinch. Cliente, not paying any attention to Gillespie, handed Holt the lead rope attached to Judge Pence's horse.

A soft growl started to arise in Tag's throat.

"Tag, play nice," Holt called as he swung up into his saddle. Ponying the judge's mount behind his own horse, he started riding toward the jail. The dog, just as eager to get away, trotted dutifully down the street next to the lawman.

Gillespie, not taking no for answer started to follow Holt, hollering, "Who found him?"

At that point, Blue walked right in front of Gillespie, briefly breaking the reporter's line of questioning. Not speaking to nor even looking at the reporter, Blue continued walking, completely ignoring the man in the ink-stained coat and shirt.

Blue approached Cliente and Vaca, quietly suggesting they leave now and finish the business they originally headed into town to do.

"You don't want to speak to that man," Blue cautioned in a low voice.

Cliente smiled with a wink and said, "*Sí. No habla, Englais,*" and the two Lazy S men took off toward the tack and general store.

Undeterred, Gillespie adjusted his thick eyeglasses again and started walking in the direction of the jail where Holt was headed. He had taken only a couple of steps before Deed stepped in front of him. Arms folded, Deed's words were measured and direct. "My brother just gave you some very sage advice," he said, his voice and demeanor like a coiled snake. "If you don't want to wear that notepad in a place where it chafes, I'd find something else to do." Two finger pokes to the bespectacled man's chest emphasized Deed's next words. "Right. Now."

Scowling at the reporter, Deed climbed aboard his horse. Blue, now mounted as well, quickly joined his brother. Spurring their horses purposefully to kick up dust in the direction of the reporter, they loped quickly to catch up with Holt.

Coughing and regaining his composure, the writer was suddenly aware that a shadow had loomed in front of him. A wide figure now stood in the path of the *Wilkon Epitaph's* only employee, blocking his view down the street.

"Konnichiwa!" Silka nodded agreeably. He smiled at the reporter and thumped his own chest. "I will speak."

Gillespie peeked around the stocky man at his main targets, now well down the street. Thwarted, but relieved to have *someone* cooperate, he composed himself. Readying his notepad, Gillespie asked, "What can you tell me about the judge?"

Silka began. *"Shiranu ga hotoke…"*

The former *samurai* was only too happy to regale the reporter about a great many things. His presence literally holding the writer in place right there in the street, Silka told the little man that *what you don't know can't hurt you*. He lectured about the richness of life and the importance of bravery and honor. He even spoke of his love for sugar in his coffee. None of it even remotely related to what just happened to Judge Pence.

And all of it in his native Japanese.

Deed looked back and chuckled at what he knew was happening.

CHAPTER FIVE

M arshal James Hannah carried a loaded double-barreled Greener as he prowled around inside the barricaded jail. He coaxed the fire in the stove and started a fresh pot of coffee. It wasn't cold enough for the fire and he didn't really need the coffee, it was just something to occupy time. It wasn't nerves, just pent-up energy. Back during the war, right before engagements, he would check and re-check his weapons as well as relieve himself several times, each time carefully re-tucking his tunic. He just needed something to do until it was time to act.

Hannah unlocked the hinged heavy plank that shielded one of the barred windows and opened it just a crack. He took care not to show himself or leave the big wooden shutter open long. He mainly tried to pick up sounds, anything that might alert him to trouble—or the return of Sheriff Corrigan and Deputy Wheeler. Bolting the shutter closed, he broke open his Greener and rechecked the loads. He looked at Bradley, whose attention was focused on the prisoners. Stepping over behind the desk, Hannah checked the rack of rifles and shotguns, making sure they were all loaded. Again.

The coffee was ready, so he poured himself a half mug of the hot brew. He was taking his first sip when a knock at the jail door switched the gunman-turned-lawman to battle readiness. A grim nod at his young assistant signaled: Get ready. Four hammer clicks from their two shotguns were ominous punctuation.

"Who's there?" Hannah called out.

"It's Holt. I'm with Blue and Deed."

"If you're the Corrigans, who did I meet first?"

Deed's reply came immediately. "We met in a stage-coach, having a tea party hosted by some Comanches."

Relieved, Hannah smiled his relieved affirmation to Bradley, but the young man kept his weapon readied. Just in case.

Returning the hammers on his own shotgun safely to rest, he lifted the heavy brace that was barricading the entrance and opened the door. Holt, Blue, and Deed breezed through the entrance and with them came the brilliance of the day and fresh air. Tension escaped from the room like turning up a lamp.

Tag entered as well, bouncing cheerfully among their legs, seeking attention. His tail whipped back and forth at the whole idea of being surrounded by his friends. He was just happy to be included in this gathering.

Holt shut the door and set the brace back into position.

Bradley eased the hammers on his shotgun back to a setting position. The arrival of the Corrigans meant the threat inside was lessened at least a little bit. He took a deep breath. And a few more. The tenseness in his shoul-ders gradually eased, but he did not move from his position nor take his eyes off the prisoners. Hannah had not asked the young man whether he had ever been in a situation like this before, and Bradley had not said. The young man was comfortable around guns and a proficient hunter, but this was the first time he had to be ready to use his weapon against another man. He wanted to prove himself to the Corrigans and Marshal Hannah.

The brothers grouped around the desk with the marshal. Holt tossed the judge's saddlebags in the middle. "He's dead, James. Some bastard stabbed him, over and over," he said softly, sadly.

Hannah exhaled a deep sigh of dejection and tossed his shotgun down next to the saddlebags. "Goddammit," he uttered, shaking his head in disgust. Taking off his eyeglasses, he slumped in the desk chair and began cleaning them with a handkerchief.

"I need some coffee," Holt declared. "Any made?" He went to the small stove and checked the pot.

It was nearly full. The aroma was strong, hot, and welcoming.

Holt approached the mayor's son with the coffeepot and an empty mug. "Thanks for helping, Bradley. I really appreciate it. Want some?"

"Glad to help, Sheriff. I'll pass on the coffee." The young man kept a firm grip on the gun to hide his still-trembling hands. "Maybe a little whiskey when this is over, thanks."

Deed went to a corner of the office near a small table that held a water pitcher, metal basin, and towels. From a vest pocket he offered a small piece of jerky to Tag. He poured some fresh water from the pitcher into a small pan on the floor that had been set for Holt's "deputy." The dog eagerly lapped it up.

"Hey, how 'bout some coffee fer us?" The gruff belligerence of Rhey Selmon broke through the room. "You take better care of that mangy dog than us!"

"Shut up, Selmon," Deed retorted without looking at the outlaw.

"You shut up. You know the only reason I'm here is that no-good Apache bitch stabbed me with some scissors," Selmon sneered.

Ignoring the outlaw until just then, Holt's question shot out like a gun. "What did you say?"

"You heard me."

"I did. Here…have some coffee!" He threw the entire contents of the pot of scalding hot coffee at Selmon. The outlaw screamed with pain and rage.

"You talk that way again about my brother's wife, I'll shoot you where you stand."

Blue moved next to Holt, a wry smile on his face. "I appreciate that, little brother, but save your bullets." He turned to glare at Selmon and the smile left his eyes. "I'll shoot him." The ferocity in Blue's eyes made Selmon take a step back.

Grabbing the empty coffee pot from Holt's hand, Blue said, "You kind of wasted that. Let me help you make some more."

Two days earlier, during a town celebration, Selmon led a group of Bordner outlaws on a brazen mission to rob the bank and kill the Corrigan brothers once and for all. Marshal Hannah stopped the robbery before it really had a chance to begin. In a last-ditch effort to escape, Selmon and his half brother took two women hostage— Bina, Blue's wife, and Atlee, Deed's fiancée. Caught in a stand-off, the crooks were surrounded by guns pointed straight at them. Bina, a full-blooded Apache, stabbed

Selmon in the stomach with mending scissors she was carrying in a handbag. Atlee used her purse to club Selmon's brother, both women freeing themselves from the grasps of their captors.

Even with the cell bars now separating them, Selmon waited for Blue to walk out to the stove before shouting, "If I *ever* figger out a way to get shut of here, you and yer kin won't live long!" He continued trying to wipe the coffee from his eyes and face. "All of you!" Steam rising from the thrown coffee gave his anger a comical effect.

"God almighty, Selmon, seems like you're always yellin' at us from behind bars." Deed laughed. "And that dumbass bear coat. It stinks as bad as you stink as an outlaw."

From the back of the cell, Pickles laughed and started singing a song he just made up. "You stink, dumbass."

Hannah called toward the lockup. "Selmon, you're nothin' but a loudmouthed asshole who can't back up his bark."

"How about we open the door and let you pick a Corrigan to finish this conversation?" Holt suggested. "Prove Marshal Hannah wrong. Maybe you're more than words."

Deed grinned at the idea. "Let's do it." His smile was lethal.

Nothing but silence came from the cell, except for Pickles's giggly "stinky dumbass" chorus.

"Quiet, Pickles," grumbled Selmon, ignoring the challenge.

"I thought so." Deed smirked, shaking his head.

Calm now, Holt mused into his empty mug as he addressed Selmon. "So, Selmon, you don't know how you're getting out of here? C'mon, you're expecting someone besides a Ranger escort, aren't you?"

"Go to hell, Corrigan."

"Yeah, go to hell, Corrigan." Pickles imitated Selmon's surly retort with a snicker.

"No one else waiting in the weeds to kill us and spring you with the rest of this trash?" Holt coaxed.

"We got friends," Selmon countered.

"There ain't nobody left, stinky dumbass." Pickles chuckled. "They dun shot ev'ryone else."

"Shut up, Pickles!"

"No more vengeful Bordner men or Selmon family?" Holt continued.

Pickles kept up his story, singing, "Rhey was Agon's fav-rite, but the big man caught that there guy's knife." He pointed at Deed. Bordner's *coup de grâce* in the courtroom shoot-out had been Deed burying his throwing knife deep into the evil rancher's heart.

"Georgian, shut him up!" Selmon thundered at the hulking man lying on the bunk.

Ignoring the man in the big coat, Pickles carried on. "Ya all kilt Rhey's lil' brother. He ain't got no more friends…'ceptin' whores…and us two." He began repeating "No friends, just whores," in a tune that sounded a lot like his previous song.

"I said, shut *up*!" Selmon abruptly launched himself at the little man, enveloping his hands around Pickles's throat. The simple-minded bandit's eyes instantly filled with terror as he clawed at the iron-like fingers and hands throttling him. He was no match for Selmon's strength.

"Hey! He's just funnin'." Georgian sat up and moved to separate the pair. "He cain't help it. Put 'im down!"

Selmon tightened his stranglehold on Pickles, whose

face was turning blue. Georgian swung a huge fist and forearm down across Selmon's shoulder. Both Selmon and Pickles dropped immediately to the floor. Pickles writhed there, choking and gasping for air that would not come. It took Selmon just an instant to recover from the blow before springing to his feet and turning around ready to pounce. Selmon attacked the huge man in fury. In response, Georgian's two huge hands grabbed Selmon's head in a vise-grip and in one brutal motion twisted sharply. The sharp crack instantly signaled the end of Rhey Selmon's life, but not before he had produced a long thin dagger hidden all this time in his bearskin coat. As he let Selmon's lifeless body fall from his hands, Georgian looked down at the front of his shirt. A rapidly expanding blossom of crimson was spreading away from the knife that had been driven deeply into the left side of his chest. Eyes widening at the horror he suddenly found himself in, Georgian tried grabbing at the blade. Instead, he crumpled to the ground into an awkward sitting position. A moment later, he fell over with a heavy thud.

The whole incident happened suddenly. The men out in the office were stunned by its violent swiftness. Only Tag had reacted, barking at the commotion.

Gathering himself, Holt blurted, "Dammit! Cover me." He threw his pistols in Bradley's lap. Big keys clanked and he threw open the cell door. The heavy steel hinges shrieked as if responding to the savagery of what just happened.

There was no doubt Selmon was dead. He lay in a heap where he was dropped. Holt stepped over the body and looked down at the hulking form of Sear Georgian. Selmon's knife was sunk deep, inflicting deadly damage. The huge man's life was spilling onto the floor.

"How about it, Sear?" Holt kneeled. "You want to set things right? You know who killed the judge, don't you?"

Georgian struggled with the words. "Selmon…an' his lil brother…planned our break…from the Rangers…an' the robbery." Speaking and swallowing were becoming more of a struggle. "We's all that's left…we di'nt kill no judge." His voice was now fading along with life. "I knew we shoulda run somewhar's else." He was quiet for several moments. "Guess my boots are on," was the final thing he uttered as light left his eyes.

Holt drew his attention to Pickles. The strange little man didn't have much time left either. Selmon's choke-hold had crushed his windpipe.

"Pickles. Pickles!" Holt hollered, trying to keep the outlaw focused on this life a few moments longer. "Pickles, who killed the judge? What'd you hear?"

The dying outlaw croaked. "Selmon…suppos'd…ta kill…Deed…" His breath came in raspy rattles now. "We suppos'd…to git…you. Thassit. No one…cared about… the judge…" A long, strange moan emitted from his throat as he breathed his last.

Holt stood. He clanged the door shut as he stepped out of the cell.

Everyone stood around the desk in silence. What the hell just happened?

Blue broke the stillness. "Bradley, go get Claude. Tell him we've got three down in here."

Holt added, "Do it *quietly*."

Marshal Hannah sat at the desk and scratched his unshaven chin. Holt took off his hat and rubbed his head vigorously. Maybe that would bring the last several minutes into focus and make sense. Blue said a silent prayer for all the souls in the room.

"You heard those bastards," Deed finally said. "They said no one was left. If they're to be believed…"

"No more Bordner vengeance," Blue finished the thought.

"Livin' up to our reputation. 'Kill Town.'" Hannah chuckled darkly. "Dammit."

"Better not let that Gillespie yahoo hear you repeat that." Holt scowled. "He doesn't need the encouragement."

The feeling of relief that the Bordner reign of terror might truly be over was instantly replaced by the stark apprehension that crept menacingly across the room: Who killed Judge Pence? If Bordner's evil game was over, what new devilry were they just dealt?

Cassidy County Sheriff Holt Corrigan put his hat back on and touched the cardinal feather in the hatband.

"The man's a federal judge. We've got to inform the important people he's dead. Starting with the governor and the Rangers," he declared. "Then we hunt down the bastard who murdered him."

CHAPTER SIX

As word spread of the demise of the remaining Bordner clan, the shadowy veil that weighed on the spirit of the town lifted. Afternoon bustle crowded the streets and more people than usual packed the boardwalks and stores. At the same time, a swarm of activity buzzed around the Wilkon jail.

The undertaker arrived with a wagon to cart away the bodies. Unsolicited, Mayor Cooke sent two of his lumberyard employees to clean up the cells and the office. Of course, it was essential that he hang around to supervise their work and hopefully glean a few juicy details from the lawmen that he could dish out as he held forth around town.

Without going into gory particulars, Hannah shared with the mayor a glimpse of what had happened. Before Mayor Cooke could bombard them with further questions they had no intention of answering, Holt informed him that a telegram response from the capitol would be coming soon. They had telegraphed the governor about the judge's murder, and also wired the Texas Rangers about Pence and the death of the criminals they no longer needed to escort to prison. It was only proper that Wilkon's mayor acknowledge the governor's reply.

"You'll be sure to sign for his honor's answer and let us know it arrived?" Holt affirmed.

"*Danke*, Herr Corrigan. *Ja*, 'tis *sehr gut*." Mayor Cooke brightened. "Very good." All his curiosity about the nastiness in the jail went away. The governor was wiring Wilkon! He had to go and be prepared.

"And tell Bradley thanks again. He made a great deputy!" Hannah hollered as the mayor hustled away.

Mayor Cooke's employees did a good job of mopping up the gory mess in the cell as well as giving the whole building a much-needed cleaning. The copper smell of blood and the reeking odor of dirty outlaws and stinky bearskin no longer pervaded the jail. The biting odor of lye replaced the foulness. Even the wall lamps had been cleaned and readied for their next use. Holt slipped both men a few coins as an extra thank-you for their efforts.

Blue Corrigan headed home, riding with the two Lazy S men back to their ranches. Everyone there would still be anxious and want to know what was happening. Deed and Silka stayed with Holt. The three sat with Marshal Hannah out on the planked boardwalk in front of the jail. Contrasting with the earlier storm that had occurred inside the cell, the day outside had actually become pleasant.

Sitting there in the afternoon sun would have been a good opportunity to relax, but the reverberations of the day's events ricocheted through their minds. The relief over the end of the Bordner saga played tug-of-war with the concern over Judge Pence's senseless murder. Tag took the opportunity to nap for everybody.

The heavy front door and two windows were thrown wide open in a further attempt to air out the office and cells. Holt made a mental note to bring in some sage to burn. The spirits would be pleased and it would make the place smell a lot better too.

They needed to go through Judge Pence's belongings, but it was so nice outside. Even for men who spent a great deal of time outdoors, the warm sunbath was refreshing. Besides, the gusty bitterness of December and its freezing partners, January and February, were just around the corner. All too soon everyone would be bullied inside by cold, wind and snow. A warm fall afternoon deserved to be savored. The reality of digging into what was stowed in those saddlebags could wait just a bit longer.

Holt knew he should be focusing on what lay ahead, but the balmy pleasantness made his mind wander like a stream finding a new course. His thoughts drifted back to how this day started.

———

Ironically, he had been savoring a little peace and some well-earned quiet. The last of the Bordner gang was still alive and behind bars. Texas Rangers had been alerted to cart them off to their final judgments. He had put on a pot of coffee and thrown a short log into the cast-iron stove to chase away the edge of dawn's cold that had settled into the jail office. He pulled out his medicine stone. Soon, thoughts of the new schoolteacher, Claire Baldwin, had begun to crowd his mind as they had since she arrived in town. His imagination replayed the moment he first saw her. He wished he would have gone up and introduced himself right then and there.

At that moment, she had knocked at the jail door. Given recent events, Holt was still on edge, even drawing one of his pistols. "Come in," he had said, cocking the gun. "With your hands empty." And, from daydream to reality, she had stepped through the door.

Claire Baldwin was a vision in blue…stunning in a blue-and-white herringbone suit with large navy buttons and a short cape…a large sky-blue hat that set off her blond hair…and matched her sapphire eyes. She had sought him out at the jail and was thoroughly intoxicating.

Hesitant and awkward, it had taken a few moments before he could find the words to introduce himself. For a man who had faced all kinds of circumstances, dangerous and otherwise, it was unexpected that he would act so uncomfortable around women. He had fought through the clumsy shyness and finally offered Claire a chair and some coffee. She had seen the stone lying on the desk and asked about it. She thought it looked magical. Could she hold it? Holt had explained the stone's significance, surprising himself that words just came jumping from his mouth as he shared things of his life that no one outside his family would know. Their chat had stretched more than an hour. As they talked, her eyes danced with his and time was forgotten.

But then the rider had come. A heavy knock at the door. The body of Judge Oscar Pence had been found. He had to go. Now.

"Of course, I understand," she had said, smiling. "I want to continue this conversation, so I will wait to hear of your return."

The vision of her standing in front of the jail waving to him as he rode out of town played like a repeated melody in his mind.

Deed's voice jerked him back to now. "Big brother, your little notepad pal looks to be heading this way." He smirked, interrupting Holt's daydream and the tranquility of the porch.

Sure enough, newspaperman Leroy Gillespie was again headed in the direction of the jail. With the reappearance of the reporter, their afternoon's reverie was over.

"I'm surprised he's kept away this long," Hannah replied.

Holt sighed. "Let's go see what the judge left behind." Then he disappeared inside the jail.

"Aiiee, I stay here. Greet ink man." Silka grinned. "With Tag." The dog happily accepted a good ear-scratching from the pony-tailed warrior.

Deed and Hannah were a step behind Holt, shutting the door behind them.

On his march to the jail, a storefront display momentarily caught Gillespie's eye. When he looked at the jail porch again, all that was there was the big Japanese man with a large sword propped next to him, seated in a chair playing with a floppy-eared dog. Pursing his lips and adjusting his thick glasses with an ink-stained hand, he abruptly spun around and strode quickly back to his printing office.

Inside the jail, the three men carefully spread Judge

Pence's possessions across the office desk. Two other small tables were pulled over to organize his effects.

On his way out of town, Blue had stabled the judge's horse in the town livery. Before riding out, he and Holt stripped the animal of Pence's gear. Now, stacked neatly in a corner back by the cells was a nice, but well-worn saddle, a blanket, canteen, and a long slicker that was rolled up around a gum blanket.

The first things laid out were the belongings Holt found on the judge's body. His wallet and soft leather folder of papers were left on the desk as was the newspaper and flower found in his hands. These required more attention. Valuable items, the gold pocket watch and his shoulder holster holding the long-barreled Smith & Wesson, were sorted onto one of the small tables. From the bandanna Holt used to wipe off the judge's face came the loose items. The coins from his pants pockets were placed with the pistol along with the silver dollar and key from his vest. A handful of loose cartridges, the pouch of chewing tobacco, an old pocketknife, handkerchiefs, and the stub of a pencil went to the other small table.

Holt threw the neckerchief dirtied by the judge's face into the stove.

A quick rap on the door preceded the energetic entrance of Tag with a happy-dog smile and a grinning Silka. "Ink man saw Silka and did face-about," he reported.

"An about-face?" Deed laughed.

"Yes, is so."

Soft chuckles spread around the desk.

"Maybe he got the hint," Holt said and shook his head dismissively.

The saddlebags were next. The left side held a tightly rolled, but clean, white shirt, a black cravat, a change of socks and long johns, a half-full box of cartridges for his pistol, a leather journal holding a pack of blank writing paper and two pencils, a nice knife with an elk antler handle in a leather sheath, a gavel, and two books— Alexander Pope's translation of *The Iliad* and Dumas's *The Count of Monte Cristo*. The other side of the bags held a new pouch of chewing tobacco, a tin with two lantern candles and a box of waterproof lucifers, a marble, a pocket-sized Bible, small bags of horehound squares and sorghum drops, peppermint sticks packaged in paper, a few strips of beef jerky wrapped in cloth, a can of peaches, a nearly empty bag of corn dodgers, a rawhide kit that held a shaving brush, straight razor and comb, three small rocks, one that looked like a tiny ram's horn, and two with imprints of leaves, and a pocket-sized, but full, flask of good-smelling whiskey.

"I hate this part," Hannah sighed, looking at the judge's writing journal. "Going through what someone left behind."

"Never stopped to think about it much...*before*..." Holt reflected. "This isn't like wartime when you quickly rifled through a dead man's things, looking for maps, ammunition or food. You took what you needed. For survival. This is different. This is an accounting of a man's life." The distinction hit Holt hard as a fist and he paused a moment before continuing. He gestured at the items spread before them. "This is Judge Oscar Pence." He shook his head and touched the medicine stone in his pocket. His voice got husky. "Damn. This is all that's left...of him."

Silka put a hand on Holt's shoulder. "Not all. There more to a man, if worthy."

"That's why you build ranches, create families, and make memories," Deed acknowledged. "You leave important pieces of yourself behind, not just stuff. Right, my teacher?" He smiled first at Silka, then at Holt.

"That is most good." Silka nodded and touched his *bushido* medallion, then tapped his right fist across his heart. "Judge gave new life to Holt. Never forgotten."

Holt nodded. His mother would have thought that too. She lived a life of unselfishly giving her time and energy. The power of positivity was her way to true happiness. She always said that little miracles happened all the time but, for the most part, people did not see or appreciate them. In his pocket was that mountain lion claw she had given him. She said it would remind him to keep a balance of body, mind and spirit. Like his medicine stone, it gave him courage and protected him. Recalling this and reflecting on the lives his brothers had carved out, Holt realized his mother had left a lot behind too.

"It is so, my friend," Holt acknowledged. "I will *never* forget."

Their attention now focused on the two items from Pence's jacket pockets. His wallet held a significant amount of money, about $50, and some receipts from various general stores for ordinary purchases, tobacco, jerky, candy and foodstuffs. The coins from his pants pocket totaled about three dollars.

"An interesting collection of belongings here," Deed noted.

"He was an interesting character," Holt said. "But nothing here screams out a cause for murder."

"Apparently robbery wasn't the purpose," Hannah observed, picking up the fancy knife. "Money, gun, watch, expensive knife, all stuff a low-life bandit would steal. Hell, even his fine horse. But it's all here."

"Maybe he was interrupted. Had to run," Deed interjected.

"The pistol or wallet could've easily been snatched if that happened," Hannah continued. "I dunno, seems that after going to the effort of killing him at least *one* of these things would've been taken."

"Someone wanted him dead, that's for sure. But maybe there is something missing and we just don't know what it is," Holt offered.

"Disagree," said Silka, shaking his head. "Robbery not purpose. *Akugō. Waru.* Evil…evil person…at work here."

Silence took hold of the room.

Holt picked up the leather portfolio of papers found in the judge's jacket pocket. Would they shed any light?

A variety of documents was revealed as the folded leather cover was carefully opened. Tightly packed together were reports, receipts, records from a court proceeding, dispatches, all manner of telegraph messages, a couple of letters, and several pages of notes in the judge's writing. Pressed in the midst of all the papers looked to be a thoroughly flattened remnant of a bloom of Indian paintbrush.

"Only way to see what's here…" Holt shrugged. "Everyone take a few to read?"

"Deal 'em out," Hannah agreed.

Like oversized schoolkids poring over a reading assignment, the four men spread out and concentrated on their stack of materials.

A solid knock on the door broke the stillness. "It's Wheeler," the voice from the other side called out.

Deputy Logan Wheeler did not have much to share from his search of Pence's accommodations. He reported that the cottage had been locked. No busted down door, no broken windows. The widow who owned the cottage, Almina Kasiah, had let him and Bradley in.

Wilkon was a town that lately had required a lot of the judge's attention. It was also a handy base for a number of locations in his jurisdiction. He had occasionally spent evenings with the widow so it seemed to make sense that he had recently become a boarder in her cottage on one of Wilkon's side streets.

There was not much to the small house. A tiny kitchen with an old stove. A main room with a rocking chair and stuffed wingback nestled around a small fireplace. A divan draped by a thick pinwheel quilt waited in the other half of the room. The drab bedroom had a doorless closet and held a single bed covered by an old quilt. A dresser and matching nightstand filled out the rest of the one-window room. The nightstand held a lamp that needed oil. Almina helped Deputy Wheeler look through drawers and the closet. Everything was neat and tidy. Nothing looked or seemed out of place.

The widow occupied a second bedroom. It looked to be the same size and furnished much the same way. She indicated to the deputy he was welcome to search in there, but the judge had not been in the room nor kept any belongings there.

No one was quite sure what exactly the nature of the judge's relationship with Almina was—and their ages lessened most of the scandalous talk—but it was obvious the two had enjoyed their short time together. The news of his death had greatly upset her.

"She was crying pretty hard," Wheeler relayed. "She said she would work with the undertaker to help make funeral arrangements."

"You not leave her that way?" Silka asked.

"No, she's all right. I gave her a hug and held her hand while we talked," Wheeler responded. "She has my handkerchief."

"Thanks, Logan," Holt said. "I'll take some of Oscar's belongings over there a little later and check in on her."

The deputy grabbed a few of the judge's papers and sat down to read.

The jail office was quiet as the documents were studied. Clicking noises from the stove and soft snoring from Tag drifted through the silence.

Tossing his stack down on the desk, Deed exclaimed, "I don't see anything here. No photos, no mention of family. No obvious threats."

"These reports and wire messages talk about a bunch of people dead from guns and knives, some of the victims might have been important, I guess," Wheeler added. "Lots of bad people out there, for sure. I suppose anyone the judge put away could want revenge."

"Yeah, there were some murders the judge received wires about," Hannah said, holding telegraph messages. "Two recent ones, over in Baccata and the other in Henion, a county clerk and a teacher. Two other killings about a year ago, a banker in Modlin and a miner in Bartle. These last two had an interesting connection, pages from the Bible were pinned to the dead men and were signed, 'The Angel.'"

Deed jumped in, "You didn't find anything like that on the judge, did you?"

"No, not that I saw," Holt said, his brow furrowed. "Cliente and Vaca found him. They would have mentioned something like that." He reached for the pocket Bible from Oscar's saddlebags and thumbed through it. "Nothing's been torn from here," he added, holding up the book.

"Hell if I know. I don't see any connections," Hannah said, shaking his head and placing his stack on top of the rest.

A grumbled *unh-unh* from deep within Silka's chest was his only response as he added his papers to the pile.

As he read his stack, Holt had set aside documents he came across pertaining to his amnesty—a signed statement from the judge plus a handful of telegraph messages notifying other judges and officials, and a return confirmation from the territory's Army lieutenant colonel. "Anyone see anything pertaining to me and my arrangement with the judge?" he asked.

"Here's something he wrote detailing the outcome of the Bordner trial." Deed held up a handwritten page. "Ranch holdings and business transactions. The last part talks about the deal he made with Holt Corrigan."

After the death of Bordner, Judge Pence had stepped in and put up all the ill-gained ranch holdings and businesses for return to their proper owners or auction. Taol Sanchez, the oldest son of the Lazy S patriarch, bought two of the smaller ranches Bordner had absconded with, the H-5 and Roof-M. The Bar 3, Bordner's largest illegal gain, was divided between the Corrigan brothers and Jeremy Regan. It had been owned by Jeremy's family, who were murdered by Bordner's gang. Jeremy, only six years old, was now a legally adopted member of Blue's family. The Corrigans would run the Bar 3 as well as their own Rafter C spread until Jeremy was old enough to officially become an owner of the Bar-3. The Wilkon bank, also taken by Bordner, was purchased by a combination of the Sanchezes, Corrigans and Judge Pence. The last part of Judge Pence's decrees was that Holt Corrigan be given a full pardon as a former Confederate soldier. It spelled out the cost of Holt's freedom too.

"Does the law of the town of Wilkon mind if I keep these?" Holt asked, holding up the documents. "Not everyone has heard about or approves of *Sheriff* Holt Corrigan."

"The town marshal approves." Hannah nodded. "If we ever need them, we know how to get them back."

Holt carefully folded the papers and placed them inside his jacket. He also carefully folded another document into his pocket—the adoption order Judge Pence had written giving Blue and Bina full custody of Jeremy Regan. They probably already had a copy, but a back-up was always a good thing to have.

Deputy Wheeler picked up the newspaper found rolled up in the judge's hand. "It's got a nice lil' ribbon tyin' it up. Kind of like a scroll." He unfurled the paper. "Hey! This newspaper ain't even from Wilkon. It's th' *Sweetclover Dispatch*."

"Where the hell is Sweetclover?" wondered Deed.

"Out west, near the border," Hannah replied. "Judge had to travel a lot. Maybe he had been there for a case."

"He hadn't been that far out of town recently…" Holt reacted.

Silka chimed in, "He play chess with Felix Sanchez. Many times lately."

As Deputy Wheeler thumbed through the newspaper, Holt picked up the prickly pear bloom and looked at it. "Wonder why he had this? His spit can looked like it was dropped onto the ground."

"Was he near a prickly pear thicket?" Hannah asked.

"There was some nearby, but not close."

"I don't understand." Hannah shook his head. "That's a lot of stuff in his hands when he was attacked."

"Yeah, I don't understand it either," Holt agreed. "Let's pack the flower and the newspaper away carefully. They might end up meaning something."

———

They ate an early supper after which Deed and Silka rode back to the ranch. Holt packed up a box with the judge's Bible, his books, and clothes. He included just about everything but the folder of papers and the weapons. He took the box to Almina's cottage and checked in on the widow. She was grateful for Holt's gesture. They sat and reminisced about the judge and what a character he was. As far as she and Holt figured, they were the judge's only "family." It was her suggestion that they drink a small toast to him from his flask.

He walked out into a dark night. Only a handful of stars watched overhead. Tag had waited patiently on the widow's porch. "C'mon boy, let's call this one a day," he said wearily and headed to his quarters.

The Wilkon jail was a converted warehouse that sat next to an old sewing workshop. The little factory had been turned into the sheriff's office and sleeping quarters. It was not as fortified as the jail, but it was not easily accessible unless welcomed inside. The jail office offered more room, which was where the majority of business was conducted. The good part about the quarters in the old shop was that it was quieter and did not stink of tobacco smoke, stale coffee, and cooped-up men. Although he planned on spending more time out at the ranch, a lot of Holt's gear was kept here.

Lost in thought, he lay on his bunk. He had taken the time to complete his nightly ritual of wiping down and checking his guns, touching each of them with the cardinal feather from his hat before setting them down.

The tumult of the day caused his mind to race in a strange, visual kaleidoscope of bitter and sweet. One image dissolved continuously into another, like crashing waves that could not be held back nor looked away from…Claire's intoxicating loveliness…a beautiful flower in winter…Judge Pence pinning the star on him…the gruesome scene of the judge lying dead…a prickly pear bloom in his hand…he and his brothers delivering the body to the undertaker…Silka warning of more evil…a skin-walker with outspread wings…the pinched face of the annoying little reporter…the shocking whirl-wind of death in the jail cell…Tag wagging his tail so hard his back end wiggled…going through Pence's things…rifling through a dead Union officer's coat…the horrible day Blue lost his arm…his brothers and Silka laughing around a dinner table…the table turning into a huge version of his medicine stone…his mother waving and turning into an owl that flew away…Holt himself standing alone in a beautiful wilderness…and trans-forming into a cougar…

Holt jolted into alertness. He had not been asleep, but definitely not awake. He became aware that he was holding his medicine stone in one hand and the mountain lion claw in the other. He had experienced vivid dreams in his sleep, but those he believed had been about previous lives. He wondered if he had just had a waking dream, what Indians would call a vision.

"No!" he declared into the darkness. "I am not worthy of that."

His mind still churned. What was he worthy of? What would he leave behind when he was gone? Maybe a life with Claire?

Something right then slammed through his thoughts.

"Oscar's black robe!" he exclaimed. "*That's* what was missing, Tag!" he said to his curious, now wide-awake dog. "I *know* he carried it in one of his saddlebags. Wheeler needs to go back to the cottage. See if it's there."

Even though the robe wasn't necessarily a valuable item, discovering its absence somehow settled Holt. He lay back down and Tag tucked in at his feet. As his morning conversation with Claire wandered into his mind and replayed tenderly in his thoughts, he finally drifted off to sleep.

CHAPTER SEVEN

The next morning's dawn was an hour away. Yellow and orange streaks were starting to cut swaths across the sky as Holt rode for the Rafter C. Ahead of him, grazing cattle were mere dots on a light brown canvas.

It was his brother Blue who had suggested a change to the ranch's name, to commemorate Holt's return. The LC, as the ranch was known, had become the "Rafter C." Blue said the new name represented the whole family being brought all together.

Their ranch brand itself did not need to be changed much, it already had a slash over the left top of the "C." All they had to do was register an added slash on the right side. When springtime time came, all the new calves and stock that were going on the drive would receive the new brand: a half-diamond or rafter—a little tipi as Blue's kids called it—over the C. The remainder of the stock would get the additional slash as time wore on.

Holt smiled at the recollection. Someday soon he

would be out here more, to help with the day-to-day responsibilities. Being the county sheriff was not supposed to be a full-time job.

He left today's safekeeping of the town to Marshal Hannah and Deputy Wheeler. The vividness of last night's waking dream left his head full of thoughts. Before he rode out, he instructed Wheeler to take the key they found on Judge Pence and see if it opened the cottage.

"If she's there, Almina might take a shot at you, so knock first," Holt half-joked. Either way, Wheeler was to look for the judge's black robe.

The Corrigan ranch was a good one, thanks in large part to their parents' careful selection of the land. Three protected valleys were rich in grass and water. Springs dotted the land, along with a healthy stream that cut across two of their main grazing areas. Five thousand head of cattle and a large string of horses were spread throughout their property—acres that were owned by them, truly owned, with all the necessary ownership papers. Their third valley had been bought from another rancher just after the war. The entire setup gave them a fine operation. The herds were shifted from one valley to another as needed. Blunt hills and long benches offered natural fencing to keep the animals from drifting.

Overhead, a hawk surveyed the countryside, moving across bundles of early clouds and dipping toward something unseen. The faint tracks of a mountain lion caught Holt's attention.

"We'll need to tell Blue," he said to Tag, who was giving the tracks and surrounding area a good sniff. "It shouldn't be a concern. The cat'll only hunt what it needs. Unless those prints get closer to the house, then we'll need to move it away from the kids. And you. Right, boy?" Whatever scent was there was quickly remarked by Tag as they moved on.

It was encouraging to Holt to know such an animal patrolled their land. His mother often said the graceful pounce of a mountain lion was God's illustration of power, intention, and grace. That was part of her approach to life—a balance of body, mind, and spirit. His hand sought the claw in his pocket.

He arrived at the ranch house and crossed the yard quietly. The buildings, bunkhouse, sheds, and corrals were equally silent. All hands were out working the herds. He and Tag eased past the small stone house used for storing milk and butter. A dust swirl danced ahead of them. Tag saw the imaginary enemy and chased it toward the blacksmith forge near the closest corral. His newest buddy, Deed's family dog Cooper, joined the attack, flanking from the porch.

"Looks like those guys might've been cavalry in another life!" Holt called out to Deed, who was just arriving from the Bar 3.

"Gray or blue?" Deed laughed in return.

———————

Breakfast was cleared and the men were drinking coffee around the table. Moments of sitting still were rare at a working ranch, but this morning the chores could wait. Talk was of anything but recent events. There were enough memories and still-healing scars on their bodies to remind them of the destructive violence they were forced to confront. Even though the bandages were gone, Deed, Holt, and Silka still carried the physical effects of bullets and arrows, and even punches, that sought to bring them down. They had fought for their lives these past months and triumphantly came through it all.

They now could focus on normal everyday life, like winter preparations for both ranches. This morning they discussed a possible cattle drive in the spring. They talked and bragged about horses. They asked Deed about Atlee and her kids and looked forward to their upcoming Thanksgiving wedding. It started to feel like they were truly a family once again, maybe even more than they had ever been before.

Dedrick William Corrigan was his full name, but everyone called him Deed, except their mother. Holt's birth name was Holton Jefferson Corrigan, their mother's father's name. Blue's own name was Bluemont Wade Corrigan, a combination of the names of their father and paternal grandfather. The name Bluemont had brought more than enough fistfights in school, but his brothers had always been willing to step in and help turn things around.

Of medium height and build, all three brothers looked a lot alike, even down to their once-broken noses, courtesy of each other. Deed was eight years younger than Blue, an inch taller, fifteen pounds heavier, and definitely wilder. Holt was two years younger than Blue and two inches shorter. Deed and Holt resembled each other the most in looks and temperament.

Distinctively, the brothers each held elements of their mother's approach to life within them. Deed cared about all things of nature, from snakes to birds to deer, much like that of an Indian. Holt had adopted their mother's fascination with superstition and reincarnation. His first experience in believing he had lived before had occurred during the war. Blue was spiritual too, but his beliefs were more traditional. He often served Wilkon as a part-time minister.

Both of their parents had died when the boys were young. Their mother and sister died of pneumonia when Blue was eighteen; Holt, sixteen; and Deed, ten. Their father had died six months before their mother from a broken neck when he was thrown from a horse. The days of boyish adventure over, the youngsters—with Silka's considerable help—were left to build up the family's ranch.

Three years later, Blue and Holt left to fight for the Confederacy while the much younger Deed stayed with Silka to keep the ranch afloat. While the older brothers were gone, Silka honed Deed's fighting skills. Blue returned after the war with his left arm missing. Holt returned only after Blue convinced him the war was truly over.

The three brothers and the man they looked to as a godfather lingered around the breakfast table, enjoying the morning. It had been a long time since they were in a position to just sit and appreciate each other's company.

Conversation meandered to Holt's unfinished business.

"So, have you talked any more to that school-teacher?" Blue asked with a wink toward Deed and Silka.

"Who?" Holt replied.

"Well, you're just about the worst liar ever," Blue continued. "I heard she was in your office yesterday."

"And you got all moon-faced earlier during breakfast

when the kids talked about school and Miss Baldwin this, Miss Baldwin that," chided Deed.

Holt fidgeted in his chair. "My brothers, the experts on women."

"A couple of experts with beautiful ladies at their sides, if you please." Deed grinned, raising his coffee mug.

"Indeed," Blue answered, returning the gesture.

"Is so," Silka said, leaning over to Holt and quietly advising, "remember, leave behind. Something important."

Holt nodded but refused to take the bait. The kidding had started to fade when Blue's wife, Bina, walked in to warm up her coffee from the pot by the fire. She patted Holt on the shoulder and said matter-of-factly, "Make it easy. Invite her to have coffee or something. Just *ask* her."

Deed slapped his hand on the table. "There you go, big brother! *There's* an expert on women. Listen to her!"

Blue took a sip of coffee, hiding a chuckle.

———

"Thank you, Holt. I—I just couldn't," Claire Baldwin said.

The words hit Holt as if a horse just kicked him in the gut. He had bumped into Claire upon returning to town and asked her out to have coffee. He had spotted her immediately as she headed home after finishing her long day at school. She wore a long khaki-colored skirt and matching jacket with black trim and a black Victorian blouse buttoned to the neck. Her hair was pulled back, with a few straggling hairs falling down. She was managing a basket of school materials and her handbag while navigating through town. Even when she didn't mean to be, she was lovely he thought.

"Uh…okay…I understand…I just—" Holt bobbed his head. At this moment he wanted to be anywhere but here, struggling for words almost as much as he was struggling for air.

"But how about breakfast?" she interrupted brightly. "I just can't get away for coffee. Once school starts, I'm tied up with the children."

It was almost like he got punched again, but in a good way. Holt was momentarily at a loss for words. He looked at his boots before returning his gaze to hers. Words tumbled from his mouth. "Yes, sure, that would be nice," he said, a grin finally reaching his face.

"So, breakfast it is! Rebecca can watch the school until I arrive."

Rebecca Hannah, the marshal's wife, had temporarily taken over the schoolhouse chores when Wilkon's former teacher quit because of all the violence in town. When Claire was hired, it had been a natural extension for Rebecca to help out from time to time.

"Tomorrow then, six o'clock?" Claire asked brightly.

Holt regained enough composure, nodded his head and managed to say, "I'll meet you at the Silver Spur?"

"I look forward to it, Holt." Claire beamed at him as she turned to walk away but turned back to see Holt waving goodbye.

———

The next morning, Holt sat nervously at the Silver Spur, thirty minutes early. His hair was neatly combed, his hat hanging off the back of his chair. He shaved the night before, bringing his mustache under control. No bleeding nicks this morning. He checked often to see if there was coffee dribbled on his new shirt. The Silver Spur might not be the biggest, most popular restaurant in town, but it was his family's favorite. Good food, but more importantly they had no problems serving their partner Silka and their friends, the Sanchezes. The Corrigans appreciated that integrity and ate at the Spur often.

Last night's sleep had been fitful. Why was he so nervous?

Yesterday, after Claire agreed to meet him for breakfast, Holt had been antsy. He spent the rest of the day making rounds through town, even at the risk of bumping into the busybody reporter. He visited the general store to stock his quarters and the jail with fresh coffee and sugar, and also bought a new shirt. Stops at the bank, telegraph office, and the tailor's provided conversation and helped time pass. Later on, he checked in on the various mounts he had stabled at the livery. He told the operator that he would soon be moving most of his horses out to the Bar 3.

He had visited the bathhouse last night as well. It was nearly the final thing he did on a day when he could not sit still. Knowing he was meeting Claire, Holt was anxious and keyed up. Not on-edge like knowing Comanches could attack out of thin air or staring down a skirmish line of Bluebellies. This was another kind of fluttery sensation that had him wound up. He wondered if this was what poems meant by "butterflies in your stomach."

The Silver Spur was blossoming with morning business. He nervously smoothed the restaurant tablecloth with his hands and checked his front once again to see if he had dripped coffee.

And like a breath of fresh air, she walked in.

Holt stood and caught her attention. This time, he had rehearsed manners in his mind and held out a chair for her. She was dressed for school and a long day of wrangling children, but to Holt she could not have been more beautiful. Her blond hair was pulled up and she wore a simple long-sleeved, cream-colored blouse and dark-navy calico skirt. A navy-colored wool cape to ward off the morning's chill was tied at her neck. Holt helped her as she removed her cloak, hanging it carefully over an extra chair. As she sat, he smelled the deliciousness of her, a little like lilacs. And the fresh smell of soap. It was enchanting. He could not stop smiling and staring.

"Where's your dog?" she asked to break the ice. "Tag, isn't it?"

"Yes, it's Tag. He's always welcome here, but I thought he could keep James company for a while." He grinned sheepishly. He had not wanted anything to interrupt this meal so he purposefully left Tag behind with the marshal. "Tag will forgive me." He chuckled. "I'll make it up to him with something from the kitchen here."

Unlike most Western people who ate in silence, Holt and Claire became lost in conversation. Eating became secondary. They shared stories and tales that pulled back the curtains of their lives. She loved doing jigsaw puzzles and was fascinated by the healing abilities of a Shawnee Indian medicine man she knew as a child. Holt told the story of how Tag adopted him during a shoot-out and the time Deed tried to raise a fawn by himself. They thoroughly enjoyed one another's company and gazed into each other's eyes. Her smile made him shout inside. Time flew. Holt was totally smitten with Claire—and she seemed equally charmed.

She said that the town had been very warm and welcoming to her. She had heard so much about all the trouble in Wilkon that she almost decided against coming.

"If I had known there were brave men like you and your brothers, I wouldn't have hesitated." Her tone was earnest and genuine.

Now, she described settling into life in Wilkon. She was boarding with a family in town, the Freeburgs. Les Freeburg was a wood carver and the town's furniture maker. He and his wife, Goldie Mae, ran a furnishings store at the end of town near Mayor Cooke's lumberyard. Their oldest son was still back in Missouri recuperating from losing a leg in the war. They had another son who was still in the Army, stationed near Santa Fe as well as a daughter who lived near Fredericksburg, outside Austin. The Freeburgs had volunteered the room and board for Claire, which helped stretch her meager salary. In gratitude, she helped them around the house with cooking, cleaning, and shopping.

"Well, someday, Wilkon will have more kids and we can afford to pay you more," Holt chimed in and then blushed at mentioning having more kids in Wilkon.

She talked about the expansion of Wilkon's educational resources and innocently revealed that Meden Taliff had invited her to dinner to discuss the future improvements.

"Taliff? Mister justice of the peace?" Holt reacted, surprising himself at the tinge of resentment in his voice and expression.

The tone of the table changed instantly, and Claire tried to correct it.

"The whole plan for the community building was Mr. Taliff's. He's overseeing the whole project," she pointed out.

Meden Taliff, an attorney who had recently moved to town, was almost immediately asked by Mayor Cooke to become Wilkon's justice of the peace. Earlier in the fall, Holt, Deed, and Silka had to track down Bordner men who robbed the Wilkon bank. On their return home, they were forced to fight a running battle against Comanches. While they were away, a traveling priest had come through Wilkon. During the visit, Father Beltran and Taliff discussed the town's need for a multi-purpose building, something that could serve as a schoolhouse, meeting hall, theater, and church. Father Beltran had counseled that a town like Wilkon needed something like this, "to bring the community together." Taliff had agreed.

With the assistance of Mayor Cooke and his lumberyard, work on the new structure had begun almost immediately. In fact, with Taliff's money and Cooke's direction, construction was progressing rapidly.

"Because it'll be the schoolhouse, Mr. Taliff said he needs my input," Claire explained. "He's busy during the day and I'm at school. That's why I said yes to supper," her explanation apologetic.

Her response made Holt feel a little better and also a bit sheepish for acting the way he did. *She can eat with whoever she wants*, he scolded himself. Before he could restore their conversation to the mood they had enjoyed before, James Hannah walked in.

Seeing Holt, the marshal strode directly to the table.

His Victorian black suitcoat flared open to reveal the butt of a silver-plated revolver in a shoulder holster. A black bowler leaned forward on his head.

He adjusted his spectacles. "There you are. Been a hard target to find," he declared. Remembering his manners, he touched his hat. "Sorry, miss. Sorry to interrupt, Holt. Business," he said. "There was no black robe at the cottage."

"Okay, James," Holt acknowledged. "Thanks, but you didn't have to light your hair on fire to tell me." His eyes glanced at Claire, sending a "Why interrupt?" signal to the marshal.

Hannah continued, "There's a telegram from Texas Ranger Captain Laird McCoy. Thought you'd want to see it right away."

Nodding agreement, Holt excused himself and stepped away from the table to read the message:

SORRY TO HEAR ABOUT JUDGE PENCE.

A FRIEND AND TRUE GENTLEMAN.

NOT AWARE OF ANY THREATS TO HIS LIFE.

END OF BORDNER GANG GOOD NEWS.

CANCELLED ORDER FOR PRISON WAGON.

I COULD USE HELP.

WOULD CORRIGANS CONSIDER BECOMING

RANGERS?

MCCOY

Holt scoffed. He knew Blue and Deed would not be interested. And he...he looked over at Claire...he had lots to do around here.

Holt tapped the message, disappointed. "No ideas of why the judge was killed or who might've done it."

"Maybe there's nothing more to it. A tragic happenstance. 'Kill Town' strikes again."

"Okay, 'Gillespie,'" Holt said sarcastically, shaking his head, frustrated and a little upset that the marshal kept repeating the reporter's nickname for Wilkon. "We got enough people spooked without you adding to the flame."

"I think I earned it. We've all been close enough to the fire," Hannah said. "Anyway, I thought you'd want to see the note from Captain McCoy, with the Ranger thing and all."

Holt deflected answering the not-so-subtle query. "Bina and Atlee would be angrier than wet wildcats if their men picked up Ranger badges." Changing the subject, he asked, "Are you and Rebecca coming to Deed and Atlee's wedding? Bina's got a big Thanksgiving dinner planned. The wedding will be dessert."

"Wouldn't miss it. Rebecca's really looking forward to it."

"I was thinking about inviting Claire," Holt whispered, indicating his breakfast partner. "But she might get the wrong idea."

"Wrong idea?" Hannah chortled. "You're thinking that if you bring her, she'll wonder if you're hankering for the two of you to get hitched?"

"Well, yeah, I thought I'd move carefully."

"Gawdalmighty, Holt. Good thing you're not like this dealing with men." He chuckled and left the restaurant.

Holt returned to the table, apologizing for being called away.

"I need to get to school and start the day for the children. Thank you so much, Holt. This was wonderful." Claire smiled broadly.

"I enjoyed it too…Claire." Holt grinned back. He briefly touched the cardinal feather in the hat band as he put his hat back on. He wrapped up the remainder of his steak in a napkin.

"For Tag. In case he missed me."

She moved closer to Holt and put her arm through his. Warmth shot through his whole body.

As he walked her outside, he nervously asked her if she would like to go with him to his brother's wedding on Thanksgiving.

"Oh Holt, I'd love to!!" She kissed him quickly on the cheek and hurried off to school.

CHAPTER EIGHT

Mid-November saw a sparse lunch crowd at Carter's, one of Wilkon's popular watering holes. The saloon generally did not fully spring to life until later in the afternoon. Sun poured through the front window and open door. Grimy oil lanterns, hanging from the walls, tried their best to help brighten the rest of the space. The bar itself dominated the room. Behind it was the owner's brother-in-law, Owen Kissick. He wore a bright, multicolored shirt and carried a cap-and-ball Navy Colt from his days in the Texas Brigade, fighting with John Bell Hood. The saloon owner, Deke Carter, usually did not come in until shortly before supper and would work through the wee hours.

Two older gentlemen were seated at a far table, nursing mugs of beer while engrossed in a game of chess, even though the set was missing a white castle and a black bishop. Shot glasses stood in for the missing pieces; the bishop's glass had a cigar band folded inside of it. A white-haired man watched their game, sitting on a chair turned backward, his arms resting on the top rail. He had called the next game and watched intently as he held a thick, half-eaten beef sandwich in one hand and dill pickle in the other. Three young Mexicans sat at a table by the door, on an early lunch break from the lumberyard down the street. Four dirty, motley-looking drovers stood at the far end of the bar, laughing and telling loud stories over Carter's cheapest whiskey. Two tired-looking saloon girls leaned against the other end of the bar, talking with Owen and keeping an eye on the few customers.

At the door stood a wiry, dark-skinned man. Handsome and dressed in well-worn, but clean, cowboy garb, he took a moment for his eyes to adjust before stepping inside. Even with less than a full crowd, the saloon was warm and musty. The stale smell of beer, tobacco smoke, and old sawdust reached his nose and he shook his head in reaction. The Negro's spurs clanked as he walked inside and pushed the wide-brimmed hat back from his forehead. He nodded at the lumbermen by the door as he entered. At the end of the bar, the four drovers stared at him, their loud stories suddenly hushed. He walked up to where Owen was talking with the waitresses and tossed down a nickel, asking for a beer. Owen's smile was warm as he presented a full mug to the stranger.

The man laid his hat on the bar. "Thank you. The name's Travis. Travis Dean."

"Make it Owen," the bartender responded. "New to Wilkon?"

"Pretty much," Travis said. "Lookin' for work."

"Kind've a tough time-a year," Owen responded. "Ranches are mostly done with fall round-ups. With winter comin' on, things're kinda shuttin' down. Tried the lumberyard?"

"It's next. Looks like they've closed up for lunch. So here I am," Travis explained with an easy grin.

"Wa'll, good luck to ya." Owen nodded and left to attend to chores in the storeroom behind the bar. One of the waitresses took a turn around the room, checking on customers. The other saloon girl stayed to chat with Travis.

From the end of the bar, Con Trumbull, the biggest of the drovers, tossed back a shot and slammed his glass on the bar. Tossing his spent cigar to the floor, he rubbed it out with a big, dirty boot and walked toward the Negro. His hard face was set and clenched like a fist. A scraggly beard only made him look filthier. Trumbull's wide shoulders and thick arms were built for brawling, an amusement he resorted to often.

Unaware of the advancing man, Travis sipped his beer and continued his chat with the waitress.

A heavy hand pushed at Travis's right shoulder.

"Di'nt know they allowed darkies in here," Trumbull declared, his eyes brimming with hate and too much drink. Snickers came from his drover friends.

Without turning, Travis replied, "Looking for work is thirsty business."

The saloon girl spoke up. "We ain't got no rules about who can drink at Carter's. Yer here ain't ya?" Wider, louder chuckles came, this time from around the room.

"Shaddup!" Trumbull growled. One of his heavy arms shoved the saloon girl aside and she fell to the floor.

As Travis immediately reached down to help the

woman up, the big man yanked him forcibly backward. "I'm gonna learn you some manners, boy," he snarled.

Travis did not expect being wrenched like that and found himself lying on the floor. He was ready though, as Trumbull poised his heavy boot to stomp on his face. The Negro—no weakling himself—grabbed the man's lunging boot with both hands and shoved it upward.

Knocked off balance, Trumbull crashed to the floor.

Travis gathered himself up to assess his attacker's next move. The bigger man was unpredictably agile, already rising to his feet. Travis instantly reacted by hurling himself forward. The top of his head rammed like a bighorn into Trumbull's face, the collision crunching the drover's nose. Trumbull recoiled away in pain, his two hands holding his face that dripped crimson and felt like it was now on fire.

As he stood, someone seized Travis from behind. In a heartbeat, he spun away from the hold, driving his left fist deep into the unprotected gut of a scrawny, stunned drover. The lanky man felt all the air abruptly leave his body. Before he could struggle for breath that would not come, Travis delivered a sharp, right uppercut to the man's chin.

The scrawny cowboy teetered backward, flailing his arms. Travis propelled him the rest of the way, driving his left foot once more into the cowboy's stomach with a side kick. The man flew into a table, knocking over its chairs.

A blow sledge-hammered the side of Travis's head, popping open a cut along his left eyebrow, nearly knocking him off his feet. A third cowboy, a red-headed Irishman, waded into his sneak attack intending to finish off this no-good. Travis swung once, twice, not striking anything, but it kept the attacker at bay, buying time to steady himself.

The realization jolted through Travis that he could very well die, right here. His survival instincts kicking in, he instinctively deflected the man's roundhouse with his left arm and stepped into a crushing right cross to the Irishman's unprotected cheek, finishing with a devastating left hook. The red-headed cowboy dropped like a sack of potatoes, his mouth gushing blood.

Travis's left eyebrow was split and bleeding. He had a brief moment to wipe some of the blood away, steeling himself for the fight he knew wasn't over.

Trumbull had regained his senses. The scrawny cowboy had staggered to his feet as well, but still bent over clutching his stomach. The sight of his own blood sent Trumbull over the edge. Pushing aside his lanky friend, the enraged drover rushed toward Travis.

"Gonna make you sorry you were ever born, boy," the huge man roared.

As he wound up a roundhouse swing, Travis drove his boot into the man's groin. Pain exploded through the drover like a lightning bolt. Trumbull leaned over to try to ease the agony and was clubbed in the back of the neck with doubled fists. Trumbull grunted and slammed against the floor of the saloon.

Travis was suddenly grabbed from behind again. The fourth drover, a fat man with heavy sideburns, had hesitated to join the fray until now. He held Travis's arms behind his back and spun him toward the scrawny cowboy who still held his stomach with one hand, but now had a pistol in his other hand. The other two drovers were slowly getting back on their feet to surround Travis.

"No more messin'. Yer black ass is gonna die," the lanky man snarled, raising his gun.

A deafening crack of a rifle shot boomed from the door and a voice shouted in the void that followed.

"Drop that gun! Now!" Corrigan Bar 3 foreman Harmon Payne strode into the saloon. The first shot from his Winchester had gone into the ceiling. A second shot was levered into readiness. The lever-action's "click-clock" was heavy in the silent room.

"I said drop that gun." Harmon's rifle was now pointed directly at the scrawny cowboy with the pistol, but his gaze shifted toward the fat drover. "And you, unhand that man."

"Or what?"

"Guess. It involves lead."

"There are four of us, mister. How are you gonna manage that?" The fat cowboy laughed.

The Bar 3 foreman brought up his rifle and sighted it directly at the face of the man with the gun. "You all don't count real well. Look around."

Angry, they glanced around the saloon. Nearly everyone in the room was now standing. Eight guns were pointed at the drovers, including the bartender's cap-and-ball pistol. Although she was not pointing it at the drovers, one of the waitresses had the shotgun from under the bar in her hands.

The scrawny man dropped his gun and it thudded heavily on the floor.

"The rest of ya unbuckle real slowly," Owen ordered from behind the bar. The drovers meekly complied. "Now, move away from them, careful like." He gestured with his pistol.

"We're meetin' someone about a job," the fat cowboy spoke up. "Tolt us ta meet him right here, he did."

"And who would that be?" Harmon asked.

The fat drover continued, "We're s'posed to meet a Mr. Payne of the Bahr 3. Said they might be needin' ranch hands."

Ignoring the four attackers for the time being, but keeping his rifle pointed at them, the foreman acknowledged Travis, "You okay?"

Travis was now at the bar, holding a wet neckerchief to his eye and brow. "Much obliged, sir," he said. "Sure glad you came along when you did."

"There isn't any call for that. Anywhere," Harmon said grimly, then directed his attention back toward the drovers.

"I'm Harmon Payne, foreman of the Bar 3. And I can tell you there isn't a job for the likes of you on my crew. In fact, there isn't one reason for the likes of you to be anywhere in Wilkon."

"They need a doctor," the scrawny cowboy said, indicating the redhead's bleeding mouth and Trumbull's busted nose.

"Here I am, not caring," Harmon said icily.

Trumbull groused, "What about our guns?"

James Hannah had followed Harmon by just a few moments. He had been standing quietly at the doorway.

"What guns?" Hannah smirked and walked the rest of the way inside, eyeing the patrons around the bar. Everyone shrugged with him. "Whatever's on the floor stays here."

"These'll stay here too," Deed announced, bursting through the door with two old rifles in his arms. "Found these on those sorry-assed horses out front." He tossed the guns with a loud clatter onto the saloon floor.

"Who do think you are?" Trumbull sneered.

"Deed Corrigan."

"D-Deed Corrigan?" the scrawny man said wide-eyed. "Herd o'you."

Deed ignored the statement and walked over to Hannah.

The marshal took over, his tone poisonous. "I'm Marshal James Hannah. Six months ago, when I wasn't wearing a badge, I'd have lined all you assholes up and shot you. Thrown your carcasses to the hogs. But with my badge, you get this one chance. Ride clear of this county, now. And you'll live. Understand?"

The four drovers, looking miserable, said nothing.

"I asked if you understood."

Mumbled words of comprehension came from the beaten cowboys.

"If I ever see any of you again, I will kill you," the marshal stated simply. "No warning. I will draw and you will be dead." The heat of his stare made the drovers look at the floor. "Now get!!"

As the four rode out of town, Hannah and Deed watched them from the sidewalk.

Back inside, Travis did his best to clean himself up. The swelling of his eye had slowed and the bleeding on his brow subsided. He approached Harmon. "Mr. Payne, it sounded like you might need some help on your crew. I'm looking for good work."

"Ever work on a ranch?" Harmon asked.

Travis nodded. "Yes sir. I know horses. Done some blacksmithing. I can ride anything you can saddle. And

I'll outwork any five men you got." He spoke earnestly, without a hint of boastfulness.

Harmon smiled. "You got sand, my friend. I want you to talk to my boss."

"Yes sir," Travis said. "May I ask, who's your boss?"

"That's him." Harmon smiled and indicated with a tilt of his head. "Deed Corrigan. Let's have the doctor look at that eye and then get you something to eat while we talk about that job."

CHAPTER NINE

D awn's cool breezes disappeared, and the sun had decided its warmth would take control. Streaks of bronze and gold were turning the land into a rich presentation of Thanksgiving Day. This year's holiday would be a memorable milestone for the Corrigan family. It marked the first time Blue, Holt, and Deed had been together for the occasion.

After the war ended, there were some Southerners who still did not celebrate the new Thanksgiving holiday. The Corrigans were not among them.

Blue had taken to heart President Lincoln's proclamation when he established the first national day of giving thanks for "a year filled with the blessings of fruitful fields and healthful skies." Even in the time of war, Blue felt this was an important pronouncement and vowed to embrace it fully when he returned home. He took to heart their mother's lessons about life in its fullest being best experienced by contrast.

"In a world of turmoil and disruption," she had often

said, "one must stand tall against life's hardships. The bitterness of life is always accompanied by sweetness that only faith and courage can know."

His mother instilled that belief in all her boys and he had seen it again and again in life. Blue had even based a sermon or two on this very topic.

There was indeed much to be thankful for and the Corrigans celebrated accordingly. Making this day even more special, it was the day of Deed and Atlee's wedding.

The bride, Atlee Forsyth, ran the stage station outside of Wilkon. She was put in that situation after her husband, Caleb, had been killed in a Comanche raid. The raid was kept from being a total annihilation by Deed Corrigan and James Hannah. Both were on the stage the Comanches attacked as it arrived at the station.

It was unique that a woman ran such an operation, but she was strong and resourceful, and her station was now considered the line's best. Her two children, Benjamin and Elizabeth, were twelve and six years old. It had been rough losing their father. Deed was there at the worst time in all of their lives and was an immense help keeping the station operational. Affections sparked between Atlee and Deed, but she had been conflicted over those feelings. She asked Deed to wait for her until the time was right. He told her he would wait forever.

The entire Corrigan clan and close friends were at the Rafter C for the day that forever became special for Deed and Atlee. Blue's kids, Matthew and Mary Jo and stepson Jeremy, played in the yard with Atlee's son and daughter. The soon-to-be cousins were having a grand day. The Corrigan dogs, Tag and Cooper, had been moved to the riders' bunkhouse before everyone arrived and given large bones to keep them happy and occupied. Holt and Blue dressed in their best suits and complimented each other on how good they looked.

Graciously greeting everyone to the happy occasion were Silka and the German couple employed at Atlee's stage station, Olivia and Hermann Beinrigt. The widow Almina Kasiah, stuck close to Silka, relying on him for introductions to guests she did not know.

Mingling through the guests on this special occasion were Marshal James Hannah and his wife, Rebecca, who were newlyweds themselves.

The Sanchezes, Felix and Maria, plus their oldest son, Taol, and youngest son, Paul were dressed in beautiful Mexican finery. Paul had mostly healed from being shot by Bordner's men. The Sanchez's lovely daughters, Tina and Lea, were also there to celebrate even though they each at one time had crushes on Deed.

Mayor Patterson Cooke and his wife, Evangeline, would not have missed this party for the world. Their son, Bradley, had volunteered to stay with Deputy Wheeler and be a lawful presence in town.

In the kitchen, the Rafter C's cook, Oliver Gistele, a short, Black man everyone called "Too Tall," held court. He had proclaimed his Thanksgiving feast would be worthy of a king and queen.

Two people were not part of the celebration: Meden Taliff and Claire Baldwin.

A few days before Thanksgiving, Taliff decided that his mostly completed community building was the perfect place to host a county-wide dinner for those who could not afford a Thanksgiving meal. He shortly expanded the invitation to those who simply did not want to go to the trouble of preparing such a large feast. Taliff hired the kitchen staff of Wilkon's Cedar Bluff Hotel to prepare several turkeys and mountains of food. He appealed to Claire that he needed her to help host and serve food to those attending. Because some guests would be students whose families needed the support, she reluctantly agreed to be there.

Yesterday afternoon, Claire tearfully told Holt of the change in plans. "I'm so, so sorry, Holt, forgive me," she wept. "I didn't know what to do. I couldn't say no if students are involved. Please understand."

"I understand," Holt said, giving her a brief hug that had all the warmth of stale coffee. Walking away from the front of the bungalow where she lived, he could not avoid being angered at Taliff and disappointed that she chose to not be with him at the wedding. It gnawed at Holt that Wilkon and the surrounding county did not have a large population to begin with and those who would not be able to feed themselves were a relatively small number. He realized that his mother would scold him for his prideful thoughts.

For late November, the day was beautiful. The Rafter C front yard and main house were spruced and scrubbed, the details overseen by Bina. Tables were set all around, awaiting the feast of turkey, venison, cornbread dressing, potatoes, corn and biscuits. Too Tall had outdone himself. Much to the delight of Silka and the kids, lots of apple and pecan pies with homemade ice cream were promised for after the ceremony.

The grand feast was completed and cleared away. It was time for the family and guests to take their places.

The natural lay of the yard would put the couple at the top near the porch, with the family and guests situated down a gentle slope looking up at them.

The brothers gathered inside, just the three of them. They stood in front of the huge stone fireplace. A well-banked fire was burning evenly. An occasional blue flame told Holt that spirits were close. He decided they were the spirits of his parents and sister.

He presented Deed with a bluebird feather. "Something old, something new...I believe is how it goes," he said.

"Isn't that for the bride?" Deed laughed.

"So, give it to her when you see her," Holt replied. "This signals prosperity and wonderful tomorrows," he continued earnestly. Their mother talked often about the need for happiness in a person's life and the ability to find it in every day. Of course, she also saw good and bad luck omens in all manner of occurrences. "And remember where you got it. It's borrowed, right?" he reminded.

The three went silent and took in the moment. No words, just smiles.

Blue, who had heartily agreed to officiate the ceremony, said, "It's time."

Deed beamed. "Yeah, let's go see my bride."

Holt nodded. "It is well."

And the brothers walked out into the sunshine.

Atlee stood radiant in the back of the ranch yard, surrounded by Bina's landscaping touches. Bushes and plantings of sunflowers, alyssum, marigolds, and firebrush made the yard into a garden just as beautiful as any cathedral, maybe more so. Gorgeous in a new pink gingham dress, Atlee also wore a pink silk scarf, an earlier gift from Deed, which was tied around her neck. Her brown hair, usually pulled back into a tight bun, was now undone and flowed down past her shoulders. Her long, wavy locks were held away from her glowing face by a beautiful wreath of fall asters and mistflowers, all set off by Atlee's deep-green eyes. The late, warm fall allowed for a few pink shrub roses to still be in bloom, which she now carried in a small bouquet.

Hermann Beinrigt escorted her down the aisle. His hair was slicked back and he was outfitted in his best—only—suit which had been brushed and pressed for the occasion. Hermann had not been this dressed up since his own wedding day many years ago. He was deeply honored to have been asked by Atlee to walk her down the aisle and incredibly nervous that he would goof something up.

Deed wore a new black broadcloth suit, a gift from his brothers. His long brown hair hung loose. He took great care shaving this morning. It was during this basic ritual when he realized he just might be a tad nervous. In one fell swoop he was going to be a husband *and* a father. In his heart, he knew he was ready.

He no longer could imagine a life that did not include Atlee and her children. They would move into the Bar 3 and join Silka in helping run the operation. Atlee would continue managing the stage station, shuttling back and forth as needed. Yes, it was time. He touched the *bushido* medallion at his neck. For the first time since he could remember, he was not wearing the throwing knife attached in the back. Atlee insisted.

Doing more escorting of Mr. Beinrigt rather than the other way around, Atlee reached the improvised altar where Deed stood. Her eyes danced with his. Benjamin and Elizabeth, also in new clothes, stood on either side of Atlee and Deed. She handed the roses to her daughter and all four held hands. Elizabeth was on her mother's left. Benjamin stood next to Deed, looking up admiringly at him. The bluebird feather was in Deed's hand that held Atlee's. With an arched brow, her eyes silently sought an answer from Deed.

He grinned and quietly said, "Holt."

A smile and giggle warmed her face and heart even more.

Blue's service and messages of Scripture were appropriate for Deed and Atlee. He spoke about love of nature, love of all things, and love for each other. One of the passages he had chosen to read was from *1 John* 4:12. "No man hath seen God at any time. If we love one another, God dwelleth in us, and his love is perfected in us." Blue described the passage as articulating the power of what loving someone means. Not only for the person receiving the love, but also the one giving it.

On counsel from Deed, he subtly addressed the death of Atlee's first husband and spoke about not having to stop loving someone just because they are no longer around. "Beginning anew does not mean that you're in any way dishonoring the life you had before. You have chosen to share your life again. God believes it is okay to love and be loved again." Blue smiled. "You are choosing love, a gift from above. A new family has been created and will now become part of a larger circle. May peace and contentment rest over you with the bright colors of happiness and well-being."

Originally, Silka had hoped to include some traditional Japanese aspects into the ceremony. Atlee had not

been too keen about all that. Deed—and Silka—understood, promising to let Blue lead the ceremony down a
more conventional path. However, to leave out the man
who had meant so much to the family, and someone who
mostly raised Deed, simply could not be. The final part
of the ceremony was given over to Silka.

Silka stood before the couple with arms outstretched
and proclaimed in a resounding voice, "*Anata no jinsei
no kono atarashī tabi de subete no seikō to kōfuku o
negaimasu. Shiawase eien ni.*" He beamed. "Wish you all
the success and happiness in this new journey of your
life. Happiness forever. It is so."

Deed's eyes met Silka's. Their eyes welled. Blinking
his vision clear, Deed softly said, "Thank you," and put a
hand to his *bushido* medallion. Silka replied, "Love you,
son," and repeated the gesture.

Blue happily pronounced Deed and Atlee man and
wife. They came together and kissed—a kiss that lasted
longer than a traditional ceremony peck. A soft murmur
of chuckles rippled through the onlooking family and
friends.

"I love you, Deed."

"I love you, Atlee."

One more kiss and they turned hand-in-hand to greet
their guests. Whoops and hollers and applause greeted
Mr. and Mrs. Deed Corrigan.

The first congratulations for the new family came
from Silka, who enveloped all four in the most joyous of
bear hugs. Then he grabbed up both Benjamin and Elizabeth in his embrace. "Ice cream and pie, yes?" his joyous
voice roared.

"Yes, Uncle Silka!" Giggled Elizabeth.

"I think some of each, Mr. Benjamin. Agree?" The

boy nodded his head enthusiastically. Silka threw back his pony-tailed head, his laughter booming skyward.

Looking on, Blue and Holt grinned from ear-to-ear, an arm around each other's shoulders. Over the joyful hubbub, Holt said to his brother, "Thank you for making me see where I belong."

CHAPTER TEN

As the wedding of Atlee and Deed was going on at the Rafter C, a few of the cowboys stayed on the property to ride its perimeter, casting for strays and keeping a lookout for trespassers. The remainder of the wranglers rode over to the Bar 3 to help with operations there. While the Bar 3 was under ownership of the crook Agon Bordner, the crew had been populated with gunmen, not ranch hands. As a result, a lot of the labor and preparation that were necessary in the daily life of a ranch fell by the wayside. Today was a good time to have extra hands help get caught up on much-needed work.

At the end of the day, all of the ranch hands were served a delicious Thanksgiving feast put together by Boody Barreto, the Bar 3 cook.

Finishing his meal, foreman Harmon Payne grinned and wiped his mouth with a napkin. "Boody, this is mighty fine. The boys and I thank you very much."

"Yes sir, thank you," the new farrier Travis Dean added. "Very tasty."

"The sausage was a little *sussie* to the dressing," Boody said. "Different than some are used to. A little Cajun savoury for all you Texans."

"Well, we appreciate it," Harmon added. "I'll tell Deed and his brothers the same."

The two men and the rest of the hands put their dishes and utensils in the sink. Boody was usually good-natured when cooking and talking about cooking, but his temper could flare in an instant if something brought inefficiency or disarray to his kitchen. Everyone was careful to show Boody respect and clean up after themselves.

As he walked outside with Harmon, Travis asked about the cook's nickname.

"Boody's a chef from New Orleans, although some suspect he may have been a pirate. He told everyone to call him 'Boudin,' which, I gather is a kind of sausage. Well, that was too big a mouthful to say, so the boys shortened it to 'Boody.' He didn't take a cleaver to anyone, so it stuck."

Travis chuckled.

The two reached Harmon's horse tied up in front of the house. The foreman asked, "Tomorrow, can you manage things around the barn and corral area here? I'll give you two men to square away the barn and hayloft, and work on the fences. I'm going to swing a wide loop around the property and check out how our water sources are looking."

Blue and Deed had moved Harmon Payne from the Rafter C to be the foreman of the Bar 3 ranch. The three of them had been diligent in hiring good men to bring the Bar 3 back to where it needed to be.

Travis Dean was one of those new employees. Harmon had rescued Travis when the Negro was

ambushed in a barfight at Carter's. His timely interven-
tion kept the outcome from turning deadly. Ironically, the
Bar 3 foreman was at the saloon to meet the four thugs
who hoped to work at the ranch.

Generally a gentle and gregarious man, Travis was
always smiling. Well-educated and well-read, he and
Harmon had really hit it off. Not much else was known
about Travis and he had yet to share details. Some
thought he came from up north, others thought Califor-
nia. It did not matter; Travis was proving to be a top
hand.

Harmon's suggestion to leave two men for him to
manage caught Travis by surprise. The new farrier
gestured toward the barns and corrals. "Yes sir, I can
manage things here." He paused, then spoke again,
"Thank you, sir. For…the responsibility."

"The shell must break before the bird can fly,"
Harmon said, swinging up onto his horse.

"That's Tennyson, isn't it, sir?"

"He wrote it," Harmon replied. "But it fits you. And
call me Harmon. I'm no officer."

"Yes,…Harmon. Thank you again."

———

The day's weather had held its glorious promise for the
wedding celebration, but threatening clouds appeared at
sundown. As he was headed to turn in, the smell of rain
in the air led Travis to decide to bring in all the horses
from the two corrals. He had been giving six horses from
their remuda extra attention in order to break their bad
habits. They were led into the barn, joining three other
mounts already there.

Nightfall brought a healthy downpour. From the farrier's area of the barn's tack room, Travis listened to the rain pounding on the roof. Silka was asleep in the tiny room built at the other end of the barn. Usually, that room was for nights when Harmon stayed near the house instead of the foreman's cabin or if someone needed to keep a vigil over a foal being born. Tonight, Harmon was out in the foreman's cabin. Silka insisted on bunking in the barn, giving the newlyweds, Deed and Atlee, the privacy of their house. Atlee's children were having a sleepover with their cousins at the Rafter C.

In the comfort of his tack room cot, Travis lay awake for a while. His mind wandered from a list of tomorrow's chores to the wonderful Thanksgiving feast all the hands had enjoyed, to his newfound job and life.

As he tried to settle into sleep, a sound caught his attention. Faint, barely perceptible above the rain. It was probably nothing. Then he heard a soft whinny. Just one of the horses restless with the storm?

No. He locked into what he heard—and felt.

Someone was trying to steal the horses!

He bolted from his bed, not stopping to put on his boots. He edged out of the tack room with a pistol readied, cartridge belt slung over his shoulder like a bandolier. A second revolver was shoved into his belt.

His eyes were already used to the darkness. His bare feet allowed him to stalk silently, avoiding uneven portions of the floor that would creak. He could feel—and see—definite movement that was not stabled horses. Rustlers had anticipated that the commotion of the day's events would leave the occupants of the Bar 3 distracted and tired.

The horse thieves moved with a purpose. Like phan-

toms in dusters, they silently opened stalls, gathering the
horses. Not only were these fine animals, these were
horses from Deed Corrigan's ranch run by Harmon
Payne. The rustlers' paths had crossed with the Bar 3
men in town. Deed and Harmon—along with Marshal
Hannah—had taken their guns and told them to ride. No
one gets away with that, they had vowed.

Since being thrown out of Wilkon, the disgraced
drovers had spent their time squatting in an out-of-the-
way Sanchez Lazy S line cabin and plotting their next
move. They pilfered two old pistols and some canned
goods from the shelter. A good haul of horses from the
Corrigan Bar 3 could be turned into cash in a neighboring
town, staking the thieves with a nice bankroll. If they
managed to pick off that no-good smiling Negro and
meddling foreman—or even Corrigan himself—that
would be a bonus.

Con Trumbull, the huge man with a scraggly beard,
held up his hand to warn the other thieves to go easy and
keep the horses quiet. Two blackened eyes and a need to
breathe through his mouth was a constant reminder of his
broken nose from that ill-fated bar fight. Another reason
to get that uppity buck, he steamed. A big bay, agitated
by the rustlers, reared, knocking the hat off one of the
thieves, the scrawny man. He could feel Trumbull's glare
through the darkness.

Travis knew shooting now was reckless. He could
see, but not well enough to be certain what was man and
what was horse. He was not sure if the thieves would ride
out with horses ponied or just make them all run from the
barn and round them up when they were well away. He
closed in. The third thief, the red-headed Irishman swung
bareback onto a tall roan. In his hand were lead ropes

attached to a couple of buckskins. He nudged the roan toward the opened barn door. Heavy rain poured down just outside. If Travis waited any longer, the thief would vanish into the wet night with three good horses.

Now was the time. Travis aimed his revolver and pulled the trigger, fanning three times. The roar of the rapid fire was thunder and lightning inside the barn. The redhead tumbled from the horse as the animal reared in terror. Someone moved in front of the frightened animal to block its escape. The door slammed shut. Travis heard some whispered Japanese and the horse settled where it stood, stomping its hooves and snorting. A second thief ran for the barn door. An explosive *boom-boom* of a shotgun detonated at the movement. In the brief flash there, Travis saw the outlaw buckle into a stall gate, a bare-chested Silka brandishing the smoking gun, his huge sword belted across his back.

The farrier heard a groan at his feet and fired a shot at the body, quieting the Irishman for good.

Con Trumbull saw this last gun flash and launched his huge body through the darkness. A huge Bowie knife in Trumbull's hand slashed at the farrier. Travis side-stepped the brunt of the attack and fired but missed. Trumbull swung his knife again and Travis barely deflected the big man's arm before the blade could do major damage. The thief smashed his other hand onto the wrist of the Negro's gun hand and drove the revolver to the floor. Travis reached into his waistband with his other hand and drew a second pistol. As Trumbull raised his knife to finish him, Travis fired repeatedly, emptying the gun into the large man.

In moments, it was over.

Travis worked hard to catch his breath, sweat

drenching his body. He realized, as he looked down, that sometime during the struggle Trumbull's knife had left a grazing slice across his chest.

"Silka? Are you okay?" Travis called out. "That's all of them. In here, anyway. But we'd better check for sure."

"*Hai*," Silka responded, now carrying a lantern and his large sword. "Silka fine. Travis bleeding though," he said, indicating the bloody cut on the Negro's chest.

Travis shook his head. "It's not deep," he said, looking again at the wound. "Took six shots to knock him down, or I'd be wearing that knife."

Silka set down the lantern and handed him a bandanna from his pocket.

"Thank you." Travis smiled. "These are the idiots who jumped me at Carter's. There were four of them then."

"We check stalls now," Silka said. "Get horses settled down."

Travis quickly shoved more cartridges into his empty pistol.

The lights were on now in the Bar 3 house. From the porch, Deed stood shirtless in his drawers and boots, a rifle in his hands. He peered through the rain and yelled toward the barn. "Silka! Travis! Are you all right? What's going on?" He levered his Spencer into readiness.

Silka appeared in the doorway of the barn. He raised his lantern and hollered, "Aiiee. All done here. Horse thieves. Maybe one more…out there." He gestured out into the yard.

Deed hollered at the door of the house, "Atlee, lock the door! Get away from the windows!" He jumped down from the porch into the rain.

Deed, Silka and Travis spread out and carefully eased through the night, their senses alert. As they neared the small cooling house in the back near the kitchen, they heard a distinctive Cajun voice holler out, "*Arrete toi!*"

Boody had been up late, cleaning and winding down from the big day in his kitchen. When he heard the gunshots in the barn, he doused the lights and stepped out onto the back landing.

The Cajun cook hollered again, this time in English, "Stop you!" He moved menacingly toward a creeping silhouette.

Suddenly, in the rainy night, one gunshot rang out followed by a cry of distress. Deed, Silka and Travis ran toward the back of the house from where the sounds came.

By the cooling house, Boody stood over the body of a fat man with heavy sideburns. The Cajun cook looked up at his approaching friends. The final horse thief lay on his back in the wet, muddy ground, his smoking rifle lay next to him. Blood was spreading out from a nasty hole in the middle of the downed man's belly. A long, cast-iron rotisserie spit jutted out of a similar hole in the man's chest, skewering him into the ground.

Boody responded to their unasked question. "He did not stop when I asked. So, he got stuck. Like a pig." He looked up. "Horse thieves?"

Travis nodded affirmatively. "There are three more like this in the barn."

"Saves us the trouble of hanging the *couillons*," Boody said calmly. He turned to go back inside. "Get yourselves dry. I'll have a little *lagniappe* for everyone."

Shortly, Deed and Atlee, Silka, Travis and Boody were gathered around a table in the Bar 3 kitchen. They were soon joined by Harmon, who had heard the shots from his cabin and came running. Boody had re-stoked the fireplace and brought out the remnants of the earlier feast. Silka had doctored the cut on Travis's chest. Boody drank from a big glass of wine, more animated in his conversation than usual. The other men sipped glasses of whiskey. Atlee turned down coffee or whiskey but agreed to a small glass from Boody's bottle of wine.

As he had hustled to the house with his Winchester readied, Harmon came across four tied-up horses, the thieves' original mounts. They were stabled inside the barn for now. The bodies of the four rustlers were stacked together in one of the stalls to keep scavengers away from the yard.

"Tomorrow morning, I'll have a couple of the hands load those lowlifes in a wagon and drive them way off into scrub land," Harmon said. "Dig a big hole and dump them in."

"Horse thieves don't deserve any more than that," Deed agreed. "I'll send word to Holt and Marshal Hannah that the drovers who jumped Travis at Carter's attacked the Bar 3."

"I guess I'm to blame for all this," Travis said sheepishly, looking at his full glass of whiskey and untouched plate of food. "I'm very sorry. I don't want you to think that trouble travels with me. I'll move on, no hard feelings."

"If we thought that, we never would have hired you," Harmon said.

Deed looked Travis straight in the eye. "That's not something I'd even consider, Travis. Most importantly, I'm glad you and Silka are all right. You also saved a barnful of our horses. I can't thank you enough for that."

"The way he handle trouble, he is warrior," Silka chimed in, touching his right fist to his heart. "We certain he not a Corrigan from somewhere?" He grinned from ear to ear. Good-natured laughter spread around the table, even from Travis.

Harmon gave him a couple of "well done" thumps on the back. "I'd say you're family."

Deed let the laughter die. He took a deep breath and raised his glass. "Join me, my friends." He beamed. "To my beautiful bride, Atlee."

She tilted her head slightly, a blush rising to her face.

"I promised her a wedding she would always remember!"

CHAPTER ELEVEN

Wilkon's main street surged with movement. A December day without biting wind or blowing snow invited people outdoors. Wagons and freighters crisscrossed the main thoroughfare, mounted riders moving between them. An occasional brave soul dashed from one side of the road to the other. The early evening found Holt and Marshal Hannah sitting at a table in the restaurant of the Cedar Bluff Hotel. Holt was sipping coffee. Hannah was enjoying a small glass of whiskey before collecting his wife, Rebecca, for dinner with the town doctor and his wife. Claire Baldwin was going to join Holt for an early supper. After the disappointment of Thanksgiving and missing the wedding, she had suggested getting together. She wanted to see him and apologize once more.

Hannah was still jabbing around the edges about Captain McCoy's telegram, curious about Holt's thoughts on joining the Rangers. Their conversation turned to Holt's role as county sheriff. Although the amnesty was permanent, Judge Pence had only named Holt the interim county sheriff. If Holt wanted to keep the job, he would need to be voted in during the next election in June. Holt was a bit surprised at the question of whether he was considering staying on and running. He honestly had not spent much time thinking about it.

Hannah changed the subject, teasing Holt about eating in the hotel.

"It's no Silver Spur, but they might have better coffee here," Holt appraised. "Besides, I guess I have to spread my business around a little now. Earn some votes."

"I see, the whole 'two birds with one stone' gambit." Hannah laughed. "Very savvy."

"As long as 'Mr. Wilkon' doesn't object to my running." Holt chortled sarcastically, referencing Meden Taliff. The newcomer had made his mark on Wilkon in the short time he had been in town. "Or try to take my job."

"Yeah, I know," Hannah nodded. "He doesn't seem to be a bad guy though. Rebecca and I have both spoken with him. He's pleasant. He's generous. I know we just went through hell with another rich fustilarian, but he's no Bordner."

"I suppose so," Holt acknowledged, using his hand to smooth his mustache. "Not that he needed to stick his nose in but he's more than a scoundrel. Remember he didn't do a thing when Rhey Selmon and his half brother were trying to cut us all down. He just stood and watched."

"Fair point." Hannah looked at Holt over the top of his eyeglasses and teased, "His attention to Claire have anything to do with your sunny assessment of him?"

"Aw hell." Holt shook his head.

"Speaking of you-know-who..." Hannah said,

motioning his head toward the large inner door which opened into the hotel lobby.

Meden Taliff was a tall, handsome man, one who liked to make an impression. He walked through the hotel lobby slowly and confidently, resplendent in knee-high black boots with gray striped pants tucked inside them. He wore a blue tailored vest with matching silk cravat. A black regency tailcoat which set off his full head of golden hair completed his outfit. A short-brimmed fedora was in his hand. He obviously had money and dressed accordingly. He stood at the lobby entrance to the restaurant, sizing everything up. Seeing the two lawmen, he strode immediately over to their table.

"Good afternoon, gentlemen." He smiled and shook their hands. "Or is it evening? I never quite know what to call this interesting time of day."

"I guess it depends on what you have left to do," replied Hannah. "'Evening' feels like the day is about done. 'Afternoon' sounds like you got a little more time." Genial chuckles circled the table, even from Holt.

Taliff wanted to inform them, before anyone else, that he had bought the general store from Flavian Rose. "I first offered to just become her partner. Even suggesting that I'd build her a bungalow rather than have her live in the loft over the store. But she's decided to sell and move to Cincinnati to live with her sister."

Her husband, Malcolm, had volunteered to ride with Holt, Deed, and Silka in the posse to retrieve the town's money stolen in the Bordner bank robbery. Although he had served with the Union during the war, he was a meek, ordinary store clerk and was ill-suited for the cruel ruggedness of such a mission. He was killed by Comanches as the posse fought to return home.

"Yeah, she's put up a brave front ever since she lost Malcolm," Holt said. "But you could tell things weren't the same. They couldn't be."

"Poor thing," Taliff nodded solemnly. "That would be rough. She's not leaving until spring, though, when the weather will be better. She's agreed to help break in the new folks I've hired to run the place."

"Who've you hired, Meden?" asked Hannah.

"Billy Jorgenson and his wife are going to run it for me," Taliff answered.

"Billy's steady. Former deputy here. A good man." Holt nodded. "Took a Bordner bullet to the shoulder. That convinced his wife to 'persuade' him into retiring from wearing a badge."

"Guess that makes him a smart man, too." Hannah laughed and offered a chair to Taliff, who accepted the invitation. Coffee was brought by an attentive waiter.

Holt shot Hannah a quick glance. Guess somebody has to be nice to people like Taliff and Gillespie, the odious reporter. That thought was immediately followed by a deep breath and mental reminder about re-election and needing to get along with everyone.

"Say, I'm thinking about buying or even building a saloon," Taliff said, settling in at the table. "Something a little different. Not too high-class, but a place that offers a gambling and sporting element instead of just standing and drinking. Faro, monte, twenty-one, roulette, chuck-a-luck, of course. But also something like darts or billiards. Maybe even a bowling lane or two." He was visualizing the thought as he explained. "The law wouldn't have any

objections to another saloon around here, would they?"
He smiled, first at Hannah, then at Holt.

"Sounds like a good idea," said Hannah. "We'll have
to police the 'fun and games' a saloon usually generates,
but other than that, I see nothing wrong." He looked over
at Holt who offered a non-committal shrug. "Guess we'll
need to warn the doc about a rise in dart wounds!" the
marshal joked. They all had good laugh at the notion.

"Well, maybe not darts," Taliff added. "But you get
the idea."

"You're a man who seems to like building things,"
Holt noted. "I'm curious. No doubt we're in need of a
few things around here, but why us, why Wilkon?" His
question was sincere, without a hint of scorn.

"Good question," Taliff acknowledged. "There's
good land surrounding us here. Lots of room to grow
inside and outside of town. I'm not a rancher or a farmer,
I like *business*. The whole equation of commerce has
always fascinated me. It blossomed when I studied the
law. Creating, buying, selling, the whole cycle. Wilkon's
situated in a good spot. Positioned for real growth. If we
can get the railroad's attention, the possibilities for businesses and jobs for Wilkon get even greater. To me, that's
a good thing. That's what drew me here."

"Nothing wrong with the money all that growth
brings in, eh?" Hannah chimed in.

"One shouldn't be going into business to fail. New
businesses create jobs, attract people, and give hope."

"That sounds more like a politician," Hannah further
observed.

Taliff appraised Hannah with a nodding smile, but
before he could respond further, his attention was drawn
elsewhere. Claire had just stepped through the outer door

of the restaurant. Talk of commerce and railroads and politics halted. Taliff smiled when he saw her walk in. Leaning into Holt and Hannah as if sharing a secret, he gestured over his shoulder with a thumb, "She doesn't know it yet, but that lady is going to be my wife."

It was Hannah's turn to shoot Holt a quick glance.

They all stood as Claire approached. Hannah greeted her and excused himself to go find his wife. Taliff greeted her enthusiastically. Holt smiled and said hello.

"Good afternoon, Mr. Taliff. Hello, Holt." Claire said.

"Please, I've asked you to call me 'Meden.'" Smiled Taliff. Claire did not reply, having already moved past him to where Holt was holding out a chair for her. He helped remove her cloak, and she sat, beaming at Holt who sat down across from her.

There was an awkward moment of silence as Taliff stood there.

Looking up at him, Holt smiled and shrugged. "The lady invited me to supper."

It took another moment for the situation to sink in before Taliff bowed his head in acknowledgment. "Good evening then. Miss Baldwin. Sheriff." He turned and left the restaurant.

Claire and Holt smiled at each other.

CHAPTER TWELVE

Mid-December was quiet. A peace the town had not seen for a while. Maybe the cold weather helped to force the issue. People only went out and about because they had somewhere to go. And they did so in a hurry.

Following breakfast at the Silver Spur, Holt and Marshal Hannah made their early rounds through a battened-down Wilkon. Now congregated in the warmth around the desk in the front part of the jail, they spent the morning getting caught up on paperwork and answering wires. Tag had put himself in charge of guarding the stove. The men took turns stoking the fire to push the cold air into the corners and keep the coffee warm.

"We've been spending too much time sitting around in here," Hannah said, looking into the pot. "This is the last of our coffee."

Holt nodded his agreement. A wry grin crossed his face. "It has been quiet. First time since I've known you."

"Me? Hell, ever since I met you Corrigans it's been

like living *Henry the IV.* Shakespeare would have loved you three."

Holt chuckled at Hannah's remark. His paperwork now completed, he picked up a pistol to clean. His Russian Smith & Wessons were always in good shape, his attention was now focused on four .44 revolvers of mixed origin. All of the guns were taken from outlaws. Good back-ups were important to have. These pistols would be ready should the need arise. As he finished cleaning and oiling them, each gun received a simple touch from his cardinal feather.

Hannah finished writing out answers to wires from other lawmen around the region. He would give them to the meticulous telegraph operator, Mr. Hayes, to handle from there.

"This is going to sound dumb," Hannah said, "but what is the telegraph operator's name again? I can never remember his first name. Is it Clark?"

"Nah, it's something you wouldn't guess. He's so precise and perfect, the name doesn't match. I think it's Opie."

"Opie? Opie Hayes? That can't be right. Aw hell, never mind. It doesn't seem right to call him anything but Mr. Hayes anyhow."

Hannah made a mental note to drop by the general store after visiting the land and telegram office, to get more coffee and supplies. But all that could wait a little longer. He picked up the latest copy of the *Wilkon Epitaph* lying near the pile of papers he had been working on. An older copy of the *Epitaph* served as Holt's gun-cleaning pad.

"You think there's anything to this talk of a railroad?" Hannah asked, peering at Holt over the top of the paper.

"Seems we've heard it before."

"Wilkon could get big soon, very big," Hannah continued. "People like Taliff and *Mayor* Cooke are really pushing for growth. Real growth, legal-like. It's a bit overwhelming, more business means more people, more people mean…"

"…more bad guys," Holt finished the thought.

"Not quite what I meant, but things aren't finished changing," Hannah said, pushing his glasses back up his nose. "We could be as big as San Antonio in a few years. Gillespie says big towns equal big Bordner-like problems."

"Not like you to go on about stuff like this. That little twerp is just trying to sell papers. You know that, right?"

"I know, I know. But Deed and Silka got me thinking the other day, about 'leaving things behind.' You know, leaving a legacy. Rebecca and I have been talking about buying a place or building one and starting a family. I want to do all that without having to worry about mayhem every time I turn around."

"Life is tough, everywhere. Small towns, big towns. Down here, up north. There aren't any guarantees. You've been around. You know that."

"Yeah, but what is it about here? Wilkon? We've been on the knife-edge from the get-go. Even on the run I had time to enjoy the finer things…" His voice trailed off. "Don't listen to me, I'm tired." Then he finally added, "Rebecca's been worried. That's all."

"Always going to be bad people wanting the things good people have. Seems like there are more than a few chapters in the Bible teaching us about that."

"I know, I know…" Hannah shook his head.

"You're not tired, James. You're just realizing you've

got more to live for than you ever did before. You're a lucky man with a good woman. Keep making those plans you're talking about."

Hannah folded up the newspaper and slapped it down on the desk. "And stop reading so much of *this* crap."

"And stop reading the crap," laughed Holt.

———

The early winter sun had been only a mere shadow of its summer brawn. The late afternoon shadows had hosted brisk pockets of nippy air and now gave way to a night-time cloak of frost.

Bradley Cooke appeared at the doorway of the jail. "There's some trouble brewing at Carter's," he warned. As if to punctuate his report, a shot rang out from the direction of the saloon. Carter's wasn't the wildest saloon in Wilkon, but on some nights it could be.

Deputy Logan Wheeler threw on his well-worn blanket coat and grabbed his Henry rifle. Be alert—and calm—he cautioned himself as he trotted down the street.

Bradley stayed behind to fill in Hannah, who sat at the desk. "Marshal, this might be more than some yahoo blowing off steam," he continued. "It's some drunk who looks an awful lot like that Selmon idiot with the bear coat."

Down at Carter's, the tin-panny piano had stopped playing. A second shot rang out. And another. As Wheeler trotted up, he saw the saloon's piano player sitting outside on the planked walkway, working hard on lighting a cigar that would not cooperate.

"Watch yerself," the musician cautioned Wheeler. "Lotta dumb in there."

Wheeler carefully peeked around the entrance and eased through the door. He had not been in Carter's much. It looked like most saloons to him. Smoky. Filled with men from all walks of life. A big mirror behind the bar. Four scantily dressed women serving drinks and smiles. A cluster of card tables controlled the main area. All were filled with customers, but only a couple had active poker games going. By the door, a table was filled with Lazy S riders, including José Vaca. Four well-dressed men were playing poker in the corner. Chips, gold coins and certificates were scattered in front of the players. At another table, five drovers played for drinks. The drovers' game looked to be more serious. Most of the clientele was trying to ignore the commotion with little success.

Wheeler briefly locked eyes with Vaca and gave a short nod.

A scrawny man with stringy dark hair was holding court at the far end of the bar. A scruffy buffalo coat, fringed leather leggings and revolver belted at his waist made him out to be a seasoned gunslinger. In his reverie, he was attempting to regale the patrons—and impress a waitress or two—with his pistol expertise. He had cajoled a barmaid to toss shot glasses into the air so he could draw his gun and shoot them. His drinking partner, a squatty cowhand with a full beard and a bald head, kept anyone from interfering.

As his bottle of whiskey neared its dregs, it became more apparent the gunslinger role was just a masquerade. Three glasses had been lobbed in the air. Three shots had been fired. Three untouched, fully intact glasses had shattered when they hit the floor.

Tightly released chuckles bespoke a saloon on edge.

There would have been more laughter, but drunk obnoxiousness and a loaded gun had a way of keeping mirth locked down.

"Shaddup!" the scraggly man sneered loudly. "When we're done thish pisshant town ish gonna feel shome lead!"

His drinking partner next to him, kept up the encouragement and wouldn't let the barmaid go. "Ya ain't throwin' it high enuf, honey! Not high enuf. Now do it right, gawdammit!" he heckled. He turned to the bar and grabbed at his beer mug, sloshing some of it on his torn Confederate trousers. Startled, he tried to put the mug back down, but instead he set it cockeyed on his old kepi cap, spilling beer all over the bar. "Give the lady 'nother glass, gawdammit! An' set me up with 'nother beer!"

The owner of the saloon, Deke Carter, ignored the request. He also had moved the stack of empty shot glasses while the annoying drunks were preoccupied.

Now standing about halfway down the bar, Wheeler hollered out, "All right, show's over!" His Henry rifle was in full view. "Boys, you're disturbing the peace. This ends now."

Two townsmen dressed in wrinkly suits standing next to Wheeler moved quickly to be nearer to the door.

"That badge an' 'Enry don't shcare me, mishter," the buffalo-coated man swayed.

"I know, friend, you're not someone to mess with." The deputy spoke calmly and continued slowly toward the man. "Now, unbuckle your gun and put your hands in the air." Wheeler's voice cut through the smoke. The levering of his Henry cut through the noise.

"Damn right I'm tough!" the drunk sloshed. "My new boss'll have you fired a'fore you kin blink."

"And who might your boss be?" Wheeler was in front of the man now, his rifle pointed at his midsection.

"Whell, he ain't my boss yet, but he owns thish town an' haff of El Paso. I'm signin' on as…as shoon ash he gets 'ere."

"Until he gets here, you're gonna come with me, peaceable like. We got a nice cot for you and some coffee in the morning," Wheeler said, trying to be friendly. But then his voice turned serious. "Unbuckle that gun and put your hands in the air. Now! You too, laughing man," he said, shifting the rifle toward the fat Confederate. The bald man answered by raising his hands to where the deputy could see them.

The drunk in the buffalo coat used that movement to clumsily reach for the gun at his hip. The butt of Wheeler's Henry rocked the drunk in his stomach. The lanky man doubled over, his air leaving him like a gale, brown liquid retching onto his boots. Recoiling in the direction of the fat Rebel who had dropped his hands, Wheeler swiveled his hips and in one motion, hammered the stock of his Henry square into the fat Rebel's nose. The smash made a hollow crack, rolling the man's eyes back into his head. His nose became a waterfall of red and he crumbled off his stool onto the floor.

As the exchange between Wheeler and the drunk drifters was taking place, a massive, bulldog-faced brute of a man entered the bar from the alleyway. A shock of dirty red hair sat atop a head that looked like it connected to his shoulders without benefit of a neck. An ugly, flat nose and a thick, droopy mustache added to his almost comical appearance. He had been urinating in the alley when his friends were being dealt with by Wheeler. Coming back into the bar, he realized they were in trouble and came careening through the hazy room, plowing through chairs and patrons alike, his pistol drawn.

Wheeler heard the commotion behind him and spun around just as thunder roared from the door. Wheeler's eyes widened as the huge man's shirt blossomed with a crimson circle in the center of his chest.

Bradley Cooke stood three steps into the saloon, his Army Colt smoking from his first shot. The young man's second shot was an eyeblink later, blasting a hole in the big man's forehead. The bulldog-faced man's unfired gun dropped to the floor before he did.

The drunk in the buffalo coat caught his air enough and attempted to use the distraction of his bulldog friend being cut down to try again to reach for his gun. The pistol was not even halfway out when Wheeler's Henry bellowed, tearing into the man's shoulder. A shot from Bradley followed an instant behind, slamming into the scrawny man's heart. He was driven from his spot like giant invisible hands had grabbed his body up and tossed the bloody shape onto the floor.

Standing next to Bradley was Marshal Hannah. His gun was drawn, but he hadn't fired his weapon.

The rapid gunshots were followed by acrid smoke sucking all of the sound from the room. Five drovers sitting at a nearby table resumed their poker game. The barmaids peeked out from various points of the bar where they had hidden. Loud conversation slowly cranked back up and began swirling throughout the saloon. Wheeler walked to the unconscious man and took his weapons. He then went to the other dead men, kneeled and unstrapped their gun belts. Like a farmer picking weeds, he went through the pockets of the dead men's clothing, looking for anything that might identify them.

"Anyone know who these peckerheads are?" Hannah asked coolly, while Wheeler shoved new loads into his rifle.

Deke Carter shook his head from behind the bar. "They came in well on their way. Didn't know they'd turn loco."

One of the drovers playing cards spoke up. "Marshal, they was jus' some foreheads from Missouri. All talk."

Vaca and another Lazy S rider now stood next to Hannah and explained. "The one in buffalo coat talk about a man named 'Wagon Boarder' who was hiring guns," the rider said, shaking his head. "He thought he would be one of them. *El estaba muy loco.*"

Vaca added, "*Sí.* He not even know his name. Also not know Bordner was dead."

"They threatened the town and tried to draw on ya. Got whut they deserved," another drover chimed in.

The two townsmen at the bar mumbled something about "not needing any more Bordner nonsense" and flagged down Carter for another round.

The man lying on the floor with a crushed nose was regaining consciousness. Carter threw a dirty rag at him to mop up the blood plastered all over his face.

"C'mon, pretty boy, we got a nice place for you," Wheeler said. He picked up the still-dazed man by a blood-soaked jacket lapel and looked around. "Hey, where's Bradley?"

The piano player hollered through the door. "Marshal! Deputy! Out here!"

After the shooting had died down and the reality of the moment sunk in, Bradley had stumbled outside. He was now on all fours on the walkway, vomiting onto the street.

Hannah kneeled by the young man. "I'm sorry, Bradley," the marshal said quietly. "You can never know what it feels like to take a man's life. Until you do. He drew first and it had to be done." He patted him on the back. "I know that probably doesn't help much right now."

Wheeler looked on, holding the lapel of the prisoner. "You saved my ass in there, Bradley. Much obliged for that."

Bradley let out another body-heaving retch. He had nothing more to bring up from his stomach.

"Let's get back to the jail," Hannah coaxed. "Set you up with a little whiskey or something."

"No, I'm okay," Bradley said, spitting into the dirt. "Maybe later." He stood and wiped his mouth with a sleeve. Adjusting his hat, he took a deep breath and walked back into the saloon.

He called to the drovers playing cards, "C'mon, let's give Carter a hand and get this mess out of here."

———

The next morning, Bradley came to the jail. Holt was the first to greet him. "You don't look the worse for wear," he said quietly. He put a hand on Bradley's shoulder. "You doing all right?"

"I'm okay. I didn't have time to think, just react. Plenty of time to think now," the young man answered.

"It's natural, to look back," Holt said reassuringly. "But don't let it eat at you. You did the correct thing. You saved Logan's life, and probably yours, and the marshal's."

"You did good in there, Bradley," Hannah added. "It might not feel like it, but you did. Thank you."

Bradley nodded. He realized this memory would be with him forever, but he also knew he stood taller in the eyes of the sheriff and marshal, and that was what mattered.

"I gotta admit when Bradley came in here talking about a 'big coat' like Selmon's, I immediately thought it just might be more Bordner trouble." Hannah laughed weakly. "The *Epitaph* keeps speculating we haven't heard the last of that gang."

"That's not much of a guess by the paper," Holt retorted. "Hell, James, that fat bastard was looking to hire an army, or at least a regiment. You actually took his money. Even I heard he was looking for guns. All that scary 'Bordner's not done' crap is just trying to sell copies."

"These were just some drunk pissants from Missouri." Wheeler chuckled derisively. "Not good at much of anything. They heard a rumor and figured they could get an easy paycheck throwin' their '*gun skills*' around."

"There you go," Holt continued. "The *Epitaph* belongs in an outhouse. Hell, if Taliff wants to open a bunch of new businesses, he ought to start up a newspaper. Not everything is an amazing gun battle or legendary killer lurking around the corner. Bordner's done, James. Let it go."

Wheeler changed the subject. Gesturing back to the cells, he said, "When're we cutting this one loose?"

"When he wakes up, I suppose," said Hannah. "Not

sure if he's out because Dr. Sandor fixed his nose or just sleeping off his drunk."

"At lunchtime, awake or not, get him out. Point him back to Missouri," Holt said scornfully. "Let him have his gun. Empty. Someone follow him out of town."

"A big question I have…" Hannah asked with a grin. "Bradley, just what the hell were you doing in Carter's?"

Rather sheepishly, Bradley answered, "A couple of my friends and I go there ev'ry so often to play poker. If you can ignore the rowdies, it's actually a good place to get an honest game."

"Maybe we should find you something better to do," smiled Holt. "What do you think, James? Will the mayor give us enough money to make him a permanent deputy?"

CHAPTER THIRTEEN

Claire was delighted at Holt's invitation to take part in finding a Christmas tree for the ranch and help the family decorate it.

"It's a tradition," Holt said.

Of course, this actually was the first Christmas he would enjoy at home since the war started. Before that, the young Corrigan brothers and Silka had struggled so much to keep the ranch afloat that Christmas usually was not much more than maybe some extra venison on the table from a lean pantry.

Christmas was about a week away, but the hope *was* that the coming weekend's tree party would become a family tradition—all three Corrigan men and their families bundling up, selecting the perfect tree to bring home, and setting it up by the fireplace. The children were already making decorations to hang. The thought of Claire being part of that tradition—a lasting part of that tradition—glowed within Holt.

That glow, however, dimmed a bit when Claire turned down Holt's offer to join him for dinner right then and talk about decorations. "Mr. Taliff" had asked first, she told him. "He wants to talk about what kind of desks the new schoolhouse needs and maybe even the idea of building a stage inside the building. The Freeburgs will be eating with us too," she explained, trying to make things better.

She offered to change plans, but Holt declined, his enthusiasm tamped down. "Another time," he responded dryly.

———

The next day, the widow Almina Kasiah stopped by the jail. The afternoon sun had mustered all its might and warmth only to fall a buttoned jacket shy. Even with the sun patrolling as best it could this time of year, a braggart wind pushed its way down the street. Her entry to the jail brought in a rush of cold air, dust, and dead leaves. In addition to her visit, Holt was pleased to see that exactly eight leaves found their way inside. Leaves coming inside was a sign of good luck. And the number eight was a sign of power and strength.

Tag looked up from his new bed near the stove—an empty Arbuckles coffee crate stuffed with a small foot rug—displeased with the slice of winter that had interrupted his nap. He had declared this a good, warm spot. The dog decided the visitor and the dead leaves were not a threat and could be investigated later.

After stepping inside the jail, Almina explained that she had received a delivery from the Real Estate, Insurance & Telegraph Office. Mr. Hayes, the telegraph operator, had been safekeeping a leather satchel that Judge Pence left with him before a recent trip. No one had come to pick up the briefcase, so Hayes returned it to her, the judge's nearest family.

She handed the satchel to Holt. "I figured you would know what to do with these. It's a bunch of maps and papers."

"Maps and papers? Do you know anything about them?"

"I really don't. He never said anything to me about them. I'm afraid I'm not much help."

"Well, I appreciate it." Holt remembered his manners. "Would you like some coffee? It'll help warm you up."

"That's very kind, but no thank you." Almina smiled. "I've been meaning to come by anyway, but this briefcase arrived and got me thinking."

Holt's expression was a question.

"In addition to this bag, I want you to have the judge's horse."

"Thank you, Almina. That's…that's really generous," Holt said, visibly touched by the gesture.

"You've been taking care of it. I think Oscar would want it that way."

Holt gave Almina a hug with one arm and quickly wiped the sleeve of the other arm across his eyes. Releasing his embrace, Holt gently patted the widow's shoulder. "Blue and Deed's daughters have been doing a good job keeping flowers on Oscar's grave."

It was Holt who had insisted that the judge be buried in the Corrigan family cemetery at the Rafter C. An old oak tree just up the hill from the ranch house shaded the graves of their mother, father and sister. And now Oscar Pence. The grave was decorated with a temporary marker Silka had made. He burned JUDGE OSCAR PENCE with a running iron onto a small, nailed-together cross. A permanent engraved stone marker was ordered and would arrive in the spring.

"That's very thoughtful. Please tell Mary Jo and Elizabeth how much I appreciate that."

"You could tell them yourself if you'll consider coming out when we decorate our Christmas tree. We'd really like that. I can pick you up in the buckboard."

"Only if you let me bring pie and treats for everyone."

———————

The afternoon settled back into stove-stoked doldrums. After Almina's departure, Holt placed the judge's satchel on the desk and thumbed through the contents. Like the folded leather cover he found on Pence the day he was murdered, this satchel held the same kind of court documents, receipts and wire messages, only more of them. Some of these papers were a couple years old. At first glance nothing stood out beyond the ordinary.

The maps were a riddle, however. The folded stack contained various maps of Texas and Louisiana as well as the New Mexico and Arizona territories. Little handwritten X's and O's dotted places here and there on each map. Some of those locations were places Holt was familiar with or at least had heard about. But he could not draw any connection as to why some towns got an X and others an O or why they even got a mark at all. He could find no notes anywhere explaining the markings. Holt knew the judge was just peculiar enough that maybe this was simply his way to keep track of good places to eat or locations to avoid.

"He was a character, Tag," Holt said to his relaxing

dog. "I wish he was here to tell us about these maps. I wish he was here right now spitting into his chaw can and telling stories."

Spurred by the generous offering from Almina, Holt decided it was time to collect the horses he was stabling at the livery. For a long time, he had found it a hard-scrabble effort to have just one horse. During the war, it was especially difficult to keep a horse—any horse—healthy and alive. Now, he considered himself horse-rich. Before winter got especially nasty, it was time to move them out to the ranch.

He had lost his prized buckskin to a Bordner ambush but had since accumulated a variety of new mounts—the youngish, lively Appaloosa that used to belong to Judge Pence; two Comanche mustangs, a buckskin and a grulla he had acquired while chasing down Bordner bank robbers; a couple of athletic bays; a tough, trail-hardy buckskin; and a good-looking sorrel he had recently bought from Kornican Tiorgs, a local horse rancher.

Holt wanted to move his whole string out to the Bar 3 where he could work them better. He also wanted their new farrier, Travis, to give them a good look-see.

In a few short weeks, Travis had become the main manager of the remuda for both ranches. Holt was not sure if Travis was as good a rider as Deed, but he was close. There were not many who knew their way around horses and how to care for them like Travis. This was probably what drew Deed into agreeing with Harmon and hiring him right away. With Travis in charge, horse care activities—like pulling their shoes for winter—had become a smooth and efficient operation.

Because Holt was going to take them to the Bar 3, he enlisted the help of Deed and his stepson, Benjamin, to help bring the string back to the ranch. The trip would be a useful exercise for both the horses and the young rider.

The morning of the move dawned crisp and clear. Deed and Benjamin rode into town early and joined Holt for a quick breakfast at the Silver Spur. Gathering Holt's horses at the livery went smoothly. It was not clear who thought this was a bigger adventure, Benjamin or Tag.

Holt rode one of the powerful bays, one that he had come to like. It had a white blaze down the middle of its face and four white socks. Deed was aboard Warrior, the Indian horse that he had tamed. Benjamin rode an older bay named Chester, an earlier gift from Deed.

Since it was his first venture at leading a horse, Holt gave Benjamin the Comanche grulla to lead to the ranch. It seemed to be even-tempered and just might be a good next horse for the boy.

Along the trail to the ranch, Tag sniffed around some faint mountain lion tracks. Holt pointed them out to Deed. "Nothing to be worried about. It's only after what it needs to live. Pay attention though if those tracks get too close to the house or it starts picking off too much of the herd."

"Yeah, I've been noticing big cat signs as well," Deed said. "It seems to be heavier between here and the Lazy S. We might even have a breeding pair."

"Wouldn't that be something?" Holt smiled.

The ride to the Bar 3 was uneventful. Holt and Deed watched the boy proudly. Benjamin was becoming a good young horseman. Confident in the saddle.

Arriving at the ranch, Holt called out, "Let's put the Comanche mustangs in the second corral with this sorrel. They've been in the livery, but they're still getting used to all this white man stuff. The others can go in the main corral."

The second corral was often where the "rough string" went, horses that had acted out during fall roundup and had been pulled from the cowboys' individual strings. Most had bad habits that needed correcting like biting, kicking, or pawing.

The trouble caused by Bordner and his former Bar 3 henchmen during fall roundup season had left little time for important details like working the horses, but thanks to Deed, Travis and Harmon, things were getting straightened out. In addition to Holt's additions to the rough corral, there were three other horses that needed some extra attention.

Watching all of his horses get used to the corrals, Holt told Benjamin, "If your dad and Travis think it's okay, maybe you should ride that grulla more often. It came from a Comanche, so it won't understand spurs, but I think it could become a really good trail drive horse. For you."

The boy's face could not get any brighter or happier. "Thanks, Uncle Holt!"

"Thank me if he doesn't toss you on your butt." Holt grinned and winked at his brother.

———

Around the Corrigan table, everyone had come to the Bar 3 for supper. Blue, Bina, and their kids rode over. The evening was going to be a lively committee meeting to plan the Christmas tree adventure, maybe even a sleep-over for the children. After eating, the kids ran off to organize the supplies for making ornaments for their tree, supervised by Cooper and Tag.

Supper completed, conversation around the table started. Deed mentioned the *Wilkon Epitaph* article that announced the sale of the general store to Meden Taliff. He said the article speculated that Taliff might open a saloon or even a flour mill in town.

Holt noted that Taliff looked to be bent on building an empire. "Like he's bucking for governor or something," he commented dryly. "I wonder if we'll have to change the name of the town."

"At least he's open about what he's doing," Blue joined in. "The general store was bought fairly. Good people are taking Mrs. Rose's place. Taliff is using his money for things the town needs. Providing jobs too. There's talk of starting a fire department."

"Yeah, I heard," Holt acknowledged. "He's got Jimmy Todd and his crew hopping all over the place. He's got him looking at digging a well and constructing a water tower there in town. When the weather clears, I hear he's sending them on a project to Baccata."

"He wants Jimmy working over in Henion too," Deed chimed in.

Atlee said that talk coming through the stage station was that Wilkon was being considered for a railroad contract. The rumors were that it could significantly hurt the stage business. "Is that because of him?" she asked.

"Even with railroad construction heating up again after the war," Holt said. "The line your station is on is still an important route."

"He's right. The railroad can't run everywhere. Yet."

Deed said reassuringly. "People will still need to go where it ain't. Your station is too valuable."

"And talk is just that. Talk," Holt added. "It's cheaper than a newspaper, but often just as wrong."

"It may be disagreeable, but there's nothing illegal about it. Wilkon's growing," Blue noted.

"James said that too." Holt shook his head. "He's a bit overwhelmed at the thought of Wilkon changing, bringing big-town problems. People like Mayor Cooke and Taliff spurring things on make him nervous."

"Seem like Taliff try to add more than businesses," Silka remarked, with a twinkle in his eye.

"Yeah, how is Miss Baldwin?" Deed joined in, trying to sound innocent.

Holt didn't take the bait. He just shook his head with a half-grin on his face and stared into his mug of coffee.

At that moment, Blue's daughter, Mary Jo, marched through the dining room, looking for a doll. "Mr. Taliff brought lunch to Miss Baldwin at school!" she said matter-of-factly. A quick, raised-eyebrows look from her mother, Bina, ended Mary Jo's report on classroom visitations. She sent a similar look at Deed.

"Well...I'll just have to watch him," Holt said. "If Taliff does something wrong, I'll be there to stop it."

Silka blew on his coffee and chortled. "That be Wilkon business or Claire business?"

———————

The last of the roof and other finishing touches to the exterior had been put on Wilkon's new community building. The structure was a simple, yet sturdy, single-wall construction consisting of vertically stacked wood plank interior walls which were covered by exterior horizontal wood siding. The construction had been completed rapidly, a feat Mayor Cooke took great pride in due to the fact that it was his crew and his lumber at the project's heart—and Meden Taliff's money. The building would soon serve as the schoolhouse, meeting hall, and location for all manner of community events, like plays and lyceums. A raised plank floor would be installed when Mayor Cooke's lumbermen could not work outdoors because of the weather. An old used stove would heat the place until a new one arrived.

Finishing the meeting hall was a major accomplishment. Mayor Cooke, with prodding from Taliff, decided a party was in order. A grand opening celebration was scheduled.

Mayor Cooke and his wife planned the event, working with newspaperman Leroy Gillespie to help get the word out. Taliff thought it was a good idea to sell raffle tickets for prizes with the money going to help buy a fire wagon for Wilkon.

Taliff said he received a message that Father Beltran would soon be passing through town. He wired back to the priest that it was only fitting and proper that he help christen the building; after all, Father Beltran had inspired the idea to build such a place.

Taliff strongly encouraged Claire to attend the celebration, pointing out her presence was needed for the occasion. What would the grand opening of the school be without the schoolteacher?

Claire reluctantly said yes but regretted all of it. The grand opening was set for the same time as the Corrigan's Christmas tree decorating party.

CHAPTER FOURTEEN

Christmas came and went. While autumn had touched the trees and bushes with beautiful, rich color, winter had delivered a heavy one-two combination of chilly gray and white, knocking the world into frosty shapes. Wintry conditions enveloped the Corrigan Rafter C and Bar 3 spreads. Still, the new year brought talk of springtime, roundup plans, and ranch improvements. The look ahead helped keep everyone's thoughts warm, even when fireplaces could not.

For anyone daring to go outside, a bleak sky was unable to stop the cold shadows that seized the frigid landscape. Long coats were buttoned and collars raised high. White breath smoke swirled around faces. Leather work gloves were used more for warmth than protection. Some hardy souls took to tying bandannas around their heads to cover their ears. Most folks just did not venture out unless it was absolutely necessary.

Holt was hurt by the fact Claire missed the family tree decorating. They had not crossed paths since then. He hadn't even attempted to see her. He chewed on the anger. Of course, the celebration that conflicted with Claire's joining him was a worthy event that was beneficial to Wilkon. The Corrigans did not call off their own plans, but instead provided Mayor Cooke a sizable donation to be put toward the construction of desks and the purchase of books for the new schoolhouse. It ground on Holt that an event Taliff arranged *just happened* to be on a day he had something special planned with Claire. *Again*. He was not sure if this kept happening because Taliff purposefully created occasions to keep her away from him or if Claire simply liked Taliff more. Either way, the resentment clouded his thoughts and he no longer was as certain about a future with Claire—or if he even wanted one.

He spent the weeks since Christmas at the ranches. Mostly to provide much-needed help with chores, but partly to avoid town. And her. The Christmas gift he had picked out for Claire, a red silk scarf, was given to the widow Almina as a gift from all the Corrigans.

Holt enjoyed this time with his brothers and their families. When the weather cooperated, he relished riding across their land, giving his horses good workouts. He was always ready to saddle up and check on how the herd was wintering. It had felt good to wrap up the final year-end chores like storing plenty of cut hay, damming up washes to hold water, and cleaning regular water holes.

When he was out on-property like that, Holt sometimes left Tag at the Bar 3 with Cooper. The two dogs had naps to take, bones to chew, and children to herd. Holt laughed. He wasn't sure Tag even knew when the dog had been left behind, like this morning.

Dawn found Holt ponying two of his horses back to the Rafter C. With better weather coming, he did not want all of his mounts at the Bar 3. The trail-hardy buck-skin and the Appaloosa from Judge Pence followed along easily, enjoying the stretch of their legs.

The first brushes of daybreak's rose and yellow sky touched the horizon. The sun was just topping the land, the brightening glow heralding its arrival. Holt appreciated crisp mornings like this, diamonds of dew frost spread throughout the land. The forceful puffs of breath smoke released from himself and the horses were fascinating. This visible evidence that life was churning through each of them felt like some kind of divine message. He touched his medicine stone in silent gratitude.

An owl saluted as it glided through the trees in search of something to eat. Holt was surprised to see the night-time hunter at this time of day.

"Good morning, friend!" he called out.

Owls always brought a sense of comfort and wonder to him. He knew that a lot of tribes, Apaches in particular, believed that an owl could be an unlucky omen that meant death was on its way. But other tribes looked at the owl as a summoning call to the spirit world, a symbol of wisdom and knowledge.

"The energy from an owl helps you observe and be aware," his mother often told him.

Owls often came to Holt in his dreams and he always felt they spoke in the voice of his mother.

Holt felt good, as if a huge weight had been lifted. Was this sensation related to a previous life? He believed that many such happenings had their birth in another time.

After breakfast at the Rafter C with Blue and his family, he rode into town. Although Wilkon had continued to be mostly quiet, it was time to see how the town was getting along and to check in with Marshal Hannah and Deputy Wheeler.

Holt brought something with him he had been thinking about since the crazy day when the last of the Bordner gang killed each other in that jail fight. A large bundle of dried sage was stuffed into a saddlebag. The jail and cells still reeked a bit from the dousing of lye soap they received after the dead outlaws had been removed. Plus, Holt was sure the spirits would enjoy the smoky tribute.

In a new building just across the wide street from the jail, Meden Taliff had recently set up his justice of the peace operations in addition to keeping a private office upstairs. The building also included a small official office for Mayor Cooke, as well as assay and engineering offices.

Taliff owned a white Arabian, which he loved to ride. The horse was magnificent, but not exactly what usually was chosen as a mount in these parts. Jesse Littleson, the livery operator, charged Taliff double to stable the high-strung horse. Taliff owned a more trail-suitable black gelding too, but it was not as eye-catching as the Arabian, so he did not ride it as much.

Holt's good feelings continued when he noticed that neither of Taliff's horses were tied out front of the new building. He arrived at the jail, stomping the cold from his boots as he stepped inside. The jail was empty. No one in the cells was a good sign. Hannah was likely sleeping in and Wheeler was probably seeing to some late breakfast. Holt went next door to make sure everything was squared away in his quarters. Tied to the door handle was a stick of peppermint with a ribbon around it

—a small Christmas remembrance from Claire. It had been battered by the elements.

Holt took the little gift and headed back next door to the jail. There was a mostly full pot of coffee, but it could use some warming. Stoking the stove, he poured a mug and set it next to the pot so it would be ready quicker. He threw the candy's ribbon into the fire and stuck what was left of the peppermint into the mug of coffee.

Opening both windows, he unwrapped and lit the sage. He offered the smoking bundle in all directions. As the smoke from the sage danced among the recesses of the jail and hunted its shadows, he allowed daydreams of Claire to escape along with the other negative spirits.

CHAPTER FIFTEEN

Springtime summoned the sun and invited friendly temperatures to join it. Like daffodils and crocuses poking through the warming soil, people restless from winter idleness started peeking out their heads and spending more time outdoors.

The first Saturday of spring was a social event in Wilkon. The town would be busy. Folks would be out soaking up the sunshine and visiting all around. Ranch families rolled into town, kids tucked in the backs of wagons along with goods to be traded. Basket lunches were packed for a full day's outing.

Marshal Hannah stood on the boardwalk outside the jail and surveyed his town. Lots of people doing the things of everyday life…getting horses shod, having saddles and harnesses repaired, buying what they needed from the town's stores. Men found friends in the saloons and talked crops, cattle, weather, horses, Comanche. The usual. It was a time for a new beginning, a time to prepare for the rest of the year. As he walked through town, Hannah was pleased that he heard very little talk about the Bordner ugliness or the judge's murder.

Springtime. Rebirth. Wilkon was back to being "Wilkon." He smiled in contentment.

The Corrigan family pulled into town on a variety of wagons and horseback. Silka peeled away when they hit the main street, headed toward the barbershop for a shave and a bath. There was a young Chinese woman working there who always gave Silka special attention.

Holt and Tag came with the caravan as well. He planned to spend a few days in town. People needed to see the county sheriff on duty, even in peaceful times.

There was a large shopping list to work through for the Rafter C and Bar 3 ranches, staples such as flour, salt, sugar, and coffee, plus nails, chicken feed and other basic goods. The Corrigan children were growing, so needles, thread and fabric for new clothes were also on the list.

Both ranches needed to plant their kitchen gardens. The Bar 3 was essentially starting from scratch, so Bina and Atlee sent the boys off to find seeds for beans, squash, peas, melons, and cucumbers along with bulbs and tubers for potatoes, sweet potatoes, and onions.

The unmistakable aroma of the general store was pleasantly familiar for many who had not been in town for a while. The blend of ripe cheese, pickles, kerosene, produce, feed, cured meats, fabrics, leather and tobacco smoke was like an old friend. The young Corrigan boys were drawn to the displays of Barlow knives, single-shot rifles, and harmonicas, working their sales pitches on their fathers, Blue and Deed.

Holt rode up to the jail and noticed a horse tied out front that did not belong to either the marshal or deputy.

This one was a lithe, muscled bay. Good belly. It looked like it could run forever.

The door was open on this mild day, airing out the jail from a long, battened-down winter. He chuckled to himself that Hannah and Wheeler probably did not care for his sage-burning. He was surprised to find out the horse belonged to Texas Ranger Captain Laird McCoy who stood inside, talking with Marshal Hannah. A thin man with a long goatee, McCoy seemed more like a Presbyterian minister, gentle-spoken and modest, which contrasted with other elements of his character. He was aggressive and direct, and expected the same from his men. His Rangers administered harsh treatment to brutal men in a rugged land.

McCoy had been close by in another town and swung through Wilkon, purposefully to ask the Corrigans about joining the Rangers.

"Since I didn't hear from you, I thought I'd come over myself. We sure could use some good men, like the marshal here, and you and your brothers," he said. "Marshal Hannah already turned me down."

"My brother, Blue, has a young family," Holt explained. "My brother, Deed, just got married. They won't want to go gallivanting across Texas. And if you persuade them otherwise, you will rue the day their wives set on your tail. You'd rather face down Hannah here, or Hickok."

McCoy nodded and chuckled. "That leaves you," he replied. "I know Judge Pence spoke highly of you. How 'bout it?"

Looking through the open jail door at Taliff's Arabian tied up across the street, Holt tugged at his ear and said,

"I'll think about it, Captain. It would be an honor. Much to do here though."

"Fair enough." McCoy accepted Holt's answer. "I'll be over in Baccata in case you need to find me. We got our hands full. There's a crazy bastard on the loose."

Holt remembered the items from Almina. "Captain, speaking of the judge. You got any interest in looking at papers and maps of his? A lot of them looked like they were related to cases. Some of those cases may still be unsolved. They might be of more use to you all."

The captain smiled. "You're probably right. But I don't have the time or the men right now for puzzles. Hang on to 'em. There'll come a day."

CHAPTER SIXTEEN

Like other families, the Sanchez clan took advantage of the first Saturday of spring and headed into town. The adventure would be a welcome change. Along with the ranch hands, one of those staying behind was the patriarch of their family, Felix Sanchez. Now, as it appeared the Bordner threat had finally been overcome, he was determined to enjoy a peaceful Saturday morning alone.

He relaxed in his *bodega*, the splendid tack room that was part of the grand Lazy S hacienda. The size and success of the sprawling estate was the result of many years of hard work for he and his wife, Maria, and their family. Theirs was a solemn and gracious way of life marked by diligence and commitment, to the land and each other.

The silver-haired vaquero used his *bodega* as a study and craft shop. He enjoyed working on various leather projects, reading quietly, and playing hide-and-seek with his grandsons. The adobe walls of the big room held temperatures well, keeping out the heat of summer and retaining warmth in cold months. Everywhere were Mexican artifacts, paintings, Indian pottery and handwoven rugs. A massive, hand-engraved wooden table commanded the far end of the room and was surrounded by heavy, ladder-backed chairs. A paneled pine chest, ornately carved, was placed along one wall and held woolen blankets. Along an opposite wall sat a solid, plain sanctuary bench. At the other end of the room, in front of a large stone fireplace, two wingback chairs, over-stuffed and covered in soft cowhide were paired with two solid, simple pine chairs and a matching table. Nearby, an old roll-top desk stored important papers and hid candy treats. A big coffee pot hung above the hearth on a chimney crane. A stack of buckets used to hold water for soaking and cleaning rawhide rested neatly alongside sturdy wrought-iron fireplace tools.

A chessboard with pieces hand-carved from bones and antlers was set up on one of the tables in the room. The board, like Felix, was always ready for a game. His sons liked to play but could rarely beat their father. Felix had never beaten Silka when they played at the Bar 3 and Silka had never won here. Before his death, Judge Pence had also become a regular Lazy S visitor, enjoying spirited games over cigars. Felix enjoyed the judge's fascination with this chess set and the fact Oscar always wanted to play the black pieces. More often though, during his last few visits the two had been engrossed in looking at old maps and drinking Spanish wine around Felix's big desk.

Leatherwork was the theme of the *bodega*. Felix's work on saddle and tack dominated the middle part of the great room. Bridal reins with *romal*, *bosals* and hackamores, new *reatas,* and sets of chaps in various stages of repair hung on the walls by heavy hooks.

The Lazy S patriarch was an excellent horseman and took pride in the quality of leather and rawhide equipment he crafted for his ranch's use. He braided his own reins and bull ropes and taught his sons the skill. He was now enjoying introducing his grandsons—his little *cabritos*—to the craft, starting with teaching them to make pigging strings and rope. To him, weaving a rope, or *reata*, was a work of art, requiring great proficiency and patience. He was exacting in the way his rawhide was worked so it was pliable with an even firmness throughout the strand. If some parts were stiffer than others, the reata would not have the right balance or sail easily for accurate throwing.

The craft area held two saddles on which Felix was working. One, a worn saddle in need of repair, sat on an old barrel half with a frame of heavy mesquite. Underneath it was an open storage area organized with tools, soft brushes, and tins of saddle soap, tallow and lard. The other project was a brand new, ornately worked saddle for his son Taol's birthday. The new saddle sat on a large stand made of pecan wood. The rack stood taller than waist-high, so Felix could comfortably work on it standing up or seated on a stool. A large storage cabinet with a door to close it up was built in underneath.

Well after the family departed for the big day in town, Felix heard a commotion outside. Thinking it was Santo, their large tabby cat, keeping the hacienda safe from mice and snakes, he renewed his attention to the cabinet area under his larger saddle stand. As a result, he was startled when a dark, barrel-chested man wearing a traditional *serape* suddenly confronted him. Felix lunged for a pistol in his desk—guns were kept out of reach due to the small grandsons—but was thwarted in the effort. He fought briefly, but surprise provided too much of an advantage, as did the appearance of a second assailant. Otherwise, *mano a mano*, it would have been a fair fight.

The silver-haired vaquero was forced at gunpoint to be tied down with his own ropes. Wet rawhide bound his wrists and ankles to a ladder-backed chair. The room became a silent witness to the brief, but fierce, struggle. Felix's precious chess pieces were scattered during the scuffle. The neat stack of large buckets was toppled over like an uprooted tree. Tins of soap and other implements of leatherwork were strewn about. Of no use at the moment, a large rack holding a dozen rifles and three shotguns rested frustratingly idle.

The two intruders had arrived just before daybreak and had hidden behind the stone fence that surrounded the ranch yard. They watched the family take off for their day trip to Wilkon before advancing, encouraged that the elder Sanchez was not with them.

A Lazy S ranch hand had approached the house at the wrong time and surprised the assailants, causing the commotion Felix heard. The wrangler now lay unmoving, tucked under some Apache plume bushes near the bodega entrance. Other Lazy S crewmen were away from the hacienda, working on chores out in the pasture lands.

The second assailant went back outside to take up watch, hidden by the cedar elm, paw paw, and persimmon trees that ringed the house. The barrel-chested man with skin the color of a gunstock and a messy mop of shaggy brown hair bent menacingly close to his prisoner. His hateful voice hissed venom into the ear of the silver-haired rancher. "The problem with possessing mammon such as yours is that there are always those who crave it and want to acquire it for themselves."

Normally, Felix's stern appearance belied a deep love of nature and affectionate sense of humor for his family. Now, his face was fixed with grim determination, eyes ablaze with vehemence. The rawhide pigging strings he had braided with his grandsons now secured his hands and feet to the wooden structure of the chair. His thick fingers and strong arms toughened from years of working with horses and crafting leather equipment were of no use. Being powerless was not something the old rancher had experienced often.

The intruder stood and glanced around the room, noticing a painted pine *trastero* that held a small library of bound books along with earthenware crocks, rowled spurs, and new leatherwork brushes. Sacks of coffee and sugar sat next to stacked mugs atop the cabinet. He walked around his hostage, relishing in the old rancher's discomfort.

"I see you're a well-read man," he observed. "I am reminded of the great writer, Matthew, who told us that no one can serve two masters, for either he will hate the one and love the other, or he will be devoted to the one and despise the other."

He drew a bayonet from a sheath strapped below his knee. "You cannot serve God and money. I see all around me which master you serve," he sneered. The tip of his blade sliced open the sacks of coffee and sugar, the contents pouring down to the floor.

Felix struggled to shout through the bandanna restraining his mouth and fought unsuccessfully to respond to the intruder's challenge. The assailant smiled at his prisoner's immobility and inability to speak. "Shakespeare lauded that 'Men of few words are the best men.'" He smirked at his own joke and began to pontificate around the room. "Who then can snatch the plunder of war from the hands of a warrior?"

A descendant of a conquistador who invaded Mexico with Cortez, Felix's roots sank deep into Texas. He served as a mounted gunman in the Texian militia that was part of the Republic Army and took part in the surprise attack launched against the forces of Mexican General Antonio Lopez de Santa Anna at the Battle of San Jacinto. The rout forced the signing of treaties recognizing Texas sovereignty. After Texas won its independence, Felix served in the Army of the Republic of Texas, distinguishing himself for bravery and leadership. In addition to being one of the largest in the region, his Lazy S ranch was one of the oldest, acquired well before the War Between the States.

"Yes, my friend," the intruder continued. "I am here to collect. The apostle Luke wrote that Jesus said, 'Watch out! Be on your guard against all kinds of greed; life does not consist in an abundance of possessions.'"

The old rancher stiffened in his chair, not from fear, but from a lifetime of reacting to danger. Of fighting back. Old nerves and muscles were tautly coiled, ready to strike at the threat. The rope that tightly harnessed him to the straight-backed chair prevented him from doing more.

"After you and I send your family my message, I am told this land will see great change," he hissed. He moved directly behind the silver-haired warrior. The razor-sharp bayonet danced at the old man's throat. Catching a glimpse of the opposite wall, the barrel-chested man paused as he spied an aged, well-used saber hanging on the wall by the double rings of its scabbard. A pair of old-fashioned dragoon pistols were fastened above the sword. Next to the weapons, a shadow box displayed the medals Coronel Sanchez earned while defending Texas. The intruder stopped his soliloquy to walk over to the cherished mementos, shoving the bayonet back into the sheath attached to his leg.

Grinning hatefully, the assailant removed the saber from the wall. Drawing it from its steel scabbard, he thumbed the saber's edge. The blade was kept sharp after all these years. "Your land and money, I care not about... but others will." He turned with the sword in his hand. "The Lord said, 'Vengeance is mine,' but down here angels deal in a different manner of currency..."

Felix Sanchez gathered his strength, coiling himself for a desperate attempt to break free and fight back against this deranged intruder.

"I am one of those angels," the killer intoned.

An angry growl from the silver-haired rancher was instantly silenced as the saber sliced his neck wide open. A sheet of crimson erupted down the front of his embroidered vest and white shirt as the old man's life cascaded along with it. The burst of violence echoed through the room.

The stranger hunted through Felix's roll-top desk. Two detailed maps caught his attention and were carefully rolled and stowed in a Confederate haversack worn inside his *serape*. Twenty or so strange-looking rocks sat on a tray atop the desk. He emptied all of the rocks into the bag under his cloak, shoving the tray into a drawer. He ignored the two small chairs sitting next to the desk, chairs specially made for little ones to sit near their Papi while he worked or read.

When the lifeblood of the old vaquero had ebbed away, the killer cut him free from the chair and laid him reverently on the floor. He felt there was something satisfying about slitting an enemy's throat and knowing the soul would leave the body. The saber was forced into the grasp of Felix's right hand. Going back to the army shrine once more, the murderer took two medals from the shadow box on the wall and laid them ceremoniously on each of the victim's lifeless eyes. From his haversack, the killer took a handful of blue chicory blooms and stuck them in the dead man's open mouth.

As he left the room, he picked up a small memento, but did not notice the little puddle which had formed under the large saddle horse cabinet.

———

After another patrol of the town's busy streets, Holt headed toward the millinery store where he thought he would find his brothers winding down their visit. Blue and Deed were sitting outside. Blue's boys were playing with their brand new harmonicas. Deed was showing Benjamin how to safely handle his new Barlow pocketknife. The girls were shopping with their mothers and had not yet met their new dolls. All of them sucked on peppermint sticks, except for Jeremy and Matthew who had to wait until their harmonica recital was done.

"Want one?" Deed offered the sack of candy to Holt.

"I think I'll wait for a cigar," he declined, then told them about McCoy.

"Texas Rangers, huh?" Deed mused. "Be interesting

to actually get paid for what we've been doing the past few months."

"I already dealt you two out," Holt explained. "Told the captain that Bina and Atlee would be on him like a mess of angry hornets."

"Hornets the size of buffalo." Blue laughed.

Just then, Tag growled a little. Turning around, they saw Meden Taliff walk out of the nearby furnishings store, followed by Goldie Mae Freeburg and Claire Baldwin. Holt reached down to pet the dog and quiet him down.

"Ahh, *all* the Corrigan men!" Taliff smiled and tousled young Matthew's hair. "Big day in town! Great to see everyone out!"

The boys mumbled their hellos and went back to their new purchases. Blue and Deed gave friendly nods.

"Good morning, Meden." Holt half-smiled back. "Mrs. Freeburg, Miss Baldwin," he greeted the ladies with a polite touch of his hat.

"Hello, Holt. How have you been?" Claire smiled broadly. She wanted to stop and chat, but before Holt could really answer she was scooted along by Taliff and Mrs. Freeburg. Claire hesitated, but then followed her shopping partners. "We have to order window dressings, but can we talk later?" she called back to Holt as the trio hustled down the boardwalk. They continued down the walkway. Shoppers moving in and out of stores interrupted their line of sight, preventing Holt's answer and any further attempt at conversation.

Tag still had a little growl in his throat as he watched the group walk away. "You might be right, pal." Holt chuckled to Tag, patting him on the head.

"You look like you swallowed most of a 'possum belly," Deed teased.

"Give your Uncle Holt some of that peppermint," Blue said to the boys. "Something didn't agree with him."

———

"OH DIOS MIO...PAPI! Oh dios mio, Papi!"

Shrieks of horror echoed through the Lazy S hacienda. Maria Sanchez found the gruesomely murdered body of her husband and collapsed to the floor. Her hands covered her mouth in horror and grief so overwhelming she could no longer make a sound, her body quaking in shock.

In a panic, Taol and Casta looked about the room for their young son, Mateo. He had insisted on staying home with his Papi. The fact he was not immediately visible sent them into a frantic search.

Tina and Lea guided their hysterical mother away from the *bodega*, taking Taol and Casta's other toddler, Dante, with them.

Paul was putting a blanket over his father's body when he noticed small, bloody feline prints that left a trail throughout the room. The paw prints disappeared into Felix's large saddle stand.

Faint whimpers and soft stirrings from the saddle stand led Taol and Casta to inspect the cabinet underneath. They opened the storage door and exposed daylight revealed a tear-stained face. Casta cried out in relief. Mateo sat hunched over, cross-legged in the cabinet underneath. He held their cat, Santo, and rocked slowly back and forth. Tears of relief flowed down

Casta's face as she reached in to pick up her son. The cat had walked through the pool of Felix's blood. Now the boy and the cat were both covered in sticky gore.

Hugging and caressing the child, she checked to see if he was physically okay. A puddle of yellowish liquid stood underneath the saddle stand, evidence that Mateo had wet himself with fright. The boy stared off unresponsively in his mother's arms and did not want to let go of the cat. With his father and uncle soothingly telling the boy that Santo needed a bath, Mateo reluctantly released the cat and buried his face into his mother's chest.

CHAPTER SEVENTEEN

Gloomy weather, like the town's mood, hung like a shroud over Wilkon. In the days that followed the news of the horrific murder of Felix Sanchez, people were in shock and scared. Like the murder of Judge Pence, this killing made no sense.

A percussion of emotional waves buffeted the Sanchez family with anger, horror, and grief continually washing over them. The Corrigans reached out to their neighbors, bringing food and helping with ranch chores.

Taol showed Blue, Holt, and Deed where they had found his father as well as young Mateo's hiding spot. He pointed out that robbery did not appear to be the intention. The tambour was up on Felix's roll-top desk, but it was always up when he was in his bodega. A sack of old Mexican gold coins still sat conspicuously in one of the top drawers. Papers had been rummaged through on the desk, but nothing looked to be missing. The ranch's beef book was sitting intact right on top where it should be. Even the rack of rifles and shotguns was untouched.

Taol quietly informed the brothers that when they had

found his father the saber that killed him was shoved into his hand. "His own saber!" Taol reported, his eyes and teeth gritted in fury and sorrow. He explained that two Army medals were placed over his father's eyes and chicory flowers were stuffed into his mouth.

Little Mateo continued to be unresponsive. Not talking, not really eating. Crying often. It was obvious the little boy witnessed everything that had happened. They hoped that time would calm his fear and bring him back.

———

Wearing a full-length hooded cloak over his black suit, Father Miguel Beltran rode his mule slowly and humbly into Wilkon. Two riders, his assistants, rode with him. Both of them wore wide-brimmed hats and serapes that at one time were vibrant in color. The three tied up in front of the Cedar Bluff Hotel and took in the sad streets of the town.

Father Beltran removed the hood and opened his cloak, revealing a large, silver-finished metal cross on a heavy chain. The cross had exquisite green glass details. He was pleasant-faced and, for a large man, had a comforting voice and manner. His skin was russet, topped with thick brown hair greased into place, like that of a military officer. He reached into his mule's saddlebags and retrieved a small leather satchel and a Bible.

A wire message from Mayor Cooke had caught up with the priest to inform him of the horrific news. He immediately responded with an offer to officiate Felix Sanchez's funeral.

Father Beltran had last been in Wilkon at Christmastime to help celebrate the opening of the new community building. That had been a joyous occasion. This would be the first time the town used the facility for a funeral.

The priest was greeted outside the hotel by Meden Taliff and Mayor Cooke.

"Good to see you, Father," Taliff said, shaking the preacher's hand. "Thank you for coming."

"*Ja*, glad you could be *mit* us during a time like this," Mayor Cooke joined in.

"That's very kind, bless you." Father Beltran nodded.

"Let's go inside, shall we?" Taliff offered.

Stepping into the lobby of the hotel, the two assistants moved off to the side to wait. Blue Corrigan was waiting there as well.

The mayor introduced the priest to Blue.

"Blue fills in from time to time when you circuit preachers aren't available," Taliff explained.

"The Sanchezes asked if I would help with the service," Blue clarified, offering his hand. "Told them I'd be honored."

"Always a pleasure to meet a man of the Spirit," the priest said, shaking Blue's hand. He took note of Blue's missing arm and the large 12-shot pistol at his side. "I'm curious how the Sanchez family is faring. Have you spoken with them? Been able to give them any comfort?"

"Our family has been there a lot. They're more than neighbors to us. Maria and everyone…they're pretty torn up. Heaven should have come much later for Felix. I'm afraid there's a hole in their hearts that will never heal."

"The Lord is close to the brokenhearted and saves those who are crushed in spirit," Father Beltran said, quoting from *Psalms*.

"Amen," Blue said. "He heals the brokenhearted and

binds up their wounds." He continued with another *Psalm*.

"Amen," the priest said.

"The mayor and I have other business to attend to, Father." Taliff smiled. "You and your assistants are set up here in the hotel. Your usual room."

"*Ja*, we shall leave you *und* Blue to discuss *das* service for *Herr* Sanchez," Mayor Cooke added.

CHAPTER EIGHTEEN

The day of Felix Sanchez's funeral dawned gray and drizzly. Low clouds hung somberly, wrapping the town in a mournful pallor. Not a full rain, the heavy mist served to turn Wilkon's earthen main street into a tacky coating of dirt paste. Sticky mud clung to boots, wheels and hooves, anything that dared step onto the thoroughfare.

Inside their room at the Cedar Bluff Hotel, Marshal James Hannah was getting dressed for the funeral and talking with his wife. "When I was little, I was told if you're not on the trail, you always wear your best suit to bury a good man," he said, looking into the mirror hanging on their hotel room wall. "I didn't understand quite what that meant, why it was important."

Rebecca watched over his shoulder, observing him fiddle with his collar.

"During the war," he reflected, "we were always on the trail. We couldn't bury even the good ones. After the war...on a different trail...I didn't see many dead men who were good, much less stick around to bury them."

Rebecca moved around to the front of her husband and smoothed out his lapels. She knew that, even with his past experiences, he had been concerned with the recent violence in Wilkon. He had told her that, before she came along, he did not have as much to lose.

"I never had to care before," he said. A pensive look came to his face. "And I never had to wear a good suit as much as I have these past few months," he noted.

"Daddy used to ask if we had on our 'best bib and tucker,'" Rebecca said, adjusting his collar.

"I guess we're bibbed and tuckered," he said, holding her shoulders. "We're burying a good man."

———

At the Rafter C, Deed pulled into the ranch yard aboard a covered wagon. Atlee was seated next to him, their kids riding in the back, all dressed for the solemn occasion. They were going to eat breakfast with Blue's family and Holt before they all headed into town for the funeral.

The five kids asked to play on the porch. A caution from Atlee for the children to stay clean—and dry—was reinforced by Bina. "No roughhousing and getting all sweaty, we have to go to church soon," she called out. "And stay out of the rain." The mothers' warning took the enthusiasm out of being on the porch and the kids moved inside to play.

The brothers and Silka sat with coffee in front of the large fireplace and were joined by Atlee and Bina. The men, still in their twenties, had been born into a rugged land and grew up in a time of bitter turmoil. They had rarely faced death on peaceful terms. Once again, they were about to bury a friend who had died an undeserved, violent death.

"That poor family. Losing Felix…" Bina said and did not finish. "It's just so…so…awful…I hope his soul can find its way." A Mescalero Apache, Bina knew her ancestors looked upon death and the afterlife quite differently. Her understanding of both Apache and Christian beliefs gave her a unique blend of how to view life and all its wonder.

"I don't recall burying many folks who died quietly or at least on their own terms," Deed stated solemnly.

"Always seemed to be something took them away before it was time. Even our family," Blue remarked.

"Pa died after being thrown from that horse," Holt said.

"Ma and Poppy were taken by pneumonia," Blue observed.

Deed sighed deeply. "Aww, Poppy. Our Calliope Rose. What a sweetheart," he said, reflecting on their sister who died when she was only seven. "I wonder what she would have grown into," he said wistfully.

"Poppy had Blue's seriousness." Holt smiled, nodding his head at his brother. "She loved flowers and reading."

"But she was superstitious like you and Ma." Blue laughed in spite of himself, pointing back at his younger brother. "And cared for animals, maybe even more than Deed did."

"Didn't she have a frog for a while?" Holt asked.

"It was a turtle," Deed answered. "Named Sam. She also tried naming all our horses and animals."

"I believe she named my old dun, 'Bear,'" Blue remembered.

"I think mine was 'Green Bean,'" Holt said.

"And the milk cow was 'Candy Cane,'" added Deed.

They chuckled a bit, then silence took over the room as the brothers lost themselves in memory.

Silka watched the men he helped raise speak of a time before he became a part of the Corrigan family. "That always bad part. Of death," he spoke up. "Earthly body get taken. The soul stays. Only good part." He touched the brass medallion at his neck and tapped his right fist over his heart. "The soul lives on in those left behind. It is so."

Atlee spoke softly. "Losing someone you love is awful hard. Especially when you didn't get to say good-bye. Awful hard." Her thoughts weighed heavily on her first husband. "But you learn to live on. You learn to love again. It's what saves you." Deed reached over and squeezed her hand.

———

Back at the hotel, Rebecca spoke about losing her parents. "Ministers always sound so contrived. When your world follows a loved one into the grave, words are...just...empty."

"Grief is a powerful master," Hannah said. "It wants to control everything."

"I never could get over those awful remarks about Mother and Daddy 'being in a better place.' Well-meaning, my a—" She caught herself and spoke again. "The better place was here with me, dammit." She shook her head. "If I hear anyone say those things to Tina and Lea and Maria today..."

Hannah cocked his head and smiled. "That's why I love you." He reached for his wife's hands.

"It's been five years since Daddy died," she said, looking into her husband's face. "I wonder if the pain will ever fade."

"It doesn't get better," Hannah said, pulling his wife into a long, warm embrace. "It just gets different."

CHAPTER NINETEEN

The funeral for Felix Sanchez was held in the new community building, converted that morning into a place of worship.

Felix, being a longtime leading resident of the region, drew a huge crowd of people who gathered to pay their respects. Despite the weather, the building was packed. Even the townspeople uncomfortable with Mexicans begrudgingly admitted that he was a gentleman who had done much for Wilkon.

Claude Gausage and Les Freeburg had built pinewood pews that would also be used as seating for concerts, plays and town meetings. Not all of them were finished, so chairs from the Silver Spur were brought in to handle all of the people who turned out. Even with the extra chairs, there were people standing in the back of the room. A nice pulpit, crafted by Freeburg, was placed at the front. A long table was covered in white linen and sat behind the pulpit. A brand-new two-foot-high wooden crucifix sat in the middle of the table. Earthenware pots of sweet alyssum sat on either end of the table.

Because it was not an actual church, men in the audience were not quite sure what to do with their guns. Most left them on except for Blue. His huge Walch revolver and gun belt were rolled up and tucked into the back of the pulpit.

The Sanchez family was seated in the front row. Behind them, the Corrigans. Silka was standing in the rear, near the back door. He usually was not one to go to church but wanted to be there to say goodbye to Felix and support his family. He, like the Sanchezes, was sometimes the target of prejudice from certain parts of Wilkon.

Today, everyone set all that aside.

The room was filled with the town's leaders and business owners. In the back was Meden Taliff, standing near Marshal James Hannah. Also in attendance, but not seated with Holt or the Corrigans, was Claire Baldwin.

Two worship assistants who traveled with the priest led a procession through the middle aisle of the assembled throng. They were dressed in simple sack cloth prayer robes and carried humble candlesticks that held lit candles. One helper was dark-complected with a heavy mustache and long, black hair that was braided like thick black ropes on either side of his head. The other associate was clean-shaven, his skin the color of a terracotta water jug, with a head of short brown hair and one long silver earring. Holt observed that they looked more like Comancheros than altar attendants. *The Lord moves in mysterious ways*, he nodded to himself. The assistants placed the candlesticks on either side of the new crucifix at the front of the room, then each peeled off to stand on either side of the room.

At the end of the procession were Blue and Father

Beltran. Blue wore his best black broadcloth suit, cleaned and pressed for this solemn occasion. The priest wore a simple black vestment and the chain with the substantial metal cross. With his broad, deep chest, the formal robe, and large cross about his neck, he appeared as a glorious, albeit imposing, man of God.

Reaching the pulpit, Blue and Father Beltran turned and faced the gathering. Blue began in a loud, clear voice. "Grieving is a heart-wrenching time in our lives. No one travels through life without, at some point, experiencing the loss of someone or something dear. The passing of a loved one is one of life's most difficult challenges and the pain can be overwhelming."

The priest continued the introductory response. "But you are not left to suffer alone. No, God has many angels to watch over you and take care of troubles in times of need."

Along the front row, Felix's widow Maria, dressed in black with a black veil, was inconsolable, completely brokenhearted. Her sons were seated on either side of her, trying to comfort their mother and be strong for her, but their eyes revealed deep wells of sorrow.

Father Beltran said, "Let us begin with a reading of the 23rd Psalm. Read along or say it with me...

"The Lord is my shepherd; I shall not want..."

Little Mateo Sanchez stood on the pew next to his father, Taol. He still had not spoken since the murder. His arm was draped across his father's shoulders and his tired head rested there. His face was expressionless and forlorn. He heard Father Beltran speak, raised his head, and his eyes flew open in fright.

"Yea, though I walk through the valley of the shadow of death,

I will fear no evil..."

"Hurt...Papi..." he whispered once. Twice.

Taol looked at Mateo and put his arm around the boy and kissed him gently on the head. "Yes, yes," Taol soothed and held on to the boy. "Papi got hurt and is gone now."

Mateo continued his soft uttering, "Papi...Hurt..."

"*'Surely goodness and mercy shall follow me all the days of my life...*"

Father Beltran heard the little boy and looked down at the pew where the stirring was coming from. The two locked eyes. The boy stared at the priest and was instantly riveted in place, trembling with fear. The front of his brown twill trousers blossomed with wetness, the liquid running down his leg and wetting his sandals.

"Amen."

His mother, Casta, noticed the accident and took the boy from Taol, who quietly wiped up the small puddle with a handkerchief. Casta carried Mateo to the back of the church, holding him tight to her chest, cooing loving words to the distraught child and comfortingly stroking his hair. Even though they were moving further away from the priest, the boy could not take his eyes off him. The boy repeated, "Hurt...Papi..." over and over, getting louder each time.

When they reached the back of the church, something in the boy clicked and he was finally able to gather himself. He pointed directly at Father Beltran and screamed, "*He hurt Papi!*"

CHAPTER TWENTY

Like the deafening quiet just before a tornado, an immediate hush took the room hostage. Silence engulfed, waiting to be unleashed.

The boy screamed again. *"Papi! He hurt Papi!"*

The worship assistant standing nearest to the side door was closest to the boy and his mother. When the boy screamed, the man fanned open his robe. Drawing a pistol, he pointed it toward the outburst. Silka saw this and moved instinctively toward the gunman—and in front of the mother and child. As he rushed forward, he drew the large sword hanging off his back.

With the disturbance, Father Beltran turned and threw a huge roundhouse punch into the side of Blue's jaw and darted to the side door, flung it open, and bolted outside. The sneak attack buckled Blue. The congregation broke out in a flurry of commotion and shouts.

The child continued screaming, *"He cut Papi! He cut Papi!"*

The gunman opened fire and emptied his pistol toward the charging Silka.

Cries of terror and panic exploded into pandemo-
nium. People dove to the safety of the floor, while some
tried to run out the back door. Chairs were upended. Men
and women hollered; children screamed. An old woman
sat straight up in a pew, motionless, hands clenched
together at her chest and eyes shut tight as her mouth
worked through a fevered prayer.

Silka fell to his knees. He dropped his sword and
collapsed.

The other assistant squeezed off two random shots
and followed Father Beltran out the side door. The man
who emptied his pistol at Silka immediately drew another
gun to cover their escape.

As soon as the first weapon was drawn, Deed and
Holt instinctively shoved the Corrigan women and children to the floor under the pews and crouched on top of
them. They drew their guns, eyes instantly surveying the
situation.

In an instant, Holt ran to the pulpit and checked on
Blue, who was gathering himself and standing up. "Your
family's okay!" he hollered and fired twice at the
billowing robes of the assailants as they reached their
horses. Seeing that Blue was all right, Holt took off after
the escaping criminals.

The flurry of shooting inside the church appeared to
be over. Shouting, crying and chaos still swathed the
room, but the immediate danger had moved out to the
street. Blue and Deed calmly urged the families to stay
put right there on the floor. Blue grabbed his gun from
the pulpit as he and Deed advanced through the crowd
toward the open door.

Hannah, who had been near the back of the room,
stalked through the chaos in the direction of the gunmen

and had managed to fire two shots at the fugitives before he nearly tripped over a motionless Silka.

At the same time, Taliff sought out the area where Claire was seated. She was cowering safe on the floor with the Freeburgs.

Seeing Blue and Deed move en route to the door, Hannah shouted to them through the commotion. Blue was already at the door and did not hear him. Deed heard and looked toward the marshal. He saw him bending over a body. His adrenaline kicked into an even higher gear with the stunning realization that the figure on the floor was Silka.

"My god, Silka!" He rushed to his downed friend and mentor.

Oblivious to everything but the men he was chasing, Holt neared the open door and warily made his way outside. Two shots blistered the doorframe near him, hurling a shower of splinters.

Deputy Logan Wheeler, on duty at the jail, heard the shots from the other end of town. Tag was keeping him company, so the deputy closed the door to keep the dog safely inside. He stepped out onto the porch, his rifle readied. Down the street, he saw three men rush outside from the community center, firing back into the building as they ran. They swung into their saddles and, as a group, pounded down the muddy street in full gallop. The wild flapping of the gunmen's flowing robes made quite a scene as they thundered by. The street and boardwalks were nearly empty on account of the funeral. The few folks out and about screamed and ducked into alleys or storefronts for cover.

Wheeler kneeled behind a water trough and fired at the fleeing men as fast as he could lever his rifle.

Halfway through town, the riders veered onto a side street and used the buildings as cover for their escape. Although the drizzle had let up, one of the rider's horses slipped and nearly fell as they took that hard turn.

Pinned near the door when the priest and his thugs peppered the building with pistol fire, Holt finally advanced into the street, chasing the attackers on foot. As he ran, he snapped off more shots at them from his revolver. Blue, not many moments behind, fired at the outlaws with his big 12-shot revolver and followed their escape down the side street. With all the lead being thrown around, it was unclear whether any of the bullets found their mark on fugitives or innocents.

"We gotta ride!" Holt hollered as he reached the jail. He checked the cinch of the horse tied next to Wheeler's mount and swung up. Wheeler was just a heartbeat behind. Spurring the horses hard, they were at full gallop in a few strides, following the tracks raised by the fleeing outlaws.

Back at the community center, in the chaos, Deed dropped to the floor next to Silka, who was lying face down. He quickly turned the big man over. The sight punched him hard. Silka had been shot three times, maybe more; it was hard to tell, his huge chest was a sea of red.

"Silka, I've got to stop this bleeding!" Deed said frantically, ripping open the wounded man's fancy vest and white shirt.

"I-I am in good hands now." Silka strained to speak. He coughed. "I see wife…and children…th-they smile."

Desperately trying to stem the flow of blood, Deed ripped a handkerchief in half and stuffed it into two of the wounds. He pressed his hand down hard directly onto a third bullet hole while searching his pockets for more cloth. "C'mon, Silka, stay with me," Deed begged.

"*Akugō...Waru*...Evil...evil person...was here." The injured man feebly lifted an arm and tried to point toward the pulpit. "Silka knew. Evil..." His eyes were unfocused, he could not keep his arm up.

"Ssshh...ssshhh... Silka, rest. Easy. Easy," Deed urged. He grabbed a bandanna from Silka's pocket and tore it in two. He packed the material into the dark holes on top of the cloth already stuffed there but could not hold back the oozing flow. "Stay here, Silka. Breathe. C'mon, *samurai*, breathe!"

But Silka's breathing was becoming irregular, rattling. "You need to fight, Silka! Fight!" Deed pled, using both hands to apply direct pressure to the wounds.

The damage was done. Silka's life continued to escape onto the floor.

"My son...I go...see wife Toshie now..."

"No, Silka, no..."

With a long, raspy exhale, Silka breathed his last.

The shock hit Deed like being yanked from the saddle. He looked at his blood-soaked hands as though they did not belong to his body. Agony ripped at his soul. Deepening pain tore at his heart. He squeezed shut his eyes to hold back the roar of emotion. Some of it escaped out the corners of his eyes. Unable to restrain himself any longer, a wail burst from his mouth and tore into the room, more like the cry of a badly wounded animal than the sob of a distressed man.

CHAPTER TWENTY-ONE

I t only took a few strides for Holt to realize this was Marshal Hannah's horse he was riding. His own horse was in the livery that morning. He kept riding though. Hard. The sorrel had a smooth gait and was ready to run. He was getting used to the animal and the horse to him. He readjusted his hat in the rushing wind and touched his cardinal feather.

"The priest was on a big mule and the others had bays," Deputy Wheeler shouted. "You saw the lead we threw at 'em, dunno know if we hit anything though."

"That bastard killed Felix. I bet he killed the judge too," Holt yelled back.

They galloped for a good mile then eased their horses down to an easier ground-eating lope. "Can't run 'em into the ground when we've just started," Holt hollered.

Following a narrow creek bed, they crossed a wide strip of sand and cactus, and traveled along an uneven line of oak and pecan trees. The land opened into a wide expanse clotted with mesquite and presented some surprising gullies. The outlaws, for now, were easy to track in the rain-soaked ground. Mule and horse tracks showed they were moving fast, with no attempt to disguise their trail. It did not look like they were planning to stop, but the assumption could get the lawmen killed.

A couple of long hours passed and they moved out of the soggy ground. The rain had not reached here. They rode through clusters of yucca, mesquite, ocotillo and prickly pear among sparse clumps of grass. In addition to the bandits, coming upon a raiding party of Comanche or Apache was a concern. Holt and Wheeler passed thickets of juniper bordering a long wash, alert for a possible ambush.

"We need to let these guys blow and water them," Holt said. "This creek has to run out somewhere along here, maybe swells into a pond. Unfortunately, they're going to figure it out too," he observed.

"Good place for an ambush," Wheeler acknowledged grimly.

"We've pushed these horses hard, we don't really have much choice. We'll take turns watering."

The end of the creek would provide a good place to rest their horses. It appeared the outlaws had stopped there earlier and moved on. A small pond definitely marked the end of the creek, at least above ground. A few scraggly cottonwood and ash trees and buckthorn scrub were doing their best to surround the water.

The horses were led to the creek one at a time. Holt got down first, his rifle out. Wheeler watched the land around them. Horse and rider drank their fill. Holt remounted and rode over to a slight rise as the deputy got down to give himself and his horse relief from thirst.

Holt reined up and studied the broken land ahead of them. It was mostly prairie, marked only with rocks, strong-willed plants, and a few tumbleweeds interested in going somewhere else. He hoped to see dust in the distance that would indicate riders but saw nothing.

Crack! Crack! Crack! Crack! Crack!

Rifle fire bloomed from an area of rock ahead of them. Wheeler spun to the ground, a bullet creasing his side above his hip. He returned fire from the ground. Dismounting, Holt fired at the sounds. His first three shots were off target. Low. He looked at the Winchester and checked its sighting.

This is Hannah's rifle, dammit!

Crouching, he sought better cover. He adjusted his aim and his next shots found their mark. One ambusher tumbled from the rocks. Both lawmen continued firing. Soon, it was apparent their shots were not being returned. They held their fire and listened to the silence.

They watched as four riders galloped away from the rocks, Father Beltran on a mule followed by three other gunmen. Wheeler and Holt squeezed off a couple more shots at the fleeing assailants.

"Well, the men from the church had help," Holt observed. "You okay?"

"Yeah, I think so," grunted Wheeler. "I'll check the horses."

Keeping cover in front of him as best he could, Holt crept up to where the outlaw fell. He kicked the body in the ribs. No reaction. Flipping the body over with his boot, the man was obviously dead. A Mexican or maybe a Kiowa. But not one of the men from the church. The man's pockets held nothing that would answer any of their questions, just some old candy, loose cartridges and cigarette makings. Holt smashed the man's rifle against a boulder and threw it as far as he could, clattering up into the rocks. He shoved the man's pistol, barrel first, into nearby mud. The dual cartridge belts on the outlaw were mostly full, but held .45's, useless to them.

Wheeler had gathered the horses, but it took some effort. "Comancheros?" he asked and held on to one of the horse's manes, feeling slightly dizzy.

"The dead one might be Kiowa," Holt responded. "Hey, are you all right? You're limping. Thought you said you weren't hurt."

"Yeah, guess they had better aim than I thought. It's justa scratch. I'm not carryin' any lead."

"Let me take a look," Holt said, moving near the deputy. Pulling up Wheeler's bloody shirt, Holt quickly affirmed the assessment of the wound not being serious was accurate. A bullet had burned a long, ugly crease along the fleshy part of his right side, just above the hip. Holt was relieved it wasn't worse, but it was bleeding hard. Cut flesh was angry and puffing. Wheeler handed him a bandanna to use to help stop the bleeding.

"Lie down, let me do some quick tending. Hold this in place while I go get some bandages and water," Holt ordered. He retrieved a canteen from the horses and an extra handkerchief.

"There's an old shirt in my left saddlebag," Wheeler said. "You can use it as a bandage."

Holt grabbed the shirt. He swabbed the wound to clean it and tore the shirt into long strips, using one to tie a tight dressing around Wheeler's middle. "Well, that'll have to do for now. Keep an eye on it. If it really starts bleeding, we'll need to do something more."

He helped Wheeler stand. The deputy was a little wobbly from the loss of blood but was determined to stay on his feet. The shock was wearing off, with pain searing right behind it. Holt helped him into his saddle. Mounted, they scouted the ambush nest. The mule and horse tracks were easy to read. Footprints coming and going and empty cartridge casings were a silent story of the attempted trap. A small patch of blood indicated at least one other rider was hit. The stains on the rocks were in a different place than where the ambusher they downed had been. Not far away, more spots of blood trailed toward where their horses had been picketed.

"Looks like we hit 'nother one," Wheeler remarked, feeling light-headed but trying not to show it.

"But not enough to keep him from riding away with the others."

The horse belonging to the dead man wandered to the creek to drink. Holt carefully approached, not wanting to spook it. It was a decent mount, a smaller grulla. At one time, it likely belonged to a Comanche or Kiowa. "We'll take it with us," Holt said. "Never know if we'll need it." Gesturing to the body, "We'll leave him. We've got to keep moving."

They followed the obvious trail left by the outlaws through the day and into the evening. The fugitives were pushing hard. Holt had a feeling they were slipping further and further away, but Wheeler was nearly done in. The deputy had spent the last couple hours wondering if Holt should tie him to his saddle. The wound had bled on and off throughout the day and he had lost a fair amount. He needed some food and a chance to rest from the pounding of the saddle.

At the end of a ravine sat a small but deep pool of water. To the right was a long rock shelf. Near the pool, a small cluster of cottonwoods held a meeting. It was not the most secure camp, but it would have to do. It was time to stop. Holt picketed the horses near some good grazing grasses and weeds, keeping them away from the water until they cooled down. He made the decision to not take off their saddles but loosened the cinches. Wheeler refilled the canteens.

Shadows started to lie across nearby rocks, creating all kinds of strange-looking shapes. A batch of wind-blown willows struggled to keep watch in a narrow hollow. Holt checked the horses' hooves to make certain they were still in good shape. Not being certain how the bandit's grulla would react if there were nighttime visitors, he picketed it between their own horses.

During the day's ride, Holt had found some yarrow and stuffed a few handfuls into Wheeler's saddlebags. Before it got completely dark, he built a small guerrilla fire near the cottonwoods to heat up some hot water and a little coffee he found in the deputy's saddlebags. It was not yet dark enough for the tiny flames to be a beacon and any smoke generated was dissipated by the overhanging branches. With the water hot enough, he stuffed the yarrow into a mug. He would make a poultice with the leaves and apply it to Wheeler's wound.

The deputy also had a little bit of salt pork in his saddlebags. Holt rolled a few strips of it on sticks and stuck them over the fire to roast. They ate the fatback and drank up the pot of coffee in silence. The coals from the fire were rubbed out.

With the last remaining light, Holt took the horses one at a time to water at the pool. It was getting dark quickly. After the horses were set for the night, it was time to tend to the wounded deputy. While Holt was seeing to the horses, Wheeler was supposed to go through all the saddlebags and inventory their supplies. But when he returned from the pool, Holt found the wounded man fast asleep, seated against a tree, his Henry across his lap.

Holt was concerned. He knew what it was like to get shot. Although they had kept an eye on the gash during the day, there was no way to keep it from opening back up from time to time. As such, the deputy had lost enough blood to make him weak. At least it looked like infection had stayed away—for now. Holt needed to keep Wheeler hydrated and let him rest as much as possible to avoid opening the wound again. He mashed up the steeped yarrow into a paste and put it on a handkerchief.

"Logan. Logan." He quietly woke the deputy. "Let me get this on you. It'll help the healing and keep infection away." He placed the poultice directly on the angry crease and tied it into place with another strip of shirt. "Get some rest now. We'll set out early."

"Th-Thanks. I'll be ready in the morning," Wheeler mumbled.

There was no way Wheeler could stand watch in his condition. Holt missed having Tag as company, but he also missed the dog's nose and instincts. The horses should supply some indication of warning, which was better than nothing.

Holt took a position near where the horses were tied. From there he could see in all directions. He withdrew the small tobacco pouch from his coat pocket and poured a handful of shreds into his hand. He tossed them in all directions around the campsite as tribute to the spirits. In his nightly ritual, he wiped clean his pistols and Hannah's rifle, touching each of them with the cardinal feather from his hatband when finished.

Propping himself against a tree, his Winchester lay at

his side, levered but not cocked. One of his Russian Smith & Wessons was in his hand. Before closing his eyes, he pulled the sacred stone from his vest pocket and asked the spirits of the land to help him. His own way of praying. He fell asleep with the stone in his fist.

He startled awake, senses on full alert. He sat perfectly still, listening. The horses were settled nicely. Wheeler was sleeping soundly. Holt was not sure what got his attention. Night sounds were all around. It seemed nothing was close that shouldn't be. False dawn was flirting with the shadows, little more than an hour away. He was surprised. He had not meant to sleep that long. He looked at the medicine stone in his hand and returned it to his pocket.

As the earliest blush of dawn was stretching itself over the land, Holt assessed their situation. An inventory of what was in their saddlebags revealed meager supplies.

Chaos and gunfire had erupted in the middle of the funeral and they chased after the outlaws purely on instinct with no preparation. Hannah's saddlebags were packed more like a teacher's travel kit, with extra clothes, a couple of books, and an extra pair of eyeglasses. There was practically no food, just a strip of beef jerky and a tin of sardines. He did have a couple of boxes of cartridges and an extra pistol and derringer. Wheeler's saddlebags offered only a few more provisions—a nearly empty package of salt pork, a couple strips of beef jerky, not quite half a sack of corn dodgers, a small bag of coffee, and a half nose-bag of grain for his horse. He checked the gunnysack tied to the outlaw's horse. It revealed only a half-bottle of tequila, a small pack of tortillas, some hard biscuit knots that looked moldy, and a small sack of beans.

Holt built another hatful of fire and started a pot of coffee. He set half of the beans to cook. Wrapped in the outlaw's tortillas, that would be breakfast. They would save the rest for another meal. He also rewarmed the rest of the yarrow paste. Wheeler would need some fortification for strength and a fresh poultice on his wound. Holt noticed the fire was crackling with occasional blue flames and was happy to see that spirits were near. Wheeler stirred and awakened. The deputy got up to relieve himself, very sore and beat up, but the dizziness had left for now.

Holt realized that to continue following the outlaws would invite trouble in a variety of ways. Although there were two of them, one was hurt. Not seriously, but enough. They had hardly any food and no extra water. About all they had was ammo and too much ground to cover. They were ill-prepared and did not have the time to live off the land.

He made up his mind and laid out how things stood to the deputy.

"Don't turn back 'cuz of me. I'm fine," Wheeler insisted.

"I know that, Logan," Holt said, acknowledging the deputy's resolve. "But look at our situation. Those bastards hit out of nowhere. The heat of the moment put us on their tails. We took off unprepared to be tracking anyone for days."

"After this, I'm keepin' my bags ready for the trail at all times," Wheeler declared.

"I'm thinking that's good advice for all of us. Let's get back. They're obviously headed somewhere south.

We've got descriptions now. I'll wire all the authorities with details."

Their trail home took them by the location where they had been ambushed the day before. They decided to retrieve the body of the bushwhacker they killed, if there was anything left of him. They approached the area and saw a man kneeling over the body. As they rode up, they laid their rifles across their laps in front of them. The man stood and held his arms out, palms open, to indicate he was unarmed.

By his dress, he looked to be an Apache. He was older, but hard to tell just how old. His long, black hair hung loose with no braids. A simple cloth headband that looked at one time to be blue in color was tied around his head. He wore deerskin leggings and high-legged boot-like moccasins. His long, fringed deerskin shirt was dyed a shade of indigo. A dark belt was fastened around his waist.

He had not touched or disturbed the dead body. No one else looked to have come through either. Surprisingly, scavenging animals had not touched the body. The dead man was just as they had left him.

Holt felt a strangeness in the Apache's presence, but a peacefulness also. Was this a glimpse of another life? Was this man with him in another time?

Holt was certain there was a mysticism to the world, more than just this one life. He was afraid of heights and thought that might have been how he had died in a previous life, falling from some high place. There were times during the war when he had the strong feeling that he had been in that battle before, only with different weapons and against a different enemy. At times there was great sorrow within him, a sadness that seemed to well up from somewhere else. During the war, Holt had heard that the actions in one life had a direct effect on the next. A person must be reborn endless times until he found the purpose God had for him. If so, what was his purpose? At those times he sought out the medicine stone in his shirt pocket. Most would say it was a silly superstition, but it seemed right. For him.

Holt shook his head to focus. He swung down from his horse, sheathed his rifle, and faced the man. He said the Comanche words for "medicine man" while he made the signs, putting his fist at his forehead, extending two fingers skyward, then spiraling his fist upward, followed by holding up one finger. He knew the man was Apache but did not know any of their words. A few Comanche words and signs were all he knew.

In response, the Apache made a simple gesture as though requesting permission to speak. The Indian looked guardedly at Wheeler, who was still on his horse and kept his rifle casually pointed in the direction of the stranger. The Indian returned his gaze to Holt and spoke quietly, "*Entiendes español?*" asking if Holt understood Spanish.

"*Sí, un poco.*" A little, Holt replied. He knew more Spanish than Comanche, but not much.

"*El hombre muerto aún no ha sido molestado por los depredadores,*" the Apache gestured down at the dead man. "*El cuerpo es demasiado malo, los animales ni siquiera se lo comen.*"

He finished speaking and turned and walked away toward the rocks where the original ambushers had hidden. "*Usted necesita estar en casa,*" was a final instruction he made over his shoulder. He moved up into the rocks and disappeared from their sight.

"Logan, you up to helping me get this jackass lashed to a horse?" Holt asked. "We need to bring him back and figure out if anyone knows who this guy is."

It was a painful chore to get down and move around, but Wheeler did not let it stop him. They threw the body over the extra horse and lashed it to the saddle. "You gonna tell me what the hell it was that injun said?" Wheeler asked.

"He pointed out that this dead man hadn't been disturbed by predators yet. He said the body was too evil, even animals wouldn't eat him."

"Good god..." Wheeler gasped.

"He also said I needed to get home. Not liking the sound of that."

"I don't wanna be out here like this any longer'n we have to," Wheeler responded.

Holt looked grimly toward where the Apache had gone. "Let me help you up," he said. "We gotta ride."

CHAPTER TWENTY-TWO

Not chasing anyone, their ride home was slower. It was early morning the next day when Holt and Wheeler arrived back in Wilkon. They were dirty, hungry, and worn out. Leading a horse with a dead man slung over it meant townsfolk gave them a wide berth. Onlookers stopped what they were doing to stare at the riders and chatter among themselves. The dejected lawmen reined up outside the jail.

Wheeler tied up his horse and limped into the building as Marshal Hannah stepped out to greet them. Tag came barreling out too, eager to see his master. Holt kneeled down to give Tag big hugs and welcoming pats on the back.

"Tag was a bit worried when you didn't say good-bye," Hannah said as he walked to the extra horse carrying the dead man. Picking up the head by the hair, he got a good look at the man's face. "Wooo, this boy is gettin' ripe." He grimaced. "He's not familiar though. Kiowa? Maybe Comanchero by his choice of employment."

"He was riding with that bastard Beltran, but he's not one of the gunmen from the church. We'll send out a wire. Maybe he's someone the authorities know about," Holt noted dolefully.

"I'll look at the sheets, send out word," Hannah said. "I already sent out word about '*Father*' Beltran."

"Yeah, we can add that they're definitely heading south," Holt acknowledged, giving Tag's back another good pat. He stood and said, "We need the doc to take a look at Logan here…where'd he go?" He hadn't realized Wheeler had gone inside.

"Bradley!" Hannah called to the jail. While Holt and Wheeler were gone, the mayor's son had helped Hannah once again.

The lanky twenty-year-old with long blond hair, darted out to the boardwalk. "Is Logan all right?" he gestured with his head back into the jail. "He's asleep on a cot in one of the cells."

Holt nodded his head tiredly and scratched his unshaven face. "Yeah, he'll be fine. Got creased on his side. Lost some blood. Could've been a lot worse. He needs a good meal and some rest."

"Bradley, take this smelly mess down to Claude's," Hannah instructed. "Tell him the law will pay. And send back Dr. Sandor to look at Logan." Bradley started untying the outlaw's horse to lead it down the street.

Holt couldn't wait any longer to ask, "What happened *after*…?"

"Blue and Deed and their women and children are all fine," Hannah immediately assured Holt, who looked instantly relieved. "The little Sanchez boy and his mother are fine too," the marshal continued. "Old man Martin took a bullet through his shoulder, but Dr. Sandor says he'll be OK. One of the lumber clerks got grazed in the arm, a nasty burn. And Bradley's mother bumped her head pretty good when she fainted."

Right then, Claire stepped out of the furnishings store and walked back toward the middle of town. Following her like a puppy was Meden Taliff. She caught sight of Holt talking with Hannah down the street in front of the jail. She tried to hurry to him, but Taliff gently slowed her down. "Thank god Sheriff Corrigan has made it back!" he declared. "He appears to be busy with something though," he said to Claire, motioning at the scene that included Bradley Cooke with the outlaw's horse and dead body. "Perhaps we shouldn't be interrupting the lawmen right now. Let's let them do their work and we can catch up later." His calm voice soothed as he guided her into the millinery shop.

"Sorry I took your horse," Holt said to Hannah. "He was there, mine wasn't. No worse for wear. He's a good one."

"Sure-footed and responsive. The way I like 'em."

"Well, thanks. Your rifle shoots a little low though."

Hannah pointed at his glasses. "You weren't wearing these." They half-chuckled. "Look, Holt, everything is under control here, you should get out to the ranch. They'll need to see you, know you're okay."

"It's a deal," Holt said. "I'll take your horse with me to the livery and have Jesse give him some extra oats, maybe a bath. I'll pay for it."

"Deal." With a heavy sigh, James Hannah watched his friend walk away. He knew Holt needed to hear about Silka from his brothers.

CHAPTER TWENTY-THREE

L ost in tired thought, Holt's mind drifted back to Agon Bordner and what he had done. It was still hard to believe the man had been responsible for all those deaths and ranch seizures. Now, the brutal murders of Judge Pence and Felix Sanchez turned his fragile new world as Sheriff Holt Corrigan into complete chaos. Lives lost to Bordner men were victims of outnumbered ambush or outgunned assaults. These new killings were vicious, beyond senseless. Silka had even said that evil was at work.

Holt's mind reeled. Who does such things? And why?

Riding out of a draw, he forced himself to pay attention to his surroundings. He had been riding for too long without actually focusing on where he was going. Even on a familiar trail and with Tag working his flank, it was a good way to ride into serious trouble.

His bay snorted, and immediately Holt was on alert. He was not far away from Rafter C land, but this was still not country one could assume he was safe. He lifted his Winchester from its saddle scabbard and cocked it into readiness. Soon, off to his right, a doe and her fawn bolted from their hiding place, unable to keep Tag from discovering them. Holt hollered at Tag, to keep the dog from chasing after the pair.

Before long, he was on Rafter C land. Exhausted but happy to return, he rode into the ranch yard. His arrival was preceded by Tag hailing his pal, Cooper.

With the dogs' playful outbursts heralding his arrival, both Blue and Deed stepped out onto the porch and met Holt in the yard. Bad news was a fact of life and they rarely shied away from confronting it head-on. They immediately related the shocking news about Silka.

The words crashed through Holt like a locomotive, "No! Not Silka!" His outburst shocked even him. "Hannah told me right away that you, your ladies and the kids were okay. Casta and Mateo too..." The words stopped coming and he looked down at his dusty boots. "He didn't tell me..."

Blue put his arm on Holt's shoulder. Deed gritted his teeth and blinked at the wetness that formed at the corners of his eyes.

Holt looked up at his brothers. "I want to see him."

The main house had a separate wing where Deed and Silka had lived independently from Blue and his family before the two moved over to the Bar 3. Silka was lying on the bed in his old room. Washed and prepared for his funeral, the former *samurai* looked peaceful, like he had just laid down for a nap. The serenity belied the blood-soaked violence that ripped him from this world. His weapons had been cleaned and were laid out next to his body.

Alone with the man they cherished so much, they stood in silent contemplation. Deed smiled through the pain and the tears welling in his eyes. "The first time we met him he said, 'I am Nakashima Silka. I am *Samurai*.' Put his right fist against his heart and declared, 'Warrior. In Japan. I lived *bushido*…way of the warrior. None dare challenge me.'" Deed touched the brass circle at his neck. The older Japanese man had instilled *bushido* in each of them, the "way of the warrior," a life built on honor, inner strength, determination, directed action, and freedom from fear of death. Deed was too young to fight in the war, so he had worked the most and hardest with Silka. His ability to fight with his hands and feet a testament to Silka's teaching.

Holt exhaled deeply. "Silka. Our warrior."

"Hard to think where'd we be if he hadn't come along," Blue said, bowing his head.

Holt pulled the tobacco pouch from his pocket and sprinkled some around the unmoving body. "Wherever the Great Spirit takes you, may you be protected in all directions," he began. "Thank you, my friend…for everything…you've done. We…we…w-were…you s-saved m-my b-broth…us." Sorrow and anger swelled inside him and came out in the form of hot tears. And venomous words.

"Where are You *now*, God!?" Holt shouted at the heavens. "Where?! I've tried hard to believe in You. Yes, You know damn well I have. And what have You done? You unleashed those unholy *bastards!* They killed the judge! They killed Felix! *They killed Silka!*" He had not been filled with this much hate and anger and sadness in a long time. A clenched rage like he had not felt since… since the surrender. But this…this was worse.

He turned from the body. A ferocity burned in his eyes that was savage; a cornered, angry panther about to attack. Very few men had ever seen this look on Holt's face. Even fewer were still alive. Raw fury rose and swelled within him, intensifying like a raging storm. "I'm going after them." His voice was a feral growl. "Wherever they are, I'm going to find them." He slammed his fists on the bedstand. "If it's the last thing I do in this world, I will find every last one of those sons of bitches." His voice was thick with vehemence. "*And I will kill them.*"

Deed stepped in, "I'm going with you."

"We're all going," Blue said. "But there's someone we need to talk to first."

"No, goddammit, Blue," Holt snarled. "No offense, but I'm not praying. God had His chance. He's got *nothin*g to do with this now."

He turned back to Silka and put his hand on the man's chest and spoke softly. "You heard me swear it. Rest easy now, my friend. I'll settle this for you. I promise."

Blue silently put his arm on Holt's back and guided him toward the big ranch kitchen. Seated around the large table in front of the big stone fireplace, talking quietly and drinking coffee were Bina and Atlee. And Texas Ranger Captain McCoy.

McCoy stood, looking directly at Holt. "I am very sor—"

"Captain," Holt interrupted. "I'm going after that priest or whatever the hell he is. Silka and Felix and probably the judge are dead because of that bastard. I'll take that badge now."

Deed joined in, "So will I."

"Swear us all in," Blue added.

Bina and Atlee said nothing, but both of their faces tightened like someone had slapped them. Hard.

Holt reacted brusquely. "No! That's not going to happen. You're *not* going! Neither of you. The family needs you *here*. It's spring. Both ranches need squaring away. And protection. The Sanchezes need looking after too."

"I'm…" Deed tried to start.

Holt held up his hand near Deed's face, the forefinger extended upward. Their no-nonsense father used to do this many years ago, a silent—and obeyed—gesture to be quiet. *Now.*

Holt's eyes blazed from Deed to Blue. He meant this. *No!*

Blue tried to speak. "You can't do this alone—"

"You said yourself, Blue," Holt interrupted, calmer now. "There are lots of ways to fight. Remember? In El Paso?" He looked from Blue to Deed and back. "Building a ranch is a fight." He smiled softly at Bina and Atlee. "And raising a family is worth fighting for."

"Holt…" Blue tried again. Holt's scorching glare returned and seared into Blue's eyes. Intensity like he had never seen before in his younger brother stopped Blue from saying anything more.

Holt stepped close to his older brother, his voice quiet. "It was no accident we met in El Paso. The spirits wanted us to cross paths. Your words brought me home," he acknowledged. "I need to do this. This is what *I* can do for *us*." His words were guttural, from deep within. "You know my spirit demands that I fight. That's what I am, what I've always been."

Blue knew better than to argue with his brother. "Take Travis then."

Deed nodded. "He's a good hand. Knows how to handle himself."

"You're a Ranger now," McCoy interjected. "You'll have a partner. Two Rangers will be enough."

Holt took his eyes from Blue to look at the captain. He took a deep breath and looked around at his family. That settled it. "Okay then."

Blue and Holt locked eyes once again. A different fire now burned between them. No words, just the unspoken understanding of brothers who had survived riding through hell and knew what was ahead. A brief nod between the two was all that was needed.

"Get your gear together. Some rest if you can," McCoy instructed. "We'll meet in your office at dawn."

CHAPTER TWENTY-FOUR

Holt said his goodbyes to the women and kids before heading immediately back to Wilkon. There wasn't time to be tired. He had supplies to purchase at the general store and gear to gather at his quarters. Besides, the fury he felt was enough to keep his spirit fire stoked and fed.

He had made up his mind that he would take two horses. It would be a little out of the ordinary, but he wasn't sure what awaited him on the trail ahead. He knew he definitely had to be able to move without delay. Alternating between horses should help him keep both mounts healthy and fresh enough to cover ground in time he did not have. Plus, he was in the position to have several horses to choose from.

Although he had not yet found a horse to match Buck, the sturdy buckskin killed last fall, he was becoming very attached to the long-legged, powerfully built bay he had been riding the most ever since. This gelding was not quite as full of fire as Buck, but it was intelligent—thinking first, then reacting quickly. It had a great deal of stamina and did not waste energy. He had pulled more than a few wet saddle blankets off this horse's back and knew it would be good on the trail. That would be his primary horse. Choosing the back-up took a bit more thought.

His best horse was probably the young Appaloosa that had belonged to Judge Pence. Sturdy and spirited, it could be ridden all day. Holt strongly considered bringing it as his back-up, but decided its spots were just too flashy. Blending in—or at least not standing out—was something he had to consider.

He also really liked the way the two Comanche horses were working out, but he remembered their reaction when he was fighting his way home outside of Turkey Wing. The two mustangs had not been disturbed at all by the appearance of the Indians who snuck into their picket line to steal horses. He did not want a skittish horse afraid of every shadow and dust whirl, but it should react if something is nearby that shouldn't be.

He settled on his older buckskin, a ten-year-old gelding with good endurance and a steady attitude. It was big-boned, with big hooves and a big body.

"I'm going to need every advantage out there, Tag," he told the dog while saddling up the bay. "Even with you keeping watch." The dog seemed to understand.

The buckskin followed on a lead rope as they headed for Wilkon. The checklist of supplies to get and what he yet had to do kept his mind sharp. Both horses would travel fully saddled, ready to ride. The extra mount would carry a small pack if he could find or fashion one.

In town, he stopped at the livery and found Jesse Littleson finishing up for the day and nipping on a little whiskey to ward off the coming night's chill. "I'll be hitting the trail at dawn. I'm riding for Texas now. A Ranger," Holt said, handing him some coins. "Can you make sure these two get some good water and grain tonight?"

A look of concern crossed Jesse's face. "Sure, Holt, be glad ta help."

"I'm going to need my saddle and tack on the bay and the judge's gear on the buckskin. Need to take them both out ready to ride."

Walking down the street with two sets of empty saddlebags over his shoulder, he headed to his in-town quarters next to the jail. He had basically been living out at the ranch, but his trail gear, coffee pot, frying pan, canteens and extra guns were kept here.

Holt stoked up a fire in his small stove and started a pot of coffee. He tossed Tag a rib bone that Blue's son, Matthew, had sent along for the dog. Content to work on his new treat, Tag hunkered down by the small stove as Holt headed back out to get supplies. The coffee would be ready when he got back.

Dusk was nearly ready to turn the night watch over to darkness when he knocked on the general store door. Although it was locked, there were lights still on.

Billy Jorgenson, Wilkon's former deputy, peered out a glass pane on the door. His face lit into a smile when he saw it was Holt. "What kin I do-fer yeh?" He smiled as he unlocked and opened the door.

"Billy, I'm resigning as county sheriff to be a Texas Ranger. I leave at daylight. I'm going after the bastards who killed Silka and the others, and I need some things for the trail."

"Come ri't on in then! We'll getcha set up." He beamed.

When Meden Taliff purchased the general store from Flavian Rose it was Mrs. Rose who suggested that Taliff talk to the Jorgensons about managing the store for him. Short in stature, but thick bodied, Billy outwardly appeared to be more like a quiet farmer when in fact he was a tough former infantryman who had served under John Bell Hood. His ruddy round face was genial and approachable, belying the fact that he had seen the worst of the war, surviving bloody engagements at Antietam, Fredericksburg, Gettysburg, and Chickamauga. Billy had been a solid deputy for Wilkon. He took a bullet hard to the shoulder during a Bordner bank robbery and the wound laid him up for some time. Time enough for his wife, Bev, to convince him that surviving the war and wearing a badge had perhaps used up his luck. It had been tough to accept his resignation, but completely understandable. He and his wife immediately took to their new life here at the store. They were more than eager to help Holt select his supplies.

General stores had always been fascinating to Holt, probably for the same reason they were fascinating to most young boys. Remembering his youth, he could not help taking in all the sights and smells. Tangy odors of vinegar and pickled fish swam with rich smells of tobacco and freshly ground coffee, and the sweet perfume of new leather and old spices. Everywhere were kegs, barrels, sacks and displays of everything from sugar and salt to gun powder and ammunition, to canisters of condiments and groceries. From the rafters hung whole hams, slabs of bacon, and cooking pots. The room swirled with intertwined reflections of past and present.

"Billy, I'm looking for a set of panniers, but *small*," Holt said. "Not the big, full-sized boxes like you'd throw over a packhorse and rope into place. I can't carry that much stuff. The horse will work too hard and it'll slow me down. But I need something more than what saddlebags will carry. You got anything that fits that description?"

"Well hell...not exactly." Billy rubbed his whiskery chin and took a mental inventory of the store. "But lemme see..."

Bev Jorgenson came around the corner from an aisle filled with a smorgasbord of jars of fruits and cans of vegetables. Except for her apron, she looked more like she was dressed for ranch work in a worn and faded blue shirt and a buckskin riding skirt. Like Billy, her light brown hair was graying a bit. She was the one who kept the shotgun behind the register, just in case.

"How 'bout some o'that heavy tarp made inta bags with leather straps holdin' 'em together?" she suggested. "Jes' throw some stitches on to hold it all t'gether."

Billy's face brightened. "Say! That jus' might work!" He hurried down the aisle over to a corner where big rolls of thick canvas stood next to a variety of folded tents and covers. "How 'bout a coupla bags made o'this?" He held up a heavy duck canvas tarp that had been treated with beeswax and linseed oil. "We could make a coupla bags 'bout dis wide an' yea tall," he gestured, holding his hands almost three feet apart and nearly two feet tall. "A lil' bigger'n a coupla water bags stuck together, eh?"

Holt couldn't hold back a grin. "Billy, that'd be about perfect. But how..."

"You jus' let us figger it out," he urged. "You go 'roun' the store an' gather up whatcha need."

Bev moved between them. "Gimme that," she demanded. "Hob's still nex' door." She tucked the large tarp under one arm, grabbed two wide leather belts, and headed out the back door. Holt could not help but smile. Other than their clothes and other obvious traits, the Jorgensons looked and sounded a lot alike. They made quite a pair.

"Okay." Billy smiled. "Whattaya need?" They proceeded to wander through the store.

Hob Meier, the owner-proprietor of Wilkon Saddlery and Boot & Shoe Repair, was next door, working late. He had come to Wilkon from New Mexico twenty years ago where he learned how to work with leather from the old vaqueros and saddlers. Felix Sanchez often stopped by to chat with Hob and compare notes.

Bev explained to him what it was that Holt was needing. He smiled from ear-to-ear and said, "This'll be easy."

With his large stitching machine, Hob created two sturdy bags with flaps that closed over the openings. The bags would be fastened shut with leather thongs. Using one of his store saddles as a guide, he stitched an additional layer of the heavy duck canvas to the backs of both bags, connecting them together so they could lay just right. Next, two belts were stitched in place across the connecting middle, giving the whole setup additional strength and durability. Between the bags in the area that would lay across the seat, Hob scored a small hole on the front end, where the saddle horn would poke through, and sliced an elongated cutout for the cantle. Extra rawhide thongs would secure the pack onto the saddle. Pleased with their handiwork, he and Bev hurried next door to show it off.

At the front counter, Holt was looking through his selections...a pound of salt pork, two pounds of jerked beef, a package of corn dodgers, sacks of coffee and beans, small bags of cornmeal and sugar, two cans of peaches, and some apples and potatoes. Lying next to the foodstuffs were two new bandannas and a new shirt as well as a new blanket and trail coat. A tin cup, plate and utensils sat atop a new water bag. Two rolls of bandages, three sacks of grain for the horses, a roll of buckskin and rawhide strings, rope, and a couple of good'noughs— horseshoes that could be used in an emergency. Rounding out his purchases were a pouch of shredded tobacco, a fistful of cigars and two boxes of .44 cartridges.

Holt was finishing up and starting to settle the bill, when Bev and Hob burst from the back room, holding up their creation like kids with a treasured Christmas morning toy.

"Hob, you've outdone yourself!" exclaimed Holt. "And Bev, thank you for seeing it through." The two beamed with pride at Holt's words.

"Have yeh et anythin'?" Billy asked.

"Well, no, I haven't, Billy."

"You set ri't down an' have some stew with us!" Bev insisted. "Hob, you too."

"Hard to turn that down." Holt smiled.

From the back room, Bev hurriedly brought steaming bowls of hearty beef stew for everyone. A small loaf of fresh, heavy bread was also offered to tear off and sop up the broth. The four of them sat around the pot-belly stove in the middle of the store, eating in silence, but enjoying the company and the food.

The front door rattled with a key opening and Meden Taliff walked through the door. He saw the gathering around the stove and smiled. "I wondered what was going on when I saw the lights," he declared cheerfully. "I didn't know there was a party going on!"

"Yer jus' in time, Meden," Bev said. "Pull up a chair an' have some won'erful stew with us!"

"Oh, thank you, no," said Taliff. "I ate early." And as if he just noticed Holt, "Ah, good evening, Sheriff."

Billy interjected before Holt could respond. "Our good sheriff is sheriff no more, Meden. He is now *Texas Ranger* Holt Corrigan," he declared proudly.

Taliff's look was a question.

"That's true. I'm riding for Captain McCoy and the state of Texas now. Heading out in the morning,"

"Yes, an' he stopped by ta git provisions for the trail," added Billy.

"Well, congratulations, Holt. Wilkon will be hard pressed to find a sheriff of your equal," Taliff held out his hand and Holt shook it. "I trust you found everything you need."

"Bev and Billy—and Hob—set me up right." Holt grinned.

Bev and Hob could not help but show Taliff the pack they had created for Holt. Taliff nodded approvingly. "As a small token of the town's esteem, let me pick up the tab on that. Wilkon owes you far more, but it's a start. The materials from here are on the house. Hob, please send your bill to the Jorgensons and I'll stand good for it."

"That's not necessary," protested Holt.

"It's the least we can do," insisted Taliff. "Thank you. And good luck, Holt." With nods of goodbye to everyone and a polite touch of his hat brim, he left the store.

Finished with the impromptu supper, Holt stood. "I

need to get going too. I need to pack all of this and my dog probably wonders if I left without him. Thank you all very much."

His new supplies were loaded into two boxes. He swung his new pack over a shoulder and grabbed up a box. Billy helped carry the second box of provisions as well as a small dish of stew for Tag. Bev insisted.

Billy placed the box and the stew on the walkway by the door to Holt's quarters. "Keep yer head down, Holt Corrigan, y'hear?" he said as they shook hands goodbye.

Tag greeted Holt with his tail slapping the air. The dog was curious about all of the purchases, his nose taking inventory of both boxes and their contents. Holt coaxed up the fire in the stove again and let the coffee heat back up.

"Sorry buddy, that took longer than I thought," Holt said while scratching the dog's ears. "But look what Bev sent you!" He set the stew down and Tag eagerly lapped it up.

Restless, Holt took some of the roll of buckskin and fashioned new leather booties for Tag, then spent great care cleaning guns and packing. Each horse's saddlebags would carry identical loads of gear, jerky and corn dodgers, an apple and potato, personal stuff, and an extra pistol and box of ammunition. The bulk of the provisions would be stowed in the new pack.

Everything arranged and rearranged in the pack and saddlebags, Holt forced himself to lie down in his bunk and close his eyes.

It didn't seem long before the gray light of dawn was finding the edges of the day and prodding Holt to get out of bed. There was no use trying to go back to sleep. He was eager to get started, so he walked down to the livery, Tag in tow.

Jesse was already on duty, rummaging around the stables. The bay and buckskin had a good night, he reported, both had been grained and watered. "I checked their shoes," he said. "They's in good shape. Nice an' tight." He saddled and readied the buckskin with Judge Pence's tack while Holt saddled up the bay. "Good luck, Ranger Corrigan," Jesse said, offering his hand. "Proud to know ya. Come back soon." They shook hands.

Tying up the mounts in front of the jail, Holt secured saddlebags onto both horses. Next, he set the new pack arrangement over the buckskin's saddle. It fit perfectly. The packs did not carry much weight and could be thrown over a saddle quickly. Hob Meier was a true artist. Bev too. Both horses carried a canteen. Whichever horse carried the pack would tote the water bag—and Tag when necessary. Holt's Winchester would be in the boot of the horse he happened to be riding. A back-up rifle would be in a scabbard on the other horse.

He went back inside to finish dressing for the trail. Tag watched intently as Holt sat on the bed fastening his old Rebel cavalry spurs with the small rowels. Standing, he gave his knee-length boots a couple of good stomps, carefully re-tucking his pants into the tops. He pulled on a faded blue wing tip shirt and buttoned his leather rancher vest over it. Next, he slipped on his twin shoulder holsters, checking the loads in each revolver. He eased into his coat, checking to see if his string tie was tucked into one of the pockets. Tag's tail really began to wag when Holt grabbed his narrow-brimmed hat from the bedstand. That meant it was about time to go.

Stepping back outside to the horses, Holt made one

more check of his coat. In case the Ranger badge was not enough, a couple of Judge Pence's written statements about Holt's amnesty sat carefully folded inside one of the pockets. After examining the cardinal feather in the band, put there—as always—for luck, he put on his hat and tugged on the brim. He was almost ready. Just to make sure his new pack arrangement would all work, he placed Tag on top of it. The dog fit comfortably up there and the buckskin did not seem to mind the passenger.

"All right, boy," Holt said, lifting Tag down from the saddle pack. "Go do your business, we'll be leaving soon." Seeing Hannah sauntering over from the hotel, Holt joked, "Ain't it a bit early for you?"

"What? And miss a goodbye kiss from you?" Hannah shot back.

Soon, Deputy Wheeler and Mayor Cooke filtered into the jail. Shortly after, Blue and Deed rode up with Captain McCoy. Small talk and coffee awakened the room.

To make everything official, Holt resigned as county sheriff. Hannah volunteered to take on those duties and Mayor Cooke immediately accepted, provided, however, that Logan Wheeler would step into the position of town marshal. As his first official task as marshal, Wheeler asked Mayor Cooke if he thought his son would want to be deputy. "Oh my," the surprised mayor spluttered. "That vill be up to him, *ja. Und* I'm sure he vill haff to ask his mother." Good-natured chuckles spread throughout the jail office.

All the lawmen were sworn in. Hannah and Wheeler took their oaths from Mayor Cooke. Captain McCoy swore in Holt and tossed him his Ranger badge.

Mayor Cooke left to have breakfast with his wife. He

was not comfortable in the presence of these hard men
anyway, and now he needed to talk with Evangeline
about Bradley becoming a deputy.

"He's a nervous feller, ain't he?" McCoy noted. "All
right. Here is what we know…"

CHAPTER TWENTY-FIVE

O n his first assignment, Texas Ranger Holt Corrigan would be sent on the trail of a prolific killer known as "The Angel."

"Until the other day, we didn't know exactly who 'The Angel' was," explained Captain McCoy. "Now, with what happened at the funeral, we have a description and a name, Miguel Beltran. No guarantees he'll continue using that identity. We do think this bastard is an actual priest though," he continued.

McCoy started at the beginning, explaining that it was Beltran who called himself the "Angel" and that his murders appeared to reveal a fascination with religious symbolism. He liked to leave something on his victims that somehow related to biblical angels. "I understand you are well-read with the Good Book," McCoy said, directing his attention to Blue. "Maybe there's some light you can shed."

Blue looked at Holt and nodded his silent agreement back at the captain.

The captain continued his summary, "In the past year

or so, random people across the state—a politician, rancher, judge, and businessmen—have been murdered," he continued. "All of them died by the sword, or knife as it were. And they each had odd objects deliberately placed on their bodies." He explained that with the first two murders, a page from the Bible which mentioned angels was pinned to the victims and signed, *The Angel*.

"Now, he's getting…creative," McCoy said. "Or more deranged." He described one body with a flaming dagger stuck in its chest. "The mayor over in Rushing was stabbed to death a few months back," the captain continued. "A lit lantern was left to burn the victim's chest and a lily was placed in his mouth."

"In his mouth?" Deed asked.

The captain nodded. "Another victim had a handful of juniper sprigs crammed into his mouth."

Hannah chipped in, "Felix Sanchez had two Army medals placed over his eyes. His own Army sword was used to cut his throat and then placed in his grasp."

Deed added, "Taol said that there were blue chicory blooms stuffed into his mouth." He shook his head at the ghastly words he just spoke.

"Judge Pence had a rolled-up newspaper from 'nother town jammed inta 'is hand," added Wheeler. "An' a yella flower in 'is other hand."

"For a man stabbed to death like Oscar was, it was pretty strange that the newspaper wasn't torn or beat up in any way. It had no blood on it," Holt observed. "In fact it was tied up, kind of like a scroll. I'm guessing now it was put into his hand after he was killed."

"I'd bet on it," McCoy said.

"But, wait a minute…" Holt said, recalling the awful image of the dead judge. "The flower was a prickly pear bloom. And it was in his other hand. The petals were bloody. Maybe he removed it from his mouth before he…" The words trailed off and the room was silent for a while.

"I don't remember my Sunday school talking about things like angels, Blue. Is there anything that you've run across in your reading?"

Blue sat for a moment. Finally, he spoke. "The Bible is filled with stories of angels and archangels. Angels were present when God created the world. I imagine they did great and terrible things according to His plan."

Deed added, "Silka spoke of evil being at work with the judge's murder. Before he died, he told me evil was in the room."

Blue continued, "The Angels I remember reading about were Michael and Gabriel—and Lucifer, the fallen angel who became the Devil. There were others, I suppose…"

Wheeler asked tentatively, "Are they powerful?"

"I reckon so. They're representatives of God," answered Blue. "Michael was kind of the chief angel, maybe what we'd call a warrior. He battled Satan. He stood guard for God. Gabriel was a messenger of wisdom. He brought us special words from above. There was another angel known for healing. I can't recall his name. And Lucifer… He was The Angel who betrayed the Lord or at least rebelled against him."

Wheeler hung on every word, "What was his symbol?"

"He's Satan, the Devil. He fell from heaven. I guess one of his many symbols is a serpent," Blue said. "There are other angels in the Bible. I-I'm just not recalling all of them. There was an angel who protected the Garden of

Eden after Adam and Eve were thrown out. He guarded it with a flaming sword." Murmurs of recognition spread around the room. "These are just the ones I remember. If this killer is actually a priest, he's likely way more familiar with Bible stories and their meanings than I am."

Hannah took off his glasses and cleaned them with a handkerchief. "How are these disgusting things anywhere near being symbols of angels? Objects left on bodies? Things stuffed into mouths?" he said. "Damn."

"What was the symbolism in what was left on Oscar or Felix?" Deed asked.

"The newspaper might have had a message, I suppose," Holt said. "Someone should read through it closely."

Deed shook his head in frustration. "But why? Why them?"

"Why?" repeated McCoy. "No idea. We're working on that. Lots of potential reasons. Power, money, revenge. We don't know if he's doing this on his own or for someone else. If there's a connection, it isn't obvious. He could just be a crazy son of a bitch, doing it for…who knows why? What I do know is we need…"

Holt finished the captain's thought, "…to stop this bastard."

"Gonna have you join up with one of our best," the captain said. "Orion Higbee. He'll be waiting for you in Lodgepole. He's got all of this information and can fill you in on other details. You'll go after this 'Angel' together."

"I need to get going then," Holt said, standing to make his way out the door. He shook hands goodbye with Wheeler. Tag was already waiting at the door.

"That dog's gonna slow you down," cautioned the captain.

Holt looked at the big-eared dog and smiled. "This guy's been stabbed by a Comanche and shot by a bank robber. He's one tough hombre. He's saved our bacon more than once alerting us to trouble. Besides, he's pretty particular about deciding when to obey the word, 'Stay.'"

McCoy just chuckled and shook Holt's hand. "Ride careful, Ranger."

Holt turned to Hannah, who smiled and said, "With mirth and laughter let old wrinkles come."

"More Shakespeare?" Holt returned the smile.

"It means keep your head down and come back. Cigars and whiskey on me."

"Deal."

They shook hands and nodded once.

Out on the jail porch, Holt checked the head leather and cinches of his horses. Tag got one last lift of his leg against the boardwalk before he was placed upon the small pack of the trailing horse. They were going to put in some hard miles to start.

It was time to ride. "I'll take that prayer now," Holt said to Blue.

The three brothers circled together. Blue put his hand on Holt's shoulder and began, "God did not promise us lives without pain and sorrow. But he did promise us love to see us through those tough times. And the strength to meet every day. Guide us and protect us with Your strength. May God watch over you, my brother, and bring you back safely. Amen." They hugged and slapped each other's backs.

Deed stepped up to Holt. In his hand he held out a small brass medallion attached to a rawhide thong. On it, the symbol for *bushido* was engraved. It was Silka's. They locked eyes. "Silka taught us the ways of *bushido*," Deed said solemnly. "The medallion brings strength and courage." Holt placed his fingers on the medallion and mouthed a silent tribute to Silka. "This is for you now," Deed said.

"I'm grateful, Deed. I'd be honored to wear this. But you need to pass this along to Benjamin. Teach him as Silka taught you. I have strong medicine already," he said, holding out his other hand. The small red medicine stone lay in his palm. Deed nodded and briefly placed his hand on the stone and uttered something in Japanese. A blessing. The brothers hugged each other.

Blue stepped in. "Sixes and sevens, and no fires turning hollow." They hugged each other one more time.

"I'll settle this for us, big brother. I promise," Holt vowed.

As Holt swung into the saddle, Deed looked up to him. His words were deadly, "Find him, Holt. *Degüello*. No quarter."

Holt ran a finger across the cardinal feather in his hat band and answered grimly, "Aiiee. It is so."

CHAPTER TWENTY-SIX

C laire Baldwin stepped out onto the boardwalk in front of the community building. She hurried through the jumble of traffic, headed directly to the jail.

"Sorry, ma'am," newly sworn in Marshal Logan Wheeler told her from the open doorway. "But Holt already left. 'Bout two hours ago. The captain swore him in as a Ranger and sent him after those bastards."

"Oh no, Holt..." She hung her head and started to cry.

"He'll be fine, Claire," Hannah called out from the jail office. She stepped inside wiping her tears.

"I-I came to give him this," she said quietly and handed a Bible to Hannah.

"That's mighty nice." He half-chuckled. "But you know Holt ain't much for reading from the Good Book."

"No, this is a Bible that Father Mig...that priest left behind. There are papers inside." She pointed to the book. "There are notes Holt...you...probably should read," she implored. "After the...the funeral...I helped clean everything up to get the building ready for school again. This was just lying there by the pulpit. I picked it up thinking it might be Blue's. It isn't.''

Hannah took the book from Claire and thumbed through it. Inside were two red ribbons marking special pages. One bookmark laid on a page within the first chapter of the book of *John* where a verse had been highlighted. The other bookmark was placed within *Revelation*. A verse within the twelfth chapter was underlined.

As he read, Hannah shook his head at the complete disconnect between this man's brutally senseless actions and the word of God. There is really nothing to be done except treat this creature like a mad dog and bring him down, he thought. He knew Holt realized this as well.

Other pages held underlined passages, but tucked within the book of *Psalms* were three telegram messages. Pulling them from the book, Hannah read the one on top:

MICHAEL-
BACCATA APPOINTMENT
QUEST: LAND OFFICE
QUARRY: DEPARTURE CLERK
QUELL: RAPHAEL
QUITTANCE: HUNTING MOON HOTEL 105
T.H.G.T.

Hannah looked up from the piece of paper. "Doesn't the word 'quell' mean to put an end to something?"

Claire replied, "Yes. Or to vanquish. By force."

"And what is 'quittance'?" he asked.

She thought for a brief moment. "It's like an allowance, I think?"

He shuffled to another wire message:

MICHAEL-
WILKON APPOINTMENT
QUEST: COURT
QUARRY: JUDGE
QUELL: GABRIEL
QUITTANCE: CEDAR BLUFF HOTEL 205
T.H.G.T.

Hannah quickly flipped to the final one:

MICHAEL-
WILKON APPOINTMENT
QUEST: LAZYS
QUARRY: OWNER
QUELL: URIEL
QUITTANCE: CEDAR BLUFF HOTEL 205
T.H.G.T.

All three telegrams had been addressed to "Michael" and were signed "T.H.G.T." They also each referenced an angel from the Bible.

"Aren't Raphael, Gabriel, and Uriel names of angels?" Hannah asked.

"I think so. Michael is too."

"Damn…" Hannah murmured. "This is serious. Did they leave anything else in the church?"

She shook her head no. She also said she thought Taliff might have gone to the priest's hotel room after the funeral, but she couldn't be certain. "I don't know, but I thought this was something Holt might want to know." She looked down almost apologetically. "Will it help?"

"It answers a few questions. Yes." He paused before he continued. "Can I ask you something? Why are you doing this? I mean, you seem to yank ol' Holt around and chose to be with Taliff more than a little bit. What's that all about?"

She melted into more tears and tried to explain that she really, really cared for Holt. Her time with Taliff was always for town reasons, like putting together the new community building or helping with charity events. Nothing else. "Looking back," she sobbed. "I was naïve. I think Mr. Taliff purposefully kept me from Holt." She knew Holt was probably hurt by what she had done. "I'm so sorry I didn't get a chance to tell Holt how I feel before he left."

Hannah got up from his desk and gave Claire a little hug. "Well, he…uh…did have to ride out in a hurry. Those Corrigans are tough…pretty lucky too. You can tell him all of this when he returns." He sat back down and patted the Bible laying on his desk. "Thank you for this, Claire."

Drying her tears, she pleaded, "You'll let me know if you hear anything from him? Anything? Please?" Hannah nodded that he would.

From his office across the street, Taliff saw her leave the jail and walked out to cross paths with her. She politely declined his dinner invitation, saying she had schoolwork to review.

CHAPTER TWENTY-SEVEN

Holt wasted no time putting miles behind him on the way to meet his new partner. Tag rode easily on the new pack, the buckskin not appearing to mind that his passenger also had four legs. They were not going to reach Lodgepole in a day and the mounts needed to remain strong and healthy for this journey and the next. He slowed the horses now to a walk. Tag was allowed to get down and stretch his legs. Hatfuls of water refreshed all the four-legged travelers in his little group.

Holt's mind was black. Black. Completely overtaken with thoughts of nothing else but finding and killing Miguel Beltran. He felt anger seeping into his very core. And deep sadness too, dragging a malaise of spirit that would not go away. His body and mind were slowed by thoughts of Silka's death. *All* of the recent deaths.

Kill Town.

Maybe Hannah and Gillespie were right. Who in their right mind would come to a town such as that? Or stay?

Upon leaving Wilkon, he removed his Ranger badge

and placed it safely in his inner coat pocket where it nestled near his medicine stone. The weight of both was comforting, yet strangely at odds. With this badge, he rode for Texas. He would fight for what was just. Fight for his family and friends. But there would be no real legacy, no *leaving behind* as Silka counseled. No Claire. No *anyone* for that matter. He shook his head and shoved the inner commotion to another realm. He must focus on what was around him now. This was dangerous country. Serious trouble came to those who were not ready.

"Right Tag?" he called out. "You and me, boy. A couple of strays. We got this."

A few more hours passed. Trees began to thin out and the land lay wide and open before him. Birds chattered angrily at being interrupted. Shallow inclines looked empty until they rode close. A band of outlaws or a raiding party of Comanche or Apache could hide in any one of them.

He rode alongside a spotty, but determined, creek that curved around bunched hills and kept a small grassy meadow from stretching too far. Dismounting, he loosened the horses' cinches a little to give them a breather and let them graze on the grass but kept them from the water until they had cooled down. A piece of jerky and a corn dodger would be a brief lunch. Tag sniffed at his piece of the dodger before chewing it gingerly. The jerky he was offered was eaten more heartily.

As he sat leaning against a small tree, his mission shoved its way into his thoughts again. The whole "Angel" business was as perplexing as it was shocking. Murdering—no, *butchering*—people. Leaving objects on the victims that Captain McCoy seemed to think were related to biblical angels. But why? Why *these* unlucky souls? It did not seem like power was a reason. What was to be gained? Some of the victims were not rich or in positions of significant authority. If it was for money, what was the connection? Who was behind this?

Intense mental imagery toyed with him and engulfed his mind with disturbing thoughts. Felix lying dead, his throat cut, hands from an unseen enemy placing two Mexican Army medals over his eyes. Judge Pence with stab wounds all over his back, a newspaper fluttering down to him like wings and rolling up to jam itself into his dead hand. Silka, drawing his sword against a never-ending hail of bullets, forever falling.

Holt had seen plenty of dead bodies—before, during and after the war—of friends and foes. It was not death that disturbed him here. It was the senseless nature, especially of these last three deaths, plus the macabre ritual of decorating the bodies that chilled him. It was beyond brutal. It was...well...*evil*. Almost otherworldly. Revulsion raced through him. Disappointment too. He realized he never read what was in the newspaper the judge held. Did it mean something?

And Silka. *Silka*. A man who had seen so much and fought through so much his entire life. Cut down by these inhumane bastards. He surely did not want to die, but he did die. Died a *samurai*. Moving forward. Protecting. Battling.

"We owe you, Silka," Holt said to the wind. "We owe you *everything*."

He did not want to think what would have happened to him and his brothers without the big Japanese man. The unanswered questions swirled around his head and pummeled him, telling his brain it was time to get moving.

He took a long, deep breath and ran his fingers across the cardinal feather. *Degüello*.

The canteens and water bag were filled from the creek. The horses got plenty as well. There was still ground to cover before stopping for the night. Tag would ride atop the pack again.

They rode over uneven country, passing live oak and pecan trees and struggling mesquite. The long afternoon stretched into the time of lengthening shadows. Daylight would be leaving soon and he needed to find a place to camp. Shadows held secrets, some trustworthy, some hostile. Pulling his rifle from its saddle scabbard, he let the bay have its head, riding through clusters of cat's claw and mesquite, over fallen limbs and coarse bunch grass. The trees gave way to a small meadow cut by a some-time creek.

He glanced over his shoulder to check his backtrail as he crossed the shallow water and climbed up its top slope. He paused. Not yet liking what he saw, he urged the horse on. After a few more minutes of riding, he let the bay and buckskin stop and get a quick drink from another pencil-thin stream that was trying to re-establish itself from winter.

"This isn't the place," he affirmed to Tag. "Doesn't feel right." They moved on.

Finally reining up among a cluster of scrawny blackbrush and alder bushes, he saw something encouraging: an elevated piece of ground, the advent to a thicker stand of cottonwoods and oaks. Nearby was a sunken bowl of land where buffalo once rolled. Or maybe it was a grave.

The rise up ahead gave a commanding view of the ground that stretched around it. Boulders on one side, cottonwoods and oaks on the other, looked promising.

The cottonwoods and faint animal trails signaled that there should be some water there. Maybe another new spring trying to build itself into something larger or at least a rock seep that pooled into a small basin.

He eased his horse onto a faint deer trail that led up through a thicket of brush and into the grouping of trees that stood beside the boulders. As hoped, a small spring greeted him as it meandered haphazardly.

The area appeared empty of life, but he approached with his Winchester levered, but not cocked. Ready for anything. No tracks had been made within the past day or so and no fresh scat was around. Superstitious as ever, Holt was heartened to see some faint bear sign. He touched the medicine stone in his pocket.

Satisfied they were clear of immediate threat, he swung down and lifted Tag off the buckskin, letting the dog stretch his legs and explore. Keeping an eye on Tag for any signs of discovered concern, Holt removed the saddles from both horses. He brushed their backs with a handful of weeds and checked their legs and hooves. He left their bridles on, with the reins tied long enough for easy grazing in the pocket of buffalo grass and weeds outside the rocks. When they cooled sufficiently, both horses would be watered and hobbled for the night.

Before the darkness took possession of the land, he checked their surroundings once more. Rifle in-hand, he walked a wide perimeter with Tag. Faint wildlife trails snaked their way through the terrain. Snagged in a thicket, a small, gray-brown feather from a horned owl caught his eye. He picked it out and pocketed the feather for safekeeping.

They returned to the little camp. He took the horses to the spring to drink their fill. After they watered, he picketed them away from the water and rewarded the bay and buckskin with little nosebags of grain. It was now dark. Bright moonlight gave birth to friendly shadows.

Some coffee would taste really good, but he did not want to chance a fire. He ate an apple, a hard biscuit and some jerky, which he shared with Tag. They washed down their meal with some clear, cold spring water.

He was comfortable here. He felt at home.

Suddenly he was aware that, around him, the sounds changed. He knew the singers of the night have a lot of information they share with each other. Sometimes it was buzzes and chirrups of identification or directions to food. Or warnings of danger. Worse yet was when the night world went silent. But this was not a communication of threat or menace. Rather, the tone of the sounds transformed, like a choir just changing its tune. One of the horses blew softly and stomped once. Not agitated, but aware. Tag sat and stared intently into the congregated darkness.

A feeling embraced Holt that he was not alone. It was an inner sensation of stillness he had felt before.

Across the camp, an Apache stepped silently out of the shadows and into the moonlight. His peaceful gaze locked firmly on Holt. *It was the same man as before!* Once more, he appeared with his hands open, arms stretched out at shoulder level, again indicating he was weaponless. Holt knew there was no need to react defensively. If the man *had* been a threat, Holt would not know —he would already be dead. No, this man possessed a distinctive quality, an aura. Holt now believed he was some kind of priest or holy man. If he was even real.

The Apache was dressed as he was just days ago, with deerskin leggings and high-legged boot-like moccasins tied at the ankles for support. He wore a long, fringed deerskin shirt that was dyed a shade of indigo with a dark belt fastened around his waist. A worn, fringed medicine bag was at his side. His long, black hair hung loose with no braids and a simple, faded blue cloth was tied about his head.

Holt stood slowly, experiencing the same sense as before. He felt he knew this man—or *had known* him.

Tag, usually wary and on-guard, was not troubled at all by the Apache. He did not growl or bare his teeth. Holt quietly told him to sit and stay anyway. The dog remained calm and melted to the ground next to Holt. They both could not take their eyes off this man.

Holt faced his visitor and smiled, extending his unwrapped package of jerky to offer some to the elder. The man held up a hand and shook his head. The visitor gestured for them to sit. They sat on rocks facing each other. In the moonlight, Holt could see the wrinkles etched on the man's face. The lines told a story of a hard life lived outdoors. His eyes were full of worldly wisdom.

The Apache studied Holt intently for several long moments before finally saying, "I am Four Shields."

Noting the look of utter surprise on Holt's face, the Apache said, "I was unsure during our meeting before. The man you rode with was troubled and scared. It was not the time or place for talk. I chose not to make myself known."

"I am Holt Corrigan."

"*T'agodel. It is good*, Holt Corrigan." He explained that his education and ability to speak English came from his band of Mescaleros being educated by Jesuit priests and missionaries. He learned the white man's language because "it was good to understand those who seek to control the land."

Holt stared in fascination. He listened intently, sensing there was much to learn.

"It is well you chose this place," the mysterious man spoke slowly, almost reverently. "This is a special place, a place of strong medicine." He gestured toward the darkness and motioned across the sky. "A place where spirits stand in the shadows and whispers are carried in the winds. They brought you here. You listen well."

Four Shields told Holt that there were many spirits following the young Ranger. Spirits were all around him and in him, ones that were old as the stones. "If you listen closely, you might hear the stones speak of yesterdays and the lessons of those who came before. It takes careful listening to hear what they are saying. But, if you listen, they will tell you of the beauty that lives in each day and every living thing." The holy man leaned forward. "I believe you have heard these teachings before."

Holt swore he heard a soft, nearly silent, *whuff-whuff-whuff* of an owl's wings moving swiftly out of sight above them.

Moments of silence passed between them before Four Shields continued. "Your spirit, the *ndołkah*, has served you well in times of difficulty."

"*Ndołkah*?" Holt questioned.

"Big cat," the medicine man said. "The mountain lion is a warrior. A leader. It carries with it energy, power and strength. This spirit gives you skill, cunning and stealth. It has led you through great turmoil and strife. Although…it almost left you when you struggled with choosing the proper path to travel."

He counseled Holt that the Ranger now had new spirits walking with him as well. "They are protector spirits. Those who looked upon you highly, in life. They are your *tsét'soyé*, your bear spirits. Your *ndołkah* helps you fight, but your *tsét'soyé* will help you fight for what is good and true. Listen to them well."

Four Shields reached into the medicine bag at his side and pulled out a small elkskin pouch attached to an elk hide strap. He decorated Holt's neck with it. The pouch had a painted circle on it. The circle was colored with plant and vegetable pigments in equal quarters of blue, white, red, and yellow. He told Holt that these colors are sacred, symbolizing a balance of life and spirit. Inside the pouch was cattail pollen.

Pointing at Holt's shirt, the Apache instructed, "Your medicine stone belongs in there too."

As Holt retrieved the red stone with the white star-shape from his pocket and put it in the pouch, the elder stood. Holt went to quickly rummage through his saddle-bags and pulled out a cigar and a small bag of sugar to offer as gifts to the priest in return for the gift of the pouch. Four Shields shook his head to indicate such gifts were not necessary.

"It is well," he nodded. "I tell you of these things because you need to know that you are on a difficult journey. You are leaving the world of light to pursue someone who exists in the realm of darkness. Do not get drawn down there. Do not sink to that world."

He then raised his right hand in a blessing. "I pray upon you that you keep your eyes open and your ears open. But most of all keep your heart and mind open. Your medicine will guide you if you listen." Lowering his hand, he said, "Worry not, your people will be looked after while you are on this journey." Then, before he turned to walk away, a faint smile traced his lips. "You need sleep now. Nothing will trouble you here."

He disappeared into the darkness as quickly and silently as he appeared. Tag was still calm and came to Holt for a head scratch. Holt listened hard for the sound of movement or a horse being ridden away. Nothing reached his ear. Only the night chorus returning to its original symphony.

Holt stood there wondering whether the strange encounter actually occurred. Was that a spirit? The peculiar meeting replayed over and over in his mind as he checked on the horses, removed their empty nosebags and watered them again. To avoid other four-leggeds that might be thirsty, he picketed the bay and buckskin away from the spring near good forage that would last the night.

Starting to bed down, he began the nightly ritual of wiping down his guns and touching each one with the cardinal feather from his hat. The holy man's words continued to resonate through his soul. He knew enough about traditional Apache religion to know that it was based on the belief in the supernatural and the power of nature. As he understood, nature explained everything in life for their people.

Finally lying back against a saddle with Tag tucked beside him, he touched the new medicine pouch around his neck. He held it up, not taking his eyes off it. He could feel his medicine stone tucked safely inside.

One experience from the mystical night echoed loudly and would not leave him alone. Four Shields had declared, *If you listen, they will tell you of the beauty that lives in each day and every living thing.* And then he said he believed I had heard those words before. "My mother! He knew of my mother and her teachings!" he declared into the night. "She was here! I heard her spirit fly over us!"

He lay there searching the sky hoping for another visit.

Sleep would not come easily. This night had been strange and wonderful. A wealth of teachings was given to him in just a few moments. He had many spirits around him, some *as old as the stones*. Did that truly mean he had lived before? And new spirits, bear spirits, were with him. Bears were known for strength and courage. Could these spirits be Judge Pence? Silka?

The Apache never asked his name but seemed to know everything about him.

And how did the Apache know about his medicine stone?

He could not wait to talk with Bina when he returned home. Holding a revolver in his hand, he was not aware of falling fast asleep.

CHAPTER TWENTY-EIGHT

It was Tag who woke Holt with a lick on his hand. He sat up with a start. The first glimpses of dawn were just reporting for daywatch, taking over for the slowly retreating shadows of night, soon to be over-powered by the pouring rays of sunlight.

Holt shook the stiffness from his body and looked around. A southern morning breeze danced along his shoulders, choosing his hair as a partner. The horses were standing peacefully, just about out of grazing material. He had been bone-tired and spirit-weary. The murders. The chase with Wheeler only to return to the news of Silka's death. Becoming a Ranger and hitting the trail again. All of it had taken a lot out of him. Mostly, his mind had been troubled. But last night's encounter and undisturbed rest somehow let energy and hopefulness seep back in and begin to fill the hollows of his soul.

Four Shields was right, nothing had bothered him here. But now it was time to ride.

He munched on a corn dodger as he got the horses saddled and squared away in very short time. He would ride the buckskin today. Now tied near the spring, both mounts could water if they were interested. Tag got a piece of jerky. It was hard to hit the trail without some coffee, but it was time to go. Lodgepole and his new partner were at least a hard day's ride away.

He sprinkled tobacco in all directions and thanked the spirits for the quiet evening and for continued guidance. A pinch also went inside his new medicine pouch. He suddenly remembered the owl feather he found and retrieved it from his saddlebag. He carefully tucked the feather inside the pouch, next to his medicine stone. The pouch would be worn inside his shirt so it was closer to his heart. It felt like it belonged there.

The day's ride was marked by wanderings of the mind. Holt scolded himself often for not completely paying attention. A man could not afford to be careless and unaware. Yet, daydreams of his life paraded through his concentration and stretched on like the land in front of him—alive with contrast, handsome in its own way, but rocky, shadowy and wild.

Short bursts of vivid memories flowed through him like colorful streams, some gentle and flowing, some rushed and terrible. His father giving him a first pocketknife. Staring at the lifeless body of Silka laid out in his best clothes. Discovering Blue's battered and blasted body. His mother handing him the claw and using both her hands to close his fist around it. Being presented a small bouquet of firewheels by his sister. Standing and sweating with Blue, Deed and Silka while leaning on their tools, sharing a canteen. Opening Allison Johnson's blouse like a glorious present and learning about the soft touch of a woman. Stalking a Yankee camp, silent and solitary like a mountain lion, attacking in an explosion of shrieks, fire, smoke and lead...

A bark shook him from the past. He reflexively reached for a pistol as he zeroed in on the dog. Off to the side of the trail, Tag and a rattlesnake were having a heated argument. The floppy-eared dog had backed his adversary up against a saguaro. Coiled and hissing, the rattler was intensely defending his position.

"Tag!" Holt hollered. "Come here, boy! Hey! Now!"

The dog had closing words with the snake, barking three more times, before about-facing and trotting happily to Holt, giving him a look as if saying, "What?"

"Get up here," Holt patted on his thigh and Tag sprung up to the saddle. Holt remembered that he had never done that with the buckskin. The bay was used to Tag hopping up and down like that. Luckily, the buckskin was not fazed by the trick.

"I could've got myself tossed on my butt," he said to the dog. "Pretty damn dumb right there." He gave the buckskin reassuring pats to its neck.

As they rode away, Holt vigorously rubbed Tag's head and ears. "Maybe you were a lawyer in another time. But in this life, you know not to argue with those mean-looking guys, right?" He turned around to observe the snake, starting to relax its coil. "We'll make Deed happy today and let that one be."

He took stock of his surroundings and checked his back trail. It was time to give the horses a quick rest.

They stopped beside a small stream gurgling a springtime song. They were not going to rest long, so he watered the horses. Tying them to thick bushes, he drank from the stream himself, then refilled his canteens. He wondered why imagery and recollections of past lives usually visited when he was asleep while his waking dreams were of this life. He gave Tag a piece of jerky and took a couple of dodgers to munch on for himself. The quick refresher over, they moved on.

Holt forced himself to think. Something was trying to push through his mind. The teachings of Four Shields were always circling back into his consciousness. Letting spirits guide you was something he readily believed, even before encountering the holy man. Still, he was unsettled that there might be deeper meaning behind the Apache's words.

His thoughts ground on the mission ahead. Find The Angel. It was time to focus on that again. He would meet his new partner soon. Together, they would hunt down this evil creature. Of that Holt had no doubt. That part of the outcome had already settled in his mind as fact. But finding him…that was what he could not stop grinding on.

"Think only of the moment," he said to Tag. "You do that well, don't you, boy?"

Meeting the problem head on was Silka's training. As the former *samurai* would say, "Deal with it with all your energy and all your skill, then move on."

And move on… Once The Angel had been brought to justice, what would he do? Ride away? Ride home? Was his life a Ranger life now? Riding for the law? Or seeking vengeance? And what was this '*brought to justice*' regarding The Angel? Had he not promised he would finish him? *Degüello*?

Silka's "leave behind" advice had a way of blending with Four Shields' counsel as well as his mother's teachings. But where was it taking him? He shook his head.

"Spirits can guide you," he murmured, "but they sure don't offer a glimpse very far down the road."

Dusk found Holt reining up beside a small pond fed by a shallow creek, half-surrounded by trees and brush. This camp did not feel nearly as secure as last night's so he left the horses saddled and bridled, tied on a picket rope. Again, he decided having a fire would be unwise. His nightly ritual with his guns and the cardinal feather finished, he took off his shoulder holsters and laid them beside him with his Winchester. One Smith & Wesson was in his hand.

Tag lay down beside him, almost asleep. The dog was a wonderful companion, he thought. "Thank you, buddy, for choosing me. I wonder what—or who—you truly had been before." He leaned over to pet Tag and the dog gave his hand a good night lick.

Stretched out, trail coat for a pillow, he placed his other hand across the medicine pouch at his chest and watched the stars that gazed down on him.

CHAPTER TWENTY-NINE

E arly the next day, Holt cleared a long bluff and came upon a small town. Lodgepole was smaller than Wilkon, but still busy. Twelve buildings straddled a short main street. The Donegal Hotel and Restaurant was the largest one and dominated the center of town. Besides the Donegal, Lodgepole boasted a general store, livery, two saloons, gun shop, boarding-house, surveyor's office, bank, drugstore, and a barber-shop and bathhouse. And a jail.

Holt reached into a coat pocket and pulled out his new badge, pinning it to his vest as he rode into town. He patted the pouch at his chest, feeling the medicine stone inside. Horse and foot traffic crisscrossed all around him. A freight wagon clattered by going the other direction, the driver giving Holt a quick salute. Morning sun caught his light-blue eyes in a squint, bringing the scar on his right check into prominence. A well-dressed couple passed in front of him. He touched the brim of his hat as they passed, the woman glancing just a bit longer. Other townsfolk took notice of the long-haired Texas Ranger riding through town with two fine horses and a dog aboard the packhorse. Reining in at the front of the town jail, he swung down and told Tag to stay put.

"I'm Holt Corrigan, Texas Ranger," he announced, walking into the marshal's office. It was strange, but a little exciting to hear his own mouth say the words. Not bad for a former Reb outlaw. For good measure, he ran his fingers across his cardinal feather. "I'm looking for another Ranger, Higbee's his name."

"Vic Thresher, town marshal. Welcome Ranger Corrigan." The lawman shook hands with Holt. "Higbee? Tall drink of water. Been here a day or so. You'll probably find him at the Donegal, havin' breakfast."

"Much obliged, Marshal."

"A'fore you go…there's a wire here fer you…came in the other day."

The telegram was from Sheriff Hannah. It briefly explained that Claire brought in a Bible that belonged to The Angel. Three telegrams were inside the book. The Angel, Father Beltran, had definitely been hired for the killings in Baccata and Wilkon. Hannah explained the messages were addressed to "Michael," and came from someone who signed off with the initials, "T.H.G.T." Each of the messages also referenced a biblical angel.

The Donegal Hotel was in the middle of town. Holt tied up in front and let Tag down to stretch his legs. He threw the dog a little piece of jerky on the boardwalk and told him to stay up there, pointing out the commotion of the street. The dog took his position in the shade of the building out of the way.

The only person sitting alone in the lobby restaurant was a tall man reading a newspaper at a corner table, the whole room spread out in front of him. As Holt walked up, the man folded his paper quickly and stood.

"Holt Corrigan," he stated matter-of-factly, holding out his right hand. "I'm Higbee. Orion Higbee. Welcome to the Rangers."

Orion Higbee was several inches taller than Holt and was much older. A full shock of salt-and-pepper hair brushed back on his head, with a thick, trimmed beard now edging more toward white. His dark brown eyes were genial and pleasant. Lots of time spent in the sun resulted in a ruddy complexion and a squint to his eyes that gave a nearly perpetual smiling look to his face. He looked like a Ranger. Confident and intimidating, but not threatening. A Ranger badge was pinned to his black, buttoned vest. He wore knee-length boots with smaller spurs, not heavy-roweled Mexican ones. A shoulder holster carrying a converted Navy Colt revolver was strapped over the vest. A single-action, short-barreled Army Colt revolver, usually hidden away in his back waistband, now lay on the table next to his coffee mug. A long, black trail coat was draped over the seat next to him. A double-rowed cartridge belt, filled with .44s, and a Bowie knife sheathed to the belt sat on top of the coat. Resting on the ear of the chair was a flat-brimmed hat, pushed up in front.

"Thank you." Holt smiled, shaking the man's hand firmly. "It's good to meet you, Orion."

"Likewise. You got here a tad quicker'n I expected." Orion smiled. "Thought maybe tonight at the very earli-est. Sit. You hungry?"

"Anything with some hot coffee would hit the spot," Holt admitted.

Orion flagged down a large woman from the kitchen.

She came over with another mug and a pot of coffee. Her long, thick hair was loosely tied into what earlier had been a bun. Her smile matched her size as she greeted the Rangers warmly. Deep dimples surrounded her full mouth. She was proud of her size, especially her large breasts that pushed against her blouse, straining the buttons almost to surrender.

With the taste of coffee, Holt let out a grateful sigh. Noticing his reaction, she put a hand on Holt's shoulder. Her big eyes locked onto his for a moment.

"Young lady." Orion smiled with a big grin. "We need your best breakfast. Whattaya recommend?" His voice was filled with a soft lilt. Not a twang really, more like warm syrup.

"How 'bout the Ranger Special?" She winked. "Fried eggs, potatoes, *frijoles*, and a steak."

"Sounds mighty fine," Orion agreed. "I'll have the special."

"And how 'bout you, hon?" Her eyes twinkled at Holt with interest as she propped her arms under her large bosom. "You'll need a good breakfast before you go do all your Rangerin'."

"I'll have the special too. Uh…please."

Leaning over to Holt, she put her hand on the table. Her bosom was nearly exposed as her blouse fell open. "How many eggs you want with that?" she cooed.

"Uh…t-two. Two…please." Holt turned a little red around the collar.

Orion cleared his throat from a near-guffaw. "Three for me, miss. Thanks," he said with a chuckle.

"Anything else you want, hon…"

Her eyes went from Holt's eyes to her ample bosom and back up to his eyes.

"...We could probably arrange it," she continued. Holt tried to sip at his coffee.

"How 'bout throwin' in some biscuits?" Orion chimed in. "That'd make it extra special."

"And another pot of coffee," added Holt.

Orion grinned at Holt, who just shook his head.

Soon, a heaping plate of the "Ranger Special" breakfast was set in front of Orion. "Three eggs for you. And for you..." she said, leaning over, making sure Holt got a good look at her exposed cleavage as she presented the plate. "Two." Her eyes searched his face for any sign of interest, but Holt was watching Tag out the window.

Holt suddenly turned his attention to the woman. "There is something..." Her eyes lit up. "Could you... wrap up some leftover ham I could take with me?" Her smile dimmed just a little. "That'd be really good," Holt said, smiling. "I'd appreciate it."

She leaned closer. "I'll take care of that, hon. You just let me know if there's *anything* else I can do for you," she purred, brushing his shoulder with her breasts as she left for the kitchen.

"Thank you, ma'am, this'll do just fine."

Orion watched her leave, amused by the mostly one-sided exchange. Smiling through a mouthful of potatoes, he chuckled. "Since you're gettin' all the service, I'm gonna letcha pick up the check."

"Yeah, what'd I do to deserve all that? Or maybe... what'd *you* do?" Holt ribbed back.

They ate in silence as was the custom of Western men. When finished, they stacked their empty plates to the side and Orion caught Holt up on what had happened in the past few days. He explained that McCoy sent telegrams to lawmen throughout the region. There had been only one response and it was a couple days old. "He an' his gang stopped in a town southwest of here, a lil' place called Arriba," Orion related. "Drawin' a line from your Wilkon to Arriba, it appears this Angel fella is headed for the border. Although he doesn't seem to be troubled with hurryin'."

Holt grumbled, "Probably knew they weren't being followed."

"Heard The Angel's last coupla victims were friends of yours," Orion said.

"Last *three*," Holt responded. "The judge who gave me amnesty and a ranch owner who was a great family friend." He caught himself and swallowed hard before continuing. "And the man who helped me and my brothers after our parents died. He was killed by this bastard and his gang when they escaped from Wilkon."

"Personal, then," Orion observed over his coffee mug.

Holt replied with a grim nod, "You could say that." It was his turn to give Orion the details of the telegram he just received, confirming The Angel was hired for the killings in Baccata and Wilkon.

"Addressed to Michael, an' signed by T.H.G.T...." Orion pondered. "Those names mean anythin' to you?"

"Not yet."

"Those angel names are damned interestin' too."

The waitress returned before Holt could respond, bringing out pieces of fried ham steak wrapped in some butcher paper. "You come back anytime, hon." She smiled, drawing a finger across Holt's jawline. "There's always a Ranger special *on the menu*." Her laugh was rich and hearty.

Finishing breakfast with a last cup of coffee, Holt left

coins on the table and stood. He smiled at the thought of the extra attention and tossed down a few more. Orion was strapping on his cartridge belts and donning his coat and hat. Holt waved the package of ham steak. "For my partner."

"Didn't know you had 'nother one," Orion said, peering at the package. "Not much of an eater."

"Tag Along is my dog. He goes by 'Tag.' We met when my brothers and I were stopping some bank thieves in Wilkon. He adopted me right in the middle of a heated 'conversation' we were having with the robbers. A stray. A bit like me."

"Well, he didn't slow you down, that's a fact."

"Tough son of a gun. Good lookout to have on the trail." He explained how Tag had been grazed by a bank robber's bullet in Hammonds and sliced by a Comanche knife outside Turkey Wing. "He sits a horse well when need be."

"Sounds like I should meet this fella," Orion smiled.

"I'll introduce you." The two men stepped out onto the planked boardwalk. Tag eagerly bounced over to Holt. Scratching the dog's ears, he invited Orion over.

The tall Ranger knelt. "Tag Along, I'm Orion Higbee. Your reputation precedes you." He laughed and let Tag come to him. "I've had a few dogs. Cats too. But it's been a while. Good souls," he said giving the dog a couple of hearty rubs and pats along its back.

Holt gave Tag a couple of the ham scraps while they readied their mounts.

Orion's horse was tied to the next rack over from Holt's two mounts. A powerfully built bay, made for speed and endurance.

Holt looked over, admiring Orion's bay. "Looks like he can run."

"Like a Texas storm," Orion enthused. "That bay of yours looks like it could be this one's brother."

"Lost a really good buckskin to an Agon Bordner ambush a few months back," Holt explained. "Taking a liking to this bay though. He's strong, doesn't waste energy."

"That buckskin yours too?"

Holt explained that he knew he had to be able to move without delay but was not sure what was in store on the trail ahead. "Not an original idea, I just figured being able to alternate between horses should help me keep both mounts healthy and fresh enough to cover more ground in time I didn't have."

"Well, that explains your gettin' here faster'n I expected. An' it makes damn good sense."

"I've got both fully saddled, ready to ride," Holt explained. "My friends created this pack for the extra mount. Can't overload it and wear a horse down, but it'll carry enough so I don't need to resupply as often. When we're moving fast, Tag rides right here."

Orion clapped his hands together and rubbed them. "I say let's go get me a back-up."

Lodgepole's livery smelled of grain, manure, hay and leather as the two Rangers walked through the open doors. A bear of a man wearing an old derby perched on his head and a patch covering his left eye approached from a back stall. Holding a pitchfork and bucket, he walked with a pronounced limp. A long scar ran down the man's face behind the eye patch and a custom-made heavy moccasin protected a left foot that no longer had any toes.

"Good mornin' to ya, Rangers," he said, seeing the badges on the two men.

"Name's Holt Corrigan."

The big man's eyebrows lifted. "Holt Corrigan? Wasn't you an outlaw awhile's back?"

Holt smiled and cleared his throat. "Don't believe all the stories you've heard. I would've needed a magic horse to be in all the places I was supposed to be. What I did was in defense of the Confederacy. The war's over and I was given amnesty. Been a county sheriff and now a Texas Ranger."

"Yass-suh, hearda you. Gave 'em hell," the livery operator said. "Fought fer th' Stars 'n Bars m'self. Rode with Gen'rul Stuart. Made it all th' way through Brandy Station an' Gettysburg only ta git womped at Yellow Tavern. Thass where I went down. An' th' gen-rul did too." The man's face saddened.

"I was at Sabine, then transferred to Ewell's corps to fight with my brother," Holt shared.

The liveryman held out his hand. They shook hands warmly. The former Rebel's name was Shannon Johnson, but everyone called him "Pony."

"Always glad ta meet a fella Rebel," Pony said, pulling on the straps of his overalls.

Orion stepped in. "Pony, I'm Orion Higbee. I came to buy a horse, if you got a good one for sale. A gelding." No one questioned or mentioned anything about Orion's involvement in the war.

"You betcha. Got a couple ya might like. That bay ri't back thar. Third stall. You kin have 'im fer…say…forty." He pointed toward another stall. "Or I've got this dun, ov'r hyar. I'll letcha have 'im fer th' same price. I'll even throw in th' head leather. 'Ceptin'…I gotta warn ya…this here dun can be mean."

"Mean, you say?" Orion asked. "You ride 'im?"

"Yass-suh. I git 'long with 'im fine. He can jus' tell if sumone ain't a hoss person. Orn'ry ta them folks," Pony answered. "Gotta few more out back in th' corral. These're my bestest though."

Orion went to the dun first. It looked mean, like it could eat a cougar for breakfast. At the Ranger's approach its ears laid back, but Orion talked quietly to the horse. He put his hands on the horse's shoulder and rubbed it gently, soothing the animal. The horse's ears relaxed. Orion slowly worked his touch up the horse's neck to its face. Speaking gently all the way, he continued rubbing its ears, nose and all around its back and flanks. Next, he ran his hands along the animal's legs and checked its hooves. Its eyes and ears were on alert, but it stood quiet and calm. With its thick chest, it looked like it could run all day. Orion decided on the horse without even looking at any of the others.

"Iff'n he likes ya, that's a fine choice, Mistah Higbee. Fine choice." The huge man smiled.

"Whattaya have in the way of saddles?" Orion asked. "Broke in."

Pony showed Orion a couple of saddles that belonged to customers who had walked away owing money or just walked away and never returned. "Letcha have either one fer 'nother twenny five. I'll throw in a good blanket too."

"Mind if I ride 'im first?" Orion asked. Pony agreed. The dun took to Orion saddling and bridling him with no issues. Swinging up, Orion rode him through the livery and into the back corral, putting the horse through some quick paces. "Lotta horse here. I'll take 'im." He smiled.

"Okay, then. Lik' I said, a fine choice." Pony smiled back. "Now, whet was the tally? Aw hell, let's call it all good fer forty. The whole outfit. Hoss, head leather, saddle n' blanket. I like helpin' out fella Rebs."

"That's more'n a fair price, Pony," Orion said, climbing down from the dun. "But you should know...I wore blue. Union Navy."

The man's face did not change. "No suh. I said what I said. You be ridin' fer Texas now," he said, swallowing hard.

"I 'preciate that," Orion continued. "But you said sixty-five. That suits me better." He held out his hand.

"Much obliged, Mistah Higbee." The two men shook hands.

Business settled. Orion rode the new dun out of the livery, his bay in tow. "Ride well, Rangers!" Pony called out after them.

They tied up at the general store and Holt gave the dun a once over. Its ears laid back as Holt drew near, but quickly relaxed as Holt patted its shoulder and rubbed its neck and forehead. It did not seem to mind or even notice that Tag stood there with the Rangers.

"Lot of horse," Holt said. "I was a little worried when I heard Pony said it was mean."

"Mean is justa habit. Every now an' then, you need a horse with a lil' more fire than might be safe for some. Keeps you on your toes. Kinda like women. The good ones should scare the hell outta you sometimes," Orion said playfully.

He purchased a new set of saddlebags for the dun at the general store along with an extra water bag. While there, they stocked up on food and supplies, including canned peaches and vegetables, some potatoes and apples, plus several sacks of grain for the horses.

Orion snapped his fingers like he just remembered something. "You got any fireworks left over from Christmas?" he asked the clerk. Holt's expression was an amused question. "Just checkin'." He grinned at Holt. "Loud noises an' balls of fire are good to have sometimes, you know."

The clerk responded. "Yes, I think there are some Roman candles, a few Sky Rockets, and a Star Serpent left."

"I'll take 'em!" Orion said, a huge grin on his face. Looking at Holt, "How're you fixed for cartridges?"

"Not bad. Always room for more," Holt responded. ".44s."

"All right. I'm low myself," Orion said. Gesturing at the ammunition display, he asked the clerk, "How full is that case of .44s?"

"Looks to be not quite half. Four boxes," the clerk replied.

"Okay. I'll take those." Orion nodded. "We'll need a box of those cigars an' a good bottle of whiskey. Irish," he added.

"I'm sorry, we don't have any Irish whiskey right now," the clerk said. "Got some good bourbon though."

"Mmm, no thanks," Orion said, looking at Holt. "Unless my friend is inclined otherwise?"

"I ain't particular." Holt grinned. "We can wait to find some good Irish."

Orion acknowledged Holt's reply and turned back to the clerk. "Throw in a coupla boxes of matches an' that'll 'bout do it, I believe."

As they were finishing their purchases, Marshal

Thresher walked into the store. "Got a telegram for you two. Must be onta somethin' big. Wires shore been burnin' up for y'all." Neither Ranger responded to the implied question as the marshal handed the dispatch to Orion. Holt thanked the lawman for the delivery.

"They've been spotted in Sweetclover," Orion read. "A priest named Miguel and four riders. One arrived injured. Stopped in Sweetclover needin' provisions an' a doctor."

"Five riders?" Holt questioned. "There were five that ambushed me and our deputy. We got one and four rode away."

"Says here, five," Orion said, holding the telegraph message. "Gotta assume someone down there can count."

Something instantly dawned on Holt. "Wait…Sweetclover?" The name jolted through his memory and stopped him in his tracks. "The newspaper I found rolled up in Judge Pence's hand was a copy of the *Sweetclover Dispatch*."

"That doesn't smell like a coincidence," Orion said with a wry grin.

"Time to ride," Holt replied.

Their four horses were evenly packed and squared away quickly. Orion stuck a cigar in his mouth and handed one to Holt. The older Ranger fired up a match, and they lit their smokes.

"Let's go find this bastard." Orion grinned.

They left Lodgepole in a hurry with Tag atop Holt's buckskin.

CHAPTER THIRTY

The midday sun was showing more strength than its customary springtime self. The Ranger duo rode hard for a while, then eased their horses to a walk, before kicking in to a land-eating lope. Tag traveled along without a problem, riding atop the packhorse when they needed to move fast.

Holt took stock of his new partner. Orion was likable and gregarious. He was quick with a smile and appeared to know no strangers. Like a typical Ranger, he seemed hard, but fair, and naturally inclined to be suspicious. Holt figured him to have a slow fuse, but once riled up, he would be like a mama grizzly separated from her cubs. Orion outfitted his rig with a saddle holster that carried a long-barreled pistol. His Henry repeating rifle sat in a saddle boot. Usually wary of someone new, Holt was already liking this lanky Ranger.

Orion turned to look at Tag, half-asleep on Holt's buckskin. He had never traveled with anyone who had a dog riding shotgun like this. He had to admit having the back-up horse was a good idea. He was deep in thought evaluating the colleague he just met. Outwardly, Holt looked like a rawboned gunfighter. Even though he wasn't a big man, he was an imposing presence. Orion figured the long scar on Holt's right cheek had to have been from the war. Even with the ivory grips, he knew Holt did not wear those serious Russian Smith & Wessons tucked into twin shoulder holsters for show. Orion decided this man seemed like a cougar, all coiled strength—silent and cautious—yet ready to strike with a fury. By all accounts, Holt Corrigan seemed to measure up. Orion was taking a shine to this new Ranger.

Walking their horses once more, they continued their talk about The Angel that started at the breakfast table.

"He was actually a pleasant-faced man, barrel-chested, with a quiet voice and manner you would expect from a religious man. Wore a big silver cross inlaid with brilliant green beads or stones," Holt said, describing The Angel. "Before the shooting started, I did think his two henchmen looked more like Comancheros than altar assistants."

"One of the wires I got before you arrived described 'em the same way," Orion responded.

"The rider Logan and I downed after they ambushed us wasn't one of the shooters from the funeral," Holt continued. "He appeared to be Mexican, but maybe was a Kiowa."

Orion listened carefully to Holt's account, then said, "Not many people know this information. It's too grue-some an'…well…too damn scary to have this known by a lotta people. Definitely don't want any newspapers gettin' hold of it. Rumors spread like wildfire."

He then filled Holt in on more of the particulars of The Angel's victims. Holt had heard some of it before, but not all of the details. Orion explained that the Rangers had known of a killer calling himself "The Angel" for about a year, but it was only in the past few months that they discovered just how widespread his murderous activities had become.

He described the first victim as a banker in Modlin who was killed a little more than a year ago. He was tied to his desk and had his upper thighs flayed open, bleeding to death on the floor of the bank. A page from the Bible was shoved into his mouth and signed, "The Angel." Not long after that, a miner in Bartle had his throat cut. A Bible page was found in the mouth of that body too, again signed "The Angel." A couple of months passed until the mayor of Rushing was found stabbed to death. For this murder, multiple stab wounds took the man's life, but a lit lantern had been left on the victim's chest to smolder. A white lily was stuck in his mouth. A few months later, a college teacher was murdered in Henion by a flaming dagger thrust into his chest. Purple wood violets were found in his mouth as well. A month after that, a county clerk from the land claims office in Baccata had his throat cut. "An' a coupla breams placed over his eyes."

"Breams?"

"Yeah, *brims*, you know, perch."

"Fish?"

"Yeah, that's what I said, an' some juniper sprigs… just stuck into his mouth," Orion reiterated, shaking his head incredulously. "An' then, 'bout two months after that, your judge was killed." He paused. "You know the rest."

Holt absorbed the information silently, giving each detail careful thought.

"These're just the seven we know about," Orion added. "There may be others that haven't been discovered or reported. This mad dog may have killed even more."

"Yeah, Captain McCoy explained there isn't an obvious connection," Holt said. "No apparent pattern to the victims or the locations. Nothing to tie them together other than the brutality and odd objects."

"Yeah. He didn't butcher seven mayors or seven bankers. Would've made more sense. You know what I'm sayin'. Random places an' victims are hard to figger."

"So, what is connected?" Holt wondered aloud. "We know The Angel likes using a knife or bayonet. Every victim was stabbed or cut. And each victim was decorated with some kind of token that was supposed to represent something biblical."

"But what do those decorations really mean? Besides bein' scary as hell."

"Damned if I know," Holt said, frustrated.

They paused and looked up as a red-tailed hawk squeed high overhead.

"I didn't think he was actin' alone," Orion declared. "These new wires found in Wilkon are an interestin' development. Someone else is pullin' his strings. Wonder who?"

"And do the angelic symbols somehow relate to the victims?" Holt questioned. "Maybe they explain in some way why those men were chosen."

They rode as quickly as they dared toward Sweet-clover, alternating between hard lopes and walking, especially to let Tag down to stretch his legs, and loping again. Miles went by, passing knots of cat's claw, mesquite and prickly pear, all kept company by coarse bunch grass. The gravity of their mission weighed heavily.

Slowing to a walk for a while, the only sounds were the humming of insects, the soft padding of their horses' hooves, and the creaking of saddle leather. A prairie hawk, munching on a dead field mouse, watched them from a high branch.

Holt broke the silence. "What's tucked in your saddle sheath there? I can't quite place it."

"It's a Navy Starr," Orion replied, pulling the gun. "Single action. Converted. Gotta second Starr with a shorter barrel in my bag. Hard to find 'em now." He spun the gun around his trigger finger and reholstered it in one smooth motion. "I used to carry a Walch here instead. You know, one of those heavy damn 12-shot monsters."

"My brother, Blue, carries one," Holt replied. "Twelve shots come in handy at times." He did not mention Blue carried a Walch because twelve shots was a very practical feature for a one-armed man. Nor did he mention that Blue had taken the gun from a dead Union officer.

"Yes, indeed. Two triggers, two hammers. Lotta gun. It shot .36 cap and ball though. I moved all my guns to .44 cartridges, so I stopped carryin' it," Orion added.

"Makes sense."

"Couldn't help but notice your pistols," Orion continued. "Unique grips, you got there. The ivory, are those panthers?"

Holt ignored the question about the grips. "Came by these on my travels. Smith & Wesson made these for the Russian army. Accurate as hell. The top-break comes in real handy for reloading."

"Now I remember…" Orion responded. "Didn't I hear about folks callin' you '*el Jaguar*?'" There was a pause before he threw in, "I hope you don't mind me askin'."

"Fair enough question." Holt realized his new partner would be curious about his past and deserved to know. "After Lee and the others gave up, a bunch of us vowed never to surrender and tried to keep the Confederacy alive by robbing Union banks, military payrolls, and stages carrying Yankee gold. Anything trying to disrupt the Army we'd spent four long years fighting against. I guess some sympathetic Southerners took to calling me that. Someone saw the guns and started writing about it in a damn newspaper." He did not mention anything about his belief that he had been the animal once. No one knew that but his brothers.

"Just wonderin'. Thanks."

"I never killed anyone robbing a Union bank," Holt continued, realizing he had not spoken much about his post-war actions. "Wounded some Yank soldiers who pursued us." Then he chuckled a little. "After a while, every bank robbery and stage holdup in Texas was supposed to have been done by me."

Orion was curious. "What made you stop?"

"I was in El Paso this past summer," Holt recounted. "We were scouting the bank there when I heard that Agon Bordner had put a big target on my brothers and our ranch. The spirits saw to it that my path crossed with my older brother there. Blue convinced me that coming home to save the ranch and asking for amnesty wasn't a fool notion."

"Knew a coupla Rangers who were nosin' 'round that Bordner business," Orion said.

Holt laughed. "A couple of Rangers from Captain Waters's company did come around. No offense, but they pretty much bought into Bordner's charade. They weren't aware that fat bastard had brought in his own law. They convinced the two to arrest my brothers. They didn't know I had returned. When I came home to Wilkon, my brothers, our partner, and our neighbors, the Sanchezes, were the only ones that kept him from becoming the emperor of northwest Texas, despite the Ranger presence." Holt half-chuckled at the thought.

"I heard that Bordner had Willard Dixon an' Degory Black on his payroll," Orion offered some of what he knew.

"Yes he did. Those two *and* Dixie Murphy, Macy Shields, and Sear Georgian. Rhey Selmon too. Plus a small company of chee-chalkers looking to make names for themselves."

"Ho-lee damn," Orion exclaimed, shaking his head. "You boys took down *all* those owl-hoots?"

"Well…most of them," Holt cocked his head. "We had the last of the gang…Selmon, Georgian and some locoweed named Pickles locked in the Wilkon jail. They got into an argument and ended up killing each other right there in the cell."

"I remember Cap'n McCoy mentionin' they wouldn't be headin' to prison. Didn't know why that was."

"Bordner even tried hiring James Hannah to kill my younger brother, Deed." Holt chuckled. "He didn't know James and Deed had already become friends."

"Hannah. Hired gun. He's marshal now in Wilkon, right?"

"Was. He took over for me as county sheriff when Captain McCoy swore me in," Holt answered. "Anyway,

Judge Pence took what I did to help rid the state of that mongrel Bordner and offered me amnesty. He figured a lot of the newspaper stories about me were generated by Bordner. His only condition was that I take over as county sheriff."

"Seems reasonable." Orion grinned at Holt. "Everythin' I've heard, you took to bein' sheriff as if you were born to it. Cap'n McCoy sure has sung your praises."

"The judge gave me my life back," Holt mused. "Things haven't calmed down much since. He was murdered only a few weeks after the Bordner trial and shoot-out. We worried that his killing might be more Bordner crap. The same day the judge was found dead was the same day Selmon and Georgian killed each other. We had peace and quiet during the winter months, then Felix Sanchez had his throat cut. Our partner...I'd guess you'd call him our godfather...was shot down when The Angel and his men were exposed during Felix's funeral."

"This godfather the Japanese fella?" Orion asked.

"Nakashima Silka. Former *samurai*," Holt replied. "I was about sixteen when our father died. Broke his neck when a horse threw him. Our mother and sister died of pneumonia shortly after. Blue was eighteen, and Deed, nine or ten."

"You were just kids. Damn." Orion listened intently. "A lot to deal with."

"We were about done in. No money. No hope. Then Silka came along. He guided us, helped us grow the ranch. Hell, he raised Deed. About three years after he arrived, the war started and Blue and I took off." Holt touched the medicine pouch at his chest. "And now, here I am." He looked over at Orion, giving him a brief nod as he smiled.

CHAPTER THIRTY-ONE

Dark clouds in the distance warned of a possible storm. Holt and Orion's afternoon plans suddenly became a search to find a camp for the night that would keep them and the animals out of the rain. The quickening wind brought the faint smell of smoke. Holt gathered up Tag to sit on the pack and they eased the horses into a smooth lope.

Before long they came across a settlement, a sad gathering of dilapidated buildings with a mess of crooked and splintered boardwalks.

Orion eyed the shabbiness and decay that surrounded them as they picked their way down the street, just an accumulation of hardened wagon ruts. "What's this for a place?"

"Says 'Kendrick Livery' and 'Hotel Kendrick.' I'm guessing that's the name of this place or the name of a really crappy businessman."

"Not much of a goin' concern is it?"

Whatever activity that created Kendrick had not only failed but took its energy with it as well. Amid the collection of boarded-up structures, only a saloon, livery and general store appeared in operation.

A distant flash of lightning reminded them of why they rode in. "Till we figger out what that storm's gonna do, let's see what this place has to offer," Orion said, reining up outside the general store. The accompanying rumble of far-off thunder accompanied the tying up of their horses. He peeked through the window of the store. Seeing no movement, he walked across the rutted street to the livery.

Holt told Tag to stay with the horses and walked next door to the saloon. Even in desolate places like this, there always seemed to be no shortage of whiskey. *At least they might have a decent bottle of Irish suitable for Orion's taste*, Holt thought.

His spurs jangled as he stepped inside. The stale smell of beer, smoke, and man sweat hung in the air. Grimy oil lanterns were working hard to brighten the darkening afternoon.

Nine men sat intent with their poker games, five at one table, four at the other. Three more watched from a nearby billiard table. Only a few even bothered to glance Holt's way. He did not know anyone in here and did not expect he would. His icy blue eyes had seen both sides of the law and many saloons like this. It was obvious now why Kendrick still hung on. All of these were men likely on handbills somewhere. He thought about his and Orion's decision to not wear their Ranger badges. They had wanted to see what this settlement was all about first. Counting the guns around him, he knew they made the right choice to blend in.

Two men stood lazily at the bar. The bartender was a large, brawny man, his skin the color of pecans. Wearing a dingy white shirt and a beat-up calfskin vest, he was adorned with an old bone-and-bead choker and an earring made of dentalium shells hanging from his left ear. Both pieces of jewelry appeared to be of Sioux origin.

"Good Irish whiskey, if you've got it," Holt said to the bartender. "A bottle."

Without saying a word or even acknowledging Holt's request, the bartender turned and walked away.

"Hey! Where're you going?" Holt's voice was louder this time, calling after the bartender. "How about the whiskey!?"

At the billiard table, a bald-headed player in a dirty coat quietly said something to the man in a forage cap next to him and both left slowly, one at a time, out the back door.

Holt turned to a cowboy with a huge mustache that turned into bushy sideburns. "Guess he didn't hear me." Holt frowned. The man was wearing a hat with what looked to be a bite taken out of the brim.

"Yeah, Goose's like that." The cowboy chortled. "Really. He cain't hear. Leastways, not very well."

Holt looked to the end of the bar. Goose the bartender had disappeared. He asked the cowboy, "Where do they keep the good stuff?"

The man hesitated a bit, then pointed. "Under thar."

"Thanks," Holt said. He walked behind the bar and pulled out a bottle, eyeing it carefully.

A breathy voice, louder than needed, called out, "*Hey!* You cahn't doo that!"

Holt looked up to see the large bartender coming toward him, two bottles in his hands. Goose walked up and stood before Holt. He held the bottles up in front of him and gestured at them with his head. Then he made a grand show of presenting the two bottles onto the bar.

"Eye-rish," Goose said carefully in an overloud voice and nodded once. The man was deaf or nearly so.

Holt looked away for a brief moment before looking back into Goose's eyes. All he knew was a few words and signs in Comanche. He did not know the words for "I'm sorry," so he made the signs for the words, "I" and "mistake," followed by the signs for "I" "heart" "on" "ground." As he signed, he spoke the words, "My mistake. I feel very bad." He paused to see if Goose understood what he was trying to say, then continued with the signs for "Make" and "peace" followed by "Now" "friends" as a question.

Goose stood for a moment, only blinking. Then he signed and spoke to Holt, "You...okay." They smiled at each other.

Holt chose a bottle and handed the bartender a gold coin.

At one of the hitching posts outside, a bald outlaw in a dirty coat moved quietly on the boardwalk. He positioned himself to the left of Orion, who had returned from the livery and was rummaging in the bags tied to his bay. The filthy outlaw kept a rifle hidden at his side. The dirty man's partner, a gaunt cowhand in stovepipe chaps and a forage cap, began untying the reins of Orion's dun, his eyes daring him to do something, anything, about it.

"Ya don't mind, do ya? I'm jes' gonna take 'im fer a lil' ride, old man." He sneered at Orion with yellowed teeth.

"Yessir, mighty fine hoss there," the bald outlaw added as he brought up the Winchester that had been concealed. "Ya jes' might have ta' keep 'im, Deke."

Lightning flickered off in the horizon. Orion stopped speaking to his horse and did not move, only staring at the man with the rifle.

"I b'lieve I will, Wade. In fact, why don't ya see what else this old-timer has. Mebbe he gots sum cash on 'im," the bony man said as he swung into the saddle. The dun stood motionless as the man hollered, "Alright, hoss. Gotdammit! Come on!"

"Mighty fine idear, Deke." The filthy-coated outlaw stepped closer to Orion. "How 'bout it, gram'pa? Let's see what yur carryin'."

Tag had been lying quietly by the horses, where Holt had told him to stay. At the impending threat, he sprang up, snarling and snapping at the man with the rifle. The thief took a full wind-up with his leg and kicked Tag hard in the ribs. The dog, knocked off its feet, yelped loudly, and landed stunned and unmoving off of the boardwalk.

At the hitching post, the horse thief in the forage cap jolted the dun with his spurs. Suddenly, as if possessed, the dun turned its head, bit the man's leg and detonated into a whirling fury of bucks and lunges. The lanky outlaw grabbed frantically to hang on, but it was of no use. He was thrown airborne, landing awkwardly on his left leg, screaming as it buckled beneath him.

Hearing his dog cry out in distress, Holt rushed outside.

Taking advantage of the distraction, Orion spun toward the bald outlaw who held the rifle on him, the short-barreled Army Colt revolver from his waistband in his fist.

"You wanna know what am I carryin'?" Orion hissed. "I'm carryin' lead, *boy.*" The cocking of the pistol punctuated his statement.

Under the darkening sky of the approaching storm, orange flame belched three times from Orion's pistol and drove three bullets into the filthy man. Then he walked over to his dun standing out in the street and calmly picked up the reins. "Easy. Easy. Good job, you're okay," he said, rubbing the horse's neck.

Holt was kneeling with Tag, petting and checking the dog's health. The dog was standing now, his head cowed and tail between his legs. He softly licked Holt's hand.

The saloon's customers and Goose hurried out from the saloon. Two of the poker players tried to go examine the man with the injured leg but were held silently in place by the bartender.

"Ya shoulda tolt me that hoss was a killer!" the would-be horse thief screamed in anger and pain. "I'll teach it not ta throw me!" He rolled over, struggling for his pistol.

In a flash, Holt moved toward the man and smashed his newly purchased whiskey bottle into the side of his head. The explosion of glass and whiskey jerked the horse thief's hand to a halt. Soaked in whiskey and bleeding profusely from a deep cut opened on the side of his head, the man grunted and fell over.

"Which one hurt my dog?" Holt asked Orion.

"That dirty one over there," Orion pointed. The motionless outlaw, laid in a pool of spreading blood that soaked into the old boardwalk planks. "He got called on a threat he couldn't back up."

Holt drew one of his Russian Smith & Wessons, put two shots into the unmoving body, and reholstered the gun. Holt then turned away from the crowd and moved to his horses. First, the young Ranger picked up his furry friend and carefully placed Tag atop the saddle pack.

Then he drew his Ranger badge from a pocket and held it in his fist.

"Horse stealin' is a hangin' offense," Orion declared to the assembled crowd. "Or haven't you heard?"

Yanking his Winchester free from its scabbard, Holt turned back around and announced to the customers strung along the dilapidated boardwalk, "All right, gentlemen, here's what's going to happen. One at a time, you're going to toss your guns out here." With his rifle, he motioned toward the street. "I want a nice, pretty pile."

"We di'nt do nothin'," one of the grubby poker players complained.

"Two of you tried to rob me an' steal my horse," Orion snarled. He pinned his Ranger badge on his coat.

"And hurt my dog," Holt added. "We don't know who's friendly here and who isn't. What I do know is that you'd better start following the orders of the Texas Rangers." With that, he fastened his own Ranger badge to the lapel of his coat and levered his Winchester into readiness directly at the crowd. Three cowboys flinched at the sound. Others murmured at the revelation that these rough-looking men were Rangers.

Orion pulled his Navy Colt from its shoulder holster and pointed it at a man with torn Confederate trousers. "Startin' with you, sunshine. Yeah, you." The short-barreled Colt in his other hand remained on the group.

Swallowing hard, the former Reb pulled an old, short-barreled pistol at his hip, glanced at the others and threw the gun in the street.

Holt was getting impatient. "You've got a count of five to start getting rid of those guns. Hideaways too," he snapped. "If you don't, I'm going to empty this rifle into the whole lot of you."

"Your call, boys," Orion added. "We didn't start this, but we're sure as hell gonna end it." The clicks of his Colt trigger being pulled back emphasized his point.

"One…two…" Holt began.

The man with the torn trousers pulled another gun from the back of his waistband and tossed it with his first pistol, then turned around. "C'mon, Davy…Jake…I ain't dyin' fer ya…do it. They ain't bluffin'."

Four men quickly yanked handguns from strapped-on holsters and coat pockets and took turns tossing them out onto the rutted ground.

The bartender, Goose, looked at Holt and slowly opened his vest and turned around so the Ranger could see the large man was not carrying a gun there. He signed "Open" and "Hand" to Holt, indicating he was unarmed. Another man stepped forward, said he was the livery operator and had no weapons, also demonstrating that he was telling the truth.

"I ain't carryin' neither, Ranger. Honest." A hatless cowboy held up his hands and kept them there.

"Aw hell, Hogan, come on. He knows yur holdin'," the grimy-faced man said.

Grim-faced, Hogan walked over and ceremoniously dropped a large Colt onto the pile. Orion swung a pistol toward Hogan. "There's one in your boot too, Hogan."

The man leaned over and a pulled a derringer from a boot holster and threw it out into the street. The rest followed suit.

Satisfied, Orion eased the trigger forward on his Navy Colt, holstered it, and returned the short-barreled gun to his back waistband. He walked to one of the saloon patron's horses hitched out front. He untied the coiled lariat from the saddle and tossed it at the feet of the assembled cowboys.

"Loop it 'round the horse thief's ankles," he said. "Make it fast."

The man with the torn trousers grabbed the rope and moved off the planked walk toward the unconscious man. The thief groaned and stirred as his when the rope was tightened.

Orion grabbed the reins of his dun and swung into the saddle. "Now, give me the other end," he snapped.

"Any of you try to get your guns," Holt threw in. "I'll start shooting. At everyone."

Goose's loud voice rang out, "No...one...will."

Orion eased the dun forward and drug the outlaw's body across the street to the livery. At the corral, the Ranger swung down from the saddle, loosened the rope from the man's ankles and fixed the loop around his neck, pulling it tight. He tossed the long end of the lariat over the crossbeam of the old corral gate. Remounting, he looped the end of the rope around his saddle horn and backed the dun up slowly. The body started dragging along the ground toward the tall gate frame.

Hogan snarled, "He cain't do that to Jethrum..." and stepped toward the pile of guns. "I'll be damned if..."

From behind, Goose drove a huge forearm down onto Hogan's shoulder and sent him crashing onto the decrepit walkway. Two others stepped between Hogan and the street, keeping him from the weapons.

Orion continued backing the dun clear across the street, stopping in front of the hitch post. Holt had readied the other horses and was up on his saddle, a recovering Tag placed on the packhorse.

The struggling form of the would-be horse thief was now hanging several feet off the ground from the old gatepost. Dark clouds in the distance rumbled and flashed, giving the scene a macabre look. The outlaw was awake now, panic-stricken. His legs kicked wildly as he grabbed at the lariat around his neck in horror, the loop strangling the life from him.

Pulling up next to Holt, Orion drew the big Navy Starr pistol from his saddle and aimed it at the thief, whose body was swaying frantically in desperation. Two quick shots from Orion's pistol rang out. The rope above the outlaw's head frayed and quickly snapped, dropping the man to the ground. The rope's tension on his neck was relieved. However, the fall broke the outlaw's leg even further, shoving bone through his skin and trousers. He gulped life-giving oxygen in between raspy screams of pain.

"He just got better'n he deserved," Orion sneered at the patrons, holstering the big gun and throwing the remainder of the rope off his saddle. "You tell that miserable slush bucket if I ever see his face again, I'll kill 'im. *Nobody* tries to steal my horse."

Amid the muttering of the crowd, Goose stepped forward and held out a new bottle of Irish whiskey to Holt.

Holt accepted the bottle with a nod of thanks and reached back to tuck it into his saddlebags. With his rifle still readied, he yelled at the group, "Now, back inside! Everyone! Move!"

After the motley crew had all shuffled into the decrepit saloon, the Rangers spurred their horses, looking back over their shoulders as they loped out of Kendrick.

CHAPTER THIRTY-TWO

Orion finally spoke up when they were well away from Kendrick, "Well, that was a bust." He paused before speaking again. "I do believe that storm's gonna keep shovin' west though. Gonna miss us, I think."

Deep in thought, Holt did not respond at first, still angered by the events in the rundown town. His rifle still laid across his lap. "Sorry, Orion. Just thinking about what happened back there."

"We didn't do anythin' a Ranger isn't supposed to do. If that's what you're thinkin' about."

Holt was disappointed in himself about judging the bartender and told Orion about it. He was also still seething about what had happened to Tag. The dog appeared to have regained most of his happy energy, but was still a little reserved, likely nursing some sore ribs. They would look at him closer when they stopped.

"You didn't know 'bout the bartender," Orion observed. "Sounds like you made a friend in the end."

"I suppose. He seemed to be the only good thing

about that place," Holt said, shoving his rifle back into its saddle boot. Several minutes of silence passed before Holt spoke again. "I thought you were going to let that jackass hang," he observed. "I was taking your lead. Horse thieves deserve to swing."

"Sent a message to all those apple-knockin' pig thumpers," Orion scoffed. "Likely more'n a few of them on handbills somewhere. Besides, that broken leg an' busted head may end up doing what the rope didn't." He paused for several moments. "Gettin' time to find a spot for the night," he announced. "Whattaya think?

"Horses need some rest," Holt responded. "Coffee sure sounds good. Let's see if we can find a spot where we can get away with a small fire."

A long hour passed and the storm still made its presence known. Lightning flashed beyond the horizon and thunder grumbled in the distance, but it was moving off and the night would be dry. The Rangers rode through mesquite and stubby blackjack with its gnarly roots, following a slope of dead grass and crumbled rock. It was land no one wanted or lived on, except Comanches or Apache.

A mile back, they had crossed a trail of faint tracks from a string of unshod ponies. The tracks were days old, as was the scat. If it were wild horses, their dung would likely be all together. What they saw was not. It was scattered. This had been a group of Comanche or Apache, maybe even Kiowa. Tracks like these weren't uncommon and didn't mean they indicated imminent danger, it just reinforced the need to remain vigilant.

They reined up and studied the scrappy land ahead of them. A vast landscape with a few scraggly cottonwood, ash, willow and buckthorn did their best to surround some big boulders.

As they closed in on the rock formation, the horses and men were weary, thirsty, and hungry. They could tell the horses thought they smelled water. The animals eager to advance. It was possible anything could be here—predators of both the two- and four-legged variety—watering or waiting for prey to come by.

"Good spot for an ambush," Orion said.

"Thinking that too," Holt said. He handed the lead rope of his buckskin to Orion and eased his rifle from its scabbard. "You boys stay here. I'll ride close and see what's going on." He patted Tag sitting atop the pack and told him to stay put. A quick touch of the cardinal feather in his hatband accompanied his clicking the bay to move out.

Approaching the rocks with great care, Holt was on alert. Although the site was open and would afford good refuge and views once inside, there were plenty of options here for ambushers to strike the unwary. He worked his way around the location in an ever-tightening ring. If there was evidence of human footprints or horse tracks, the elements had ridded them many days before. Faint wildlife tracks showed this small oasis was not exclusive. It looked as though a bear had watered here not long ago. Holt took that to be a good sign and touched his medicine pouch.

The area was clear of threat. The horses' noses were correct. There was good water collecting in a rock seep, surrounded by boulders on one side and a couple of cottonwoods on the other. Clusters of blue grama, buffalograss and blue stem would provide good forage.

He let the dog down and Tag ran around, happy to be

moving again. Holt smiled that his pal showed no apparent ill effects from his Kendrick encounter.

The animals were attended to first. The Rangers removed the pack and saddles, wiped their backs, and let them roll. Orion meticulously checked each of their hooves and legs while Holt filled canteens and water bags in the seep. He was impressed with the way Orion handled the horses and the way they responded to him.

They both examined Tag closely. There weren't any protrusions in his chest or ribs and he did not cry out or whimper when they were feeling around and carefully pressing on him.

"We'll keep an eye 'im," Orion said. "If he starts a cough or has trouble breathin', that might mean a bruised lung or somethin'. We'll watch his eatin' too." They let the dog go explore the neighborhood. After wandering the edges of their camp, he trotted back to pronounce the area safe from invaders. He had even found some dinner as well, presenting a pocket gopher to the lawmen.

"Good boy," Holt smiled, pleased that Tag was showing an appetite.

A small fire beneath the low-hanging branches of a buckthorn tree would provide heat for coffee, a can of beans, and a quick pan of bacon with potato slices. Not yet full dark, the sticks for the fire were dry and what little smoke they created would dissipate in the tree's leaves. Cooking bacon, potatoes and beans with some apples and hard biscuits with a pot of coffee felt like a feast. Holt was pleased once more to see tiny blue flames in the fire and knew it meant spirits were close. He assumed the spirits were friendly and greeted them silently.

Their horses were watered and hobbled for the night.

They grazed calmly in a pocket of green just next to the boulders, their saddles and blankets airing out nearby. Holt dug in one of his bags and handed the bottle of whiskey to Orion.

"Your friend Goose took care of us!" Orion smiled.

"You kinda used up the other one."

The two Rangers spread out the remaining coals of their fire and moved to a secondary rock shelf overlooking the horses.

The shelf afforded them a good defensive view of the surroundings, but not so high that it required a lot of climbing up or down. They could get to the horses just as quickly from here. Tag could also move around easily and, if nature called in the night, it would not be a risky scramble down for the men. Saddlebags and trail coats made a cozy nighttime nest. Holt engaged in his nightly ritual of wiping down his weapons and touching each of them with the cardinal feather.

Orion walked up the little pathway to the outcrop. "No more fire, but this'll keep us warm," he grinned and handed the bottle back to Holt. "Glad you thought of it."

Holt uncorked it and sniffed. Good Irish whiskey. He took a swig. "You mentioned you were in the Navy," he recalled. "Figured you to be cavalry."

"I was. Started out in the 3rd Illinois Cavalry. I switched 'round a bit from there," Orion said. "I didn't enlist right away. Not many of us up north did. Figured the whole ruckus wouldn't last long."

"Thought we'd come to our senses, huh?" Holt half-chuckled and handed him the bottle.

"Somethin' like that," Orion grinned and took a good pull of the smooth, pale gold liquid. "I lived near Quincy, on the Illinois side of the Mississippi, just north of St.

Louie. Owned a deliv'ry company. Good-sized one too. Steamboats an' railroads linked to Quincy made business good."

"Illinois?" Holt reacted. "What brought you to Texas?"

"I was born in Texas, basically grew up on the water. My father was a river pilot in Galveston. He died of pneumonia 'bout five years before the war. Ma didn't want to leave the river, but St. Louie wasn't to her likin', so I moved her up with me an' my wife."

"You've got a wife?" Holt asked, reaching for the bottle.

"Had a wife." Orion laughed dryly and took another quick swallow from the bottle before handing it over. "Let's jus' say we parted ways. We were on opposite sides of most everythin'." He paused reflectively for a moment, then asked, "You ever been married?"

"No," answered Holt, taking a mouthful from the bottle. "Had a childhood sweetheart promise to wait for me. She didn't."

"Ever think 'bout her?"

"Not for a long time," Holt mused, corking the bottle and placing it between them. "If you don't mind me asking, how does a Union cavalryman get himself into the Navy?"

Orion laughed heartily. "Simple story, I got tired of horses gettin' killed out from under me."

"No..." Holt half-smiled, unsure if Orion was kidding.

"Yeah," Orion continued. "I enlisted in the fall after the war started, like I said. In the 3rd Illinois Cavalry, formed there right by home. My company's first engagement was at Warsaw, Missouri. Captured a *big* store of supplies. That's when I lost my first horse. Reb sharp-shooter dropped 'im instead of me. We built a bridge there across the Osage River, which was where I lost my second horse. Broken leg."

"I didn't know there was that much war going on in Missouri."

"Oh yeah, that's about all we did for the better part of a year, just chasin' General Sterling Price's troops around through there and Arkansas. At Pea Ridge, I lost three horses."

"It was obvious from the start you Yanks had more means than we ever did," Holt observed. "That's five horses you alone lost in a year, yet you still got new mounts every time. We wouldn't have been so lucky. Good horses, hell, any horses were hard for us to come by."

"It gets better. Or worse," Orion replied and picked up the bottle for a fresh swig. Re-corking it, he recalled, "I lost three more horses when we spent the next few months bouncin' from Arkansas to Missouri to Missis-sippi. Those were tough times."

Holt reached to take another swallow from the bottle. The movement briefly woke up the sleeping dog curled against him. He carefully rubbed Tag's back until the dog closed his eyes again.

"Finally, we were ordered to join the forces movin' on Vicksburg. We'd be under the command of General Sherman himself," Orion continued. "We rode in Admiral Porter's river transports. I got pressed into service helpin' load horses an' mules. They hadn't figured out yet that a horse'd rather swim than get on a damn boat." He chuckled heartily.

"Never thought about that before," Holt mused.

"Horses can get all kinds of squirrelly around water, that's for sure."

"I got assigned as some kind of cavalry liaison over-seein' the horses an' mules on these transports. I lost my ninth horse to artillery shrapnel in a charge at Chick-ashaw Bluff. One shell blew up near us an' he reared, throwin' me. Another shell came in right after an' tore him up. Lotta that flyin' metal was probably meant for me..." His voice trailed off.

Holt just shook his head. "Tough to see a good horse go down."

"Sure is," Orion said, lost in memory. A few moments passed before he spoke again. "I vowed right then an' there to not lose another horse. I spoke with Admiral Porter's staff about becomin' a permanent part of the Mississippi River Squadron."

"And you ended up with the best parts of your world, horses and boats," Holt surmised.

"An' artillery n' explosions." Orion smiled. "Lord a'mighty, we had some big naval guns. Some big boomers were aimed at us too. You Rebs weren't lackin' for firepower."

"For a while anyway..."

"After Vicksburg, Admiral Porter's boats were ordered to take part in a campaign to control the Red River in Louisiana. It was a disaster. General "No Brains" Halleck couldn't manage an ice cream social. We didn't accomplish a single objective."

"And I thought *we* had more than our share of bungling generals who couldn't follow orders or read maps," Holt observed.

Orion just shook his head. "After that, they trans-ferred Admiral Porter an' his big ironclads over to North

Carolina. Some of us stayed behind with a handful of monitors an' tinclads. We spent the rest of the war usin' those military boats to *appropriate* contraband."

"You mean seize cotton and ship it north." Holt gave a knowing smirk in return.

"Half right," Orion said. "Seize and *sell*. Rather than confiscatin' cotton, sugar an' rice to ship north in acts of war, a few of us decided to base our operations more hidden from pryin' eyes, if you know what I mean. We started peddlin' our wares from New Orleans all throughout Texas."

"So, cavalryman to sailor to pirate."

"I preferred the term, *privateer*, if you please." Orion chuckled in return. "You want any more of this?" He held up the bottle.

"If I have more, I'll want a cigar and we'd be up all night trading stories. Don't want to sleep too soundly either."

"More for another time," Orion agreed. "Good stuff."

CHAPTER THIRTY-THREE

Morning came without incident. Breakfast for Tag and the Rangers was hard biscuits, the rest of the apples, and a couple strips of jerky. The horses had grazed and watered well throughout the night. Both men decided to ride their back-up mounts to start the day, giving their bays a rest. The terrain was going to be rocky and prickly so Holt put the leather socks on Tag's paws and let him start the day on foot. Tag happily got used to the booties and trotted around the area to investigate.

"Fancy-steppin' fella, right there," Orion remarked. "You thought of everythin'."

"I made his first set when we got ambushed and were stranded without a horse in that frying pan on the other side of Turkey Wing. He doesn't seem to mind, knows what they're for."

Red fingers of dawn crawled across the land and soon it was bright once more. The sun proclaimed its heat would take control of the day. They rode through lowlands that hosted outcroppings of limestone and shale colored in an earthy rainbow of yellow and brown with touches of red. The valleys were awash with waves of broken sandy terrain and brimming with squadrons of mesquite trees and grass as well as cacti and scrubby desert brush. Just out of reach from the thirsty basins, sentinels of mountains teemed with lush oak, piñon, and ponderosa pine trees. It was hard to believe great cattle country was just a few days' ride from here.

After a couple of hours, they stopped to give the horses a breather and let them drink canteen water from their hats. Tag was ready to ride for a while. Holt tucked the dog's boots into his saddlebags. Overhead, a hawk dipped low to examine a cluster of prairie dog holes, swooping skyward when none appeared.

"Got the feelin' you faced a different war than I did," Orion observed as they resumed their riding. "Heard you was at Sabine."

"Yeah, that I was," Holt answered. "My brother Blue and I enlisted right away, even before all the shooting in South Carolina. We were part of the Texas Mounted Riflemen, which sounds more impressive than it was. Basically, we were supposed to protect the Texas borders between the Red River and the Rio Grande. All we really did for a year was ride around and protect ranchers and planters—and Yank sympathizers—from Indians. Our enlistments… well…the entire regiment's enlistments ran out in the spring of '62."

"Sounds a bit wasteful," Orion remarked. "Like our piddlin' around in Missouri."

Holt nodded in agreement. "Blue decided he wanted more action and left to fight with Stonewall Jackson's Second Corps. Ewell's boys," Holt continued. "He caught up with the Second at Fredericksburg, just in time for winter. A few of us remained in Texas and volunteered to fight with the First Texas Cavalry Regiment. We got sent to New Orleans, which sounded promising. But rather than go fight, we immediately hunkered down to defend the city. We got involved in a couple of skirmishes around Baton Rouge, but nothing to speak of. Finally, we were ordered to sail from New Orleans as part of the Sabine Pass expedition, only to find out we were being sent as reserves. I knew some Irish boys fighting with the Davis Guards at Sabine, so a couple of us left to go fight with them."

"I'll say you did," Orion exclaimed. "Forty-seven men an' six old smoothbore cannon took down 6,000 Federals. Damn! Even as a Yank, I had to admit that was mighty damn impressive."

"We had a huge advantage, we knew the ground," Holt explained. "Our guns were fixed on the narrow channel where they had to sail through, already sighted in where the boats would be."

"Kind of a big turkey shoot."

"Yeah, it was. Those cannons quickly cut into their parade of boats. We went down and cleaned up the troops on the transports we hit."

"'Bout a hundred Yanks killed or wounded an' more'n 300 captured," Orion confirmed. "That got everyone's attention, for sure."

"And we didn't lose a man," Holt added. "Our one big day."

Near midday, they stopped beside a small creek given new life by a distant cloudburst. The Rangers settled under a scrawny oak and ate some jerky and corn dodgers. They drank from the stream and topped off their canteens, then watered the horses after they had cooled down. Both men decided a cigar would make a fine dessert and lit up two from Orion's saddlebags.

Tag began to growl, a teeth-tightening warning.

Off in the distance, a sizable group of riders on horseback appeared over a shallow ridge. Even without field glasses, Holt knew they were Indians by the way they sat their mounts. Orion retrieved his naval spyglass and surveyed the group.

"Comanches," he said coolly, puffing on his cigar. "Twenny-four. Painted for war. Horses got feathers in their manes an' tails."

"I'm guessing it was their tracks we saw outside of Kendrick," Holt assessed.

"Well, they've seen us now," Orion added calmly, collapsing the spyglass. "Checking out our horses no doubt."

"They likely have been sniffing around our trail more than just this morning," Holt said, stowing away their packages of food. "We aren't going to lose them no matter how fast we ride."

Orion pointed at a big outcropping of rock and boulders about a half mile away in the opposite direction and declared they should make a stand there. "Looks like a good place to hole up and fight if it comes to that."

"Oh, it'll come to that," Holt chuckled grimly. "They see four good horses and only two men."

"We can protect the horses better there too," Orion added. "We'll have the high ground."

Holt grabbed Tag and tossed him aboard the bay and mounted his buckskin almost in one movement. Both Rangers and their four horses took off for the sanctuary of the rocks at a full gallop. The Comanches were surprised by such a sudden response and only warily advanced to the other side of the basin.

Reaching the outcropping, the Rangers tied their horses in a small nook. The entire area inside the rocks and the surrounding space was occupied by stubborn burrograss and grama grass. The recess where the horses were tied was not completely sheltered, but it would have to do. It gave the mounts a place to graze and hopefully remain calm during what was about to take place.

In case the Rangers needed to make a fast getaway run, Orion tightened the cinches on all the horses. He grabbed an extra pistol from a saddlebag and shoved it into his waistband. He retrieved a flat box from the other bag as well as a brown paper package and stuck them under an arm. He unsheathed his Henry and headed to the wall of rock.

Holt had his Winchester in-hand and an extra pistol shoved into his belt. He grabbed two boxes of cartridges and set one by Orion. He arranged himself in a good firing position behind the rock wall and made sure that Tag was safely down by his boots. He moved his panther claw to an outer coat pocket and drew the medicine pouch out from underneath his shirt. He held the pouch over his heart and asked his spirits for strength and guidance.

Orion took a position to Holt's left. The imposing boulders at their backs rose too high for anyone to come down at them from behind. Their sides might be another story. They would have to be vigilant. Although they were on higher ground, they needed to take care to not get flanked and hit from several angles. They noted the Comanches had moved closer but had yet to charge.

"Wonder what they're waitin' for?" Orion asked.

"How many did you say there were?"

"Twenny-four," came Orion's reply. "There're twenny-two now, aren't there?"

"They're holding two horses in the back of the group, out of sight," Holt observed. "Watch our flanks."

Orion alternated keeping his awareness out in front and readying the contents of the thin, flat box he brought from his saddlebag. Inside the box were three strange-looking darts. Ketchum grenades. Each dart had a tapered, oval-shaped iron body about the size and shape of two shot glasses stuck together open-end to open-end. Each body was packed with gunpowder. On the top end was a small, circular plunger. Affixed to the bottom end was a six-inch wood strut tail with hard-paper fins. Orion was carefully removing the circular plungers and applying percussion caps to the stick ends that went inside the body. He carefully and methodically inserted the plungers back into the bodies.

"What do you do with those?" Holt questioned without removing his eyes from the terrain outside their defensive position.

"You throw 'em!" Orion replied, eyeing the group of warriors in the distance.

"And?"

"An' they explode, tearin' the hell outta anythin' near it! Surprised you never ran into any of these. We'd throw 'em at Reb sharpshooters takin' potshots at us from the riverbanks."

"Only Union Navy boats I saw didn't get many shots off. And the only explosions I dodged came from those damn Napoleons and Howitzers you Yanks never seemed to run out of. The ones that used to wither our lines and scatter men in panic. They're what took my brother Blue's arm at Spotsylvania."

"I am truly sorry on that," Orion said, looking Holt in the eye. "Goddamn war."

"So how do they work? You light them or something?"

"Naw, you throw it at 'em. When this nose hits… *Boom!*"

"What if it doesn't hit nose first?"

"You shoot it."

Holt half-smiled, half-shook his head at Orion's matter-of-factness. "We should try getting a few of them before they get close enough for you to throw those things."

"That too," Orion said, taking a long pull from his cigar, letting the smoke waft around his face.

All at once, the group of warriors on horseback broke as one toward them. The sounds of their shrieks and battle cries reached them moments later. Riding as if they were part of their horses, the warriors had long, black hair decorated with feathers, glass beads, silver conchos and pieces of fur. Most of them carried painted war shields. Half were waving rifles or revolvers, and the rest, bows and arrows or short lances. Holt touched the cardinal feather in his hatband.

Tag looked out from around a boulder next to Holt and resumed his growling. Holt set his rifle down and drew a revolver as Tag's teeth became a snarl. A Comanche sprung up at them from the right, the Indian's body covered in dirt and sand. A knife flashed in his fist. The warrior had been crawling a long way.

Holt's gun blasts tore at the man's face and chest. The Comanche was dead before his lifeless body hit the ground beside him. Tag snarled and grabbed the warrior's arm, shaking free the knife. "Sshhh, Tag. Get down! And stay!" The dog sniffed the dead Indian one more time and moved back to Holt. Shoving the revolver into its holster, Holt grabbed his Winchester again, touched his medicine pouch, and resumed the watch on the warriors closing in on horseback.

Orion forced himself to scan the tall grass in front of him, instead of the Comanche riders still a ways off. His eyes had caught movement. It wasn't conspicuous, more of a sense than something tangible. He cocked his Henry rifle, pointed it in that direction, and waited.

A brown body slithered through the undergrowth. Deliberately. Steadily advancing. It reminded Orion of a cougar stalking its prey.

Orion anticipated where he thought the man was likely to crawl. He tightened his finger against the trigger and aimed the Henry. He saw movement and fired at a leg. The Henry thundered and the warrior rolled up on his side, then crumpled with Orion's second shot.

Six warriors outraced the rest of the war party and were closing fast on the Rangers' left, closest to Orion. Four other outriders had swung to the right flank closer to Holt, with the main group screaming directly toward their center.

Orion fired at the closest warrior, killing his horse, sending its rider cartwheeling onto the rough terrain into a broken lump. He fired at a second warrior, whose face, chest, and leggings were dotted in yellow. His bullets punched into the Indian's stomach and he buckled backward off his horse. The other four spread out their charge. One of them, with his lower face painted white, drew an arrow from the handful he held next to his bow. Orion

fired, missing twice. The warrior's arrow sang menacingly close to the Ranger as Orion's next two shots
slammed into the warrior's chest and shoulder.

Amid the sound of more steel-tipped arrows slicing
through the air, Orion quickly reached for a Ketchum
grenade and threw it in the direction of the three
screaming riders. It detonated with an explosion of fire,
hot metal and basin dust. The warrior closest to the blast
was blown completely back, along with his horse, both
shredded by the grenade's shrapnel. A piece of the hot
metal zipped through the air right at Orion, slicing a thin,
ragged line from his cheek to back under his ear.

"Wooo, like th' Fourth o' July!" Orion hollered,
ignoring the shrapnel's close call. The detonation had
knocked another warrior from his horse, the frightened
animal fleeing in terror. Suddenly on foot, the warrior
was dropped by two shots from Orion's Henry. The
remaining warrior had reined up, spurring his horse away
from the sudden eruption of fire and debris. Orion took
the brief moment of calm to wipe at the blood on his face
and shove more cartridges into his gun.

Holt fired twice at the warrior fleeing from Orion's
flank, missing both times. Tag moved again to get a
better look. "Dammit, Tag! Get down!" Holt hollered and
reached over to push the dog toward his feet. An arrow
struck the rocks where Holt's head had been. Two shots
from his rifle stopped the warrior trying to notch another
arrow.

A warrior with blue paint across his eyes like a mask
swung his lathered horse closer. As he shrieked a war cry
and aimed a pistol, Holt fired his Winchester three times.
The roar sounded almost like a single shot. The blue-
faced warrior disappeared in a plume of red mist and

toppled from his horse, his pistol thudding into the sand and dirt.

Bullets sang past Holt's head as a warrior with his mouth painted in a red handprint drew a running bead on Holt's position with a rifle. Before the Comanche could squeeze off another shot, Holt's Winchester bucked three more times, its bullets ripping at the throat and shoulder of the red-painted warrior, driving him from his horse.

A short-haired Comanche, face and body painted half blue, had charged close to Holt and cocked his arm to throw a short, brutish lance. Holt fired his Winchester and missed the warrior. He used the rifle to block the warrior's thrust and throw. The force knocked the Winchester from his hands. The Comanche launched himself from his horse and tackled Holt. Tag snapped and snarled at the Indian wrestling on the ground with Holt. On his back, Holt drove the heel of his right hand up and smashed it under the Comanche's chin. In the instant before the warrior could recover, Holt reached across his body with his left hand and drew one of his Russian Smith & Wessons and pumped four shots into the attacker. He shoved the dead warrior off of him, fired once more into his head and holstered his pistol.

"We're okay, Tag," he gasped, patting the dog. Out of breath, he picked up his Winchester and inspected it. It appeared no worse for wear and he pushed a few cartridges into the loading gate. His cigar, long since played out but still in his mouth, had been smashed in the struggle. He threw it on the ground and Tag sniffed at it indignantly.

The main party of eleven Comanches galloping barreling at the Rangers' center were joined by the warrior who escaped from Orion's first explosive and were almost on top of the lawmen.

Orion hollered, "Duck!" and threw another Ketchum. The grenade exploded in the midst of the charge, sending the middle three warriors into a tangled mess of bloody men and horses. "Look at that, didn't know what hit 'em!" He cackled with laughter. The surviving warriors on either side, wheeled away in withdrawal. The Rangers both fired twice at the retreating Indians, missing with all four shots.

The remaining nine warriors from the raiding party gathered around their war leader who had hung back out of the fray. He wore a Union officer's vest and carried an old cavalry carbine. In his scalp lock were two eagle feathers attached to a silver concho. Two yellow jagged stripes, like a lightning bolt, were painted down the right side of his face from his forehead down across his eyelid to his jawline. A similar lightning bolt graced his medicine shield. He studied the rocks, where his adversaries were reloading their guns and firing into a couple of still-moving warriors laid out in front of their position. To quit now would mean his disgrace; no warrior would ever follow him again into battle. He had to prove his medicine was still strong. He raised his shield and rifle to the sky, then crashed them together twice. The gesture was made to strengthen his war medicine.

A hundred yards from the Rangers' position, nine warriors raced forward with their war leader to comply with his command.

As they closed in, Orion readied his last Ketchum and hollered, "Duck again!" as he threw the grenade at the charging warriors. The grenade bounced harmlessly on the ground as the Comanche thundered right by it.

"Ho-lee damn," Orion exclaimed as he brought up his Henry and began firing. Three shots from his Henry took down a warrior wearing a Confederate infantry tunic. Two shots from Holt and his Winchester dropped another.

A menacing warrior with black-and-white face paint and wearing a white woman's dress veered off to the left; another warrior wearing leggings and an open Rebel tunic peeled off to the right.

Holt's first two shots at the warrior in the tunic missed. He had slipped to the side of his pony, making him a difficult target as he positioned to fire a revolver from under the horse's neck. Holt had seen the maneuver many times before and had even used it himself. He stroked the cardinal feather in his hatband and aimed. His first shot brought a scream from the Indian pony. It stumbled and fell, toppling the Comanche under him. The warrior's pistol skidded into a scrubby mesquite bush. Holt fired two more times, making sure the horse did not suffer. The warrior under the horse was dead.

Orion was focused on the war leader, who was screaming and exhorting his men in between firing shots from an old rifle. Shifting his cigar to bite down on it, Orion cocked and fired his Henry. The war leader's cry jerked to a stop and he folded from his horse, his head a bloody mess with a huge bullet hole in his forehead. Orion puffed on his cigar to keep it lit.

Suddenly, the warrior in the woman's dress appeared in the rocks just to Orion's left, his tomahawk raised to strike. "Orion, look out!" Holt yelled, swinging his Winchester at the shrieking attacker as the warrior leaped at Orion. He fired his Winchester four times as fast as he could lever the gun, the man falling where Orion just stood.

"Much obliged, Holt!" Orion shouted. "You saved my bacon." He fired his Henry into the bloody body to make sure.

Their war leader dead, the last five warriors turned to ride away.

"Holt! Holt!" Orion hollered. "Fire at the Ketchum! Sting 'em some more if we can."

Both Rangers opened fire at the grenade with their rifles. They didn't know which one of them hit it, but it suddenly exploded in a ball of fire, knocking three of the warriors from their horses.

"Woooo!" Orion reacted. "That did it!"

Holt continued firing until his rifle emptied, felling the two Comanches still on horseback and one on foot. He immediately shoved a handful of cartridges into the gun.

Orion reached down into the package he brought and pulled some fireworks from it. The remaining two warriors, now horseless, recovered their senses and were running away as were all the riderless horses.

"*These* are for scarin' the hell outta them an' any of their horses still dumb enough to be here," he proclaimed. He lit a Roman candle with his cigar. It sizzled and began shooting fiery exploding balls at the retreating Indians. Orion laughed hard at the effect. "Here, hold this." He handed the still-sizzling tube to Holt. "Careful, it's gotta few more balls to go." Orion quickly fixed a Sky Rocket into a boulder crack and lit it. The rocket took off with a noisy *whoosh* and exploded well over the heads of the running Comanches, echoing loudly throughout the basin. At the sharp report from the sky, one of the warriors stumbled and fell. He immediately got to his feet, trailing dust from his body as he ran.

"Lookit 'em go!" Orion cackled. The two running warriors were not quite out of range, but Holt decided to let them continue running.

Orion lit another Sky Rocket, lowering this one's trajectory. And he lit the Star Serpent. Both fireworks took off with loud *zhooms* of fire and sparks. The Sky Rocket blew up in another sharp report. The Star Serpent lived up to its name, flying wildly in a flaming corkscrew before exploding in a bloom of fiery stars.

"Hooweee…that one'd be good to see at night!" Orion was so tickled he dabbed at a little wetness at the corners of his eyes. "That's good stuff."

The only one not enjoying the display was Tag. He was hunkered down by Holt's feet. "*Now* you decide to hide from loud noises," Holt joked and kneeled by the dog. The sudden quiet and Holt's ear scratches brought the dog back to his feet, tail wagging happily.

"Wonder what story they'll tell back in camp." Orion grinned, watching the Comanches who were still running.

"Let's get out of here before they get brave again," Holt said, finishing the reloading of his rifle.

Grabbing the remaining fireworks and the box of bullets, Orion picked up his rifle and made his way back to their horses. Before gathering up his weapons and extra cartridges, Holt left a tobacco tribute and thanked the spirits for watching over them.

At their little picket area, several cracked and broken arrows that missed their marks laid on the ground among the forage grass. "Aww, look here," Orion called out. "Somethin'…an arrow or ricochet burned a mean scratch 'cross my bay." The flesh on the horse's upper thigh,

back near its tail, was cut and bloody. It was not a deep
nor particularly debilitating wound, but serious enough it
would need to be watched.

"You're bleeding too," Holt said. In addition to the
thin slice across the right side of his partner's face, Holt
noticed that Orion's coat and shirt along the top of his left
forearm was torn and bloody.

Orion pointed at his face. "Did this to myself. Piece
o' that first Ketchum," he said, shaking his head. He
looked at the damage to his coat and arm. "Guess one of
those bastards got kinda close here. Good thing it was
this one," he said, holding up his wounded arm. "Didn't
affect my throwin' with this one." He smiled, holding up
his other arm.

"You match your horse. Not sure which looks nasti-
er," Holt said. "You need to give both of those a quick
rinse," he instructed as he went to his saddlebags and
pulled out a canister. Orion dug in his saddlebag as well,
retrieving a canteen and the bottle of whiskey.

Orion gave his face a quick cleanse with a
bandanna from his coat pocket and water from a
canteen. Rolling back the torn sleeves on his left arm
exposed a ragged, bloody groove rasped across the top
of his forearm. He poured water from the canteen to
flush the wound. Next, he poured some of the pale gold
liquid from the bottle into the bandanna and wiped the
cut on his face with it. As the alcohol hit the open
wound, he inhaled sharply between gritted teeth. He
took a big slug from the bottle and held it out for Holt,
who shook his head. Orion then poured some whiskey
onto the bloody slash along his forearm. "Hoo-*ewww*!
Mother jumpin' frog bangers, that stings!" Corking the
bottle, he took a few deep breaths to steel himself.

"Saint Patrick be doin' his magic inside an' out! Ho-leee *damn*!"

Holt opened the tin container that once held pipe tobacco. Inside, it was packed with a thick mixture that smelled a little bit of turpentine mixed with hog's lard, beeswax, arnica and cedar. "An old Navajo remedy," he said, giving the container a whiff. "Don't know how or why, but it works," he said, giving both of Orion's wounds a quick slather of the concoction. "We'll wrap that bandanna around your arm for now," Holt instructed. "Let's put a little on the horse too," he suggested.

"Better let me," Orion said with a laugh. "No one, even a horse, likes doctorin' around their butt." Talking softly, with his hand rubbing the horse's chest, then its neck, he moved slowly and poured some water from the canteen on the horse's wound. The horse flinched a little, but made no other sound or reaction, its eyes fixed on Orion. Continuing to talk in a soothing voice, Orion reached for the tin in Holt's hand. He took a dab of the ointment on his fingers and slowly and easily smoothed the mixture across the bloody crease on the horse's haunch.

"That feel better, boy?" Orion said to the horse. "Hard to tell exactly, but I think he knows that stuff is s'posed to help." He sniffed his arm. "Smells like it should do somethin'." He chuckled.

Everything got squared away quickly in their saddle-bags. Tag was placed on the pack with Holt's bay. Orion hopped on his dun. His bay had enough adventure for the day. Before he mounted up, Holt placed the medicine pouch inside his shirt, holding it briefly against his heart.

They rode away, rifles on their laps in front of them

and their heads on swivels, taking care to make sure they were not being followed.

"We got 'bout two, maybe three hours before dark," Orion guessed. "Let's get far away."

"You know what yarrow is?" Holt asked.

"My grammy swore by it for colds." Orion smiled.

"Keep an eye out for some. Or goldenrod. It's good for bullet and arrow wounds." Holt smiled back, pointing at Orion's arm.

They spent the rest of the afternoon in a steady lope, stopping only occasionally for their horses to get hatfuls of water. Orion searched their backtrail with his spyglass. No signs of riders, not even indications of distant dust.

CHAPTER THIRTY-FOUR

D usk was beginning to lengthen the shadows in the basin when Holt pointed to the edge of a forest above them. The line of trees marked the beginning of a small mountainous area that patrolled the outer edges of the region. "How about settling up in there for the night?"

"Good cover," Orion observed. "There's been no sign we've been followed."

"We stung 'em pretty hard. You took down their leader. We'll be far away before they rally around a new one."

They tucked their camp up inside the thick forest, the open, boulder-strewn basin spread out just below. Holt and Orion tended to their mounts first. The horses had worked hard today. Their saddles were pulled and their backs were rubbed down with handfuls of grass. Their hooves were checked carefully.

A spring provided a small pool with just enough cold, refreshing water for the men and horses. The seven creatures in their group drank the small pool dry. After the fight with the Comanche war party, the Rangers were worn out and hungry. They decided to risk a small fire tucked behind some rocks and an old stump.

Holt laid strips of salt pork into a frying pan, placing it at the edge of the fire. The coffee pot readied dark, hot brew which would be most welcome. An extra tin mug steeped hot water for the yarrow they found along the trail, with which he planned on making a poultice for Orion's arm. As the meat began to sizzle, he then cut chunks of a raw potato, letting them drop into the pan. A handful of wild onions lay near his boots to be added to the fry.

Pleased with the progress of dinner, Holt asked Orion, "What was he like? Sherman. I always wondered if he was as big a son of a bitch as we suspected." He laughed.

Orion chuckled in response. "He was somethin' else. Bigger'n Grant. Actually, Sherman was a pretty scary peckerhead, if you ask me. The man was *intense*. He had no tolerance for fools."

"That sounds like everything I've heard."

"He was 'bout your height. Had a real presence. If he was nearby, you could feel 'im. Red hair, grizzly beard, he didn't care as much 'bout his appearance like a lotta generals did, but he wasn't as grubby as Grant could be."

"Strutting peacocks, most generals," Holt interjected and stirred the pan with his knife.

"Fools, on both sides. Too many politicians an' rich assholes playin' soldier."

"And pissing matches between each other that got too many good men killed."

Orion nodded. "Sounds like our war was similar in that regard," he said with a touch of sadness.

From the cover of the wooded area, they could survey the basin below as they enjoyed the hot meal and coffee. As darkness took over, they agreed that cigars and a couple of mouthfuls of the Irish whiskey would be nice, but decided they should avoid enjoying themselves too much. Letting their guard down would be inadvisable. Their afternoon still weighed heavily.

"In fact, Orion…you know what?" Holt suddenly declared. "This is a good spot and all, but I'm thinking we ought to pull out of here tonight. Now."

The idea was on Orion's mind as well and he immediately agreed.

It did not take long to repack their gear and resaddle the horses. Their small fire, already dying to embers, was rubbed out completely. They emptied the tiny spring-fed pool again, topping off their canteens and letting the horses get their fill.

Although they were moving on, pushing the horses was unwise. "I don't like to run a horse at night, too easy to hurt 'em," Orion said.

"No need to unless we have to. They're tired too. We can still put some more distance between us and wherever that Comanche camp is though."

They kept the horses to an easy trot, which ate good ground. Even with the slower pace, Tag rode on the pack. About two hours in, they came across a small road—more of a rutted wagon track—but it did indicate civilization at one end or the other. They kept well away from the road, letting moonlight guide their way.

Tag sat in his usual place and dozed, growling occasionally as he dreamed. The rhythmic gait soon had both men feeling the long day. Before drowsiness totally took over, Orion spoke up. "My full belly an' this easy-gaited sonvabitch is makin' me dozy. I gotta talk about some-thin' to keep me awake." He paused a moment and said, "Mind if I ask you what happened after Sabine? I ain't pokin' for any reason, jus' curious to hear 'bout other pieces of the war. You can tell me if I'm proddin' too close."

Holt didn't mind. He had never really looked back at all of it before, much less talked about it. Besides, it would keep him awake too.

"Well...the Yank boats turned around and left. The Guards admired their medals from President Davis. The First Texas boys headed back to Louisiana to sit and defend taverns and restaurants," he said sarcastically. "I sure as hell wasn't going back to New Orleans or sit at Sabine, so I decided to go find my brother, Blue. I caught up with his regiment as they were digging in at Mine Run on the Rapidan, just as Grant started playing his game of battle chess with Meade and General Lee."

"Battle chess." Orion chuckled. "That's a good way of puttin' it."

"At the Wilderness, we stopped Grant from moving on Richmond. A few days later, at Spotsylvania, Blue got hit by artillery and lost his arm. Damn near died. I didn't think the doctors were caring for him properly," he said, shaking his head at the bitter memory. "Nearly shot both of those white-coated buggers. Some major threatened me with a court-martial and I almost shot him too."

"I hated goin' near those hospitals." Orion shook his head. "The smell was enough to knock you sideways. Damn sorry about your brother though. Hope to meet 'im someday."

"He's just as intense as I am." Holt laughed. "But

he's focused it on the ranch and his family. Part-time preacher too. My brother, Deed, is the wild one."

"Think I heard 'bout 'im." Orion nodded. "Took down some bank robbers over in Austin. They had the drop on 'im an' he took 'em all with his bare hands. No gun. That right?"

Holt grinned. "That would be Deed. True story. He's settling down now. Just got married. We'll have you out to our place, the Rafter C, when we're done here."

"I look forward to that." Orion smiled.

Holt resumed his story. "I guess I stayed with Blue until I knew he was going to pull through. He was moved to a hospital in Tennessee and I followed. I sure as hell wasn't going back to fight for Ewell or Early. They couldn't find their butts with either hand. I heard that General Hood was put in charge of the Army of Tennessee, so I rode straight for him. Even with only one good arm and leg, that man liked to fight. That's where I wanted to be. I caught up with him in Atlanta just before Sherman closed in."

"So you *have* met General Sherman." Orion chuckled.

"In a way," Holt acknowledged, finding memories that had been shoved aside for a long time. "You know, looking back now, I've got to hand it to him. Sherman was the right man for the job and exactly what *we* didn't need. Destroying our railroads and supply lines would make us leave Atlanta. That's how he'd done it in the past and that's just what he did. At the time I didn't like it one bit, but it's exactly what I would have done. No question, no quarter. Simple as that." He smiled to himself, thinking that Sherman and Silka would have had an interesting conversation.

"All that burnin' an' slashin' mighty unpopular around these parts," Orion said.

"Unpopular as hell where we were, I can tell you that," Holt recalled. "They cut our supply routes and we evacuated. Left Atlanta at night. General Hood ordered an entire trainload of ammunition and other supplies destroyed. You could see the fire and hear the explosions for miles." He got quiet for a moment, reliving that awful night—ammunition blasts startling men and horses, an otherworldly inferno flickering at their backs. He snapped back to now. "A lot of men lost their will to fight that night. It just made me mad."

"I guess a lotta people'll never forgive 'im for what he did on that march," Orion observed. "I wonder how he'll be thought of when all of us are dead an' gone."

"It'll be flavored by those who won," Holt remarked with no emotion. "It already is." He picked up his train of thought. "We didn't know we were all but finished then. Just hanging on, tooth and nail. We conducted a bunch of pointless frontal assaults against fortified positions at Franklin and Nashville, but they were like Pickett at Gettysburg. Foolish. Disasters. We were fighting on pure pride and empty bellies."

"Damn. I read about that. Never talked with anyone who fought through the end there. From either side." He touched the raw cut along his cheek. Holt's healing mixture still protected it.

"It wasn't pretty. When the end did come, I just couldn't bring myself to admit the South had lost. I just couldn't."

"I said it before." Orion nodded in solemn appreciation. "You faced a diff'rent war than I did."

"You know the rest of the story... After the surrender,

a group of us started hitting Union payrolls and the like. Guess we thought it would bring back the South. It didn't. It just made me a wanted man." Holt pondered the thought. "Nobody's fault but mine."

"An' here you are! Ridin' for Texas an' Cap'n McCoy. I'm damn proud to ride with you, Holt Corrigan." He paused. "Thank you again for savin' my life."

"Don't mention it. You'd have done the same. That's what partners do."

They rode another hour, mostly in silence, then made a cold camp about a mile off the tiny, rutted road. Their camp was nestled on a grassy plateau that gave them good vision in all directions. A dry creek wandered around the edge defining the plateau, so the horses drank canteen water from the men's hats. Unless they ran into water between here and Sweetclover, what remained in their canteens and water bags would be all they had, so they needed to take extra care. They kept the horses close, hobbled and saddled, loosening their cinches just a little. The ties could be removed quickly if necessary.

Holt was dead tired but maintained his nightly ritual by quickly wiping down his weapons and touching them with the cardinal feather. Tag snuggled up to Holt's leg. The men slept with their boots on, pistols in-hand. Holt's medicine pouch lay on his chest, out from underneath his shirt.

CHAPTER THIRTY-FIVE

A day later, Holt and Orion paused at the outskirts of Sweetclover to get their bearings and affix the Ranger badges to their coats. Somewhere a small sparrow whispered an inquiring song. Holt wondered if it was some kind of a sign. He decided it was a good one. How could a bird singing be an indication of something bad coming?

A Conestoga wagon rattled by, headed south. Its driver waved at the Rangers and snapped his whip to make certain the team of mules understood who was in charge. Distant metallic clanks of a blacksmith's hammer greeted their ears.

The midday string of carriages, buckboards, and riders pushing through this border town was constant. The boardwalks were thick with people of all walks of life—clerks and merchants, dirty cowboys and aristocratically clad men, well-dressed women and dancehall ladies, drovers and farmers, whites, Mexicans, immigrants, and Blacks. The town of Sweetclover seemed like a big tumbleweed to Holt, people and buildings all jumbled together, everyone in a hurry to be somewhere.

He considered letting Tag down to stretch his legs but thought better of it. The traffic and heavy commotion unfolding before them was not conducive to the health of anything small…children, dogs, or even hesitant pedestrians.

The noontime sun commanded the street. Holt and Orion were a contrast to the commotion, easing their way through the hustle and bustle around them. Outside the livery stable, two Black men hitching a buggy stopped to watch the Rangers ambling by.

In front of the marshal's office, they dismounted and tied up their horses. Orion gave his animals a quick assessment. Holt stretched out his legs from the long spell in the saddle and examined the hooves of his bay and buckskin. He poured some water into his hat and let Tag get a drink. He retrieved a small piece of jerky and laid it up on the planked walkway by the jail door. Tag could sit there out of the way while they visited inside.

Frank Gentry, the marshal of Sweetclover, greeted the Rangers warmly as they stepped into the jail. He was an older man, older than Orion, dressed neatly in a black sack coat, gray canvas work vest and a clean white shirt with trousers stuffed into long, mule-eared boots. A black leather gun belt holstered an Army Colt at his waist. Gentry was very methodical and particular. His precise nature served him well as a lawman, as it had many years ago as an outlaw riding through Kansas and the Indian Territory.

His desk was heavily scratched, but quite orderly. A few papers were organized in a wood tray on the corner.

The rest of the desktop was empty. A black stove was working to keep a coffee pot ready. One wall held a framed photograph of Sam Houston.

A rack of rifles and shotguns occupied the adjoining wall. Barred windows with evenly spaced rods let air and light into the jail while deterring intruders from getting in or those in custody from getting out. Heavy wooden shutters that could be closed and braced from the inside added to the building's security. Three wall lamps had been recently cleaned and refilled. The back half of the jail had a gated iron-barred wall that separated—and secured—three fortified cells.

Gentry offered the Rangers coffee as they sat around his desk. He had heard of both of them. Orion Higbee had brought a number of cattle thieves to justice up and down the Rio Grande valley. Holt Corrigan was a name he was familiar with on both sides of the law.

"Understand you've had some trouble lately," Orion began. "Riders comin' through, one maybe masqueradin' as a man of the cloth?"

Gentry nodded in affirmation. "More than a week ago now, we had a return visit from a priest named Miguel. Father Miguel Beltran," he recounted. "He came through here several months ago as well. Both times two men rode with him, reservation Kiowas, maybe mixed Comanch."

Holt and Orion glanced at each other.

The marshal continued, "The priest was big, barrel-chested, but seemed to be a gentle man doing God's work. The two riders seemed a little out place, rough-like, not the usual clergy. At the time I thought the Lord worked in mysterious ways, but who am I to judge?"

"You wouldn't be the first town taken in by this... *Miguel*...and his men," Holt said.

"The first time, Father Beltran rode through town and spent almost a week. He conducted a couple of church services. He lent a hand to raise money for food to help folks in need. It didn't connect at the time, but our general store and newspaper office were broken into and robbed while he was here. Looking back, it had to be his orchestrating."

"How long ago did you say?" Holt asked.

"That first time was about six months ago," Gentry answered. "This last visit, Father Beltran was only here for a couple of days. He seemed a bit distracted this time. One of his two helpers had a shot-up shoulder. The father claimed that bandits had waylaid them. He still held a worship service for us. A good one too, if I may say so. Even conducted a ceremony to baptize a baby," he reflected. "What we didn't know was that two more riders, Mexicans, probably Comancheros, had snuck into town. During the baptism service, those two robbed the bank. The priest's assistants *just happened* to be nearby and helped with their escape."

"Damn," exclaimed Orion. "Got away, did they?"

"Mostly," Gentry said. "There was a flurry of gunfire outside the bank. A lot of lead was thrown back and forth. Our buildings still have the holes and splinters. Ike Wall, one of the bank tellers, and Del Halsey, a store clerk, were killed in the shoot-out. Good men. One of the outlaws was wounded."

"Wounded?" Holt asked.

"Yes," Gentry confirmed. "He's recuperating over at the doctor's office. Shackled until he mends and can stand trial."

"We need to meet this owlhoot," Orion declared. "But what happened to the priest?"

"After the engagement in front of the bank that included his two worship assistants, I led a posse after the three robbers who escaped with the money," the marshal explained. "While we were gone, no one paid much attention to the priest. Some folks carried our wounded townsmen to the doctor, but there wasn't much that could be done for them. Del was already dead. Ike died a couple hours later. The shot-up outlaw was dragged to the doctor as well. In the commotion and chaos, no one noticed that Father Beltran got on his mule and rode right out of town."

"Which way did they head?" Holt asked.

"We followed the three outlaws south and west to the Rio Grande," Gentry said. "We couldn't go any further when they crossed."

"And the priest?"

"His mule tracks took a different path to the river and disappeared across. When I returned with the posse, the telegram from Wilkon was waiting. I knew exactly who Father Miguel Beltran was."

"So, the priest an' four riders came to town an' a total of four left," Orion repeated, more to Holt than the marshal.

"Any idea where they were headed once they crossed?" Holt asked.

"No idea. And, as usual, there's no help from the Mexican authorities. They don't know and don't care."

"Where can we visit this recuperatin' outlaw?" Orion inquired. Neither he nor Holt mentioned anything about "The Angel" or his activities.

The two Rangers and Tag followed the marshal out of

the jail. Holt made sure Tag stayed close, right next to him. Even three men with shiny badges were barely enough disruption to slow the traffic bustling in all directions.

As they approached the hotel, Clark Worthington, the bulldog-jawed mayor of Sweetclover, stepped out onto the boardwalk. He had watched the marshal advance across the street with the Rangers. Crossing their paths was not a coincidence.

Gray strands had long ago given up hope of covering the mayor's head. Only a ring of hair remained, partly hiding his huge ears. Just below that sparse outcropping, two wide, sprawling eyebrows flourished and flinched with lives of their own. A dark brown buttoned vest and brown herringbone frock coat struggled to cover his girth. A four-in-hand tie that looked like it hadn't been undone in weeks garnished a shirt spotted with gravy stains. The heavy-jowled man preferred being called "Colonel Worthington" or just "Colonel."

Straightening his coat and vest, the mayor hailed the marshal. "A very fine day to you, Marshal Gentry," he called out. "Who are these gentlemen? Texas Rangers from the looks of their badges, yes?"

The marshal introduced the men with him. "Yes, indeed, Mayor Worthing…"

The mayor peered at the marshal, his bushy brows arched in slight disapproval.

"*Colonel* Worthington, this is Ranger Orion Higbee," he said. "And Ranger Holt Corrigan."

Worthington shook Orion's hand, but his eyebrows jumped at hearing the name of the second Ranger.

"*Holt Corrigan?*" he asked. "We've heard that name

in the newspaper. Surely, you're not the same Holt Corrigan who robbed the El Paso bank just a few months ago?"

Gentry started to step in and explain.

"No, *Mayor.* I *am* Holt Corrigan. Obviously, you've heard of me, but I never robbed the El Paso bank," he coldly corrected. "In fact, the president of that bank was someone I fought next to during the war. At Sabine. He and I are friends." His eyes bored into the fat, self-important man. "Surely."

"Ranger Corrigan received full amnesty," Orion added. "Pardoned by a federal judge an' recruited to ride for Texas by Cap'n Laird McCoy."

Holt's eyes did not let up and he did not offer his hand to the pompous mayor.

"Um, hmm, McCoy, I see…very well," Worthington stammered. "That is…interesting. We all had to do our part…during the war, that is. Glad it's over…uh, glad you're riding for Texas now."

Orion's face looked a little like a hot pepper went sideways down his throat. "You'll excuse us, Worthington. We've got important things to take care of," he said and walked away with the marshal down the boardwalk.

Holt waited for Tag to finish peeing on a lamppost next to the fat man. "Come on, boy." He smiled. Holt touched the brim of his hat and nodded in the direction of Worthington. "*Mayor…*" he said, with more than a hint of derision to his voice and turned to follow Orion and Gentry.

"I shoulda slapped the mouth offa that gotdammed pasty-faced pumpkin roller…" Orion grumbled when Holt caught up to him.

"He isn't worth it," Holt said. "Just a gasbag. Steak dinner says he didn't serve anywhere on any side."

Gentry walked next to the men. Although he did not add anything to the conversation, a broad grin crossed his face.

The drug store was quiet, an oasis of calm from the Sweetclover thoroughfare. Orion and Holt followed Marshal Gentry into the back where town doctor Bren Gustafson had his office and examination rooms. The clerk behind the front counter, a smiling Negro woman named Mary, offered Tag a pan of water while the dog waited for Holt to return.

Dr. Gustafson met the trio out in the hallway. Holt quietly suggested to Orion that he have the doctor look at his forearm. Orion was hesitant, but Holt insisted.

Stepping into Dr. Gustafson's office, Gentry and Holt looked on as the doctor unwrapped the bandanna posing as a bandage. The doctor inquired, "How did this happen?"

"Arrow," Orion said. He did not say anything about the possibility the gash could have been caused by shrapnel from one of his own Ketchum grenades. Holt stayed quiet and provided support to his partner.

"This looks to be healing nicely. As does that slice across your face."

"My medicine man right there is responsible," Orion said, pointing at Holt. "Some kinda Navajo paste an' a yarrow poultice."

"Well, it's done a good job of keeping infection away," the doctor said. "Let me wash those wounds and apply some ointment. And give your arm a better bandage." He tended to Orion's injuries. "Keep these clean and they should be just fine," he advised.

Dr. Gustafson then ushered the three lawmen into an examination room guarded by Don Baldwin, one of Gentry's deputies. He sat just outside the windowless room with a double-barreled shotgun across his lap.

Gentry quietly explained to the Rangers that his deputies were watching the door to keep the outlaw in custody, as well as to discourage any townspeople from trying to visit. "Plenty of folks rightly upset by the killing of their fellow citizens," he added.

Holt stared at the man lying there. One of the prisoner's legs was shackled to the bed and partially covered by a blanket. The patient's eyes were closed, but Holt could tell he wasn't asleep.

"This is the man wounded in the robbery?" Orion asked.

"Yes," Dr. Gustafson confirmed. "He already had a bullet wound in his shoulder, from another time. The slug in his thigh and the graze across his ribs came from the shoot-out here in the street."

"Thank you, Doctor," Holt said. "Marshal, we'll be a moment."

Orion closed the door on the doctor and the marshal. Gentry motioned to his deputy for them to ease down the hallway. The marshal knew from many years' experience that Rangers were not bound by as many conventions as local law enforcement.

Inside the room, Holt stood over the injured outlaw, anger beginning to well inside him. Orion moved up next to him. After a few moments, Holt quietly said to Orion, "This is one of The Angel's men from Wilkon. One of the bastards at the funeral. I don't think his bullets killed Silka though. He wasn't by the door where Silka fell." His eyes were slitted in growing fury, his teeth gritting.

"That bullet hole in his shoulder came from me or Deputy Logan Wheeler."

"You don't say," Orion cocked his head. The older Ranger sat on the bed next to the wounded outlaw and glared at the man, eyeing his bandaged shoulder. He then lifted the blanket to look at the man's ribs bound in cloth.

"You Mexican, or Kiowa?" Orion asked, studying the man.

The bandit opened his eyes, looking first at Orion, then up at Holt. His eyes blinked impassively and he did not answer.

"What's your name?" Orion continued. "Is your boss Father Beltran?" He looked for signs of recognition from the bandit. "Miguel Beltran?" Again, no answer. "*Cuál es tu nombre?*" No sign of reaction in the man's face.

"No *habla*, huh?" Orion said. He reached for the bandage on the outlaw's shoulder, unwrapping it in a wad and tossing it to the floor.

"Whattaya say now?" Orion sneered and jammed his thumb directly into the bullet hole in the man's shoulder.

An ear-piercing scream split the air and filled the hallway outside the door. The deputy tried to move past Gentry to go check on his prisoner. The marshal stopped him and shook his head silently. The doctor bolted toward the scream and swung the door open. Holt stood in his way.

"You can't treat him like that!" Dr. Gustafson protested and tried to get by Holt. "That's my patient!"

"This man's a prisoner," Orion called out. "Responsible for two…three…maybe more murders." he barked, not removing his eyes from the bandit. "He's gettin' a lil' cure for a cold shoulder."

"He isn't telling us much," Holt said. "Yet." He closed the door on the doctor.

"Let's try again," Orion growled at the prisoner. "What's your name?" He paused. "No?" He pushed his thumb into the bullet wound again, deeper this time, and the man screamed even louder. Orion removed his thumb, the bandit gasping in pain, trying to recover his breath.

"You better find your words. You're gonna tell us about your priest. Where he went. And you're gonna do it...*now*." His threat was like a machete.

The man tried to catch his breath to speak, but not fast enough for the Ranger. Once more, Orion shoved his thumb into the bloody hole, twisting his gore-covered finger inside the wound.

"Stop! Stop! Stop! I'll talk," he panted in English, through gritted teeth. "I'll talk."

"Make it quick. I'm thinkin' that bullet in your thigh needs examinin' next."

The man began speaking. He was a half-Kiowa called Neemo. He and the other riders had all been recruited by Miguel Beltran, a real Mexican priest who did both good, and terrible, things. Neemo had ridden for Father Beltran for only a few months. The other riders had been with the priest longer. They all helped with the priest's church services then robbed the towns. He had never seen Beltran take orders from anyone. He had also never seen the Father actually kill anyone but knew it had happened by hearing some of the other riders talk. He said that he did not know where the father and the others had gone when they crossed the river.

"You don't know?" Orion was unconvinced. "The marshal said Father Beltran an' his gang crossed into

Mexico. An' you don't know where?" The Ranger threw open the outlaw's blanket and started unfastening the bandage around his thigh.

"No! No! Please!!" the bandit pleaded. "I'm tellin' the truth. Honest ta God. I don't know where they went!"

Holt shook at his head angrily at the audacity of the man's declaration of God and honesty. He drew a pistol and pointed it at the prisoner's head. "You miserable son of a bitch," he shouted. "God doesn't believe you and neither do I!"

"I'm tellin' you," the bandit insisted. "I don't know where they went."

"That's enough!" Holt roared. "You're wasting our time!" He cocked his gun, the end of the barrel now just inches from the criminal's right eye. This man had been part of the group that killed Silka. He needed to die. His pathetic life must end right here.

Tears ran down the man's face. A widening circle of wetness soaked through his long johns and onto the bed. "It's the truth. I'm tellin' ya…it's the truth. I've never been to Mexico. That's the truth. I've never been there. I don't know where they went. No one said." He collapsed into sobs.

A vision of Four Shields jolted into Holt's awareness. "Keep your eyes open and your ears open. But most of all keep your heart and mind open. Your medicine will guide you if you listen…" he had said. Holt eyed the bandit, but no longer looked at him as prey to strike down. This man was not who he came after. He had just served his purpose, adding a little more to what they knew about The Angel.

Holt took in a deep breath and let it out, steeling himself and tamping down the fire that had started to consume him. Pulling the gun out of the outlaw's face, he slowly eased the hammer forward with his thumb, holstered the pistol and walked out the door.

Wiping the blood on his hand off with the bandage from the floor, Orion followed his partner. Walking out the door, he calmly told the doctor, "I think his wound popped open again."

CHAPTER THIRTY-SIX

H olt and Orion retrieved their horses from the jail and made their way to the livery. They would stable their horses for the night as they plotted their next move.

Dee Kennedy, the livery operator, was a gentle man the color of rich walnut with penetrating green eyes. Despite his chosen occupation, he was wearing clean overalls over a tidy gray shirt. A wide-brimmed straw hat was pushed back on his forehead as Holt and Orion walked in.

"Always nice ta meet Rangers." He smiled as they introduced themselves. His bright eyes were warm with curiosity as the lawmen inquired about stabling their four mounts.

Dee said he would gladly take in their horses and assured them he would see to their care himself. He also pointed out that the best bathhouse in town was just across the street. "Jun's" had the best hot water for bathing and shaving. "I can personally vouch for it."

Holt chuckled to himself. No doubt he and Orion

both needed the services of Jun's establishment. Definitely he and Tag could use a little sprucing up, having been on the trail since they left Wilkon. But Holt knew that was not what the livery operator was getting at. He grinned and appreciated the earnestness of this businessman, his eagerness to provide service.

The lanky Black man admired the Rangers' horses. "This one here looks lik' he could be givin' a bear a run fer its money," he said as he ran a hand across the shoulder of Orion's dun.

"Yes sir, bought 'im not long ago, over in Lodgepole," Orion said. "Gettin' mighty fond of 'im." He gave Dee a good-natured warning, "He just might be able to wrassle a bear. He can be a stretch orn'ry. If you like 'im, he'll like you back."

"You kin tell a lot 'bout people the way they treat hosses an' dogs, an' the way hosses an' dogs respond ta them," Dee remarked. "Don' have much use fer people who're ugly ta animals an' children."

"Me too," Orion agreed.

They moved over to Orion's bay. "This one runs all day, I 'magine," Dee observed, patting its chest.

"An' then some." Orion grinned. "He's a good one all right." Orion wanted Dee to check out the ragged crease on the bay's upper thigh. "Ran into some Comanches a few days ago."

"Bet that cut was mean lookin' when he firs' got hit," Dee said, smoothing the haunch carefully. The horse did not flinch or mind. Dee peered at the long, heavy scratch and said, "It's lookin' right fine now. Ain't infected. Looks ta be healin'."

"Secret concoction my partner has." Orion grinned and indicated in Holt's direction with his thumb.

"It did th' trick alright. Injun potion?" he asked Holt as he kneeled down to greet Tag, letting the dog get used to him before bestowing enthusiastic rubs to the dog's head and floppy ears.

"Navajo," Holt said. "Some hog's lard, beeswax, arnica, a little turpentine, and some cedar, I think.

"Wooo-eee," exclaimed Dee. "That'll do it, fer sure!" Tag shared the dark man's animated assessment with tail wags and a head search for more rubs.

"Tag, meet Mr. Dee Kennedy." Holt grinned. "Dee, meet Tag Along, Ranger Dog First Class."

"Happy dog! A good one too," Dee said, standing back up, but at Tag's insistence he leaned back over to administer a few more pat-pats. "Ya got some fine animals, fer sure."

"They've had some hard miles put on 'em recently," Orion said. "There's likely gonna be a lot more ahead."

"We're going after the men who shot up the town here." Holt nodded.

Dee nodded, a serious look crossing his genial face. "Yer goin' after that no-good preacher," he said in a hushed voice. "Be careful. He's evil. Knows what he's doin' too. Jus' disappears inta Mexico. No one'll cross o'er an' go get 'im."

Orion arched his brow. "You heard anythin' about where he might've headed?"

"I don' know fer sure, but if he really is a preacher lik' some say, there's a big enuf church jus' o'er the other side of that river. He could be hidin' there."

"A church?" Holt asked.

"Yassir, a decent size church. Not far from th' border. Bigger'n what we got here in Sweetclover."

"We haven't heard of this place before," Holt explained.

"I'm jus' guessin'. The church is in a lil' town, 'bout five miles give or take 'cross th' border. Good'a place as any ta hole up. In a town called Laelia."

"La…" Orion tried to repeat.

"La-ay-lee-uh," Dee enunciated perfectly.

"Laelia," Orion echoed. "An' you know this, how?"

"I don' know this as my fact, but my missus' does. She's a clerk an' sometime nurse fer Doc Gustafson."

"Is that Mary?" Holt asked.

"Tha's her." Dee smiled proudly.

"She's a nice lady. She watched Tag for me while we had business to discuss with the marshal and the doctor. She's been to Laelia?"

"She went a coupla times," Dee acknowledged. "Helpin' th' children there. She ain't been there'n awhile, tho. Busy 'nuf here."

"Do you think she'd mind if I ask her about her visits?" Holt inquired. "Do *you* mind, Dee?"

"Not a'tall. We're glad ta help th' Rangers."

Holt and Orion made arrangements with their newfound friend to have their horses rubbed down, grained and watered. They gave Dee a big portion of the payment in advance and headed back out to the street.

"I'll go see what Mary can add to what we know," Holt said to Orion. "Why don't you get us a couple of rooms to bunk in for the night?"

"All right. Gonna send a wire to Cap'n McCoy first. I'll send one to Wilkon too."

Holt and Tag walked across the main street of Sweet-clover. The late afternoon traffic had slowed to a less dangerous pace. As he moved through town, he absent-mindedly rubbed his hand across his chest, becoming aware of the feel of his medicine pouch. As always, there was a certain comfort to it. Unexplainable, but definitely there.

He entered the drug store, urging Tag to stay on the walkway. A mother with three small children in tow was completing the purchase of some kind of blue jar. They were a little intimidated at the long-haired Ranger who held open the door for them.

The pretty clerk saw the rugged Texas Ranger and her face lit up in recognition. "You're the Ranger with the dog." She smiled.

"Uh…yeah…yes'm…" Holt stumbled through his answer. "We go along together, me and Tag. Yeah, that's him." The Ranger badge had not given him a newfound way to talk comfortably with women. Hannah would shake his head in exasperation.

"What can I do for you?" she asked pleasantly. Her rich, walnut-colored complexion set off a plain blue calico dress and perfect white full apron. "Do you need to speak to the doctor again?"

"Oh…n-no, n-nothing like that," Holt stammered a bit. "I'm certain he doesn't care to see us again."

The woman nodded with a knowing smirk.

"Are you…Mary?" Holt asked. "Mary Kennedy?"

She nodded carefully, but affirmatively.

"My partner and I have been talking with your husband, Dee. Do you mind if I ask you a couple questions about Laelia?"

"Laelia? Okay," she said. "Not much to tell."

"Dee said the town had a large church and that a lot of people went there to get help. Is that correct?" Holt began.

"That's right. It was a place where many people used to go to get food and to get care."

"Used to go?"

"The mission at Laelia was run by an old priest, Father Rogers. He took care of everyone he could. Every now and then he would ask for help from towns here on the other side of the river. I went a couple of times with some people from here. We brought supplies for Father Rogers and would help with sick or injured people, mostly children."

"How big is Laelia?"

"The town itself isn't very big. Not even half the size of Sweetclover. The people would come from all around the area."

"How long ago was this?"

"Ohh, it's been more than a year ago. Maybe even a year-and-a-half ago."

"And what happened to Father Rogers?"

"I don't know," Mary said, shaking her head. "There were no more messages from Laelia. No more requests. No one heard anything and no one went back." She looked down and searched into memories. "There was talk that the church may have been abandoned. Maybe someone else just took over and ran things differently."

"Could this Father Beltran have taken it over?"

"Maybe." She shrugged. "But we haven't heard anything like that and he didn't mention being from Laelia during his services."

"Do you think the church, the building itself, would still be there?"

"It was a big, strong building. I think something bad would have needed to happen for it not to be there anymore."

"Thank you, Mary," Holt said, touching the brim of his hat. "That helps a lot. And thanks for keeping an eye on Tag earlier. I appreciate it."

Holt left the drug store and tracked down Orion outside the hotel. "I think we need to visit Laelia," he confirmed to the tall Ranger.

"You think he's there?"

"I got a feeling. If I'm wrong, it costs us a day."

Orion nodded. "Let's go see Mr. Kennedy."

———

Dee was a little surprised, but happy to see the Rangers so soon.

"We'll be takin' off at daylight," Orion said. "Gonna leave my scratched-up bay an' Holt's buckskin 'til we get back. Hopefully gone no more'n a day."

"Bad men an' Rangers always seem ta be ridin'," Dee observed. He paused for a moment and looked carefully in all directions before speaking again, softly, "That'll mean yer gonna be crossin' th' river, don' it?"

Orion looked briefly at Holt before confirming, "Yes sir, that's what we're gonna do. But no one needs to be knowin' that, my friend."

"Yer mounts'll be ready to run for ya," Dee declared, a broad smile on his face.

———

Jun's Bathhouse had been the Rangers' first stop of the evening. They made the decision to not get too slicked up though. They would be riding out in the morning and did not want to smell like roses while attempting to sneak up on bandits. Tag got the same treatment, just some hot water scrubbing, but no fragrant soap suds. Dusty trail clothes were left with Jun's laundress and swapped for clean outfits from their saddlebags.

They now sat in the far corner of the lobby restaurant, away from the bar and its boisterous crowd. The two men looked forward to a good, non-trail meal at the hotel and a real bed. A couple of big steaks, large helpings of chili beans, sliced beets, and warm tortillas were brought out by a young girl.

"How 'bout some big fluffy biscuits too, please." Orion grinned at the girl.

"And a pot of coffee," added Holt. "Please."

They ate in silence. No one refused the two Rangers, so Tag quietly enjoyed a bowl of beef stew under their table.

A table holding Mayor Worthington and his party, boisterously carrying on, sat at the far end of the room. The pompous fat man tried hard to ignore the Rangers dining in the corner but could not help staring at them. Often.

Holt and Orion finished dinner with a request for more coffee and a couple of glasses of Irish whiskey. Marshal Gentry entered the restaurant and ambled to their table. They insisted he join them.

Sitting down, Gentry smiled. "You find out any more information?"

"Yes, we did, Marshal." Orion grinned. "An' we're 'bout to discover just how good the pie is." He held up three fingers at the young waitress. "'Nother mug too," he told the girl.

"We don't mean to be cagey or disrespectful,

Marshal," Holt said. "Best you not know exactly. I hope you'll understand—and appreciate."

Three pieces of flaky, juicy apple pie were laid in front of them. Holt cut a small piece and laid it down for Tag.

"I've been riding a long time," Gentry acknowledged. "No offense taken. I know what you're up against and where you're likely headed."

"Hopin' Doc Gustafson'll understand that we had to do what we did," Orion added.

"Doctors only see hurt that needs healing. It doesn't matter to them who's wearing the wounds."

They finished their pie and Gentry declined the offer of some Irish whiskey. It was time to make sure the deputy guard was changed at the doctor's office.

"We 'preciate your help, Marshal," Orion said.

Holt nodded his agreement.

Gentry thanked them for the pie. "Ride careful, Rangers. We used to say, 'Keep your powder dry.' How about now I just say, 'Keep your heads down.'" He shook their hands and said good night.

Holt gazed around the room. "I'll have another quick glass, but I hear a bed upstairs calling my name awful loud."

"I'm not too far behind." Orion yawned.

CHAPTER THIRTY-SEVEN

The Rio Grande was not far away and Laelia was only an hour or so beyond that. If the Catholic church at Laelia was, indeed, The Angel's hiding place, that meant he was dangerously close.

Assuming their long-shot hunch was correct, the mission to cross the border river, capture this madman, and bring him back to Texas without being detected was not going to be easy. Grabbing him would have to be successfully accomplished under the cover of night, while at least four or five—or more—of his henchmen would battle to prevent that from happening. The return to Texas with their prisoner would be a race to the border before Mexican authorities could discover or detain them. Proper timing was vital to the mission.

So was luck.

Orion was aboard his dun, Holt rode his bay. If all went well, they would be back in Sweetclover in little more than a day. They reduced the amount of food and gear they carried. Their foodstuffs were the standards designed for cold camp travel...jerked beef, corn dodgers and hard biscuits. Orion talked Holt into bringing some apples. "Mighty refreshin' when you're trekkin' in the desert," he said. Both Rangers carried extra pistols and boxes of cartridges in their bags. Orion found room for the remaining fireworks. All their extra gear was left for safekeeping with the marshal.

They left Sweetclover in a steady lope, alternating to a breath-gathering trot to keep the horses reasonably fresh. Tag rested easily on Holt's saddle in front of him. Holt was certain the dog had to still be tender from the kick to his ribs, but Tag did not appear or act the worse for wear. The floppy-eared dog was happy to be along for the ride. A swarm of sparrows, resting in a post oak, lit up the morning with songs to celebrate the riders' parading by. As was his duty, Tag kept a watchful eye, just in case any birds decided to attack from above.

The two men arrived at the Rio Grande just before midday. The sun was not quite ready to deliver the scorching presence its full summer self would bring, but it was promising to be a hot, parched day ahead. Mexico and, possibly, The Angel lay on the other side of the roiling water. Holt had never been to Mexico before, only glimpsing the land across the river on his one visit to El Paso after the war. Here, the famed boundary was mostly murky water snapping at the leash of the shoreline.

They had no intention of stopping. They needed to get to the other side, the sooner the better. Doing so without being observed was crucial. Holt immediately began looking for a good place to cross. He took a few moments to survey their surroundings and determine what he could about the footing below the surface of the river.

It was not particularly deep nor wide here, but river

crossings were never to be trifled with. What he was looking for were tracks, someplace where other animals had entered. Not cattle tracks, they would walk into an ocean drop-off, but rather the hoofmarks of deer or pronghorn. They had good sense and a knack for finding firm, gentle slopes into the water. He found some faint deer sign leading down to the river. Tag hopped down from the saddle and sniffed at the path's entrance.

"This looks to be as good a place as any," Holt called out, careful not to shout too loudly.

"You know, in our capacity as Texas Rangers we can't legally cross the Rio Grande without authorization…"

"Wha…?"

"It would put us in violation of international law," Orion continued his deadpan warning.

"Who's going to know…or tell?"

"I dunno. Just thought someone should mention it." Orion shrugged, smirking. "In case someone asks."

Holt shook his head at his partner's humor.

"Let your horse drink if it wants to," Orion instructed. "It needs to know this is natural, not a threat."

Holt did not need the coaching but did not resent the reminder either. He had already discovered that Orion cared deeply for—and knew a lot about—horses. It was just his way to share.

Tag was already starting to splash across. The water would probably get chest-high on a horse, so the dog would have to swim eventually. Touching the cardinal feather at his hatband, Holt and his bay followed Tag into the water. Orion followed just behind.

Holt stayed downstream from Tag and kept a careful eye on the dog in case the current became too much. The dog was strong and eager to get to the other side. It appeared that Holt's assessment of depth and current was fairly accurate, but he stayed ready and let the bay navigate its own way across the dark, cool water.

Reaching the bank, Holt held the reins in one hand and a big fistful of mane in the other as the bay charged hard up the bank's incline and stood in the country of Mexico. Alighting to check his cinch, he watched as a moment later Tag arrived, clearing the bank easily. The dog and the bay had a shaking contest to rid themselves of water. Holt did not want to stand out in the open, so he moved his horse to an area protected by large mesquite and ocotillo.

Orion splashed up from the bank. It was now the dun's turn to have a good shake. "Woooo!" Orion chuckled as he stood in his stirrups, "Man, when they shake, it rattles all your teacups, don't it?" The dun's movements prompted a second round of shaking from Tag and Holt's bay. Orion declared, "If there's a report to be made, this ain't even the Rio Grande. We'll call it 'Tag Along Creek!'"

Holt smiled and produced a package of jerky from a saddlebag and offered some to Orion. Tag got a good-sized chunk too.

While he was down off his horse, Holt checked the cinch on Orion's horse. "Mexico, huh? Doesn't look or feel different," he said.

"It'll feel different all right if we get discovered by some *federales*."

"Speaking from experience?" Holt grinned.

"Let's just say Rangers have often been known to cross the border to retrieve cattle that's been stolen from American ranchers. Or so I've heard."

Holt shook his head and laughed. "Your cinch is good to go." Before remounting, he left a small tobacco tribute for the safe crossing.

"I do know we need to keep outta sight between here an' Laelia," Orion said. "There won't be much time to get this done either. We best be back here by this time tomorrow, if not earlier."

"You're saying we're headed for a picnic then," Holt acknowledged.

Orion looked around, getting his bearings. "Given what Mrs. Kennedy said, Laelia's 'bout five, maybe six, miles ahead of us. Bearin' south an' a little west from here."

They stayed off roads and known trails. The gravelly landscape, washed occasionally with sandy soil, caused them to have to pick their way, slowing their progress. Tag pranced alongside, wearing his leather shoes for protection against the rocky terrain.

Ahead was a belt of rolling hills, distinguished only by a thin topping of yellowish rock and connected to a line of scraggly acacia and emory oak trees. Ground teaming with saguaro, ocotillo and other brush stretched for miles. The spring bloom was just starting. Soon, a remarkable carpet of wildflowers and cactus blossoms would provide stark beauty to this harsh land.

It was early afternoon and the spring sun washed over the mosaic of shrubs and grasses and painted a layer of gold on the underbellies of clouds. Darting among the gilt-edged fluffiness was a red-tailed hawk, appearing like a copper dart. They passed a box canyon where murky shapes lurked. It was easy to imagine that a shadow was more than darkness. Holt got the feeling that spirits were close.

The heat made the distance shimmery as they huddled by a small rock outcropping to give Tag a breather and let the horses blow. Large creosote bushes and a couple of mesquite trees had gathered near the rocks, providing a screen from the afternoon heat and glare. A piece of jerky, an apple, and some hard biscuits renewed the Rangers' energy. Tag's too. Holt's bay and Orion's dun munched on grama grass that grew in clumps on the desert floor. The horses' hooves were checked carefully. This was stone bruise territory. When they cooled down, the mounts would get hatfuls of water.

"We're makin' good time," Orion observed. "We can rest here a bit."

"Are you sure? We sure as hell don't want to be spotted in broad daylight. And we're going to need enough light to get a good look at the place."

"We can't get there too early either. We're doin' good. Might even have time for a bit of a catnap," Orion said.

"All right, you go ahead. I'm okay to keep watch."

Orion nestled against one of the shaded boulders and pulled his flat-brimmed hat down over his face. Soon, he and Tag were snoring softly.

Holt thought he heard a soft *whuff-whuff-whuff* of wings and looked up to see a burrowing owl with a large beetle in its mouth whooshing down to a rock ledge thirty yards away. He was surprised to see an owl at this time of day.

He pulled the medicine pouch from under his shirt and took out the red sacred stone, holding it in his palm. He stared at the white star-shape on the stone and ran the fingers of his other hand across it. Painful words from Silka the day the judge's body was discovered slivered through his thoughts. "Something tell Silka this not work of Bordner," he had said. "Judge's body hold…something *akugō*… More evil." And before he died in Deed's arms, Silka had claimed again, "*Akugō… Waru…* Evil… evil person…was here."

Orion and Tag resettling their nap positions caused Holt's reflections to evaporate like a gust clearing away chimney smoke. He placed his sacred stone back into the medicine pouch and tucked the pouch back under his shirt, but not before he added some more tobacco inside.

The words of Silka continued to echo in his thoughts, joined now by his own vow to his brothers, "I need to do this. This is what *I* can do for *us*."

CHAPTER THIRTY-EIGHT

What was left of daylight slanted long rays across Holt and Orion as they edged on their stomachs to the lip of a small, hilly ridge. They had hobbled the horses a couple hundred yards back against a protected rock outcropping. Tag was convinced to stay in the shade of the rocks with the horses, a piece of jerky sealing the deal. The Rangers were not going to be gone long.

A broken line of odd-sized creosote bushes took station overlooking a small dusty town. The Rangers picked two of the larger ones to crawl under, partly for concealment, partly for shade from the heat. Hats off, they slowly peered over the top of the rise and got their first glimpse down into the quiet village of Laelia.

"Does this look like the hideout of some bastard called The Angel?" Orion asked.

"It's no Kendrick," Holt said straight-faced.

They both chuckled in spite of the situation.

"Hard to tell," Orion continued. "He could be here. It sure feels like he should be."

From their vantage point they could see all of Laelia. Just as Dee and Mary described, there was a large church, which was the tiny town's distinguishing landmark. It was located to their left and marked that end of town. The main road, also down to their left, came into the village from the open emptiness they just crossed. The wide avenue made a right turn in front of the church and split the town down the middle. Four buildings and five tiny houses, along with the church and its small cemetery, comprised the whole of Laelia. The two largest buildings were the church and a cantina, which sat at opposite ends of the village from each other. The front of the cantina was where the main street veered again and continued out into the desert.

The town was silent with no activity. No people were out and about. Four or five horses and mules dotted various hitching posts along the street. A rickety wagon carrying an old man and a boy drove into town. The wagon stopped midway up the main street at the general store and both ventured inside.

The church was plain and looked to be like most houses of worship—a big block building with one very large room where services were held. It was modestly constructed with thick adobe brick.

"It doesn't look run down to me," Holt said quietly. "Mary and Dee guessed it would still be around."

"Yeah, the roof's still in decent shape," Orion said. "It looks like it's bein' used for somethin'."

The church had one main entrance with large double doors that faced the street. Small windows flanked the doors. Two hitching posts sat out in front of the entrance. The long side of the building facing the Rangers had one big window, marking the halfway part of the structure.

They could not tell if the opposite side of the building was similar, but assumed it was. In the churchyard along their side the building, random clumps of twisted underbrush and creosote butted up against gnarled greasewood haphazardly placed there by the elements. They could see part of a small cemetery on the far side of the church. The lawmen would have to change their position to get a better glimpse of what the other side looked like.

A rider suddenly rode into town, loping at a good clip. He reined up hard in front of church and tied it to one of the posts out front. The dark-skinned man wore a weather-beaten sombrero. Crisscrossed bandoliers of ammunition glinted in the sun as he briskly walked inside.

"Think he's here for Communion?" Holt observed. "Just the one rider though."

"Only one that we can see," Orion corrected.

Far to their left, in the back of the church but still connected to the building, stood a smaller adjoining structure—maybe only one room. It was only about a quarter-size of the main part of the church and only stood about half as tall. The wall of this connecting building that faced them was also constructed of thick adobe and had a tiny window. There was likely some kind of an interior wall or door that opened this part into the main portion of the church. From their vantage point, they could not see much more of this structure.

"Anything else we need to see, we're going to have to get over there," Holt said, gesturing far to their left. "Behind it all somehow."

Orion nodded his agreement.

The men used their current position to survey their next move. They turned their attention to the area behind the church and cemetery. That would have to be their post if they were going to move against whoever was holed up here.

"There, behind the church and cemetery, see where the land slopes up?" Holt pointed behind the graveyard. "Maybe that's the bank of a wash or something that slopes down and away. Could be a good place to muster and keep our horses out of sight."

"Yeah, I can't tell if the back of that rascal is sloped or flat," Orion said. "Hope it ain't too steep."

The area they were looking at was not as high as they were now, but it was closer to the church and would still provide them with a view of the back of the building. The ridge ran diagonal to that end of town for at least a half mile or more and was scattered with scrubby vegetation of varying heights and shapes. It was hard to tell the lay of the land from where they were now. They would have to check it out to be sure.

"Even if it's a trench or a gully back there, we'll be above the church," Holt continued. "If we're lucky, we can hide behind it."

"Lucky? We're askin' to be downright charmed. All this hide-an'-seek don't mean squat if The Angel isn't here."

"Let's say he is," Holt said determinedly.

"I think he's here too."

They eased themselves out from under the bushes and edged their way down off the ridge. To be extra careful, they crouched most of the way back to the horses. Tag's tail thumped the air in greetings upon Holt's return. Hatfuls of water rewarded the dog and horses, with Holt and Orion taking a few swallows as well.

From the outcropping, they could see the road as it

stretched into town. Unfortunately, the ground sloped just enough the wrong way that they could not see back into the distance as far as they would have liked. Their next move was to cross the road. After crossing, they would need to swing a wide loop in order to come up behind the church and cemetery to the sloping area they had just studied.

To be seen out in the open making these moves would risk getting caught. And they had already observed a rider, a possible Angel henchman, journey into town from that direction. But to attempt this exploration in the dark, unaware of the terrain and not seeing their final location, would be foolish.

They decided to wait just a bit longer for shadows to lengthen. Even fifteen minutes would help make a difference.

They kept their eyes on the road coming and going into town. All clear. It was time. Tag rode in front of Holt on the saddle. Orion led the way. They took care to keep their dust down and rode single file across the road, swinging over to rocky ground rather than leaving imprints in the softer, sandier soil. Clear of the road, the Rangers hugged close to larger creosote bushes and mesquite, anything to disrupt their horse-and-rider silhouettes.

Dusk was nearly upon them when they arrived at their target behind the churchyard. It turned out to be a dry gully with a bank that inclined steadily up to a rounded crest that sloped down toward the church and cemetery. Holt left Tag and his hat on the saddle and handed his reins to Orion. He crossed the gully and scrambled up the bank. Peeking over the top, he saw the back of the church laid out in front of him. Moving back down to Orion, he reported the location would be good enough to work.

Holt and Orion tied the horses on the closest bank of the gully behind a small family of bunched mesquite and stunted cottonwoods waiting patiently for the next rain. Tag guarded the mounts and happily worked on a piece of jerky.

The lawmen carefully scrambled up the bank together to get a better look.

The first thing they noticed was something they could not see from their earlier vantage point. There were four more horses tied to a hitch rack on the far side of the church.

"They rode out of Sweetclover with four total," Holt said.

Orion stared down at the church and chewed on his lip. "There's five tied up here now. But no mule." He sniffed and exhaled.

Holt mumbled quietly, "The hand isn't dealt yet." He did not take his eyes off the church. Momentarily, he pointed out, "The stove attached to that chimney in back is cranking out smoke."

"It just occurred to me…I believe this back part is where a priest is s'posed to live," Orion said. "I believe they call it a *rec-tory*."

"I'll take your word for it," Holt said, studying the yard below. "Is it big enough for five or six men?"

"I don't know 'bout that," Orion answered. "But they got a big ol' damn church they can spread out in too."

They noticed there was a tumbled-down structure up against a wall behind the church, likely the remnants of a small shed. It was difficult to discern its original purpose. Maybe it had been for storage. The roof looked to have collapsed straight down, now lying flat on the ground. It would not present any concern for the Rangers.

They waited patiently as darkness closed in. Sundown was beginning to suck the warmth from the earth.

In their position elevated from the street, they could hear faint clip-clops growing louder. Entering town from the far end, two riders approached, one atop a horse, the other riding a mule.

In the dusk, the lanterns of Laelia helped illuminate two dark-skinned riders. The man on horseback had a heavy mustache and long black hair with familiar thick braids. The rider on the mule had russet-colored skin and thick brown hair greased into place.

"That's The Angel," Holt said in a dead calm voice.

"You're sure?"

"That's him all right. That braided bastard was with him in Wilkon. He's the one who killed Silka."

"We're charmed indeed. Now we can open the ball."

The Angel and his henchman tied up their mounts in front of the church and walked through the main doors.

Right down the bank from them, the door of the rectory opened and a bandit leaned out to throw a pan of liquid out into the yard, slamming the door shut when he finished. From where they hid now, the Rangers could see anyone coming or going through that door. Like the side they had already inspected, the wall of this smaller building that faced the cemetery also had a tiny window.

Lights suddenly spilled out in front of the church. Boisterous voices followed. From the lawmen's perch, they could not see anything until three men appeared in the street. The church had no exterior gaslights or torches. This side of town was lit only with moonlight and a few lanterns from further up the street trying to help.

One of the bandits came around to the side of the church and untied a horse. Rider and horse took off loping up the street. The other two bandits shouted something in Spanish at him as he turned at the cantina and rode off into the desert. These two, now in full view, walked up the street in rowdy conversation. The distance kept Holt and Orion from hearing exactly what was being said, just hearing faint talking and laughter.

The bandits' stroll ended at the cantina and they went inside. Before long they re-emerged, each carrying a large, covered basket and big jug of something. They headed back down the middle of the street to the church and entered once again through the main doors.

"They don't appear too concerned. Looks like that dinner is for more than two."

"An' drinks for more'n two."

Holt nodded grimly. "We're going to let those jugs have some effect before we go say hello."

CHAPTER THIRTY-NINE

Deep night introduced a frosty twang to the air. Holt tied a dark blue bandanna around his neck and donned his leather gloves.

Midnight had come and gone. The Rangers determined the alcohol consumed inside the church had enough of a head start. Both lawmen had taken off their spurs and anything else that might make a noise. This was one time that Holt definitely wanted the medicine pouch under his shirt to remain there. He gripped the claw inside his coat pocket and envisioned his panther spirit, the *ndołkah*, and asked that it serve him well tonight. He made sure both Smith & Wessons were ready and the Winchester loaded. He stuffed extra handfuls of cartridges into his pockets, checking to see if they rattled when he moved. Orion had also stuffed his pockets with extra bullets and was making sure his guns were ready.

Earlier, Tag had happened upon a gopher burrow and lucked into bagging two of them. An owl silently swooped overhead, probably because it smelled fresh kill, but Holt hoped its fly-over was a salute from the spirits. Kneeling and rubbing Tag's head, he quietly but firmly told the dog he needed him to watch the horses and to stay put, right here. "Stay! You hear me? I'll be right back. Stay here, Tag. Stay!" He considered tying up the dog, but worried that Tag would get frustrated and bark. Holt hoped the instruction and Tag's hunting bounty would keep the dog occupied and close to the horses.

Holt stood and looked at Orion. "Is this going to work?"

Orion responded with a brief nod, "Let's say yes."

"What's our 'rally?'"

"Our what?"

"Rally cry. All clear. I'm not going to just call out if you're still stalking. You shouldn't either. Call it a secret word."

Orion thought for a quick moment. "How 'bout 'Sherman?'"

"How about 'peckerhead?'" The response came with a quick laugh.

"I like it."

"Give me fifteen minutes and then let it rip any time after that."

"Just keep your head down, peckerhead."

Holt wheeled and started advancing across the gully, away from the church. He kept on the far side of the slope, carefully traversing the outskirts of the graveyard to conceal his movements. He moved around the perimeter, keeping to the uneven shadows, ever alert.

He pulled the bandanna up around his face. He was not breathing heavily, but the night was getting colder and breath smoke appeared as he exhaled. The bandanna would help diffuse most of that.

This was a time when most men would be on high adrenaline, with heart racing and throat dry. In fights, Holt had always found an inner quiet, like now. It just seemed to take over and almost made things move in slow motion. Maybe it was because he had been in battle situations many times in this life—and in other lives. He knew his spirit demanded that he fight. This was his inner panther. That's what he was, that's what he had always been.

The gully continued on into the desert, but Holt had traveled beyond the cemetery and cleared the chase of the Laelia lanterns. He looked with all his senses before moving again, angling stealthily down to his right. He quickly made his way to the rear of a tiny house. The little cabin stood on the other side of the cemetery, just past the churchyard. The deep, dark cover provided by the back of the building embraced him upon his arrival. Noiselessly as possible, he levered his Winchester and thumbed the hammer forward until needed.

He took off his hat and peered slowly around the corner. Shadows were everywhere. His position behind the house put him almost even with the one big window on this side of the church. Through that opening, he saw a quick glimpse of someone moving inside. Oversized silhouettes flickered on the inner walls. Leaning back into the black void behind the tiny cabin, he put his hat back on, touched the cardinal feather in the band and waited.

When Orion gave his signal, Holt would move around to the side of the house and nestle himself among some scrubby greasewood bushes. From there, he would have a clear view of the front entrance where mounts were tied, including The Angel's mule. He would also be less than thirty feet from the side hitching rack where the rest of the horses were tied. From there he would be in position to cut down anyone trying to get away.

He was not sure how long it took him to get to his position. The last pocket watch he owned lay trampled and shattered somewhere on a battlefield outside of Nashville. It didn't matter, he was ready. Silka—and war —had taught him the power of patience combined with the added force of surprise. When every instinct was to attack, there was value in waiting. Besides, impatient men usually died first.

Orion made his way over the rise and straight down the hill toward the rectory, crouching as low as possible to blend in. Although some stunted cottonwoods stood between him and the building, helping with his conceal-ment, he still needed to move quickly and carefully. And hope no one stepped outside. His next move would be the trickiest and most dangerous—at least before the bullets started flying.

Hunched over like a bear, Orion moved swiftly from the cottonwoods to the back wall of the rectory, placing himself just next to its door. He listened for any sound of discovery and took a moment to gather his breath. He crept around the corner into the dark area just outside the window. He stared at the tumbled-down shed to his right, letting his eyesight adjust to the new level of darkness.

Just then, the back door swung open. An outlaw stag-gered through the entry, the middle-of-the-night stillness giving extra volume to his boots as he clomped his way outside. Oil lamps lit up the interior, causing the open door to become a beacon. The door slammed behind the bandit as he took a few more weaving, drunken steps out into the yard. He hummed an off-key tune through a lit cigarette dangling from his lips as he proceeded to relieve himself.

A dull thud and heavy flop to the ground were the only sounds as Orion's rifle butt struck the outlaw's head. The Ranger drug the unconscious body out of sight around the corner, depositing it along the wall where he had just been hiding.

It was time. This bandit would be missed before too long. Holt would be in position by now. Orion set down his rifle, propping it against the wall.

A match strike flared the night with a snap of light. Orion's other fist held three Roman candles. The hissy *zzhsshh* of fuses was a bright cacophony in the night, as he took one step and jammed the fireworks through the little window of the rectory. He counted on the flaming balls having enough action to wreak havoc all throughout the church. He picked up his Henry and darted across the darkness back to the cottonwoods.

For a heart-stopping moment, Orion wondered if the candles were duds, but soon bursts of flashing lights, muffled booms, and shouts erupted inside the place of worship.

The back door slammed open. Exploding light and smoke streamed outside, along with a bandit trying to put out part of his smoldering coat. Orion pumped two quick rounds from his Henry into the man.

Hearing the first explosions, Holt moved into the bushes. He could see the interior of the church illuminated by a bouncing frenzy of fireballs. Orion's plan had worked! An outlaw suddenly rushed through the front doors, slapping at sparks and smoke on his clothing. Holt leveled three quick shots from his Winchester. Two of the shots hit the Comanchero in the back and another ripped into his neck.

In the main part of the church, a young Kiowa bandit had seen his buddy run out into withering gunfire ahead of him. With flaming balls careening around him, he crept up to the big window to get a look outside. He took a cautious step forward to peer out the edge of the frame. He saw nothing. Nothing but darkness outside and intense flashes around him inside.

He raised up, pistol cocked and ready, but revealed himself just a bit too much. A fireball illuminated the young bandit's profile. Holt's Winchester moved in a blur toward the window. His first two shots struck the bandit in the shoulder. The Kiowa's pistol fired reflexively, its bullet ripping into the roof of the tiny house where Holt was hiding. Holt fired once more tearing a black hole in the bandit's cheek. The Kiowa's body buckled and he fell to the floor.

As suddenly as it started, the gunfire and fireworks ended. Quiet descended over the church and surrounding yard. Holt reloaded his rifle. Minutes passed. No movements. No sounds.

Holt was not certain what was happening with Orion around back, while Orion was unsure how his partner fared. Their best estimation going in was that there were five bandits and The Angel. Holt knew he had only taken care of two.

Patience was always vital in a fight. Holt had spent years honing the skill. It was a basic tenet of battle. But there was a point in any battle, of any kind, when it was time to move out and meet the fight head on.

Like a mountain cat tracking its next victim, Holt crept to the main doors, avoiding the windows as best he could. The doors were now standing wide open. Holt paused against the exterior wall, looking at the body lying motionless near the street. The acrid smell of fireworks gunpowder from inside the church reached his nose as he stood just outside the doors.

He leaned his Winchester against the wall and drew one of his Russian Smith & Wessons, cocking it as quietly as possible. Crouching down to reduce his silhouette, he rounded the corner and edged silently inside.

The main part of the church was lit by dingy oil lamps. Smoke hung everywhere. Immediately taking cover behind a long wooden pew, Holt blinked several times attempting to get his eyes adjusted to the dusky light.

Through the haze he saw candles burning on the altar at the far end of the room. Below the flickering lights, a figure in a hooded robe was huddled over, on its knees at the altar.

Out in the stillness of the back churchyard, Orion advanced directly to the back door, cautiously, yet steadily. The body of the second bandit he downed lay in the doorway. A swift, sharp kick to the man's ribs brought no response. He levered his rifle and stepped over the form and waded into the smoldering murkiness.

In the dark corner of the backyard of the rectory, the dilapidated roof of the collapsed shed gently hinged open. As they observed the area at dusk, what had appeared to Holt and Orion to be the remains of a caved-in shack was actually the decrepit door of an old root cellar.

Skulking up from the earth below, the man known as The Angel emerged from the underground pit, a pistol in his hand.

When the Roman candles and gunfire began bursting around him, the killer priest had made his way into Father Rogers's old underground storeroom, where provisions for the poor had once been kept. He waited down there until the firework explosions and gunfire ceased. With the bangs and blasts now died away, he was determined to see who had disturbed his sanctuary. Clad in black clothing, the dark-featured Angel glided silently through the night to the back door of the rectory.

Inside, Orion stood in the entryway between the rectory and main part of the church, the large door separating them thrown wide open. The kneeling figure at the altar was just a few feet from him. He pointed his rifle at the man and demanded, "Stand an' raise your hands, or crows eat your dead eyes."

The cowled man did not move or speak. Intensity grew.

Suddenly, the figure toppled. The hooded robe fell open revealing the dead Kiowa from the window.

A voice hissed at Orion from behind. "And after the feast, the crows will have you for dessert."

Without turning around, Orion barked. "That chapter an' verse?"

The Angel smirked. "Book of Lead, the whole chapter."

As Holt began to creep out from behind the pew, a bandit lying in wait to his left sprang from the darkness. Holt's revolver roared three times in a continuous string of sound and lead. The outlaw's braided head exploded in a crimson mist and snapped backward like it was on a hinge. He folded to his knees, then collapsed headfirst into the ground.

Startled at the gunfire, Orion and The Angel were

momentarily distracted, but the evil priest returned his attention to the Ranger and cocked his gun. In a blur, a streaking figure rushed through the darkness of the rectory and pounced with a growl.

Tag!

The dog landed on the killer's arm as the gun blasted into the wooden floor. Tag's jaws locked onto The Angel's forearm in a death grip of teeth and snarls.

Man and beast struggled frantically, one to break loose, the other to not let go. The Angel could not free himself from the dog's fury. Orion could only watch the ferocious struggle. He was unable to shoot for fear of hitting the dog. He inched closer.

Using the arm that was being torn to shreds, The Angel tried to hold the dog away and unsheathe the bayonet in his boot with his other hand. With the priest in that awkward position, Orion stepped closer and swung his Henry like a club, the barrel making a heavy thud as it landed across the side of The Angel's neck and shoulder.

Staggering, the priest was momentarily defenseless. Orion immediately rammed the butt of his rifle into the man's midsection. The priest doubled over gasping for air. Tag continuing his attack on the outlaw's forearm.

Holt hurriedly moved in, his gun still drawn. He coaxed the dog into releasing its grip. "Let go, Tag! Let go!" The dog came quickly to the Ranger's side, panting deeply.

Orion knocked the pistol out of the stunned priest's hand with another sharp jab of his rifle stock and kicked the gun out of the way.

Holt stepped in front of the bent-over Angel. Rage once again blazed inside him. "On your knees, you miserable bastard," he growled. "And put your hands on top of your head." The priest, still unable to find his breath, struggled to comply.

Holt glared at the man on the floor like wounded prey. This man was pure evil. A killer who dared to perform in God's name. He aimed his pistol the priest's face. A wrath with the heat of a thousand suns exploded within him. For a moment, Holt had a vision of himself launching into the priest and literally ripping him apart. The image instantly drew back into the deep recess of his mind and he realized he was still aiming his gun.

"Nakashima Silka died because of you," Holt snarled. "You murdered Oscar Pence. And Felix Sanchez. You need to die." He cocked the hammer back.

Hate raced through Holt's very being as he looked down the barrel of the pistol. Kill him now. Vengeance served. Resign and go home. No one would say anything. The world would be rid of an evil killer.

You promised your brothers.

Everything in him wanted to scream and unload his gun into the face of this evil creature.

"*Do it! Damn you, do it!*" The Angel screamed.

In that moment, something inside Holt somewhere on the edge of his perception—a voice he felt, a feeling he heard—kindled a new light, driving away the shadows within.

He became aware of the weight of the medicine pouch around his neck. Like a pot of coffee that boiled too long, the blackness inside him burned away. Holt looked down at the priest in disgust.

"Father Whatever-the-Hell-Your-Name-Is..." he said calmly. "You'll meet your god, but not today." He eased the hammer forward and returned the gun to his shoulder holster. The movement caused his medicine pouch to move slightly. He rubbed his hand across his chest, acknowledging its influence.

The priest spit in Holt's direction. The Ranger responded with a vicious slap across The Angel's face and an equally forceful return smack with his backhand. Tag barked at the commotion. The priest tasted blood in his mouth.

"My spirits have convinced me to allow you to live," Holt hissed. "But you don't have to be healthy." He spied the cross worn by The Angel, large, silver-finished metal detailed with exquisite green glass details. "Only a man truly of God can wear this," he growled as he reached down and angrily tugged at the cross. The savage yank broke the cross's heavy chain. He stuffed the crucifix in his coat pocket.

Still holding his rifle on the priest, Orion pushed at the prisoner's back with his foot. "On your stomach, cherub," he ordered. "Now!" Holding the Henry one-handed like a pistol, Orion tossed Holt some pigging string from his coat pocket. "Tie his hands behind him. Tight."

After securing the binds to his wrists, Holt reached down and removed the bayonet from the priest's boot sheath. Holding it in one hand and placing it tip down onto the floor, he stomped on the blade with his boot heel until it bent. He tossed the weapon toward The Angel's abandoned pistol.

"Doesn't look very angelic now, does he?" Orion said. He then seized on the other part of their mission that needed to go well. "We gotta get back to Texas before the sun an' anyone sees us." He headed for the front door. "Watch him, I'll be right back," he called over his shoulder.

"Who are you?" the killer demanded. "You have no idea what you have done."

Holt ignored the man and started peering into the rectory to see what was there.

Orion returned through the front doors, leading one of the horses from outside. He tied it up securely by the altar where The Angel was lying. "Help me get this asshole up in the saddle," he told Holt.

"Where are my men? Have you killed them all?" The Angel protested.

"I'm afraid your boys are all shot up," Orion said, getting more leather and rope ready.

"I am a man of God!" he hollered, squirming on the floor. "We are doing divine work!"

Orion tugged the killer's head up by his hair so they could look each other in the eyes. "There's no god worth havin' who'd have the likes of you speakin' for him. Now, shut up or you'll be meetin' him right quick." He pulled on the hair more forcefully, hauling The Angel to his knees. Holt grabbed the priest's cartridge belt, yanking the prisoner to a standing position. The gun belt was unbuckled, dropped to the floor and kicked away.

Together they hoisted The Angel onto the horse. The barrel-chested man did not struggle. Holt drew his pistol and held it on the prisoner. Orion jammed the priest's feet into the *tapaderos* and tied his legs to the stirrups with more pigging string. Both legs were then secured together with rope under the horse as well.

"You'll thank us for all this rope handiwork down there." Orion grinned. "It'll help with your balance." Then he pulled his knife from its sheath. "Now, we can do this next part the easy way or you can die. You choose."

Holt cocked the hammer of his pistol for punctuation.

Orion cut the leather that had bound The Angel's arms behind him. "Hold your hands in front like you were praying," he ordered. The priest obeyed, and his wrists were quickly re-bound. "Now grab the saddle horn," he continued. Rawhide and more pigging string tied the prisoner's hands and wrists directly to the saddle and pommel.

Holt picked up The Angel's pistol and bent bayonet. He emptied the bullets from the gun. Both weapons were shoved into the captured horse's saddlebags.

"He isn't going anywhere. I'll run an' get our horses," Orion thumbed over his shoulder. "You might take a quick look 'round. We don't have much time."

Holt hurriedly searched the rectory. At a large desk, he spied two maps laying on top. "What the hell?" he exclaimed. One map was an elaborate topography of Texas. The other was a detailed layout of the Sanchez Lazy S property. The Texas map was adorned with the same X's and O's as on Judge Pence's maps. Lying underneath the maps was a thick leather satchel that appeared to be filled with a mass of paperwork, newspaper articles, and more maps.

Holt gathered up the two maps and the leather satchel. He peeked his head down into the root cellar. The boxes and packages sitting down there were not food or medicine, but stolen treasures and other loot. There wasn't time to search or investigate. A large set of open saddlebags stuffed with money was closest to the entrance. He slung them over his shoulder. Sweetclover can have something back, he thought.

Orion hollered into the rectory, announcing his return with their horses. As Holt stepped out into the backyard,

Orion was moving between both of the bodies lying out there and firing a shot into each head. "Can't have anyone talkin'."

"Tie these on your horse," Holt said, handing Orion the money-filled saddlebags. He stowed the two maps and satchel in his own saddlebags. "I'll swing out front, get my rifle and see what's on his mule."

Out in front of the church, Holt grabbed his Winchester still propped outside the main doors. Remembering Orion's words, he fired a shot into the head of the Comanchero lying there. He knew the other outlaws he downed were already dead. He approached The Angel's mule and removed the saddlebags.

Two wide-eyed villagers came running down the street. Holt hollered, "*La iglesia esta en llamas! Ve a buscar ayuda!!*" They scurried away in a panic.

He swiftly went back inside. Orion was attaching a lead rope to The Angel's horse. "We got company," he declared. "Two villagers. I told them the church was on fire and to go get help."

"Good thinkin'."

"Where is Judah?" the priest asked.

"Who the hell is 'Judah'?" Orion snapped.

"Judah is my mule. Am I not to ride him?"

"For one, he knows you an' you know him," Orion responded. "I ain't havin' any funny business. An' two, I hate mules. I'd rather shoot the crazy sonvabitches."

"And three, shut the hell up," Holt shot back and finished tying the saddlebags from the mule to his own horse. He walked over to retrieve Tag and to sprinkle a quick tobacco tribute. Climbing into his saddle, he unsheathed his rifle and aimed it at the priest while Orion swung up on his horse.

"You know, we may have to rethink our decision to not gag him," Holt said to Orion. The prisoner huffed but did not say anything more. Tag rested in front of the saddle as Holt managed the reins and his rifle.

As Orion looped the lead rope around his saddle's pommel, Holt smiled next to him, "'Crows will eat your dead eyes?' Damn."

"It just came to me."

Holt laughed. "Nice work, peckerhead."

Orion clicked his horse into movement. He would go first, leading The Angel's horse and Holt would follow, keeping watch on the prisoner and their backtrail.

Stars were beginning to find their daily hiding places. Early feelers of dawn announced that the sun would be joining the celestial game of hide-and-seek before too long.

It was time to ride. They left Laelia in a steady lope.

CHAPTER FORTY

O nce the mission of finding The Angel was accomplished, proper timing of sunlight was still a challenge for their return to the Rio Grande. The concern now was getting to the other side of the river before full light without anyone seeing them.

Holt spent most of the miles between Laelia and the river staring a hole into the back of the priest's head. Emotions were still deliberating heavily with his spirits. Part of him still struggled with why he didn't just kill this beast right now.

Four Shields had told him "You are on a difficult journey from the world of light to pursue someone who exists in the realm of darkness..." It occurred to Holt that they had fought The Angel in the middle of the night and, as they were nearing the relative safety of being across the river, the sun was rising.

The horse's movement caused the medicine pouch to shift slightly under his shirt. His hands were busy, but he acknowledged the spirits with a nod and a mental salute.

They reached their crossing spot from the day before.

This time, Holt was going to keep Tag balanced on the saddle in front of him.

"Here we are," Orion hollered. "'Tag Along Creek!'"

Orion spurred his dun and yanked the lead rope of the horse carrying The Angel. The two horses splashed into the muddy water. Holt and his bay followed. The river was as cooperative as it had been yesterday. They all burst out of the water and into Texas, loping for several hundred yards before reining up.

"We made it." Holt smiled. "Hannah always jokes that the Corrigans are lucky. I guess he was right this time." He adjusted his hat and gave the cardinal feather a quick touch.

"We'll let 'em blow here an' give 'em some water," Orion said. "I wanna check on our guest."

The priest spoke out. "I insist you tell me why I'm being held prisoner. Why were those men with me murdered?"

Orion rode up to The Angel with a canteen in his hand. "Do you want a drink, or do you want to yammer?" The Ranger poured some gulps of water into the priest's mouth.

"Why am I being drug across the border against my will?"

Handing the canteen to Holt, Orion pulled out a bandanna and fastened the cloth around the prisoner's mouth. "What border?" He looked at Holt, smirking, "We never left Texas. That's Tag Along Creek right there."

The Rangers poured water into their hats and gave their horses a drink, including the horse captured from the church. Tag got a good drink as well. Holt gave a piece of jerky to the dog. "Did you think we forgot breakfast, boy?" he said, giving his pal a quick head pat.

Orion proclaimed that The Angel's ties were still doing their job well. They would trot to Sweetclover from here. It wasn't far. Their horses did not need to be pushed now unless necessary. Tag could stretch his legs too.

Daybreak had arrived. Holt left a small tobacco tribute and decided he would still keep his rifle across his lap.

———

The Sweetclover morning had not yet churned into high gear when the Rangers rode into town with their prize. Most of the shops and businesses were just opening. Only the blacksmith and the saloons appeared to be fully active. The few citizens out on the walkways were treated with an interesting sight. A dusty and disheveled man with a bruised face and bloody arm led in by two Rangers was not particularly unique. That the prisoner was tied to a horse with more pigging string than a roundup would need and dressed in priest's garb was the head-turner.

Reining in at the jail, Holt got down first and told Tag to wait up on the boardwalk. He tied the prisoner's horse to the post, his rifle still at the ready.

"Hello the jail!" Holt hollered. "Marshal Gentry!!"

The jail door opened and Deputy Don Baldwin stepped out.

"Good morning, deputy!" Holt called out. "I presume you know Father Beltran."

Orion looked up and added, "We need cuffs an' a shotgun." He dismounted his dun and tied him to the rail.

Don did a double-take at the sight and the demand,

not knowing how or what to say. He stumbled a quick hello and ran back inside, shortly returning with hand-cuffs. An older, squattier deputy, Merlyn Reed, followed him, carrying a double-barreled shotgun.

Orion began cutting the prisoner loose from the horse.

Holt stepped over to the boardwalk and looked up at Don. "Marshal Gentry around?"

"He rode out at first light," Don said. "There was trouble at one of the ranches. We might have a goat and sheep rustler."

Holt's lips tightened a little as he exhaled a deep breath. That was not quite the answer he wanted to hear.

"He oughta be back by tonight," Don offered.

"Sounds good. What are your cells like? Empty?"

"All empty but one," the deputy answered. "Drunk and disorderly. We'll probably let him go before lunch."

"Send him on his way now," Holt said. "We don't need anyone else in those cells. We'll put this bastard in the cell that's farthest from any window. Does it have an iron bunk?"

"Yes," Don nodded.

"All right. Give me a hand and help get the cuffs on."

"Deputy, come down here with that shotgun," Orion ordered.

Both deputies hurried down to the street.

"Okay, now listen…" Orion instructed the deputy holding the shotgun, but the message was more for Father Beltran. "I'm gonna cut that rope under the horse an' then cut his hands from the saddle. If this hoot-owl does *anythin'* other than step off that horse, you empty both barrels into 'im. Understood?"

"Yass-suh," Deputy Reed said.

Father Beltran stepped down off the horse. Holt and Don positioned the father's arms behind his back and snapped the handcuffs into place around his wrists. Orion reached over and untied the bandanna used to muzzle The Angel.

Gathering his breath, Father Beltran declared indignantly, "You still have not told me why I'm being held prisoner!" He addressed the deputy, "Marshal, these men have killed my assistants and taken me hostage."

Don was a little confused. He was just a deputy and these men were Rangers.

Orion spoke up. "This is Texas, isn't it?" He pulled his badge from a pocket and fastened it to his coat. "I'll be damned…guess that makes us Texas Rangers."

"Now, move," Holt ordered. Tag followed the group inside.

Inside the main area of the jail, the heavy door was locked and braced behind them. The prisoner spoke up again. Arrogant in his behavior, defiant in his tone, he said, "You still haven't told me why I'm being held like this. I am wounded and need a doctor."

"Father Beltran…ah hell, Miguel," Holt barked, now wearing his Ranger badge prominently. "You sure as hell ain't worthy of being called a man of God. You're under arrest by the state of Texas, for robbery and murder. A lot of murders. Your bloody arm is the result of sneaking up behind a Texas Ranger with intent to shoot him in the back. We'll decide if you need a doctor."

"I am a minister of God!" the prisoner yelled. "How dare you accuse me of this!"

The arrogance of the priest was more than Holt could tolerate. He stepped up and bellowed into Father Beltran's face, "How *dare* you stand there, *alive*, when a trail of good people are dead because of you?" He drew his pistol and jammed it underneath the priest's chin. "You should have been dropped like a mad dog." He continued to stand face-to-face with the priest, his blue eyes blazing. The man would not, could not, meet the Ranger's eyes.

Holt took a deep breath and holstered his gun. "The spirits are all that are keeping you from being sent to hell," he said, now in a calmer, but just as lethal, voice. "But you'll get there soon enough."

"I only spread the word of God," the killer intoned calmly.

"The last time I checked, the Word of God was not about murder," Holt said and pushed the killer toward the lockup.

Orion gestured to a wide-eyed Deputy Reed that he should follow the priest, with the same instruction as before.

The adobe and stone Sweetclover jail had a large iron-barred gate that separated the main room and office from the space with three small cells. Holt was encouraged to see that two locking doors separated prisoners from the general area and vice versa. It seemed that most of time this gate was left open. That habit just changed with their current occupant, he noted.

Father Beltran was marched through the gate and placed in the far cell, farthest from any door or window. Deputy Baldwin fastened a heavy iron shackle to the prisoner's right leg. A four-foot length of heavy chain attached the other end to a cell bar by the cot. The other leg was shackled similarly. The prisoner could lay or sit on the bunk, but little else.

"Well, you ain't runnin' anywhere," Orion said

blandly as he removed the handcuffs from the priest's wrists.

"What if I have to relieve myself?" the priest asked.

Orion just stared at the man, then reached outside the cell and picked up a metal bucket sitting against the wall. He dropped the pail inside the cell with a tinny clunk, followed by a reverberating bang when the cell door shut.

"I require a Bible. Surely you won't deny me that?"

Holt watched the exchange. The prisoner looked up. Holt's eyes slashed at him so hard the man blinked and quickly looked away.

Slamming and locking the gate, the various lawmen huddled in the main part of the jail. Holt quietly asked Don, "You got any more law around? Any more help?"

"Deputy Morton went with the marshal," Don responded. "We got another one. He's probably sleeping though. He had night duty."

"Lotta deputies," Orion observed.

"We have to handle town *and* county matters," Don explained. "They haven't gotten around to setting up a county sheriff in these parts. So, lots of deputies."

"Well, everyone's on duty now," Orion said. "Go get 'im. An' Doc Gustafson."

"And, Don..." Holt cautioned. "Don't talk to *anyone*."

———

Orion had positioned Deputy Reed with the double-barreled shotgun by the locked gate.

It wasn't long before a knock at the braced front door brought the return of Don and Dr. Gustafson. Tag greeted the serious men as they entered the jail.

Orion refused to remove the shackles while the doctor washed and examined the nasty punctures and tears that frayed the prisoner's arm. "How did this happen?" the doctor inquired.

Before the priest could answer, Orion spoke up. "The prisoner tried to sneak up an' shoot me in the back. That brave Ranger dog, Tag, pounced on his arm an' wouldn't let go until I could restrain the killer."

Dr. Gustafson examined a large bruise on the priest's neck and shoulder. "What about the injury here?"

"He tried to bayonet the dog," Orion replied. "So he was introduced to the manufacturin' quality of the New Haven Arms Company."

"I don't follow," Dr. Gustafson said.

"When he tried to stab Tag, I clubbed 'im with my Henry rifle," Orion replied.

"And the bloody mouth?"

"Doc." Orion looked hard into the man's eyes. "Your job is to check 'im out an' fix 'im up. Quietly. Got it?"

Dr. Gustafson shook his head. He treated the effects of the dog wounds with ointment and a dressing pad, then wrapped a bandage securely around the arm.

"That should take care of things for now," the doctor said. "I'd like to examine him again in a couple of days."

"We'll have moved on by then an' he'll be travelin' with us," Orion advised. "You really wanna be personal physician to a murderer?" The doctor had no response for the Ranger and took his leave.

Out in the main part of the jail, Don quietly said to Deputy Reed, "Jeezus, Rangers don't mess around."

"And, goin' ta all this trubble in tha jail here?" Reed murmured back.

Holt heard the remarks and took a deep breath. "Gentlemen, I can't tell you everything," he began. "But I can tell you that, in addition to your two townspeople, this 'man of the cloth' directed the killings of at least three other people and countless robberies…"

Orion's look was intense as he interjected, "An' he himself cold-blood murdered at least seven men. With his own hands."

"This is a dangerous criminal that required Texas Rangers to do the job of tracking him down and bringing him in," Holt continued. "And we need your help."

"You can start by followin' orders," Orion added. "An' keepin' everythin' you've heard right here."

"I'm not sure what you're used to, but hell is staying overnight in Sweetclover," Holt said matter-of-factly.

The thick silence was broken by loud thumping at the door.

"That'll be Jimbo," Don said and opened the door.

A loud voice entered before the body. "Why th' hell're we lockin' th' damn door?" An overweight man in a green bib shirt strode through the door. A flat-crowned, flat-brimmed straw Nevada hat adorned the man's head —"like the kind Colonel Travis wore at the Alamo," he often bragged. The bulldog jaw, sprawling eyebrows, huge ears, and arrogant attitude gave it away. This was a younger version of the fat, self-important mayor.

"Rangers, this is Deputy Jimbo Worthington," Baldwin began the introductions. "Jimbo, this is Ranger Holt Corrigan and Ranger Orion Higbee."

Jimbo eyed Holt carefully. "Heard from my father ya rode through here. An' now yer back." He did not offer his hand. Neither did the Rangers. "Find whatchas lookin' fer?"

"Back there." Holt gestured with a nod of his head.

"Don' look like much, do he?" Jimbo blustered. "Why bother? He an' his men killt Ike n' Del. We should jus' string 'im up."

Orion stepped in front of Jimbo. A taller man than the lippy deputy, the Ranger's glare penetrated into the rotund offspring's eyes. "Deputy, I'm sure you think the world revolves 'round this lil' town of yours, but this man has caused a lotta trouble all across Texas. He's a killer, but he ain't no mastermind. We aim to find out who's pullin' his strings. An' you'll follow orders. *That's* why bother. Savvy?"

Jimbo Worthington swallowed hard.

Partly to get away from the arrogant deputies, but mostly because Captain McCoy needed to be briefed, Orion left Holt to explain the security details while he ventured out to the telegraph office. The message he sent to McCoy informed him of the shoot-out and that The Angel was in custody in the town of Sweetclover. He did not mention the location of the capture. Sheriff James Hannah in Wilkon was sent a simple message—The Angel had been captured.

Holt began explaining to the deputies how security would operate for the rest of the day and night—especially night. At least two lawmen would be in the jail at all times. The main door was to be locked and braced. No one without a badge would be allowed inside for any reason. The inner gate would be shut and locked as well. Everyone on guard inside would carry a loaded shotgun. Anyone unauthorized who tried to get in—or out—would be shot.

"Tha's a lotta precawtion." Jimbo harrumphed.

Holt tempered his patience and response. "*Son*, you think you're the first to come up with the idea of just dispatching this bastard? We have no idea who's behind all of this man's evil. We need him around to find out." A hard look came to his eyes. "Look at me. There is no telling *who* or *what* may come after *you* to get *him* out of here. Do you understand?"

Baldwin and Deputy Reed nodded earnestly. Jimbo crossed his arms over his fat belly.

The deputies were checking the rack of shotguns and the jail's coffee supply when more thumps were heard at the door. Deputy Reed slid back the small plank covering the spyhole, saw who was outside and immediately removed the brace. The door swung open and Mayor Clark Worthington strutted inside. His sprouting eyebrows always looked as if they were in a perpetual state of surprise, but this time they truly were when he saw Holt Corrigan standing there.

"G-Good m-mornin' Colonel sir," Deputy Reed stammered and hurried past the mayor on the way to the general store for more coffee.

Holt glared at Deputy Reed, then shot a glance at Baldwin who returned it with a subtle frown and shrug. Holt nodded a less-than-welcome greeting, "*Mayor.*"

"Ranger...Corrigan," the elder Worthington replied. A few awkward moments passed, before he spoke. "So... you Rangers got him. Excellent! Sweetclover thanks you."

"Since you're here, Worthington, I've got something for you," Holt said. "Come with me." He held the door for the mayor to follow him outside. He wanted the arrogant man out of the jail, but he also could serve a purpose. He stepped off the boardwalk to Orion's horse and untied the saddlebags filled with cash.

Holt explained that this was all of the money they

could recover. "I'm not sure how much Sweetclover lost in the robbery or even how much is here," he said. "This prisoner was our priority. He's wanted by the state for way more than what he did here in Sweetclover." Holt did not want to tell this gasbag that the priest had been captured across the border. He draped the set of bags over Worthington's arm. "I trust you know the proper contact at the bank who will want this."

The mayor looked down at the stuffed-full saddle-bags. He flipped one open to peer inside. When he saw all the money, his wild eyebrows arched high.

"Very well," the rotund man said.

With no further comment coming from the fat, arro-gant man, Holt shook his head disgustedly and turned to go back into the jail.

"You're welcome. *Mayor*," he said with a sneer and slammed the door.

CHAPTER FORTY-ONE

The only thing bigger than the mayor's waistline was his mouth. It was not long before he began pontificating about who was being held in his…Sweetclover's…jail.

Word that the priest whose men robbed their bank was in their jail spread like wildfire through town. Like true wildfire, bits and pieces of speculative talk were added like kindling.

The few townspeople who witnessed the arrival of the Rangers spoke of the bloody and bruised priest being tied to a horse and led handcuffed at gunpoint into the jail. At the general store, Deputy Reed told the crew hanging around the stove that the prisoner was responsible for many murders and robberies all over Texas, and that the Rangers had shotguns aimed at him even behind bars.

Unable to keep confidential what he knew, the telegraph operator violated his sworn oath and hurried to the store to add juicy details of a shoot-out and the arrest of someone the Rangers called "The Angel."

Mayor Worthington also let it be known that only *part* of their stolen money had been recovered. He tried hard to suggest that former outlaw Holt Corrigan, one of the Rangers, might have kept some. No one seemed interested in that piece of information though, only wanting to talk about the scuttlebutt surrounding the prisoner.

Orion arrived back at the jail having sent his wire messages and tracking down a Bible. Deputy Reed returned at the same time with the coffee purchase. The door was locked and braced behind them. It was going to be a long day and night. Everyone was heartened that there would be plenty of the hot, black liquid for warmth and support.

Holt assigned Jimbo Worthington and Deputy Reed to the first shift, starting now. These two appeared to be the weakest links and broad daylight was not a likely time for trouble.

Seeing the arrivals into the jail, the priest hollered from the cell asking about the Bible he requested.

"An odd request for such a man in your *line of work*," Orion said as he and Holt entered the cell area through the iron gate, locking it behind them.

"I am a man of God. The Bible is my shield."

"You're a murderer," Holt barked. "Blades are your tools." He pointed to the empty bayonet scabbard still strapped to the prisoner's leg and asked, "What was that for? An extra cross?"

"'He gives strength to the weary and *increases the power of the weak.' Isaiah*, chapter forty."

Orion retorted. "From *Ephesians*, 'Put on the full armor of God, so that you can *take your stand against the Devil's schemes.'* Chapter six."

"'Judge not that ye be judged.' *Matthew*, seven, one."

Orion added with a smile. "'Thou art weighed in the balances and art found wanting.' Book of *Daniel*, chapter five, verse twenny-seven."

"You have made a grave mistake," Father Beltran hissed. "But there is still time for you to repent. The *Psalms* tell us, 'Great is our Lord, and abundant in power; his understanding is beyond measure.'"

"And the Gospels tell us," Orion responded. "'If we say we have no sin, we deceive ourselves, and the truth is not in us.'"

Not winning the Scriptural sparring match, the priest quietly glared, "'Vengeance is mine, I will repay.'"

"Well now, let's chew on that one," Orion calmly countered as he moved closer to The Angel's cell. "That whole passage reads: 'Beloved, never avenge yourselves, but leave it to the wrath of God, for it is written, Vengeance is mine, I will repay, *says the Lord*.' Or did you forget that part?"

The priest took a deep breath and exhaled sharply. "You have the wrong man."

"Got the wrong man for what, Miguel?" Holt interrupted. "You're the man we were after. You *are* 'The Angel.'" His expression was stern, the heat in his voice progressively rose as he barraged the priest with criminations. "We know all about the banker in Modlin...the miner in Bartle...the pages from the Bible...the headless snake...the flaming sword...Rushing... Henion..."

"Enough!!" Father Beltran shouted. "I know *nothing* of those things!" he declared. "I don't know anything about what happened at Modlin...or Baccata...or Wilkon!"

"I didn't say anything about Baccata. Or Wilkon," Holt replied calmly, but the peacefulness did not reach his eyes.

The priest's face tightened.

"Father, who do you know with the initials, 'T.H.G.T.'?" Holt asked in a soft voice.

Father Beltran slowly lifted his head to look at Holt, but quickly averted his gaze.

"You can help yourself," Holt continued. "Who is 'T.H.G.T.?'"

"Man cannot help himself. We can only be saved," the priest intoned. "The Lord blesses the mighty ones who do his word, obeying the voice of his word."

Holt's brow furrowed. "Is this 'T.H.G.T.' your boss too?"

"The Creator oversees us all. My boss is a clarion, leading men to their destinies."

"Clary...who?" Orion asked.

Father Beltran had only answered with a sly smile. "Clarion. The Bible tells us of a golden trumpet. I hear the call and *he* guides me. The plan is his. I am only a messenger angel."

"Who guides you?" Holt asked.

"The blood trinity will be alert to my needs." With that, the priest laid back on the cot. As he shut his eyes, he said, "You have the wrong man."

"What you are is a crazy bastard," Orion said, pulling a Bible from his coat pocket and tossing it through the bars onto the cot. "You wanted this to read. *Second Thessalonians* would be a good place for you to start."

Without another word the Rangers turned and left, locking the gate behind them. Holt's head-tilt to Orion was a question. Orion smiled back and said, "It's th' apostle Paul's letter 'bout protestin' too much.'"

Stepping into the main part of the jail, the Rangers realized that, other than a little water from the trough, their horses had not been tended to since arriving in Sweetclover. They needed to be relieved of their saddles and given some attention. Prior to leaving, they instructed Deputies Reed and Worthington to make note of anything the prisoner said.

"Whether you think it's important or not. Even a hymn," Holt said sternly. "Anything."

Orion reconfirmed the standing order: shoot anyone coming through the door not wearing a badge. "An' that goes for the mayor. Your daddy doesn't need to be here. Got it?"

Stepping out onto the boardwalk in front of the jail, Holt turned to Orion, "I didn't want to say anything in there, but did you catch that he was talking about himself as being an angel and that we had the wrong *man*?"

Orion did a double-take. "A tricky glimpse at who's really behin' this?"

"'You have the wrong man,' he said." Holt repeated. "What did he say a clarion was?"

"A golden trumpet."

"G.T."

"That's right. 'I hear the call and he guides me. The plan is his. I am only a messenger.'"

"Besides those telegrams from a 'T.H.G.T.,' he just admitted to someone else pullin' his strings," Orion affirmed.

"'T.H.G.T.' What if 'T.H.G.T.' wasn't a person's name, but a nickname or a title or something? Worth considering."

"Let's talk to him again," Orion urged.

"Let him stew. Give him time to settle in."

"Good idea," Orion agreed. "Our horses need seein' to. An' some real food not made by us sounds mighty fine."

"Maybe a bath too. What do you say, boy?" Holt called to Tag.

CHAPTER FORTY-TWO

The livery stables were a hive of energy as Holt and Orion arrived with their mounts and the one brought from the shoot-out at the church. Livery operator Dee Kennedy met them with a huge smile and ear scratches for Tag.

"Heard you was back in town," Dee said. "Seems all anyone kin talk 'bout."

"I imagine it's big news," Holt said. "It'll pass quickly, I hope. We're riding out tomorrow morning."

Dee could not wait to show Orion how his bay was doing. The wound from the Comanche fight was looking good and starting to scab over, a sign of healing.

"Your buckskin's likin' the easy life too." Dee smiled at Holt. "Had to ease him down from the grains, don' want that belly o' his gettin' soft." He laughed, rubbing his own.

He assured the Rangers that their tired mounts would get a good rubdown as well as grain and water. They explained where the extra horse was acquired and why. Dee promised to have him ready in the morning also.

"Ya don' mind me sayin' so, but you fellers look a bit rough," the livery operator said. "Nothin' a bed an' a meal cain't fix."

"I'm afraid a bed's out of the question," Holt said. "It's going to be a long night."

"But a lil' clean up an' a meal is definitely on the horizon." Orion grinned. "We been at it for a while."

As before, they paid the operator in advance for his services. Leaving the livery, the Rangers were greeted by a welcome sight: Marshal Frank Gentry tying up in front of the jail. Both Rangers moved down the street toward the lawman with Tag eagerly following.

"Rangers! You're back!" Gentry hailed. "Good hunting?"

Holt indicated with his head. "He's inside."

"How'd your trip go?" Orion asked. "Rustlers, we heard?"

"Looks like it. Deputy Morton is still out there following up. Sorry I wasn't here."

"Mighty glad to see you either way, Marshal," Holt said.

They walked up the steps and were stopped by the locked and braced door. Gentry knocked, saw the spyhole open and smiled at the Rangers. "Your doing?"

They nodded back.

"Exactly what I would have done," he responded as they were let inside by Deputy Reed.

Jimbo Worthington leaned back in a chair, feet propped on the desk. "Hi Frank, get th' rustlers?"

"Good ta see you, Marshal…" Deputy Reed acknowledged his boss properly and returned to his post across the room.

Gentry looked around, could see the arrangement

Holt had put in place. Other than the lazy son of the arrogant mayor, the plan was sound. Deputy Reed sat by the locked gate, shotgun in his lap. Deputy Worthington was more at ease, but at least had his weapon laying across the desk nearby.

Gentry peered through the gate, back into the cell at the priest. "That's him, sure enough," he confirmed.

Holt filled in Gentry on most of what transpired, giving a brief, straight-forward account of the Laelia engagement—leaving out that it all took place across the border and not revealing that this was "The Angel." Gentry listened and nodded along, appreciating the briefing.

"You should know…" Holt continued. "I wasn't sure when, or if, we'd see you so I gave Worthington a set of saddlebags we got from the hideout. They were filled with money. I don't know how much was in it or how much your bank lost. Figured you should know."

"Thank you, the town will welcome hearing that," Gentry said appreciatively.

"We didn't have much time for rummagin' 'round." Orion smiled. "The river was risin', if you know what I mean."

The three trail-hardened lawmen chuckled.

"I'm sure Worthington thinks I pocketed some of it," Holt said. "But there ought to be an accounting of what was in those bags against what Sweetclover actually lost."

"I'll look into it," Gentry said. "But that will have to wait until we're shut of this prisoner."

"All right," Orion said. "We been at it since yesterday mornin'. If you're squared away here, we're goin' to go find a bath an' a meal."

Gentry spoke to his deputies. "I'm going to the doctor's office to tell Deputy Baldwin he'll be reporting here at six o'clock and then I'll be right back. Reed, I'll send you to take over for Baldwin at the doctor's office a little before six. Worthington, you'll be on duty here until Baldwin arrives and then you'll spell Reed at the doctor's at midnight. And keep yourselves awake. Anyone not wearing a badge who tries to get to either prisoner gets a load of buckshot. Understand?"

Mumbled understandings came from the deputies, realizing their night would be a long one.

"Sounds good, Marshal," Holt said. "We'll take the late shift."

"Yeah, bad things happen at the witchin' hour." Orion grinned.

"I'll be here with you," Gentry said. "I'm not leaving until this prisoner moves on."

CHAPTER FORTY-THREE

H olt and Orion headed to Jun's to see about a bath and pick up their clean laundry. Their clothes were ready, but the bathhouse was extra busy. Jun herself graciously asked that they come back later in the evening.

They wanted to avoid the hotel and its crowd, especially Clark Worthington's bunch, so they chose a small diner on the end of town, down near Jun's, by the livery. The restaurant was run by a Mexican family who was overjoyed to have the famous Texas Rangers in their establishment. They were even happy to host the brave dog who rode with them. Dee Kennedy and his wife, Mary, were seated in another part of the diner, talking quietly. They saw the Rangers and waved them over.

"Ya discovered th' best spot in town!" Dee beamed. "Y'all should join us!" Mary nodded enthusiastically.

"We can't interrupt your quiet meal with your lovely lady," Orion smiled. But the Kennedys insisted.

Soon, a big meal of *barbacoa* with onions and peppers, *frijoles*, rice, and fresh corn tortillas was laid before them. Tag received a bowl of eggs and ham, prepared specially for him. The Rangers had to agree that the food was excellent. Holt especially enjoyed the spiced coffee. Conversation dwindled, more because of their concentration on the delicious food rather than the custom of eating in silence.

Holt knew Mary was curious about the Laelia church so he shared with her a little bit of what he saw. He assured her the church was still standing and, in fact, looked as though it had been kept up with recent repairs. She asked about whether he saw any children.

"Thankfully, we didn't," he said. "It was late—and dangerous."

He described the root cellar, but said that it had been quite some time since food was stored in it. She was dismayed to hear the cellar was used to stash the evil priest's plunder and that Father Beltran hid in it so he could try to ambush them.

While they were absorbed in eating and talking, a burly man in a worn buckskin shirt ambled by the window of the diner. The man was noticeably bowlegged. His bandy gait was accentuated by an afternoon of whiskey drinking that made it look like he was moving across a ship when he walked. The man took careful note of who was sitting inside the diner.

Throughout the day, the tale of the prisoner the Rangers brought back to town only grew in proportion and with it, unrest. At Tiller's, Sweetclover's main saloon, drinkers stood two-deep at the bar swapping information about what they knew and what they had heard—all of it hearsay and inflammatory. Just who was this "Angel?" Was he really a priest? Why did the mayor and some of the deputies say the Rangers would not let them execute justice?

All day, many of the close friends and family members of Ike Wall and Del Halsey, the men killed in the bank robbery, had been drinking and listening to the gossip. The fact that other towns also had murdered kinfolk did not matter. The patrons of Tiller's could only focus on the loss of the two people who had been gunned down in their street.

In the middle of it all, Colonel Clark Worthington was fanning the flames of the conflagration, quietly declaring to anyone who would listen that—as mayor and acting judge—he thought the priest, this "Angel," should be pronounced guilty of murdering Ike and Del, with sentencing carried out. Immediately.

Later, at a corner table in the hotel, a just off-duty Deputy Jimbo Worthington reported to his father that Frank Gentry and Don Baldwin would be guarding the jail during the evening. The Rangers were not planning to take over until midnight.

"Them Rangers are eatin' o'er at th' El Matador right now, Colonel sir," the bowlegged man chimed in. "We gotta get over ta th' jail b'fore them Rangers get thar."

"Gawdalmighty, Turner, you know Frank an' Don wear their badges shiny. They ain't gonna just hand over th' Angel," Jimbo warned.

————

Over at the diner, their meals completed and long post-dinner conversation run out, the Rangers said their good-byes to the Kennedys. The lawmen were hoping spots had opened at Jun's bathhouse.

Jun informed them that tubs were open but she was not sure about how much hot water was on hand. If they could wait just a little longer, the water would be hotter. With a long night ahead, they turned down the offer of whiskey from Jun's assistant.

Finally, the big metal buckets had heated enough hot water. Orion sat in his tub. "This is gonna feel darn good. Just dump it right over my head!"

Jun's assistants began pouring buckets of water into the tubs.

"I'm looking forward to not smelling like my dog," Holt chimed in from the next stall.

"I'm sure he does too." Orion laughed. "Their noses are pretty advanced."

In his own tub, Holt reached over and scratched Tag's head. "You don't mind, do you, boy?" The dog jumped up on his hind legs, front paws on the edge of tub, and sniffed at the soapy water.

Leaning back in his tub, Orion hollered over the partition at Holt, "I could use a cigar 'bout now!"

"Now you remember!" Holt called out. He instructed Jun's assistant, "Leave a full basin for my dog, please." Tag barked in agreement.

———

Marshal Frank Gentry sat at his desk, thumbing through a copy of *Ivanhoe* by Walter Scott. He had enjoyed the book before, many times. Tonight, it was more an exercise in keeping his mind occupied. His deputy, Don Baldwin, sat by the locked iron gate, absent-mindedly wiping down a rifle, a loaded shotgun propped next to him. The prisoner, Father Beltran, had eaten a small supper and dozed off reading the Bible.

A knock came at the door. Baldwin immediately put down the rifle and picked up the shotgun. Gentry grabbed his shotgun and went to the door. Jimbo Worthington's eyes peered back at him through the spyhole. The marshal carefully opened the door and let the deputy inside, quickly bracing the door behind him.

"Deputy, what's going on?" Gentry said. "I didn't figure to see you here anymore tonight. You've got doctor's office duty later."

"Came here ta tell ya there's a lot of folks bin drinkin' an' gettin' ugly 'bout the pris'ner here," the younger Worthington said.

"Smells like you've been in the midst of them," Gentry observed.

"Cain't hear bar talk if'n ya ain't inna bar," the deputy said. "Anyways, there's a lotta talk 'bout stringin' him up."

Worthington actually looked a little nervous at the prospect.

Gentry's face turned grim. He returned to the spyhole and looked out. Hard to see distance through it but thought he could make out a small crowd gathering down the street. It could also just be nighttime shenanigans. He shut the plank to the spyhole. "Deputy, since you're here, you better stay. Grab a shotgun. If it comes to it, I want at least one of you inside the locked gate. Understand? No one gets to the prisoner."

Fifteen minutes passed and a loud thumping came at the door. A gruff voice bellowed on the other side. "Marshal Gentry! Open up! We want to talk!"

Gentry looked through the spyhole. The burly,

bowlegged man, Turner Halsey, whose store clerk brother was gunned down in the robbery, stood at the entryway. Behind him, Gentry could see maybe a dozen people. Three or four were holding lanterns and torches.

"C'mon, Marshal, it's Turner, Turner Halsey. Ya know me. We jus' wanna talk."

Gentry shook his head. He knew they were not there to talk. Maybe he could get them to lose interest.

"Turner, your brother was a good man," Gentry hollered out the spyhole. "Why don't you all go back and drink to his memory? Tell some stories. I'll stand good for a round."

There was no response to his suggestion or his offer. He heard shuffling on the boardwalk and peered out. Turner had turned around and was yelling to the people with him, "He ain't comin' out." Another voice hollered, "Go get that half-breed lyin' in the doc's office!"

Gentry saw a couple of the torches move away. He knew this hand he was dealt could not be folded.

He turned to instruct his deputies, "Deputy Worthington, I want you inside the gate now! Deputy Baldwin, come lock and brace this door. If it isn't me coming back through it, open fire. Understand?"

He removed the brace, unlocked and opened the door. He stood behind the heavy entryway with his Greener held out one-handed and pointed at Turner's belly. "Turner, I want you out on the street, then we can talk."

Turner moved back off the boardwalk and stood out in the dirt with the assembled mob. Gentry stepped outside, not taking his gun off the group directly in front. The door shut solidly. Ten men stood in front of the marshal in the street. Most were faces he recognized.

"You there, heading to Doc Gustafson's, get back

here!" Gentry hollered. The men crossing the street stopped and turned around to look.

"Look," Gentry began. "I can't bring back Ike or Del. No one can."

A daylong occupant at Tiller's hollered, "That's why we should string him up!!" More whiskey-fueled courage followed.

"Yeah, hang 'im!"

"Get out of the way!"

"Bastard killed our friends!"

An arrogant voice sang out from off to the side. "Marshal, looks like these people have a legitimate beef." Frank Worthington moved closer to the front of the group, a cigar in his hand. His daylong pontifications had almost as much to do with fueling this agitation as the rotgut at Tiller's. "As mayor…and justice of the peace…I say what're we waiting for?" He placed the cigar in his mouth confidently.

"The colonel's right!"

"Yeah, hang the bastard!!"

"String him up!!"

Turner Halsey and two men took a step toward Gentry. The marshal fired one barrel of the Greener straight in the air. The resounding *BOOM* stopped everyone in their tracks. He immediately leveled the gun back at the front row and drew his Colt. Two guns and Marshal Gentry stared down the crowd.

"The man's going to stand trial, by a real judge. So if any of you take one step in this direction, I'll empty these guns," Gentry growled. "Six bullets from the Colt and a barrel from the Greener. That will put holes in at least eight or nine of you. Who's it going to be?"

"Gonna be you, marshal, if ya don' put down them

guns," an arrogant voice drawled from behind the marshal.

Standing with his own shotgun in the open door of the jail was Jimbo Worthington.

Gentry turned his head slowly. The deputy he was forced to hire sneered at him with an insolent smirk.

"Marshal," Jimbo said. "Ya bes' be droppin' them guns." His thumb pulled the hammers back on both barrels. Behind him, in the light of the jail, Gentry could see Deputy Baldwin lying on the floor.

"He better not be dead," Gentry hissed at the deputy.

"Baldwin ain't dead," Jimbo assured. "Jus' a headache. Now...drop th' guns!"

Gentry eased the hammer forward on his Greener and set it down, dropping the pistol next.

Frank Worthington stepped up on the boardwalk next to Gentry and declared in a loud voice, "As justice of the peace of Sweetclover, Texas, I declare Father Miguel Beltran to be guilty of murder!"

The mob rushed through the door...

CHAPTER FORTY-FOUR

Holt and Orion sprinted across the big open lot between the hardware store and blacksmith shop. Their shirts and trousers soaked through from the inside after jumping out of unfinished baths into their clothes. Tag barked at their heels. The shotgun blast from the direction of the jail had alerted them to trouble.

Street lanterns and the remnants of torches lit up a town alive with the business of death. A crowd of towns-people, mostly men, stood in a rough circle, looking up in the flickering darkness. Heavy murmurs from multiple conversations swirled around the macabre scene.

Up in the gnarled, old mesquite trees that usually provided shade to the smithy's forge, Father Miguel Beltran and the half-Kiowa named Neemo, swung from the end of ropes, their bodies slowly revolving. The priest's final spasm of life jerking just as the Rangers pushed their way through to the front, the shackles still attached to his ankles adding to the force of his drop.

"Ho-lee damn," Orion exclaimed under his breath.

Holt stared at the bodies, stunned into silence.

Dr. Gustafson walked unsteadily to the lynching site, holding a bloody rag to the back of his head. When a group of angry drunken townsfolk had come for the prisoner in his care, Deputy Reed assisted them by striking Gustafson with the butt of his gun. The doctor stood next to the Rangers, sadness blanching his face.

"I will never understand this," the doctor said, looking up at the bodies. "Why it isn't wrong to end a life even if it ended other lives." He shook his head and looked at the bloody rag, then put it gently back in place. "I suppose now I understand why you have to do the things the way you do," he said to the Rangers.

Holt did not respond to, nor look at, the doctor.

The remainder of the mob started to disperse, including Dr. Gustafson. Orion watched the milling crowd gravitate to the street in front of Tiller's and the hotel.

At a boarding house near the livery where he kept a room and his meager belongings, Frank Gentry stepped out onto the boardwalk. His possessions were now stuffed into saddlebags, which he tied to the back of his saddle. He climbed aboard his horse and rode down the street. He spied the Worthingtons milling with the pack that had confronted him at the jail.

The arrogant mayor had a fresh cigar in his mouth, pleased with himself. His toadies arranged around him stood smiling and laughing at something the younger Worthington said. Gentry rode through the mass, directly up to the Worthingtons. "Understand this..." he started. "If I *ever* cross paths again with either of you...I will kill you and dance on your graves," his voice was a snarl. "You've had your warning."

He started to spur his horse away, then turned back and cautioned the mayor, "Tell your fat son with the shiny gun, he isn't that good—and that you'll die first if he tries."

Jimbo's hand flinched toward his pistol anyway. Gentry's Colt was drawn and pointed at the mayor's startled face before the young man could even clear the gun from its holster.

Staring at father and son, Gentry hollered out to the milling crowd. "Sweetclover!! May I have your attention! Marshal Gentry here…in case you didn't know it, the Rangers brought back your stolen money!" A buzz started to spread through the crowd as they listened to the marshal. "They gave everything to Worthington here. It might be a real good idea to get the bank to verify that your mayor returned every cent!"

He holstered his gun and smiled. The Worthingtons looked like they had been slugged in their ample guts. "Oh yeah," the marshal hollered out once more. "Clark Worthington was a corn farmer in Kansas during the war. That's the only '*kerneling*' your mayor knows anything about. He never served anywhere, except himself at a buffet!" The crowd's buzz became louder and laughter joined in.

He spurred his horse away from the throng and approached Holt and Orion, who still stood at the execution site. They watched the marshal's display with tempered amusement. Reining in, Gentry looked up at the bodies. "The town lynched two men in my custody…" he said disgustedly. "Two of my deputies helped the bastards. Worthington's useless son pulled a gun on me. I'm sorry, Rangers." He dropped his head to his chest and shook it slowly. He looked back up at them with his sad brown eyes. "This isn't my town anymore. I've got no ties here. I'm riding on." He pulled the badge from his vest and flung it into a nearby water trough. Grasping the brim of his hat with a thumb and forefinger, he said, "Somewhere down the trail, gentlemen," and spurred his horse.

The Rangers watched him ride into the darkness. "Lotta fireworks in Sweetclover tonight..." muttered Orion as he reached into the trough to fish out the badge.

The town's diminutive telegraph operator suddenly appeared in front of them, out of breath and holding out a piece of paper. "I've been looking for you two."

"Yeah, I bet you have." Orion's upper lip curled into a scowl. The only way anyone in Sweetclover knew about a killer called The Angel was because the operator had a big mouth. Orion yanked the piece of paper out of his hand. Both Rangers glared at the little man until he turned and hurried away. The wire was from McCoy. Orion read it and handed the paper to Holt.

RECEIVED WORD ABOUT THE ANGEL.

GOOD WORK.

TROUBLE ACROSS BORDER.

LOCAL ALCALDE WORRIED.

BODIES FOUND, PRIEST MISSING FROM LAELIA.

MAYBE TAKEN INTO TEXAS.

PROVIDE ANY KNOWN INFORMATION.

MCCOY

Holt tapped the paper. "He knows what happened."

"Of course he does." Orion smiled. "I'll handle it. Need to send 'im an update now anyways." He walked in the direction of the retreating telegraph operator.

Holt turned and watched the undertaker and his Chinese helpers begin the process of bringing down the bodies.

He had yet to put on his medicine pouch after the bath. There had not been time. He pulled the pouch from his trouser pocket where he had placed it for safekeeping and took out the sacred red stone. He held it in his hand and worked it with his fingers.

The bodies were lowered to the ground. The ropes removed. The Indian was placed onto a wooden cart. Father Miguel Beltran...The Angel... whatever the name, was dumped next to him and hauled away. Holt watched all of it.

His thoughts turned to Judge Pence and Felix Sanchez. He saw them vividly in his mind—not in their repose of death as had frequently tormented his thoughts, but now cheerful and smiling, at him. They were nodding happily when his inner vision dissolved to an image of his mother touching his face. The image was more sensory, the feeling of his mother and her everlasting love. Then, like his bearing in life, the intense presence of Nakashima Silka rushed into Holt's vision, laughing with him and his brothers, bursting with the joy with which he was to be forever filled.

The vivid memories of their beloved *samurai* flooded Holt's mind, some of it leaking its way out of his eyes. He put the stone back into place and slowly decorated himself with the medicine pouch.

Grasping the stone through the elk hide, Holt whispered, "It is so, my friend."

CHAPTER FORTY-FIVE

After Gentry rode away and the executed prisoners were disposed of, Holt and Orion checked in at the jail. Deputy Don Baldwin was being looked at by a worried-looking young woman. She was carefully dabbing the back of his head with a wet rag smudged a faint reddish-brown. Tag watched with concern.

"You all right, Deputy Baldwin?" Holt asked. He knew it was a dumb question, but he cared and wanted to know.

Baldwin was angry, hurt, and humiliated. "I didn't like him, but I thought I could at least trust a fellow deputy." He grimaced. "Have you seen the marshal? People said he was okay, they didn't...when they...I haven't seen him, have you?"

"The marshal quit," Orion said. "Rode outta town."

Baldwin dropped his head. He softly told the young lady she could stop. "I suppose that's what I need to do too."

"A man's got to choose his own way," Holt said.

"There'll be changes around here though. Before Gentry rode out of town, he exposed Worthington for what he was. You never know how that will shake out. Because of what happened here, Sweetclover will be different. Forever. Might be room for something good to happen."

"You did nothin' wrong tonight, Deputy," Orion said, putting a hand on the man's shoulder. "It hurts, but hold your head up an' think 'bout what's next."

Holt looked at Orion. The look in their eyes was an agreement that some of those good things needed to start happening, now. Without saying a word, the Rangers decided it was time the Sweetclover bank president received a visit.

As the Rangers headed out into the night, Tag was left at the jail with Baldwin.

———

At first, Esry Singleton III was not happy to have been rousted from bed, especially by two rough-looking men in long trail coats pounding on his door this late at night. The noise in town had already been enough. When the oil lamp he held in his hand reflected the shiny glint of Texas Ranger badges, he became more welcoming, letting the Rangers step inside.

"Yes, I received a message a little earlier about that awful business at the jail." Singleton shook his head in disgust. "Simply awful. No room for that here in Sweetclover. It must be looked into in the morning."

"Yes sir, Mr. Singleton," Holt said. "Many things need to be straightened out, but I'm afraid some of it requires attention right now."

Holt assumed that the man did not know all of what

had transpired—or at worst, was operating with the sensational version that had spread across town throughout the day. He informed Singleton that, with the capture of the priest, there had not been time for a full search of the gang's hideout. However, he and Ranger Higbee were able to recover at least some of the town's money and, more importantly, they had returned it.

"We 'pologize for the lateness of the hour, sir," Orion said. "But in our legal capacity for the state, we wanted to follow up on whether you had received this money."

"Received?" Singleton was taken aback. "This is the very first I've heard of it."

Holt and Orion looked at each other, shaking their heads dramatically.

"I was afraid of this, sir," Holt explained earnestly. "When we arrived in town, Marshal Gentry was away on duty, so the money we brought back was entrusted to your mayor, a man named Clark Worthington."

"Yes, Clark, of course I know him," Singleton acknowledged. "As you said, he's our mayor...he's also justice of the peace. A colonel from the war. One of our leading citizens."

"Well, Mr. Singleton," Holt intoned. "I personally turned over the money to this...this Worthington, first thing when we arrived in Sweetclover this morning. Have you seen him today?"

"Why yes...yes I did," Singleton said, nodding vigorously. "At lunchtime and again shortly after."

"An' he never said anythin' 'bout the money?" Orion asked.

"No, Rangers. No, he did not." Singleton's brow furrowed deeply when the Rangers looked at each other again. "What do you suggest I do?"

Holt replied solemnly. "Mr. Singleton, in the interest of Sweetclover's financial security, we would be proud to go with you now and retrieve the town's money from this Worthington fellow."

"Yes, by all means, yes. We should do that." Singleton's manner took on a tone of anxious motivation. "Give me a moment to get dressed," he said, turning back into his house.

"Better hurry, Mr. Singleton," Orion called out as the banker walked away. "No tellin' what's happened." He put his fist to his mouth to conceal a burst of laughter. "I didn't think he was gonna take time to change out of his robe an' pajamas!" He snickered at Holt.

"Shhhh, shhh," Holt cautioned. "This is serious Ranger time."

Shortly, Esry Singleton III was leading two Texas Rangers down the main street of Sweetclover. Not as many people milled about outside as before, some drifting off to end the night at home, many filing back into the town's saloons.

"There's something else you should know about this Worthington fellow," Holt said as they neared the hotel. Singleton stopped to listen. "He never served in the war. For that matter, never served in any war."

"Wha—never served?" Singleton repeated.

"Neither side. Blue nor gray," Orion said. "He ain't no colonel."

"Not a colonel. But..." Singleton was taken aback.

"He was a corn farmer," Orion added. "In Kansas."

"Makes you wonder about the man you elected mayor and appointed justice of the peace, doesn't it?" Holt asked. "I think I'd question anything he says."

"Why yes, I believe you're right," Singleton agreed, overwhelmed and stunned at the revelation.

"There's one more thing, Mr. Singleton," Holt pointed out. "Tonight, as a prelude to the lynching, Deputy Jimbo Worthington knocked out another deputy and held a shotgun on Marshal Gentry, which allowed your mayor and his mob to execute our prisoner held in Sweetclover's jail." Singleton gasped. "Another deputy in cahoots with the Worthingtons assaulted Dr. Gustafson," Holt continued.

"Assaulted Dr. Gustafson?"

"Clocked 'im in the back of head, with a gun," Orion affirmed.

"The mob grabbed the prisoner in the doctor's care and lynched him as well," Holt finished.

"That's…that's just not acceptable! That's criminal, isn't it? We need Marshal Gentry to do something about these people and these deputies right away," Singleton said angrily.

"Sweetclover doesn't have a marshal right now," Orion informed the bank official. "Because of Clark Worthington an' his assault on the jail, Frank Gentry quit. He rode outta town an hour or so ago."

Singleton looked like he was going to vomit. He hung his head. Then he took a deep breath, raised it and with a determined look said, "Rangers, let's go find Mr. Worthington."

Holt and Orion looked at each other once more. This time, their looks were truly intense; the game stakes just got higher.

"Before we talk to him, send someone to the jail to fetch Deputy Don Baldwin," Holt instructed. "Tell Deputy Baldwin that the Rangers sent for him."

The bank president wound his way through the nearly full lobby bar to a far corner. He stopped where Frank Worthington and his son were drinking. Turner Halsey, Deputy Merlyn Reed and a few other Worthington yes-men filled in the rest of the table.

Singleton cleared his throat. "Frank, as president of the Sweetclover bank, I demand you turn over the money the Rangers gave to you this morning. Now."

"Why sure, Esry, you think I'd do otherwise?" Worthington asked, a surprised look on his face. The lobby had taken notice when the Rangers entered. Now people were rapidly settling around the table, shushing each other and straining to hear what the bank president and the lawmen were talking about with the mayor.

"I *thought* you would have returned the money as soon as you received it," Singleton said calmly.

"No problem, Esry, I'll get it now," Worthington answered. "Jimbo, it's in my room," he said, snapping his fingers and gesturing with his head to his suite upstairs.

Jimbo stood and Holt quickly interrupted, "Hold it right there, Jimbo, I want you to slowly unbuckle that gun belt and let it drop."

"What? What's going on here?" both Worthingtons protested.

"You heard the Ranger," Singleton said.

"Slowly," Holt cautioned. Jimbo complied and eased the gun belt onto his chair. Holt turned to Orion. "There's no room in his overworked pants to have a hideaway. He's ready."

Orion barked at Jimbo, "Okay, youngster, let's go

find that money." They moved to the stairs leading up to the hotel rooms and the mayor's suite.

"I don't know what game you think you're running here, Corrigan," the elder Worthington blurted. "But you've got a lot of nerve being all high and mighty."

"That's *Ranger* Corrigan to you, Worthington. And at Sabine Pass they called me *Captain* Corrigan. I suggest you find some manners. Fast." Holt took a step toward the fat mayor. "And since we're on the subject, just *where* did *you* serve?"

The lobby rippled with mutterings…

What does that mean?

Is he calling out the mayor?

"Now see here…" Worthington started to bluster.

"No!" Singleton interrupted. "*You* see here, Clark. I believe the Ranger asked you a question. Where did you serve, '*colonel*?'"

Worthington stared daggers at Singleton but did not answer. The mutters became audible rumbles of discord.

"I've been informed that you were the ringleader behind tonight's ugliness," Singleton continued. "I'm told the forced execution of those prisoners is in a bit of a gray area legally, but *your actions* certainly represent a lack of moral character as a mayor and a definite over-stepping of your justice of the peace responsibilities. Consider yourself relieved of those duties."

"The town leadership decides that!" Worthington bellowed.

"And I sit at the head of that table," Singleton snapped. "We will be meeting first thing in the morning to determine your replacement."

At that point, Jimbo Worthington trudged down the

stairs, followed by Orion. The younger Worthington tossed a set of stuffed saddlebags onto the table.

"Very good. Thank you, Ranger," Singleton said. "Worthington, as I was saying, you don't deserve the office. A meeting will be held in the morning. At that time, we will determine your replacement."

The lobby exploded with a clamor punctuated by more than a few cheers.

Singleton looked at Holt as to if ask, anything else? Holt motioned with his head to behind the banker, indicating an introduction needed to be made. "One more thing." Singleton smiled. "Our new marshal has some business to tie up."

From behind the banker, new Sweetclover marshal Don Baldwin stepped forward. His hat sat gingerly on his head, but he did not exhibit any ill effects from what happened earlier at the jail.

The room settled back into silence as Marshal Baldwin announced in a loud, clear voice, "Jimbo, you might be the worst deputy in Texas. You're lazy and a yellow-bellied bushwhacker. You are immediately relieved of your duties. Place your badge on the table. Now."

Beaten, weaponless and already hanging his head, the younger Worthington picked the deputy badge off his shirt and dropped it on the table.

Baldwin continued, "Merlyn Reed, you didn't strike a fellow lawman tonight, but you attacked our town physician and are a poor excuse for a deputy. Turn in your badge now as well."

Tears welling at his eyes, Reed's shaky hand took the badge from his vest and laid it on the table.

"Now," Marshal Baldwin announced even louder,

"Jimbo Worthington, you are under arrest for assaulting a lawman, drawing a lethal weapon on a marshal, abetting the removal of a state prisoner from custody, and assisting in that prisoner's forced execution. You will be held in Sweetclover jail, pending review by a circuit judge from the state of Texas."

"Don't worry, son, I'll take care of it," his father called out.

"You'll have to take care of that for the both of you, Worthington," Marshal Baldwin said. "You're under arrest as well. You too, Reed." He drew his pistol and held it on the trio. "You know the way. Now, march."

———

Holt and Orion had decided to spend the night in the jail even before the confrontation in the hotel bar. They wanted to avoid whatever additional reverie the night's activities might inspire.

Don Baldwin locked the older Worthington in the same cell previously occupied by the priest. His son sat dejectedly in the middle lockup, with former Deputy Reed in the remaining cage.

Orion had taken great satisfaction in directing the attention of the new prisoners to the plumbing facilities, pointing to the bucket he had originally left for the priest. "You'll have to figure out a way to share." He grinned.

As the Rangers started to settle in for the night, Orion produced the bottle of Irish whiskey from the saddlebag draped over his shoulder. A generous pour into three coffee mugs served to toast the best wishes for the new marshal of Sweetclover.

Holt smiled to himself, the town had already begun changing.

"An' one more toast..." Orion beamed. "To Tag, the Ranger dog. Glad he didn't stay when you told 'im to back there at the church. That sonvabitch had me dead to rights."

Everyone chuckled their agreement. Holt gathered his dog into a big bear hug. Tag even allowed Orion to administer some well-placed neck and back scratches.

Contentment sat on one side of Holt's shoulders in the form of the different directions the night had turned for Marshal Baldwin and the arrogant Worthingtons. All parties received what was deserved. Weariness, of mind and body, weighed heavily on the other side. It seemed years ago, rather than months, that he said goodbye to his mad crusade of keeping the Southern cause alive before finally heading home to his brothers.

And here he was.

He finished the remainder of his whiskey and wiped down his guns, finishing with a touch from the cardinal feather. Before lying down, he poked through the contents of The Angel's saddlebags.

Inside one of the bags was a black robe with "O. Pence" embroidered on the inner label.

CHAPTER FORTY-SIX

The sun rose as a canopy of gold, bright amid the brilliant blue sky. The morning ushered in a fresh beginning for Rangers Corrigan and Higbee.

Provisions for the trail were purchased from the general store and repacked onto their horses. Orion was particularly excited at the idea of the canned peaches resting in one of the bags. A handful of new fireworks were tucked in there, too.

They agreed that their livery friend, Dee Kennedy, should be given the horse recovered from the Laelia church. They wrote an official note explaining the circumstances and deeding ownership, which they both signed.

Holt was aboard his buckskin, giving the bay an easier day carrying the small packs—and later on, Tag. Orion started off on his bay, letting it stretch itself after being wounded in their Comanche fight. In addition to provisions, a package containing The Angel's maps and leather satchel plus a few small items were tucked carefully away.

As the town's buildings began to disappear behind them, horse and human muscles were getting used to working together again. Tag was happy to be trotting next to his master. Holt was happy to be trotting away from Sweetclover.

He mused to Orion, "I figured Captain McCoy would be hacked off at us."

"For what?"

"I don't know, a 'dereliction of following rules' or something."

"He acknowledged that justice was served in an unexpected way," Orion half-chuckled his response. "But by the book stuff ain't his way though."

"I'm sure that *alcalde* didn't mind finding a bunch of stolen goods and money in that church," Holt added. "I'll bet he didn't mention that in all his hollering."

Orion nodded his head. "Tell you the truth, partner, I wouldn't have let that Angel bastard up off the floor if we had known more 'bout who was pullin' his strings. I know you were thinkin' 'bout it too."

"We still don't know much," Holt said with resignation. "But I think we can look through all those maps and papers with a new perspective."

A moment or two of quiet passed before Orion handed over a folded piece of paper to Holt.

"Got this while you were packin' up," Orion said. "From the Cap'n…"

RANGERS HIGBEE AND CORRIGAN:

RIDE TO EL PASO.

AWAIT FURTHER ORDERS.

NO SWIMMING REQUIRED.

MCCOY

"'No swimming, huh? We're going to hear about our adventure for a while, aren't we?" Holt asked, handing the paper back to Orion. "El Paso?"

"Always good to have a Ranger presence be seen in a town that size, even if we don't have anything to investigate."

"Sounds like a picnic compared to the last few months," Holt responded. "Whattaya say, Tag? Let's ride."

A LOOK AT BOOK FOUR:
CAST ASUNDER

Scott F. Smith, son of Spur Award-winning author Cotton Smith, keeps the Corrigan brothers saga alive and full of action.

Texas Ranger Holt Corrigan thought his nightmare was over when he and his partner, Orion Higbee, captured the murderous priest known as "The Angel." But even with the wicked man of cloth six feet under, the bloodshed hasn't stopped.

As Holt and Orion split up to unravel the deadly conspiracy, ruthless tricksters and relentless outlaws push them to their limits. With lives on the line, Holt must rely on his courage—and the strength of his scattered allies—to piece together the dangerous puzzle and keep Texas safe.

But can Holt Corrigan stop the killings before it's too late?

AVAILABLE DECEMBER 2024

ACKNOWLEDGMENTS

My undying love and thanks to Cynthia Smith. I could not have done any of this without you. In addition to being my wonderful wife, your enormous heart, sharp eye, and considerable patience helped guide me on this trail. Thank you for shining your light on my life.

To my sisters, Laura Faulkner and Stephanie Kissick. As the big brother, I have always looked up to your kindness and wicked senses of humor. Thanks for putting up with me. I love you.

To my trail ride partner, Jay Wolpert, and his lovely wife, Roz, I am grateful beyond words that our life paths crossed. My pal, as you read this from the great beyond, know that I will always treasure the mirth and banter of long days in the saddle and nights around a campfire. You found time to teach me about the craft of storytelling and the wonder of creativity. I am forever thankful for you and your family's love and friendship.

Thank you to Mike Bray, Jake Bray, Patience Bramlett, and my new friends at Wolfpack Publishing. I am indebted to you all for your belief in the Smith family.

Thank you to Johnny D. Boggs for your advice and goodwill. And to the Lost Boys...you know who you are...my endless gratitude for the shenanigans and brotherhood.

And finally, my heart overflows with love and admiration for my parents, Sonya and Cotton Smith. Your love for me and my sisters knew no bounds. I miss you.

ABOUT THE AUTHOR

Scott F. Smith continues the spirit of the Old West created by his father, Cotton Smith, author of the first two books of the Corrigan series and other wonderful Western adventures, such as *Pray for Texas* and *Behold a Red Horse*.

Vengeance Wears a Star is Scott's debut novel and is rooted in the elements that made Cotton's books great—grand themes, moral conflict, and courage. He grew up with a love of American history, reading, and Western movies and is an Eagle Scout and recipient of the Boy Scouts of America's Silver Beaver Award. He continues to volunteer with Scouting to help develop tomorrow's leaders.

As a youth, Scott was introduced to the ceremonies, customs, and traditions of the Plains Indian. Research for Western storytelling heightened his appreciation for and spiritual connection to the land. For many years, he participated in the Desert Caballeros trail ride, covering a hundred miles in a weeklong trek through the Arizona mountains each year.

Scott is an award-winning writer and producer for corporate clients and relishes the experience of staring at a blank piece of paper or computer screen and creating a story within an easy-to-imagine world. He previously taught high school media and video production, having enjoyed sharing his storytelling expertise as well as helping students bring their own tales to life.

A member of the Western Writers of America, Scott and his wife, Cindy, are global explorers but call Lawrence, Kansas, home.

You can find Scott's work at www.ScottSmithWesterns.com.